Mistaken

JESSIE LEWIS

Meryton Press
OYSTERVILLE, WA

This is a work of fiction. Names, characters, places, and incidents are products of the author's imagination or are used fictitiously. Any resemblance to actual events or persons, living or dead, is entirely coincidental.

MISTAKEN

 For information: P.O. Box 34, Oysterville WA 98641

ISBN: 978-1-68131-019-0

Cover design by Zorylee Diaz-Lupitou (all images public domain)
Layout by Ellen Pickels

Dedication

For Richard, my rock, and my kids, my pebbles

"Seldom, very seldom, does complete truth belong to any human disclosure; seldom can it happen that something is not a little disguised or a little mistaken."

—Jane Austen

1 After the Storm

Saturday, 11 April 1812: Kent

"Well, Darcy," said his cousin as their carriage rolled through the gate, "notwithstanding your unaccountable brooding, this year's visit has been a good deal more pleasurable than most."

Darcy made no reply. Fitzwilliam was perfectly capable of carrying on a conversation alone and would do so better without any objection from him.

"Astonishing what a difference a few young ladies can make to a place, even one as depressing as Rosings."

Darcy considered neither his aunt's house nor the presence of any of said ladies agreeable. He kept the thought to himself and fixed his eyes on the window through which the parsonage would *not* appear as they passed it.

"You do not agree? I hope you are not going to hold it against Miss Bennet that she did not ask me to verify your account. You know how persuasive Wickham can be. It may take time for her to learn to appreciate your disclosure."

The glass reflected Darcy's sneer back at him. He adjusted his focus beyond it. Given the *appreciation* Elizabeth Bennet had shown for his offer of marriage, he had expected no gratitude for exposing her favourite's true character. Indeed, were it not for the satisfaction of having defended his own, he might regret writing the letter at all.

"I have faith she will though, old boy. If you trust her with such a delicate matter, then I trust her to come to the proper conclusion about the perpetrator."

Darcy did trust her—implicitly. Her integrity was but one of countless qualities he admired. Perverse was the twist of fate that had given rise to the woman he held in such high regard refusing him in defence of the man who so cruelly used his sister. He gave his cousin a glancing nod so as not to invite another debate on the wisdom of revealing Georgiana's near ruin.

Fitzwilliam presently gave up his chatter and fell asleep, but Darcy's relief was short-lived. His own private monologue soon took over, recounting conversations he would much rather forget.

A rejection of marriage was not something he had ever thought to encounter. The violence of Elizabeth's refusal left him winded, gasping for comprehension. She had been merciless in her use of him, teasing and taunting 'til he was driven beyond his endurance, only to spurn the offer she wrung from him. Incensed anew, Darcy followed his cousin's lead and sought the anaesthesia of sleep. By the time he awoke, Kent's rolling hills had flattened into London's suburbs.

"I thought you would never wake up. I was forced to read this awful book of yours to pass the time." Fitzwilliam picked it up and peered at the spine. "What the devil are you doing reading this hogwash?"

"It was the first one I found in Lady Catherine's library," Darcy replied, tilting his head to release the muscles in his neck. "I thank you for your trouble. I shall not bother starting it now." He caught the book before it hit him and felt the pull of his first smile in days at the corners of his mouth. "Can I tempt you to join me for dinner?"

"I should infinitely prefer it," said Fitzwilliam, "but alas, my father has summoned me to dine with him and Ashby—and my future sister, God help me."

Darcy raised an eyebrow in query.

"Lady Philippa," his cousin revealed. "My delightful brother decided he could not bear Miss Blake's teeth after all and has staked his entire future happiness on the dental merits of an ill-tempered shrew."

Darcy almost smiled again 'til Fitzwilliam's enquiry as to his plans chased it away. His only obligation that evening was to resume his former life as though naught had changed. Indeed, other than the longing for Elizabeth—which none of his resentment had dislodged from its perch in his heart—nothing had. "I have no fixed engagements," he mumbled then picked up the book he had moments earlier foresworn and hid himself in the opening chapter.

Saturday, 18 April 1812: Kent

Elizabeth returned to Hunsford parsonage to find her friend awaiting her in the parlour. Tea things were spread upon the table in readiness, and at Charlotte's invitation, she sat down and accepted a cup.

"Did you enjoy your walk?"

"Very much," she replied, hiding behind the steam from her tea lest the lie reveal itself in her half-hearted smile. In truth, unwelcome reflections had plagued her all through the grove, as they had all week long, ruining her last opportunity to enjoy it.

"I shall be sorry to see you go." Charlotte's odd little frown seemed to suggest she had something else less innocuous to say.

"And I shall be sorry to leave you." *Though not sorry to leave.* "I hope the house does not seem too quiet without us." Looking around, she added, "Will your sister not join us?"

"She is repacking her trunks," Charlotte replied, a sly smile replacing her frown. "The poor dear was up half the night fretting that Lady Catherine would somehow discover she had not folded her gowns the right way."

"Poor Maria! Her ladyship was particularly urgent on the matter. But then there is excessive urgency to all Lady Catherine's advice."

Charlotte laughed lightly but adopted the same strange look as before.

"I am pleased *you* are not made so anxious by her tyranny," Elizabeth hastened to add.

"Oh, you know me. I try to be practical about these things. There is little point chafing at the bit, having submitted to the harness. Besides," she added wickedly, "*some* of her advice has proved rather useful."

"Is that so? Such as…?"

"Such as the several methods she has described for discouraging my husband's attentions once I provide him with an heir."

Incredulity prevented Elizabeth's amusement from turning into a full laugh.

"Do not pretend to be shocked. I know very well you are in possession of all the facts, for you enlightened me long before Lady Catherine, or indeed, my husband."

"Yes, well," Elizabeth admitted, grinning, "I probably ought not to be in possession of quite as many facts as I am. We are both indebted to Mr. Craythorne for our prescience. Were it not for his...*evident* admiration that day, I should never have petitioned my aunt for such intelligence."

"And Mrs. Gardiner probably ought never to have consented to provide it, but I must say I am grateful she did."

Elizabeth opted to drink her tea rather than answer. She disliked how closely the conversation had veered towards Charlotte's intimacies with Mr. Collins, with whose admiration she had only narrowly avoided becoming fully acquainted herself. His had been the first offer of marriage she refused—the memory of which brought her perilously close to thinking about the second.

"You have been uncommonly quiet this past week, Eliza," said her friend, taking shameless advantage of her distraction. "Will you not tell me what troubles you?"

Elizabeth surprised herself with the violence of her aversion to doing so, though she was stranger to none of the sentiments that swarmed nauseatingly at the prospect. Indignation, confusion, shame, affront—she had kept constant company with them all since Mr. Darcy's astonishing and offensive proposal and even more shocking letter. Until she settled the matter for herself, however, she could not begin to justify it to anybody else.

"Has it something to do with the gentlemen's departure?" Charlotte pressed.

"What makes you ask that?"

"Only that it coincided with your low spirits. I wondered whether, perhaps, you had set your heart on Colonel Fitzwilliam."

"Colonel Fitzwilliam? Goodness, no! He is perfectly amiable but quite above my reach."

"And not nearly so handsome as his cousin."

"Nor so insufferably proud!" she retorted, exasperated that such an inane remark should have made her blush. With a concerted effort at composure, she added, "If I have been quiet, I believe it is only that I am ready to be home. I hope you will not mind my saying so."

"Not at all. I know you must be eager to see Jane."

Seizing upon the change in subject, Elizabeth launched into an account of all the things she and her sister meant to do together in London before travelling home to Longbourn. Charlotte graciously let the other matter drop, referring to it only once, obliquely, with a firm reminder that Elizabeth could write to her at any time with any concern.

At length the chaise arrived, the trunks were fastened on, the parcels placed within, and it was pronounced to be ready. After an affectionate farewell between all parties, Elizabeth and Maria set out for London.

Saturday, 18 April 1812: London

"You are very quiet, Lizzy," Mrs. Gardiner remarked after dinner. "Are you well?"

"Forgive me. I ought to have slept in the carriage as Maria did; then I might have arrived better company." As it was, anticipation to be reunited with Jane and other, less agreeable anxieties had kept her awake for the entire journey.

"Nay, there is nothing wanting in your company," said her uncle. "You are naturally fatigued from your travels."

Jane sent her a worried look, which Elizabeth parried with a smile. Of greater concern to her was that Jane had not passed any part of the day in a carriage and thus had no reason to look as weary as she did.

"Tell me then, girls," said Mrs. Gardiner, "how are Mr. and Mrs. Collins getting along?"

"Oh, they make a fine couple, though I wonder how my sister tolerates the way Mr. Collins chews his food."

Maria's eagerness to satisfy everyone's curiosity suited Elizabeth very well. She was exhausted from the effort of diverting all talk of Kent away from the specific mention of Mr. Darcy, conscious of her propensity to blush at the merest mention of him. To avoid speaking of him was one thing; however, Jane's unabated melancholy made it impossible not to *think* of him. Her sister might have been happily engaged to Mr. Bingley presently had not Mr. Darcy separated them, a deed for which his letter revealed him to be wholly unrepentant. Perfectly ready to wallow in resentment, Elizabeth was vexed when certain other parts of the same letter obtruded on her memory. Its revelations of Mr. Wickham's true character were almost too appalling to allow, given how blithely she had permitted him to court her vanity and colour her opinions.

"Please do not make me go," she heard Maria say. "His plays are all high Dutch to me."

"Of course we shall not make you go, my dear," said Mrs. Gardiner.

"I should be happy to stay here and keep you company," Jane offered. "I have never much cared for Shakespeare either, particularly the tragedies. They are too fraught with turmoil for my liking."

"And you, Lizzy?" Mr. Gardiner enquired. "Can we tempt you with a little *Romeo and Juliet*?"

"I should be delighted," she replied, drawn to the prospect of an evening passed in contemplation of anyone's turmoil but her own. How, after all, was she ever to reconcile such an intense dislike of Mr. Darcy with such remorse for misjudging him?

"Excellent! It is settled, then. Have you any other plans, ladies?"

The failure could not be hers; Mr. Darcy was the most contrary creature she had ever met. On the one hand, he was unrepentantly meddlesome while, on the other, unfailingly dutiful.

"I promised Mrs. Featherstone we would all visit," Mrs. Gardiner said.

He boasted of consequence and duty yet, by his own admission, was motivated by sensibility.

"I should like to go shopping," said Maria. "Lady Catherine said, if I mentioned her name at the drapers on Bond Street, I would be attended to!"

"Then we absolutely must go," Jane replied. "I have no plans other than to steal as much of Lizzy's time as I can."

Elizabeth smiled. Dear Jane! How perverse that Mr. Darcy should have treated her so cruelly whilst all gallantry in defence of *his* sister!

"I cannot imagine you will find any complaint," Mr. Gardiner replied amiably. "Though before you begin, might I persuade you, Lizzy, to play the pianoforte for us?"

Most contrary of all, she thought, was that he had disdained her connections, situation, and looks and then declared his passionate admiration and love!

"Go to bed, Lizzy," her aunt said softly, closer by than she had been a moment ago. "Maria can play for us. Truly, you look very ill."

She looked up, struggling to disengage herself from her reflections. The drawing room, her aunt's frown and, over her shoulder, Jane's concerned expression came into focus. Elizabeth wrinkled her nose in defeat. "Pardon me, everybody. I am a hopeless bore this evening."

Everyone politely assured her otherwise, though no one objected when she excused herself to bed.

Tuesday, 21 April 1812: London

"Let me understand you, Bingley. This cousin of yours has inherited land in Nova Scotia?"

Bingley squinted at his friend Tindale and nodded. The whole room wobbled. He stopped nodding.

"And he has asked you to build him something on it?"

One, brief nod—still too much movement.

"Why can he not build something himself?"

"He has no money."

"Ah, and you have no land. I begin to comprehend your temptation."

Bingley tried, in his best approximation of sobriety, to explain that, in fact, he was not at all tempted. "In any case," he concluded, "it is too blasted far away."

"'Tis about to be in the middle of a blasted war," said his Brother Hurst.

"I wager they will not see a bit of fighting that far north," said another of the dinner guests from the far end of the table—Wrenshaw, Bingley thought.

"That is a gamble I should not like to make," Tindale countered. "But then, we all know how you prefer your odds."

"The material question," their host, Verney, asserted, "is what potential has the land? I could endure a good deal of unrest if my house were built on a lode of gold."

"He does not need to leave the country in order to invest in the land," someone argued. Bingley had given up attempting to fathom who said what.

"Quite right! He could stay here and invest in *mine*!"

"You cannot have much land left, Wrenshaw. Did you not recently sell half your estate to Mr. Darcy?"

"Not quite half. Only three hundred acres."

"Three hundred acres and *still* you are in deep? What the devil did you wager this time, man?"

Wrenshaw mumbled something about a horse and a duchess, whereupon Bingley gave up all attempts to follow the conversation. His legs felt heavy, and he amused himself by wriggling his toes in his shoes to see whether he still could.

"Here is a wager you can afford, Wrenshaw," Verney shouted. "Two pounds to the man who can guess which woman has put that stupid grin on Bingley's face."

Bingley laughed for show, though his cheer evaporated at the mention of women.

"'Tis not Miss Rivers is it, old boy?" Tindale said with a wink.

"No," Bingley replied, reflecting briefly upon what he had always considered to be two of Miss Rivers' best virtues. "I have long been reconciled to never becoming better acquainted with those. Just as I am resigned to the loss of Miss Bennet." He ended with a morose sigh.

"Miss Bennet? Who—"

"For all our sakes, do not ask, I beg you! It will only encourage him," Hurst interrupted. He lurched to his feet, splashing brandy down his waistcoat in the process, and hauled Bingley from his chair by the elbow. "Come now; you are too foxed by half to be brooding over women."

Bingley was also, it transpired, too foxed to object and submitted with only mild complaint as Hurst thanked Verney for an agreeable evening but insisted it was long past time they took their leave. In the time it took Bingley to correctly align all the fingers of his hands with those of his gloves, their carriage had been summoned, and the two gentlemen were homeward bound.

"I must say," said Hurst a short while into the journey, "notwithstanding your professed heartbreak, you seem to be rallying remarkably well."

"I shall not forget her, Hurst. Miss Bennet is an angel."

"So you keep saying. Indeed, I cannot altogether account for your giving her up."

"She did not love me." He sighed, rather pleased with the dramatic effect.

"A man with your fortune does not require a woman to *love* him."

"Darcy did not agree. He said her sincere regard could be the only inducement to such an imprudent match."

"That only shows how deuced imprudent a match he considered it to be!"

"But Dar—"

"Cease hiding behind the Titan and admit it. You agreed with him."

"I did?"

"Aye! He did not make you leave. You chose to do it. Besides, I do believe your spirits are more recovered than you allow. Remember, I witnessed your dance with Miss Aston Tuesday last." He waggled his eyebrows salaciously.

Bingley leant forward. "Stuff 'n' nonsense! I am in love, and I shall not be convinced otherwise by you, my sisters, Darcy, Miss Aston, or anyone else!" He poked a forefinger into Hurst's chest with each point.

"Far be it from me to disabuse you of it. God knows you are forever in love with *somebody.* Only it does seem this particular fascination is beginning to lose its power. There is surely some comfort in that."

Bingley was forcibly returned to his seat when the carriage came to an abrupt halt outside his front door. There he remained, slumped dejectedly, shaking his head. "I swear I am as in love with Miss Bennet as ever I was."

Hurst chuckled quietly. "*That* I do not doubt, my friend."

Wednesday, 22 April 1812: London

Darcy put his name to the last of the documents his attorney had brought and flicked the ink well shut. "Any other matters?" Already, he felt the tug of other thoughts and struggled prodigiously to ignore them as he concluded his meeting.

"Only that the sale of land from Mr. Wrenshaw's estate is completed." Irving reached across the desk for his papers. "I wonder he did not wait to sell to Crambourne directly."

"I understand he was not at liberty to wait for funds."

Irving looked unsurprised and vaguely disgusted. "He is popular in some circles, I understand, but I have heard several things that have given me reason to think ill of him."

Only several? Darcy thought bitterly. Since Elizabeth had *every reason in the world* to think ill of him, that gave Wrenshaw the advantage.

"I do not suppose Crambourne was in any haste, either," Irving went on, sliding the documents into his satchel. "Railways are a patient man's investment. Though Wrenshaw is the last man in the world whom I could ever be prevailed on to marry."

"I beg your pardon?"

"Um, I said Wrenshaw is the last man in the world whom I would expect to comprehend that…sir."

Darcy clenched his teeth against an imprecation, immeasurably weary of hearing Elizabeth's voice and recalling her enmity in every conversation. "Quite."

"Still," Irving said with a caution Darcy despised, for it bespoke his own insufferable distraction, "Wrenshaw approached you with the offer, not the reverse. One must suppose he knew what he was about."

"Quite," Darcy repeated, unable to keep from wincing at the memory of Elizabeth's response to his offer. His brief pause must have stretched into a long one, for Irving cleared his throat loudly before announcing his readiness to depart. Cursing silently, Darcy thanked him for his diligence and personally escorted him out. Would that have made Elizabeth think him any more gentlemanlike or merely prouder and more unlikeable for having been inattentive in the first place?

"I shall have coffee in my study now, Godfrey," he instructed the butler, as though coffee was all that was needed to silence the unending echo of her reproofs.

He had barely seated himself back at his desk when there was a knock at the door. He barked an instruction to enter but regretted his tone when his sister stepped into the room. He stood immediately to greet her.

"Pray, excuse the interruption," she begged. "Godfrey said you were busy, but I simply had to see for myself that you were better."

He flinched. As a rule, he abhorred disguise of any sort, but he had arrived home from Kent with no inclination whatsoever to discuss his time there; thus, he had feigned illness to avoid her questions. "I am—thank you."

"I am pleased to hear it. I have been very worried. And now we shall still be able go to the theatre this evening."

It took a heartbeat, but the allusion found a mark amongst the tumult of his thoughts. Damn! *Romeo and* blasted *Juliet*!

"You do look tired, though," she said, coming forward to peer at him. "I trust nothing is amiss?"

"Nothing at all." Indeed, had he not repeatedly assured himself that an alliance with Elizabeth would have been a terrible mistake? "All is as it ought to be." The ache that abruptly assailed him indicated otherwise. He inhaled sharply at the unpleasantness of it—a cold, inflexible, and altogether appalling loneliness.

"Very well then," his sister said. "I shall leave you for now."

"There is no need to rush off. Would you care for some refreshments?"

"I thank you, no. Mrs. Annesley is waiting for me in the carriage. I only stopped by to see if there was aught you needed."

Yes! Elizabeth! The ache deepened, closing his throat alarmingly, so it was all he could do to give a curt shake of his head.

"Then, I shall see you this evening."

She exchanged a brief word with Godfrey at the door as she left. Darcy watched the butler unload his tray onto the table, furious with himself for even noticing the solitary cup in its solitary saucer. He was further vexed by the almighty thud his heart gave when Godfrey presented him with a letter clearly postmarked from Kent. He resolutely ignored the chasm of disappointment that opened in his gut upon recognising the hand as his cousin Anne's.

He tossed the letter onto the table where it lay, taunting him with the possibility of its containing any mention of Elizabeth, while he lowered himself into a chair and poured some coffee. He knew not which he most wished to gratify: his desire never to think of her again or his longing to know how she fared. Reasoning that Anne was unlikely to have mentioned her in any case, he opened the letter. Then, though but a moment before he had believed his wish for news to predominate, he began to regret reading.

Rosings Park, Kent
April 20

Cousin,

Your recent visit must render any news I have redundant. Nevertheless, my mother insists.

We do tolerably well. The weather is improving at last, and I have been out in my phaeton every day it has not rained. Mr. Collins's sermon yesterday was his worst yet. You would have choked. Still, my mother seemed pleased by it.

She is to host a dinner next week for Lord and Lady Metcalfe. I do not look forward to it, for I have always thought Lady Metcalfe rather stupid. I suspect my mother only tolerates the connection as a means of relieving her occasional ennui, which might explain the peculiar interest she took in Miss Bennet. You would not credit their most recent exchange, a discussion of the differences in understanding between the classes. Miss Bennet holds that intellect cannot be dictated by accident of birth. Her example was her success in teaching one of the children of her father's tenants to read. His mother left or died or some such, and he wished to read stories to his sister—all very touching I am sure, but really! Does Miss Bennet fancy herself governess to the poor? My mother was most vexed at being required to justify her understanding of the matter, but then, she would engage Miss Bennet to begin with! I hope Lady Metcalfe proves to be an adequate proxy.

The gnawing ache of loneliness abruptly fractured into a gaping abyss, seething with insuperable memories, Elizabeth's compassion not least among them. How fiercely he cherished her compassion! Her *everything*! Her laugh, her liveliness, her wit, her figure, her eyes—dear *God*, her eyes!

"Damn it, why can I not stop loving you, woman?"

He threw the letter down and propelled himself from his chair to stalk off the intolerable feeling of loss. That he should be in love at all was absurd. That he should love a woman with so immoveable a dislike of him was unbearable. And she accused *him* of causing other people's misery! What did other people know of this pain? What was Jane Bennet's misery but a frustrated design to marry well? What was Bingley's but a necessary evil? Not even Georgiana—

He drew up short. Could Georgiana's disappointment be so readily dismissed? Could the fiend who caused it be so readily forgiven? The thought struck him with force, shame blossoming like a bruise from the point of impact. Darcy knew well the grief of seeing a sister broken-hearted, yet with what ease, what presumption, had he dismissed Elizabeth's anger. His own heart squeezed to think she must despise him as vehemently as he did Wickham.

His shame notwithstanding, a grim relief overtook him. Nothing was mended; nothing was as it ought to be, despite the lie he had told his sister. Yet, for the first time since Elizabeth entered his world and tore apart his understanding of it, Darcy knew precisely what he must do.

The arrival of a visitor distracted them, but a quick glance from the window revealed it to be an acquaintance of their uncle. Jane returned to arranging her sister's hair, aware of, but refusing to acknowledge, how she scrutinised her in the mirror.

"'Tis no good," Elizabeth said. "I cannot forgive their interference—not when I see you are this unhappy."

Jane suppressed a sigh. She had hoped the interruption might end their conversation. "I am unhappy, yes," she mumbled past the pin held between her teeth. She took it out and pushed it into a curl, adding, "But I cannot believe that either Mr. Darcy or Mr. Bingley's sisters schemed to make me so. Their motive was much more likely to protect him than to harm me."

"Whatever their motive, the consequence remains unchanged. You are miserable."

Whatever Elizabeth's motive in so obstinately pursuing the matter, it was not helping to relieve the misery upon which she was so keen to remark. "Do not blame them, Lizzy," she begged, coiling a last length of hair around her finger. "If Mr. Bingley was persuaded to leave on the basis of their recommendation alone, it confirms nothing more than an error of fancy on my part."

"I sincerely hope you do not mean to blame yourself!" Elizabeth cried, twisting to scowl up at her.

Better that than to blame Mr. Bingley, Jane thought, for if she allowed him to be as heartless as Elizabeth wished to paint him and with such awful friends, she would feel even more foolish for being unable to stop loving him.

"Keep still or it will all be undone," she chided, gesturing for Elizabeth to turn back to the mirror and retrieving the strand of hair that was wrenched from her fingers when she twisted around. "Let us talk about it no more, for no amount of reproach will change anything." She stepped back to review her work. "I am sure I shall begin to get the better of it very soon."

"I dearly hope so. You deserve to be happy. You are so good—and five times as pretty as the rest of us," Elizabeth added playfully.

Jane smiled as best she could, though her best felt rather feeble. In truth, at that moment, with her hair gleaming in the last rays of afternoon sun, a smile illuminating her face and her eyes twinkling from teasing, she rather thought Elizabeth was the prettier one. She felt a twinge of something unpleasant but dismissed it and searched in her box for a ribbon.

"Indeed!" Elizabeth persisted. "Mr. Atkinson thought so. Only you were too modest to notice."

Jane said nothing and continued working, weaving the ribbon between curls and securing it with jewelled pins. She *had* noticed, actually. There had been several young gentlemen in attendance at Mr. Atkinson's dinner yesterday, all of whom had flocked to her upon first introduction. During the course of the evening, however, their attention had gravitated towards Elizabeth, where it had then remained. It had since struck her that this was not an entirely uncommon occurrence. The more she had thought on it, the more instances she recalled of her sister's prevailing popularity. In the wake of Mr. Bingley's abandonment, these were not happy insights.

"Ow!" Elizabeth yelped, adding with a laugh, "I am sure it will look well enough without the ribbon!"

"A moment, 'tis nearly done."

When Jane had been in Mr. Bingley's company, her sister's presence or absence had gone entirely unnoticed. His attentions had never diverted to Elizabeth or anyone else—until he left. She dropped the pin she held onto the dresser.

"I believe that will do. You look very well. I am sure you will be much admired at the theatre."

Bingley sat perfectly still, gawping at his friend. He was aware of all the things he ought to have felt—anger, disappointment, and hope to name but a few—yet all he truly felt was unnerved. The man who owned to having given him such disastrous advice was the very man to whom he would usually apply for advice on what to do about it, leaving him at something of an impasse.

"I am not at all sure how you expect me to respond to such an admission," he said at length.

Darcy stared at him with exceedingly disconcerting gravity. "You have every right to be furious."

The notion of being furious with the Titan was so absurd, Bingley almost laughed. "I cannot pretend not to be shocked that you concealed Miss Bennet's presence in Town, but you have owned yourself that your inducement was to protect me. How could anyone fault you for as much?"

"I daresay it is easier than you think," he snapped and then, in a more reserved tone, added, "To persuade you against a course of action before you even sought my advice was…it was arrogant."

"But you gave more reasons to leave than her indifference. What of your other objections—connections and fortune and the like?"

"They stand."

"Then dash it if I am not utterly befogged! If your opinion of the match has not changed, what is it you came here to advise me?"

"I did not come to advise you. I came to inform you I was mistaken as to Miss Bennet's regard."

"Then you now believe there is sufficient inducement for the match?"

"I no longer believe I should be the judge of the matter."

"But you do believe she loved me?"

"Yes."

"You think, then, I ought not to have left?"

"I think I should not have *advised* you to leave, which is a very different matter."

"Then you still think I was right to leave?" Darcy looked as though he would speak but then, very unhelpfully, did not. Bingley huffed his frustration. "You think I ought to have stayed?"

"It matters not *what* I think! Make whatever decisions you will, but pray do not ask that I advise you."

"That will not do at all! Where would I be without you to tell me what to do?" Bingley replied, only partially in jest.

Darcy's voice took an edge. "You ought to have more courage in your convictions."

"Perhaps, but it is much easier to have courage in yours. You are an excellent friend; master of your own estate, you have lived in the world. It is surely to my advantage that you offer advice so freely and so often."

Having thought it a handsome compliment, Bingley could not comprehend why it should make his friend scowl so. Not knowing what else to do, he stood and rang the bell for tea. It was while his back was turned that he could have sworn Darcy murmured, *"I am Lady Catherine."*

By the time he returned to his seat, silence had taken command of the room. Silences made Bingley excessively conscious, yet Darcy's sullen glare was not conducive to intrusion. Resigned to waiting for him to cease brooding, he toyed with the torn corner of a discarded newspaper and did what people were supposed to do in moments of quietude: he reflected. The more he thought about Miss Bennet, however, the more confounding the situation seemed. Fortuitously, just as bewilderment threatened to overwhelm him, Darcy roused himself to speak.

"It seems I have mistaken friendship for patronage. I had not considered my advice officious, but I see now it was."

"Indeed, it was not. Your observations of Miss Bennet's reserve were perfectly reasonable. Despite her sister's claims, one wonders what strength of feeling existed beneath so composed an exterior." Bingley could not but smile at the irony of having such a conversation with Darcy, of all men. "Though I must be allowed some reassurance from your example."

"Meaning?"

"If we are to dub inscrutability the harbinger of indifference, you could be labelled the most unfeeling of all men. My knowledge to the contrary ought to give me hope that Miss Bennet's affections were merely under similar regulation."

Bingley was vastly pleased with this bit of logic. Darcy seemed less impressed. He took so long to answer that a footman arrived, received Bingley's request for refreshments, and went away again before he responded—and then Darcy's answer made no sense.

"She never knew."

"Never knew what?"

He gave no answer at all this time and, as though to disprove Bingley's reasoning, now looked profoundly troubled.

"Come, Darcy, you cannot have the blame for all the wrong in the world, you know. You were not the only person who suspected her of indifference. Besides, was it not you who accused me of yielding too easily to persuasion? It seems I have succeeded in proving your argument admirably, despite Miss Elizabeth's best endeavours to defend my character."

Darcy gave a tired smile. "Miss Elizabeth would argue the sky is red in defence of a friend."

"Oh ho! I see how it is! The sky is really blue, and she believed me guilty of caprice all along, eh? I suppose I must be grateful she defended me so loyally, regardless of my defect."

"I should say you were served as well by her obstinacy as by her loyalty."

"Mayhap, but I prefer to think the loyalty was all for me and the obstinacy all for you."

Darcy's smile vanished. "What makes you think so?"

"What would make me think otherwise? I got on famously with Miss Elizabeth. The pair of you quarrelled incessantly."

If only her sister had been half as animated, I would not be in this deuced fix. The thought drove off *his* smile too, and not even the inclusion of sweetmeats on the tray sent up from the kitchen could restore it.

Darcy did not want tea. He had come to redress the injury to his friend, only to be accused of a host of far worse offences, and he was in no humour for social niceties. He left it on the table and continued watching his friend unconsciously tear strips off the corner of a newspaper and roll them into balls, dismayed to be the cause of his evident distraction.

"It has been many months," Bingley said glumly. Without warning, he threw one of his pellets at Darcy's neglected cup of tea. It missed. "Think you Miss Bennet's regard has endured?"

"If I could not tell that when in her company, you can hardly expect me to know it in her absence, but her sister certainly believes it has."

Bingley fired another pellet, which bounced off the tea caddy, and another, which sailed directly over the table onto the floor. "I should dearly like to see her."

Darcy reached over to steal one of his missiles and leant back, rolling it between finger and thumb. "If your affections and wishes are unchanged, then I do not see you have anything to lose by returning." He flicked his pellet so it landed in his tea with a faint splash.

With an incredulous expression, Bingley flopped back onto the sofa and huffed. "How vastly comforting."

"At worst, Miss Bennet will not welcome your renewed attentions, but in that case, you will be at no greater disadvantage than you are now. And as long as you are at Netherfield, you will at least have the pleasant company of your neighbours."

"Pleasant company?" Bingley scoffed. "You dismissed my neighbours as having little beauty and no fashion. How have they become pleasant to your mind?"

Darcy started. True—apart from Elizabeth, he had not found the company in Hertfordshire particularly inspiring. Indeed, he would admit to taking pains to avoid some of Bingley's more tiresome neighbours, and there had been precious few he had not considered tiresome…

He clenched the arms of the chair until the urge to run a hand over his face passed. Never, 'til this moment, had he given the slightest credence to Elizabeth's charge of conceited manners.

"Was I uncivil to any of them?"

"Lord, no! A little aloof, perhaps. And, of course, incorrigibly argumentative with Miss Elizabeth."

Darcy's jaw began to ache from being clenched. "That is the second time you have alluded to antagonism between that lady and me. Actually, I found her company very pleasant indeed."

"You did? Well, good! I am not surprised. She is a lovely girl—almost as pretty as her sister—though she did not impress you at all, did she? What was it you said? Something along the lines of her being tolerable, but not handsome enough to tempt you."

"I said no such thing," he replied with the abysmal feeling of being wrong.

"Yes, you did—at that first assembly. I attempted an introduction, but you refused and made some remark about her being slighted by other men and it being a punishment to stand up with her or some such nonsense."

Blood rushed in Darcy's ears. "Pray tell me nobody heard."

"None but the lady herself!" Bingley said, chuckling as though this were not the most ruinous piece of news Darcy had received all year. "I hardly think she could have missed hearing it. We stood not two yards away."

Darcy surged to his feet. "Bingley, I am taking Georgiana to Covent Garden in less than one hour. You will forgive me, but I must leave."

He is here!

Elizabeth stared in alarm at the familiar silhouette. She had never thought to encounter him again. Certainly naught could come of it but mortification on both sides. She turned to leave—too late, for he also turned, and their eyes met. She exhaled forcefully and stepped backwards, swaying slightly. It was not Mr. Darcy after all.

The gentleman's gaze brushed past hers to an older woman who could be heard berating him for being uncivil. Elizabeth smirked. Though the man's features had not the same definition as Mr. Darcy's—his expression had none of the intelligence—he exhibited all the same hauteur of rank, and she took a good deal of satisfaction in his set down. She strained to hear what excuse he gave in reply.

"Cara is barely a twelvemonth in her grave, and you would have me flirt with these women? I miss my wife, madam."

She gasped and turned away.

"Lizzy?" her uncle enquired. "Are you well?"

She assured him she was and accepted his proffered arm, following his lead to their seats. He and Mrs. Gardiner chattered merrily 'til the curtain was raised, for which Elizabeth was vastly grateful; she was too overcome with shame to speak.

Had she learnt nothing that she would wilfully misjudge one man simply to vindicate her opinion of another? Had she not yet learnt her opinion of the other was mistaken? Oh, Mr. Darcy was still the proudest, most disagreeable man she had ever met, but he had not mistreated Mr. Wickham. His efforts to separate Mr. Bingley from Jane, however objectionable to her, had not been malicious. For how long could she continue to think really ill of him without becoming guilty of conceit herself?

"I AM ONCE AGAIN INDISPOSED AND THEREFORE UNABLE TO ACCOMPANY YOU TO THE theatre this evening. Please accept my apologies for your disappointment."

Georgiana read the note aloud and then looked up to gauge her companion's response.

"It seems a perfectly reasonable note," Mrs. Annesley said. "A little terse perhaps, but if he is unwell, that is not to be wondered at."

"He did not look particularly unwell this morning," Georgiana whispered. "Only distracted, as he usually is nowadays. I think he must still be angry with me."

Mrs. Annesley clicked her tongue. "Let us not begin that again. Your brother has told you the matter is closed."

Georgiana knew better than to argue. The subject of her misadventures with George Wickham had been well and truly exhausted between them. "But if I have not upset him, what has? He has been ill-tempered since we returned from Ramsgate and he visited Netherfield."

"It is not your place to question your brother's conduct, Miss Darcy. You had much better return to your book."

Georgiana did as she was bid though she had already determined to question Miss Bingley about events in Hertfordshire when next they met.

The intermission came, more an interlude to Elizabeth's tragic narrative than to Shakespeare's, and Mr. Gardiner was sent for refreshments. The ladies had not long been alone when an altercation erupted between two men a short way off.

"Oh, dear! Let us move away," Mrs. Gardiner whispered.

Elizabeth would have done so directly had not one of the men then mentioned he who had been uppermost in her thoughts all evening.

"…never known *anybody* so high in the instep. Well, fie on him and his righteousness! I say Mr. Darcy is a sanctimonious prig!"

She fixed her eyes on the clearly inebriated speaker, her lips pursed against all the things she should like to say but could not. True, she had accused Mr. Darcy of worse, but she was acquainted with him well enough to have received an offer of marriage. She sincerely doubted this horrid little man had any such claim to intimacy.

"I never said he was not, but he did not cheat you, Wrenshaw," the other man replied, and it seemed very much as though it was not the first time he had said it.

"How is it then that we parted with the same piece of land within two months of each other, and he made a fortune while I made naught but a fool of myself?"

"Because you are reckless with your money!"

"Piffle!" the man named Wrenshaw shouted to the tittered delight of the growing crowd. "He took advantage of me, I tell you! He is a cheat—a bounder! Do not be fooled by the stick up his bailey. No man can be that damned proper. I wager he has a whore in every bedroom at Pemberley!"

A squall of gasps flew up.

"Come away, Lizzy," her aunt repeated, but she could not leave.

"Mr. Darcy does not deserve this! He is not a bad man!"

"I confess I am surprised to hear you defend him."

"I know, but I was very wrong about him."

"Here we are!" Mr. Gardiner announced behind them. Before either lady could do more than receive the drinks he had brought, he added, "Good gracious, is that you, Harding?" and walked directly to the pair of squabbling men.

Mrs. Gardiner groaned. Elizabeth felt nothing but relief that Mr. Wrenshaw would be silenced. Within moments, her uncle was gesturing for them to join him. He introduced the quieter of the two men as a business acquaintance, Mr. Harding, and the other as that gentleman's friend, Mr. Wrenshaw.

"And this is my lovely wife, Mrs. Gardiner. She has spent a good deal of time in your part of the country actually, Mr. Wrenshaw, in Lambton. And this is my niece, Miss—"

"Lambton? In Derbyshire?" Mr. Wrenshaw interrupted.

"Yes, between Pemberley and Yewbridge," answered Mrs. Gardiner, looking as displeased with his incivility as Elizabeth felt.

"I know very well where it is, madam," he replied curtly. To Mr. Harding he said, "It was Lambton that Crambourne wished to bypass with his blasted railway. And since Darcy would part with nary an inch of *his* estate, the arrogant swine bought half of mine and sold that to Crambourne instead! Now tell me he is not a swindling bleater!" His voice grew louder as he warmed to the topic, recalling the attention of all the eavesdroppers who had begun to lose interest.

Elizabeth's vexation flared. "Upon my word, you have been very free with your opinion of that gentleman this evening, sir."

Mr. Wrenshaw looked at her sharply. "What of it? You cannot have any peculiar interest in him."

"I daresay the energy with which you have maligned him has provoked us all to be a little curious," Elizabeth replied, indicating with a glance the scores of inquisitive faces watching their exchange. "You are obviously keen that we should all agree with your estimation of his character, but none of us will be able to until you decide what it is you wish us to think of him."

His countenance reddened. "What is that supposed to mean?"

"You have accused Mr. Darcy of being righteous and depraved. I have been used to consider those opposing qualities. I am afraid he cannot be both."

"I merely suggested, *madam*, that the appearance of one often conceals the presence of the other."

"Indeed?" Elizabeth resisted a smile. "Then, it is to all our advantages that there are respectable men such as yourself to evince the difference for the rest of us."

"Lizzy!" Mrs. Gardiner hissed.

"Indeed!" Mr. Wrenshaw assured her airily, to all appearances satisfied with the turn of the conversation—until several people sniggered nearby and his brow creased in puzzlement.

His friend wasted no time engaging Mr. Gardiner on another matter. Elizabeth retreated, happy to observe the crowds and their interest dissipating and happier still when the second curtain call came and she was able to escape Mr. Wrenshaw's odious company.

Thursday, 23 April 1812: London

Elizabeth turned away from the window at a sound beyond the door. The watery hues of daybreak had crept into the room behind her, diluting the light of her candle, which blew out anyway when her aunt bustled in.

"Very well," Mrs. Gardiner began at once, holding the door ajar for a maid with a tray. "Your uncle is not here now, so you may speak freely." The maid closed the door as she left. "What transpired between you and Mr. Darcy in Kent?"

Elizabeth smiled at her frankness. Having anticipated some explanation would be required, she had resolved to relay Mr. Darcy's account of his history with Mr. Wickham, omitting any mention of Miss Darcy. That was *all* she would disclose, however, for she had not yet reconciled herself to any other part of their dealings and was certainly not ready to hear her aunt call her a fool. She accepted a cup of tea and returned with it to the window, where she watched the steam mist the glass as she told her tale.

"Were you terribly disappointed to learn this about your favourite?" Mrs. Gardiner said at the end.

"Happily, no," she replied, shamed that her undisguised partiality had fixed Mr. Wickham in everyone's minds as such. "I am angry with him, but the loss of his acquaintance will scarcely be a deprivation."

"Mr. Darcy, then, is not quite as dreadful as we all believed?"

Elizabeth rubbed a little peephole in the condensation on the window and peered through it, but the view afforded her no new, improved perspective of his insufferable pride or insulting proposal. "Not in this matter at least."

"Well, it is a lesson learnt, my girl."

"Indeed it is. I hope I never allow myself to be blinded by prejudice again. Let us be thankful I have Jane to steer me. She has an enviable capacity to see good in everybody."

Mrs. Gardiner's expression clouded slightly. "Forgive me for saying, but that is not always such a fine thing. Jane has been as much wounded by credulity as you have been by prejudice. Her desire to believe Mr. Bingley a good sort of man has seen her very ill-used."

"But he is a good sort of man!" Elizabeth pushed away from the casement and planted herself defiantly opposite her aunt, the sofa absorbing the brunt of her indignation. "Only, Mr. Darcy persuaded him against offering for Jane. He has admitted it!"

"Ah! So his friend thought to remind him of the judgement that opposed inclination?"

She set her cup down with a clatter. "His *friend* presumed to know Jane's feelings and mistook her to be indifferent. They might have been married by now were it not for him!"

"Be careful, Lizzy. Mr. Darcy is not the only person guilty of presumption in all this."

She could think of nothing to say in defence of that, and she was obliged to sit in silence whilst chagrin crept up her neck and overspread her cheeks.

"Have you told Jane?"

"About Mr. Darcy's interference? Aye, though I regret telling her that much, for she is still in very low spirits."

Mrs. Gardiner frowned. "She has had a great many weeks to nurse her low spirits. She ought to take the time to listen to you."

"It is not that she will not take the time but that I do not wish to trouble her with it. Her heart is not mended. Mine is perfectly sound. There is no need for me to burden her further with tales of Mr. Wickham's perfidy."

Or indeed Mr. Darcy's proposal, though it was that about which Elizabeth most wished to talk to her. Yet, to complain about the offer of marriage she had received, when Jane was not yet recovered from injury of the offer she had not, seemed unpardonably cruel.

Mrs. Gardiner looked as though she would object, but she was not given the chance. Her two sons burst into the room, each wailing the other had hurt him. She gathered them to her, conciliating and chastising as only a mother can do.

"You are a dear girl, Lizzy," she said over their heads. "Jane is very fortunate to have you."

Saturday, 25 April 1812: London

Bingley turned away from the implacable butler and puffed out his cheeks helplessly. He ought to have known Darcy would not be at home. It was Saturday, and Darcy invariably visited Angelo's of a Saturday morning. He looked up and down the street, hands on hips and chewing his lip, unsure what to do. He checked his pocket watch.

"Oh! 'Tis later than I thought! I might as well wait here for him. I daresay he will not object as long as I behave myself."

"Miss Darcy and her companion are here, sir, also awaiting Mr. Darcy," Godfrey replied.

"Even better!" he cried, whipping off his hat and bowling past him into the house.

"Did you enjoy the theatre on Wednesday?" he enquired of Darcy's sister once all the requisite salutations had been exchanged and he had settled himself into a chair.

"We did not go in the end. My brother was unwell."

"I am sorry to hear that," Bingley replied, though it did explain why Darcy had seemed so out of sorts. "Is he recovered? He must be if he has gone fencing."

"I have not seen him since, so I cannot say."

"If he *is* sickening for something, I might have some luck convincing him to come with me for a few weeks for some country air."

"You are going away?"

"I am!" Bingley resisted the urge to bounce up and down in his seat. "I am returning to Hertfordshire within the week for an indefinite stay."

"But you will miss the remainder of the Season!"

"You share Caroline's outrage, I see. Be assured, Hertfordshire has far pleasanter diversions than Town, as your brother reminded me just this week."

"He did? Might I enquire: Did he enjoy his time there, do you think? He has seemed somewhat distracted since he returned."

Mrs. Annesley cleared her throat. Miss Darcy glanced at her, as did Bingley. He thought he caught a glimpse of a firm shake of her head, but neither lady said anything more; thus, he could not be certain.

"I had not thought him much enamoured of the place while we were there," Bingley replied, "but he has since assured me otherwise."

"What made you think he was displeased?"

"He was forever squabbling with Miss Elizabeth, for one."

"He argued with a lady?" Georgiana cried, sounding horrified.

"Frequently and fiercely!"

"That is quite shocking! She must have been frightfully disagreeable, for I cannot believe he would have been uncivil without good reason."

"On the contrary, she was a perfectly charming houseguest."

"Oh! Was it she who fell ill at your house?"

Mrs. Annesley cleared her throat again, this time with the effect of making Miss Darcy look rather contrite.

"No, that was her sister, Miss Jane Bennet, another wonderful young lady. Miss *Elizabeth* Bennet stayed to nurse her well again."

"Then my brother has mentioned her in his letters. She was in Kent when he visited our aunt recently."

"Yes, so I understand."

After a surreptitious glance at her companion, Miss Darcy leant forwards and enquired, "Is Miss Elizabeth very handsome?"

"Miss Darcy!" Mrs. Annesley interrupted. "I think it high time you called for tea."

Bingley judged it best to say no more, but as the ladies busied themselves ordering refreshments, he reflected that the answer to the question was very simple: *Yes, she is.*

"TOUCHE!"

Colonel Fitzwilliam stepped back, tugging at his shirtsleeves where they stuck to his arms with perspiration. "Father wishes you to join his dinner a week on Thursday." Darcy was engaged in wiping his brow on his sleeve; thus, much of his face was obscured. Fitzwilliam nonetheless observed his grimace. "Come now, it ought not to be *too* dire. Only a few sundries in attendance."

The director called, *"En garde,"* and both men resumed their positions.

"Ashby will bring Lady Philippa, of course. And she will no doubt bring Lady Daphne."

"Rapture."

"Prêt! Allez!"

He lunged immediately, but Darcy parried, closing the distance between them. Fitzwilliam scrambled to retreat, but in lightening tempo, his cousin executed a sharp beat to his sword, feinted an attack in *sixte*, disengaged, and thrust in the opposite line.

The director called it. "*Touche!*"

"Damn!"

"*En garde!*"

"You will never guess who else will be there," Fitzwilliam said, ignoring his aching sword arm and resuming his position.

"*Prêt!*"

"Wellington?" Darcy said flatly.

"*Allez!*"

Again, Fitzwilliam lunged first, attempting to catch him off guard, but it was a weak attack. Darcy must have seen it also, judging by the speed and angle of his riposte.

"*Touche!*"

He wondered, on occasion, why he bothered taking on Darcy at all. He brought his feet back under him and stood straight, pushing his damp hair from his face. "Better than that. Guess again."

"Byron."

"No."

"Prinny."

"A sensible guess, if you please."

"I have no idea, Fitzwilliam, as well you know."

"You only dissemble because you believe it will be some God-awful sparrow father is promoting."

"*En garde!*"

They crouched.

"Fear not!" he continued, grinning. "Who better to protect you from all young ladies seeking to distinguish themselves by breaking your heart?" He swished his sword about in front of him to demonstrate his readiness to defend his cousin.

"*Prêt! Allez!*"

The next assault began explosively as Darcy came at him with a fierce attack. He parried frantically and retreated a step—and another—before Darcy's remise faltered, and he seized the opportunity. Parrying on the advance, he lunged forward, executing a *glissade* that saw his foil scrape down the length of Darcy's blade and land a hit on his flank.

"Ah ha, a hit! Got you!"

Spinning away, Darcy raised his sword arm, circling it around once, twice, but on the third revolution, he slashed his sword downwards in an uncommon show of pique. The colonel grinned, gratified to have riled his usually imperturbable cousin.

"*En garde!*"

"Perchance it is not protection from the ladies you require?" he said, raising his sword. "Mayhap you ought to accept one of Father's suggestions after all—scratch that itch of yours."

"I shall not dignify that with a response."

"*Prêt!*"

"Better yet, take a leaf out of Bingley's book. Choose a girl and fall in love!"

"*Allez!*"

Fitzwilliam won the next assault with uncommon ease, his cousin's usually flawless execution distinctly off kilter.

"*Touche!*"

"Who is it, then?" Darcy enquired tersely, which was stranger still, for it was unlike him to be a poor sport.

"Who is what?"

"Your father's secret dinner guest."

"'My grandmother, Mrs. Sinclair."

"I thought she was dead."

"She very nearly is. She is eight-and-seventy!"

The next assault began with a rapid flurry of feints and retreats but ended abruptly when Darcy launched himself forward in a perfectly executed *flèche*, landing a hit on Fitzwilliam's shoulder. Someone behind him applauded.

"A hit!" Darcy said with an infuriating smirk.

"Very flashy!" Fitzwilliam panted.

"Display is not your prerogative."

"I should hope not! What a dull place Angelo's would be were it not for the glut of pageantry."

The clock struck twelve, and the director called time, signalling for a man to take their practice foils and another to bring their coats. They bid him good day and weaved their way through the crowded halls to the stables.

"What brings Mrs. Sinclair to England?" Darcy enquired.

"One too many arguments with my cousin's wife. She has forsaken Ireland forever and sworn never to return unless Niamh dies before she does. Only she arrived to discover her townhouse fallen into disrepair, so she has imposed herself on my father until it has been renovated. *My father,* who despises nothing in this world more than Sinclair women!" he ended, chuckling at his father's vast displeasure.

Darcy did not join him in laughing. Looking at him, Fitzwilliam suspected he had not listened to a single word he said. "Not on top form today, Darcy?" he ventured.

It took a moment, but at length the words roused his cousin from his reverie. "By all means blame me if it will make losing more tolerable."

Fitzwilliam wasted no more time attempting to extract his secrets. He was a man grown. He would speak up if there were aught serious troubling him. "May I tell my father you will come?"

"I have a prior engagement that evening."

"That is clearly a lie."

Darcy smirked. "What of it?"

Fitzwilliam rolled his eyes, but after a little further persuasion, namely the inducement of watching Lord Matlock suffer the lamentable presence of his almost-dead mother-in-law, he extracted his cousin's word that he would attend.

Darcy arrived home to find Georgiana and Bingley awaiting him. He agreed with his sister that she would stay for the remainder of the day, but left her with Mrs. Annesley while he braved the inevitable discussion of Hertfordshire, eager to put it behind him. Despite his fears, however, Bingley began not with a discussion of that place but a wholly unexpected locale.

"Nova Scotia?" he said after his friend's haphazard account of his cousin's venture in the New World was done.

"Yes. This is the third time he has written to me. He seems determined to persuade me to his thinking."

"Is he having any success?"

"Not a jot! I should not like to be anywhere nearer than Land's End if the war were to make it that far north."

"Must you oversee the project? Could you not simply invest and remain in England?"

"That is what I wished you to tell me."

"I can certainly enquire of Irving whether he knows of any attorneys with the relevant experience."

"Capital! I knew I could rely on you."

The conversation moved naturally to the possibility and implications of a war with America. Inevitably, however, it came around to the matter that one party was eager to discuss and the other was eager to avoid.

"I travel to Hertfordshire Friday next."

To Darcy's vast consternation, the mere mention of the place set his heart to racing. He perfunctorily expressed his good wishes, then stood and moved away, unable to think of aught but what Elizabeth's reaction to Bingley's return might be.

"Will you join me?" Bingley enquired, twisting to look at him over the wing of his chair. "Your sister informs me you have been unwell, in which case a spot of country air will do you wonders." He broke into a wide grin. "Besides, if *you* come, Caroline will come, and then I shall have a hostess."

"I am sorry, Bingley. Your sister may do as she pleases, but I shall not be there."

"You are quite sure? You do look rather tired."

"I *am* tired!" he snapped with all the exasperation of the sleep-deprived and broken-hearted. Then he cursed himself privately and added, "I cannot join you. I have business in Town. Besides, I have been away from Georgiana too long now. I would stay with her for a time."

"Very well. Shall I pass on your regards to my neighbours?"

Darcy baulked at the notion of sending word to Elizabeth. God knew he longed to speak to her, to see her, to be with her—even more so after Fitzwilliam's earlier teasing. Yet, she would not wish to hear from him again. He had been certain of that even before all his recent revelations.

He rubbed a hand over his face. "If you have an opportunity to do so discreetly, I should be grateful if you could make your neighbours aware that I regret my manners last autumn."

"I really do not believe there is a need. But if it puts your mind at rest and if the opportunity arises, then I shall."

Thus, the visit was concluded. The two friends exchanged hearty farewells as they parted ways. Quashing a potent surge of jealousy for Bingley's destination, Darcy went in search of his sister and some measure of equanimity.

Longbourn, Hertfordshire
April 27

Jane!

You must hasten home immediately. I had it this morning from Mrs. Long—and it cannot be otherwise, for she had it directly from Mrs. Etheridge, whose housekeeper had it from her niece who is applying for work there. Netherfield is reopened! Mr. Bingley is returning!

It can only be for you that he returns; therefore, make haste and return this very day if your uncle can arrange it.

In anticipation,
Mama

Thursday, 30 April 1812: Hertfordshire

Their carriage had been caught behind a throng of cattle for twenty minutes before Elizabeth persuaded Jane to abandon it and go the rest of the way on foot. They were less than a mile from Meryton, the church spire already visible above the trees, and she was impatient to be home. She longed for familiar surroundings—the reflection in her own looking glass, the fire in her own hearth—*anything* that would return her to the simplicity of life before her visit to Kent.

"Slow down, Lizzy! I cannot keep pace with you."

She turned to see Jane sidling around a puddle she herself had not noticed. Smiling ruefully at the mud left on her skirts by the oversight, she went back to offer her arm.

"You are as impatient as Mama." The reproach in Jane's tone bespoke her decided reluctance to return.

"And you are unnecessarily anxious," Elizabeth said gently.

"Am I, Lizzy? I would dearly love for Mr. Bingley to renew his addresses, but I have mistaken his intentions before. What if he does not come for me at all? What if he comes only to fish in his pond?"

To Elizabeth's mind, there was no doubt Mr. Bingley had returned for Jane. The coincidence of his arriving mere weeks after she informed his friend that her sister's heart was still engaged was too great to overlook. The conclusion that it was Mr. Darcy's doing frustrated her attempts to dislike *him* even more. For in so graciously redressing his error, he had demonstrated a humility far removed from the conceit of which she had accused him.

"You may as well call it fishing," said she. "The fact is he regrets throwing the best catch back in when he was last here and has come to cast his net again in hopes of recapturing you. But it will not do for me to try and persuade you of his affections. That would make his task entirely too easy."

She lost all appetite for teasing upon turning into Bath Street and coming face to face with a group of officers, amongst them he whom she least wished to see.

"Miss Bennet—and Miss Elizabeth," Mr. Wickham exclaimed, seeming to linger over her name. "I cannot tell you how pleasant it is to see you returned. Meryton has been exceedingly dull since you went away."

Elizabeth dipped a desultory curtsey, even angrier than she had expected to be upon seeing him again. "You flatter us, sir, but I cannot imagine Miss King would be pleased to hear you dismiss her company as dull."

He gave an affected wince. "It grieves me to say Miss King's family did not look favourably on my attentions. They have taken her to Liverpool."

Elizabeth pursed her lips against an uncivil remark. Jane was more sympathetic, lamenting the interference of third parties who presume, often mistakenly, to know the depth of two people's attachment.

"He did *try* to show her the depth of his attachment," one of Mr. Wickham's fellow officers interjected, elbowing his companion. "'Tis that what got her sent away."

Mr. Wickham turned red and snarled at his friend to be quiet. His mortification and Mrs. Gardiner's education on the matter left Elizabeth in no doubt of the officer's meaning. She started in revulsion. Poor, poor Mr. Darcy, to have almost lost his sister to this wretch!

"I pray your heart mends soon," Jane said with an earnestness Elizabeth found uncommonly exasperating, particularly when her remark appeared to convince Mr. Wickham he was safe.

"I am sure it will," he replied, "now that you have brought your sister home."

His smile, the same by which Elizabeth had previously been utterly drawn in, made her cringe. "Come, Jane," she said, grabbing her sister's arm. "We had better make haste."

Mr. Wickham's smile faltered. "May I have the honour of escorting you home?"

Elizabeth resolutely, and not very politely, declined and all but dragged her sister away.

"Lizzy Bennet, what on earth are you about?" Jane exclaimed as soon as they had gone out of sight.

"Forgive me. I could not bear to be in his company a moment longer."

"Why ever not? I thought you were friends."

Elizabeth paused, still disinclined to burden her sister's heart unnecessarily. Yet, with Mr. Bingley's return, Jane's heartbreak looked set to imminently be a thing of the past. Perhaps she might confide in her after all. She began, as all revelations of any worth ought to begin, with a sigh.

"While I was in Kent, Mr. Darcy revealed more to me of his dealings with Mr. Wickham. We have been gravely misled. He was not denied a living. He was granted, at his own request, three thousand pounds in lieu of it—money he squandered in a matter of months before asking for more. It was *that* he was denied."

"Goodness—that is quite shocking. But can you be sure it is true?"

"Oh yes, there are witnesses, but that is not the worst of it. He also attempted to seduce Mr. Darcy's fifteen-year-old sister to gain her inheritance of thirty thousand pounds. And we need look no farther for proof of that than his recent dalliance with Miss King. He is a determined shark!"

"I see what you are thinking," Jane said in a vaguely condescending tone. "But you ought to be careful."

"What do you mean?"

"You are thinking that, if he had been motivated by greed, it would better excuse the abortion of his attentions to you in favour of Miss King."

Elizabeth pulled her arm from Jane's and stood gaping at her.

"I understand your disappointment," Jane persevered, "but you must take care not to allow jealousy to overrule your judgement. If Mr. Wickham's regard for Miss King exceeded his regard for you, then you must accept it as gracefully as you can."

"I shall not deny I enjoyed his attentions in the autumn, but it is not jealousy that motivates me to speak thus; it is prudence. Mr. Wickham has attempted to seduce two young girls—perhaps more—and brazenly lied about Mr. Darcy. How can you defend him?"

"Indeed I am not defending his actions, but neither am I prepared to condemn his character entirely until I know his reasons. We cannot know beyond doubt he did not love Miss Darcy or Miss King, and if he was truly attached to both, then the poor man has had his affections rebuffed at every turn for nothing more than his want of circumstances. It is too horrible. I know that pain, Lizzy!"

Elizabeth comprehended at last. Jane's obstinate support stemmed from some imagined affinity with him simply because he, too, had been jilted. Comprehension scarcely eased her frustration. Her sister was evidently not ready to hear any unpleasant truths—in which case, she was certainly not ready to hear about Mr. Darcy's proposal. No doubt, she would argue his conduct had been faultless, smooth away all insult in misunderstanding, and render his contemptuous address romantic and heartfelt.

"I understand your desire to sympathise with him," she conceded, "but I am afraid you will not convince me that your situation and his are comparable. May we at least agree he is not beyond reproach?"

To this, as well as to the appeal to preserve Miss Darcy's secret, Jane readily agreed, after which the matter was dropped. When Longbourn's chimneys came into view half an hour later, the sisters were returned to their usual harmony, their quarrel well and truly behind them.

Saturday, 2 May 1812: Hertfordshire

Kitty's announcement that a certain gentleman was riding towards the house threw Jane into an unbearable state of suspense. Elizabeth had walked out, and in the absence of her good sense, there was little to prevent Mrs. Bennet's hysterical fluttering or Kitty and Lydia's wild speculations as to their visitor's purpose. By the time Mr. Bingley arrived and the long-awaited interview began, Jane had abandoned all hope of approaching it with equanimity. She longed to observe whether he paid her any peculiar attention yet scarcely dared look at him. She longed to speak but could think of nothing to say. It seemed safest to concentrate on her embroidery and allow her mother to carry the conversation.

Though he bore Mrs. Bennet's effusions with good humour, Jane could not but notice Mr. Bingley's smile grew progressively more fixed. Gathering her courage, she exerted herself to enquire whether spring had much favoured Netherfield's gardens. He answered in the affirmative and most enthusiastically, but after that, they both fell back into awkward silence.

"I recall your saying, sir," her mother went on, unperturbed, "that whenever you were in Town, you never wished to leave it."

"Did I? But, of course, I must have if you recall it," he replied amiably.

"You did. Yet, here you are! You have left London in favour of the country. How ought we to account for it, I wonder? What is here that could possibly tempt you away?"

Jane closed her eyes, mortification burning her cheeks.

"I decided the country had one considerable advantage over London and that I should be much happier here."

Jane opened her eyes again in astonishment, and he was looking at her directly. She gasped and instinctively lifted a hand to her breast, regrettably dropping her embroidery hoop in the process. She lunged after it, but too fast, for she lost her balance and toppled after it. Stifling an unladylike screech, she reached for the nearby occasional table to break her fall.

Her recovery was short-lived, for the folding leaf of the traitorous furniture unceremoniously folded, clearly mistaking the *occasion* for an entirely different one where its services were not required. Her hand swept down towards the ground, followed by her head and shoulders as she made unintentional obeisance to the room, the stack of ribbons atop the table unfurled in a colourful fountain, and to her utter mortification, a distinct ripping sound came from under her arm.

Her sisters erupted into laughter. Her mother openly lamented her inelegance. Mr. Bingley she dared not look at as she slid back into her seat, despairing of ever regaining his esteem after such an exhibition. It was with a palpable sense of relief that she heard the front door open and the sound of Elizabeth's voice. When her sister came into the parlour, Jane turned away from the gathered company and mouthed to her urgently, *Help!*

Elizabeth judged the awkwardness pervading the parlour to be beyond salvation. She suggested they walk in the garden instead, and with a little help from her mother in dissuading the younger girls from joining them, it was agreed.

"'Tis well," she assured her sister quietly, nudging her towards the stairs. "He has come this far; a dropped hoop is not likely to put him off. Go! Change your dress and take a moment to collect yourself. I shall sing your praises until you return."

She found Mr. Bingley by the front door, and together they resolved to take a slow turn whilst they awaited Jane.

"Is your sister well?" he enquired.

"Perfectly well, thank you, sir. She is changing into something better suited to walking." It did not seem to placate him overmuch; thus, in an attempt to give him heart, she added, "We are all exceedingly pleased to see you returned."

"It is exceedingly pleasant to be back."

"And were there one person's opinion you particularly cared for," she added with a sly glance, "I daresay you may be confident of a warm welcome there also." The hope overspreading his countenance was all she could have hoped for on Jane's behalf.

"I thank you sincerely for your assurances. I hoped, from what Darcy said, that you would be my ally."

Her heart skipped a beat. "He spoke of me?"

"Oh yes, he confessed everything. I know it all."

"All, sir?"

Perhaps it was the tremble in her voice that bade him look at her with such concern. "Pray, be not alarmed that his disclosure was in any way improper. I know you did not see eye to eye with him, but I assure you Darcy is a very good sort of man—and exceptionally loyal. As soon as he realised his actions had injured me, he felt obliged to confess his mistake. I know of his misjudgement of your sister's affections, his concealment of her presence in Town this winter, and your assertion of her regard—all of it."

"I see." Elizabeth could only hope the omission of any mention of his proposal was indicative of Mr. Bingley's ignorance rather than his discretion.

"I apologise if mentioning it made you uneasy."

"No, not at all. I am only relieved my interference was not seen in a mistaken light."

"On the contrary, I cannot thank you enough for speaking up. I am quite in your debt."

She smiled distractedly, consumed by a sudden and compelling desire to hear more about his friend. With as much disinterest as she could feign, she enquired whether Mr. Darcy would be joining him at Netherfield.

"Not on this occasion," he answered. "He has been particularly busy these past weeks—rarely home to callers and unwell to boot."

"He is unwell?" She endeavoured to ignore the cloying sensation of guilt, for surely even with her vanity, she could not take credit for an ague.

"Oh, nothing serious—only a persistent cold, I think. Ah! Miss Bennet, you have joined us at last. Wonderful!"

Elizabeth gladly ceded possession of his arm to Jane and fell in behind them as they meandered Longbourn's paths. She made a poor chaperone, for all her thoughts were focused nearly thirty miles away in London on the man who had gone against all his professed scruples to reunite two people in love. Mr. Darcy would never wish to see her again, she knew. Nevertheless, though still not sorry for refusing him, she felt a burgeoning regret for not allowing herself to see him properly when she had the chance.

Monday, 4 May 1812: Hertfordshire

84 Gracechurch Street, London
May 1

Dear Lizzy,

You left us only yesterday, and already the children are wild for company. I, too, am sorry your visit was cut short, but I console myself with thoughts of our trip to the northern counties this summer—and so must you.

If your mother's raptures are to be believed, Mr. Bingley will have offered for Jane by now. Though, since he has proved himself the most whimsical of creatures, I am all anticipation for your next letter telling me he is gone off again and your sister is inconsolable. I trust you to keep me informed.

You will be most surprised to hear whom I encountered at Mrs. Featherstone's house yesterday—Mr. Craythorne! I declare the man is as hopelessly infatuated with you as ever. He would not be satisfied until I told him all your news, though I think he was only interested in whether you were yet married. When I told him you had planned to attend the soiree with me, he fair swooned. You cannot go through life making men love you so, Lizzy. It is most cruel. Did not Mr. Greyson also come perilously close to declaring himself last summer? And how could I forget Mr. Collins? No indeed, you must take pains to make them all despise you lest you invite any more unsolicited advances.

In all seriousness, while I am on the subject of gentlemen's advances, I beg you to be on your guard for Jane. If Mr. Bingley truly has returned to Hertfordshire for her, he may be keen to demonstrate his affections. Need I remind you of how Mr. Craythorne's affections manifested themselves? Mark my words—men who fancy themselves in love have improper thoughts. I caution you to be vigilant.

Enough gravity. I shall end now. Please be a dear and send a sketch for Anna, for she is woebegone without her "Li'beth."

Yours most affectionately,
M. Gardiner

With her cheeks aflame, Elizabeth folded the letter and looked up to where Mr. Bingley walked a short distance ahead with Jane. Not for a moment did she believe him the sort to behave improperly. She wished her aunt had not put the notion in her head, for she had no desire to think about his baser imaginings—and particularly not Mr. Craythorne's or Mr. Collins's or indeed any man whose improper thoughts involved her.

She stopped walking abruptly. The heat in her face spread to suffuse her entire person as it occurred to her for the very first time that Mr. Darcy had wished to bed her.

Bingley ambled down the lane with Miss Bennet's hand resting gently in the crook of his arm, attempting prodigiously hard to enjoy the moment—and failing. Not one for excessive deliberation, he had not given much thought to how he might salvage their understanding once he got here. This was their third encounter, and he was no nearer to knowing her feelings towards him than before he left London. Yet, regardless of how vexing his total want of progress was, he had abandoned her once and would not do so again unless he heard from her lips that he should. He allowed his gaze to wander as he cast about for something to say, and he was met with the sight of a ridiculously large bull energetically copulating with a complaisant cow in the adjacent field. He looked away peevishly, refusing to be jealous of cattle.

"It was kind of Miss Bingley to call on me in January," said Miss Bennet.

"Caroline called on you? In London?" This was shocking news indeed! Darcy had implicated no other party in the concealment of her presence in Town.

"You did not know?"

"I am sorry to say she did not mention it. I assure you, had I known you were in Town, I should have called on you myself."

He counted it a victory to see her almost smile and pressed his advantage by expounding on all the balls and dinners he should have liked her to attend with him. She responded with a précis of her time in London. That mostly consisted of shopping and morning calls, however, neither of which could long hold his attention; thus, his gaze soon wandered again. It fell, to his consternation, upon a pair of rabbits, vigorously obliging one another amongst the daffodils. Determined that not all God's creatures should outdo him, he let go of Miss Bennet's arm and slipped his hand about her waist, disguising the intimacy as an attempt to steer her around a muddy puddle. He threw a petulant look at the rabbits, but they were gone, and his inattention caused him to misstep, splashing mud on his boots and Miss Bennet's alike.

He was surprised to hear her laugh—a sparkling sound wholly devoid of censure—but soon realised his mistake. It was not she who was diverted but her sister, who was somewhat flushed and out of breath, having hastened to catch up with them. Bingley had to agree with Darcy's estimation that her prettiness was quite delightfully emphasised by exercise.

"Pardon me," she said, "I ought not to laugh, only had either of you been more willing to part, you might have walked either side of the puddle."

There was an encouraging thought! It even drew a modest smile from Miss Bennet. All gratitude, Bingley offered Miss Elizabeth his free arm, but she declined.

"Would you mind very much if I did not go the rest of the way with you?"

"Of course not, Lizzy," Miss Bennet replied. "Are you unwell?"

"Not at all. I would reply to Aunt Gardiner's letter before I forget all my wittiest retorts."

Bingley was rather disappointed to see their party diminished but was encouraged when Miss Bennet did not object to continuing alone. They had the distance to Lucas Lodge, where they walked to collect one of the younger Miss Bennets, in each other's sole company. He hoped that, in private, he might glean a better idea of her receptiveness to his attentions, and if he was unsuccessful there, he hoped at least he would receive no more reminders from nature as to what little advancement his courtship had made.

Elizabeth regretted her dishonesty but could hardly acknowledge the true reason for her discomposure. She bade Jane and Mr. Bingley farewell and turned homeward, forgetting them almost instantly as her thoughts returned once again to Mr. Darcy.

He had himself claimed she was not handsome enough to tempt him; thus, she had assumed he offered for her despite her looks. Could it be that his opinion of her beauty was, in fact, quite the opposite? It ought not to matter, for though she had never been insensible to his striking looks, ever since he denounced hers, she had resolved to be indifferent to them. All the same, the discovery of his admiration rather begged her to dwell upon the merits of his person—his indisputably pleasing figure, the thick, dark hair that curled over his collar at his nape, his dark, deep-set eyes that appeared almost black on occasion, his rare but becoming smile, the vertical crease that formed between his brows when he frowned…

She laughed incredulously. *Oh, yes, very indifferent! Admit it, Lizzy. He is the handsomest man of your acquaintance.*

It seemed improbable that she should have impressed him, yet her aunt had said men who fancy themselves in love have improper thoughts, and he was the only man ever to profess actual love.

She gasped and almost stumbled. Her heart pounded. Of all the things he had said to her in the course of his atrocious proposal, she had given the least credence to *that*—his declaration of love. It had seemed incredible at the time. She had dismissed it as a passing fancy. Yet, she ought to have known Mr. Darcy did not suffer passing fancies. Every report she had of him, including his own, showed him to be a man of profound sensibility with feelings immutable once formed. An avowal of ardent love from such a man could not have been lightly given. He had truly loved her, and she had refused him—nay, spurned him.

She, who took pride in her natural inclination to compassion, had been hateful in her rejection. She had hurled unfounded and appalling charges, defended the monster who almost ruined his sister, mercilessly vilified his character, and acknowledged his heartfelt declaration only insofar as to tell him he ought to have no difficulty in overcoming it. When Mr. Darcy was at his most vulnerable, his heart lain open, she had shredded it and thrown it back to him in pieces. She left the path, unable to bear any more guilt and certain anyone she encountered would immediately perceive what she had done.

Had he suffered as Jane had? Did he suffer still? She trudged disconsolately through the woods, wondering sadly who had comforted him in his distress. The bluebells beneath the trees blurred into a murky blue puddle as tears welled in her eyes. She supposed that office ought to have fallen to his wife. He had wanted her to care for him, to love him. Instead, she broke his heart. Her tears spilled over at last. She wept—out of shame for herself and pity for the man she had used so ill—and did not return home 'til all her crying was done.

"Lizzy! Whatever is the matter?" Lydia exclaimed from the sitting room as Elizabeth passed it, thwarting her hope of going into the house unnoticed.

"Nothing, Lydia. I am well."

She came to the doorway. "There must be something. You look awful. Your eyes are all puffy, and your face is a fright. Is it your monthlies?"

Elizabeth huffed a small laugh. "Really, there is nothing the matter."

"I am not *that* silly. It is clear you have been crying. Though, if it is a tricky problem that requires a clever answer, then I suppose you had just as well not tell me, for I am sure I shall be no use to you at all."

Lydia owned it—she was not the sort of girl in whom one confided. Nonetheless, very quietly and quite to her surprise, Elizabeth found herself speaking. "I have made a terrible mistake, Lydia. I have wronged somebody most grievously."

"Oh, then nothing is so easy! You must apologise."

Thursday, 7 May 1812: London

In his bed, asleep; at his club, drinking; on his horse, hurtling across the countryside; or here, at his uncle's table, surrounded by pomp and speciousness—it mattered not where Darcy was or what he was doing.

Nothing eased his misery. On the contrary, everything seemed designed to make him miss Elizabeth more. No one to whom he talked was quite as witty. No one with whom he danced was quite as vivacious. No one to whom he expressed an opinion ever challenged it. Life was muted in her absence.

Darcy had little inclination to eat, and his scant reserves of composure waned further still as dinner dragged on. He became overly conscious of the din of cutlery scouring china and the ghastly way the woman opposite scraped her teeth on her fork. He raised his hand to run it over his face, but caught himself in time and reached for his drink instead.

"Is your cousin always such scintillating company?" enquired Mrs. Sinclair, on his right, to Fitzwilliam on his left.

Before he could decide whether to be affronted or embarrassed, his cousin replied, "Not always. Sometimes he does not even trouble himself to scowl."

"I think we can all agree it would be absurd for him to go about grinning at everybody if he does not mean to speak," she replied, somehow turning the conversation so that Fitzwilliam was to blame. "You had much better carry on scowling, Mr. Darcy"—at which they both turned away to pursue other conversations.

Darcy motioned for his glass to be refilled. Though he disliked Mrs. Sinclair's incivility, he disliked more that his own disinclination to converse had caused offence. Again. He recalled Elizabeth with crystal clarity, dancing circles around him as she teased that he was of an "*unsocial, taciturn disposition, unwilling to speak unless he expected to say something that would amaze the whole room.*" He reached for his wine and attempted to pick up one of the conversations around the table, resolved to make more effort at being cordial.

"How did he propose?" he heard his sister enquire.

He set his glass down and let out a long breath. That was one conversation to which he would absolutely not be contributing.

"I do not imagine he did," his cousin Ashby replied condescendingly. "It was no doubt arranged for them."

"That is a shame."

"How so, Miss Darcy?" Lady Philippa demanded. "That is the way of things."

"It may well be the way of things, Philippa," opined her friend Lady Daphne, "but it is not terribly romantic, is it?"

"What has romance to do with a contract of marriage?" enquired Lord

Matlock. "The Pendlebury girl ought to be well satisfied with such an excellent match."

"I do not mean to suggest she ought to be dissatisfied, my lord. But it would not have hurt the gentleman to give her some assurance of his regard."

"That is a pretty notion, I am sure," countered Colonel Fitzwilliam, "though rather dependent on him having any."

Ashby snorted.

"If that be the case," argued Lady Daphne, "he ought to have employed whatever arts were at his disposal, for I can think of no occasion with more need for disguise. Every woman wishes to believe she will be respected and esteemed by her husband, even if it is not likely be the case."

"Oh, do stop, Daphne," Lady Philippa said sharply, perhaps because her friend had been looking at her when she spoke. "You are making yourself sound ridiculous."

"No, I quite agree with Miss Darcy," Lady Daphne insisted. "A woman ought to be flattered at such an auspicious moment, not treated as so much chattel."

The conversation moved on, but Darcy heard none of it over the thrumming in his ears. He stared at his glass. It was empty. Had he not assured Elizabeth of his regard? Of course he had. He made a bloody fool of himself declaring his ardent bloody love. He certainly recalled the passion with which he detailed the obstacles his attachment had overcome, the scruples he had set aside, and the injury to his consequence he was overlooking—in retrospect, hardly quixotic sentiments. He twisted the stem of his glass between his fingers, spinning it back and forth.

He was certain he must have complimented her, even if he could not recall what words he used. Though—damn! Now that he had begun dwelling on the whole infernal scene, he *did* recall excusing his want of flattery as an unashamed form of honesty, blaming her affront on her own pride. And to what great pains he had gone to illustrate he did not respect her situation, that she was not worthy of his declaration! He signalled again for more wine.

Her reproof that he had not behaved in a gentlemanlike manner, which had wounded him so deeply at the time, seemed positively generous in this new light. Any other woman might have wept to receive such insults. Yet, even as the thought occurred to him, he realised she had. Her red-rimmed eyes when he handed her his letter the next day were testament to it. He had dismissed it in his resentment—or perhaps revelled in the sense of vindication it afforded him.

"Darcy!"

He started and looked up. Fitzwilliam was standing over him, looking concerned. All around the table, the ladies were rising to take their leave. He lurched to his feet. "Excuse me."

"You look ashen, man. What ails you?" Fitzwilliam whispered.

"Naught—I am perfectly well." That earned him a dubious look, but the appearance of some exceedingly fine port on the table saved him from further questioning and eased all the gentlemen into their usual after-dinner languor. Darcy sat down and swallowed most of the contents of his glass, attempting to swill down his shame and regret with it.

"What the devil are you thinking," said one of the guests to Darcy's uncle, "hobbling poor Ashby to that hideous woman? She did naught but carp throughout the entire meal."

Fitzwilliam snorted. Ashby, at the far end of the table, did not appear to have heard, though Darcy wondered whether he would have objected if he had.

"It was his choice," Matlock replied. "He could have had Miss Blake."

"That was rather like choosing between the French disease and a venereal wart," Fitzwilliam whispered to Darcy, almost making him spit out his wine.

He could not disagree. Lady Philippa was insufferable, and Miss Blake had been worse. He waited until his cousin raised his glass to his own lips before asking, "Which one is which?"

Fitzwilliam did spit out his wine. Darcy smirked. Adrift as he was in a sea of remorse, his cousin was a lighthouse to his sinking ship.

"I know not for whom to feel more sorry," Fitzwilliam whispered, wiping his chin with a napkin. "She will be saddled with Ashby, and I doubt she was given a choice. Women generally are not, I understand."

"We will give Georgiana a choice."

"We will?"

He was not alone in his surprise. Heretofore, the list of suitors Darcy had deemed acceptable for his sister had been nominal, and he had certainly never considered her preference as having much bearing on the selection. When had that changed? He knew precisely when. He refused to think her name.

"Then she will be one of a happy few," Fitzwilliam continued, taking

Darcy's silence as answer. "Come to think on it, Miss Bennet is another. She felt not duty-bound to wed, did she? Though I doubt her parents were in accord with that particular choice."

Darcy blanched. "I…she…what?"

"Precisely. They cannot have been pleased, for it would have secured all their futures. I cannot blame her, though. She would have been miserable."

Deeply wounded he should think so, Darcy forced himself to enquire how Fitzwilliam knew of it.

"Anne told me."

"*Anne* knows?" he hissed.

"I cannot believe the fool offered for her. Heir to Longbourn or not, it was an insult."

"What? Heir to—Collins?" Several gentlemen paused in their conversations to look at him. He lowered his voice once more and repeated, "Collins offered for Miss Bennet?"

"Aye, can you imagi—"

"When?"

Fitzwilliam eyed him warily. "Obviously before he married his wife."

Darcy knew not whether to be relieved or aghast. He did not bother to suppress the urge to run a hand over his face this time.

"Truly, Darcy, are you sure you are quite well?"

He snatched his hand down. "Would that you stop asking me that! If it pleases you to have me unwell, then that will do. Let us say I have an ague. I probably ought to go home. I leave Georgiana in your capable hands."

Though Fitzwilliam tried several more times to extract some explanation for his malaise, Darcy would not capitulate. Even were he inclined to divulge his humiliation and misery, he did not think he could, for he was truly beginning to feel ill. Ignoring his cousin's concern, he made his excuses and departed.

Saturday, 9 May 1812: Hertfordshire

The carriage jounced into the High Street, its windows rattling and its driver bellowing at his horses. Mrs. Bennet flapped at the tangle of legs in the foot well, shrieking at anyone who stepped too near Jane's new gown. Mary and Kitty argued. Lydia and Elizabeth laughed. Jane turned away to peer at the looming façade of the assembly rooms.

Not even she had truly known how badly Mr. Bingley's abandonment had affected her until he returned, whereupon she discovered her confidence in both the sincerity of his affections and her ability to secure them had been reduced to nothing. Four visits, his request for the first set this evening, and Elizabeth's constant encouragement had buoyed Jane's faith in him just enough to allow a measure of anticipation for the evening ahead, but it was a fragile faith, and her grip on it was tenuous.

She and Elizabeth stepped down first and walked towards the entrance. "Once more unto the breach," her sister said, grinning.

"Pray, tax me not with Wordsworth this evening, Lizzy. I am determined to be sanguine, but it will only stretch so far."

Elizabeth gave her an odd look but said nothing more.

"I hope it is not too warm inside this evening," Mary said behind them.

"As do I," Mrs. Bennet agreed, catching up with them. "It was unbearable last month with all the fires lit."

"Oh, I have left my fan on the seat," said Jane, checking her person to confirm its absence. "One moment." She turned to fetch it from the carriage but stopped short of the door when she heard Lydia and Kitty still gossiping within.

"All that fuss over a stupid dress!" Kitty exclaimed.

"She does not look as well as Lizzy in any case," replied Lydia. "Or me."

"Would that she hurry up and secure Mr. Bingley. Then we would not have to hear any more of her new dress or slippers or any of it."

"She had better hurry up and catch him soon anyway, for she is practically an old maid. I should die if I were three-and-twenty before I found a husband."

Jane re-joined the rest of her family sans fan or equanimity and now fighting back tears. Lydia's words echoed her own fears precisely. If Mr. Bingley would not have her, who would?

"Look, Jane," her mother said in a none-too-quiet whisper as soon as they went in. "There he is! Look at the silk of his waistcoat! Oh, you are a clever girl!"

Jane looked. Mr. Bingley did indeed look fine in full evening dress, but then she had always thought he did—just as she had always admired his ingenuous, affable smile, which to her relief, he then turned on her.

"Good evening, Miss Bennet," he called, coming immediately to greet her. He bowed; she curtsied. He beamed; she smiled. Then the moment was lost as her mother pounced upon it.

"Mr. *Bingley!* How wonderful it is to see you—" She was allowed no further raptures. Elizabeth had urgent need of her elsewhere in the room, apparently. Which was very thoughtful, except it left Jane the sole focus of Mr. Bingley's attention before she had thought of a single thing she might say to him. She managed to answer his few enquiries with equanimity, but by the time he led her to join the line for the first set, her hands were shaking from the fear that she would never be easy with him again.

After all her recent revelations, Elizabeth could not but observe her family with new eyes, and she was vastly dissatisfied with what she saw. Mrs. Bennet doggedly and vociferously directed all her neighbours' attention towards Jane and Mr. Bingley, Lydia and Kitty drew attention to themselves with their shameless flirting, and Mary, in her bid to avoid any attention at all, had slighted Mr. Winters by turning down his request to dance.

How she could previously have been blind to such behaviour she knew not, but in acknowledging their impropriety, she better understood the depth of Mr. Darcy's affections. He had been willing to expose himself to the ridicule they were certain to earn him—ridicule he had once told her it had been the study of his life to avoid—so as to be with her. Rather than dwell upon it, she marched across the room to demand that Lydia relinquish Lieutenant Connor's sabre and to extract a large glass of wine from Kitty's greedy clutches and give it to Mary in the hope it might embolden her to accept the next offer of a dance.

"Good evening, Miss Elizabeth," Mr. Wickham said, stepping out from the shadows, instantly trebling her indignation. "You look exceedingly well this evening. Would you do me the honour of the next dance?"

She gave him the most perfunctory of curtsies and looked past him, searching for her partner. "I am already engaged for this one, sir," she replied, grateful it was true.

"Another then? I have not had the pleasure of your company since you returned from Kent."

His arrogant, presumptuous smirk only made Elizabeth more determined not to be compelled to talk to him. She pursed her lips and held her tongue.

"You look as though you did not enjoy your stay there," he said, quite mistaking the reason for her displeasure.

"On the contrary, I found myself in excellent company in Kent. By comparison, this evening's society feels distinctly wanting."

He pulled a face that he presumably thought was charming. "Ah, but you have not yet danced with *me*. Pray allow me to change your mind with the set after this one."

"I cannot oblige you there either, sir, for I have promised that one to Mr. Bingley."

"I shall begin to think you do not wish to dance with me," he said, laughing in such a way as bespoke his complete assurance to the contrary. "Perhaps you fear my company would also prove wanting compared to your new friends in Kent?"

"No indeed," she replied with a full smile. "I could never think any less of you."

It was a moment before he recovered his smile. "I am relieved to hear it. Evidently, somebody has impressed you on your travels, though. I confess I am intrigued."

Elizabeth at last espied her dance partner coming towards her through the crowds. With her escape guaranteed, she had no qualms in satisfying Mr. Wickham's curiosity. "There is no intrigue, sir. I believe you are acquainted with every person I saw there. Mr. and Mrs. Collins, of course, Maria Lucas and her father, Sir William, Lady Catherine and her daughter"—she turned her smile over Mr. Wickham's shoulder to her approaching partner—"Colonel Fitzwilliam and Mr. Darcy. Good evening, Mr. Greyson."

"Miss Elizabeth!" Mr. Greyson replied. "Pray, forgive my tardiness. Sir William delayed me. Shall we?"

"With pleasure," she said, accepting his arm and walking away as Mr. Wickham finally found his voice and spluttered, "Who…what…*Darcy?*"

"Sister, will you look at Lizzy," said Mrs. Philips. "Does she not dance beautifully?"

"Well, you know, she always has!" replied Mrs. Bennet. "And do they not make a fine pair?"

"Indeed they do, but did you know Mr. Greyson was returned? I heard nothing of it before this evening."

"Not a whisper! He was gone so long I began to think he would never come back, but see how he looks at Lizzy still, as though he never went away! There is no doubt he is here for her. I *knew* some good must come of her refusing Mr. Collins."

"As did I, Sister, as did I! But pray, is Jane not pleased Mr. Bingley is come back?"

"What is your meaning? Of course she is pleased."

"Well, she might like to show it. I have not seen her say two words to him all evening."

"Nonsense! She simply does not rattle on like her other sisters, and with her countenance, neither does she need to! Oh, look at Kitty dancing with Captain Denny!"

"Now there would be a happy match," Mrs. Philips agreed, "if only Colonel Forster was not taking his regiment away to Brighton next month."

It soon became clear that this was news to Mrs. Bennet, for the remainder of the first set was passed listening to her violent lamentations over the militia's imminent removal from Meryton.

After two hours of watching and waiting, Wickham finally espied an opportunity. Seeing that Elizabeth Bennet stood unattended in a dingy corner of the ballroom, he strode directly to reach her before anybody else did. She knew something. He had no idea what, but her sly remarks earlier in the evening had convinced him it was something related to Darcy, and nothing to do with that self-righteous prig ever boded well.

"Miss Elizabeth!" If not that he was already on his guard, he might have missed the flash of vexation upon her countenance. "You are much in demand this evening, but I have you to myself at last."

"So you do."

"You have danced very prettily tonight. I hope you have found all your partners agreeable."

"Aye, very much so, thank you."

"You seemed anxious earlier that Meryton's society could not please you."

"Perhaps I was, but it does not do to be too fixed in one's opinion of people," she said with a pointed look.

Blast it! What had Darcy told her? "Neither does it do to be easily persuaded of an alternative opinion."

"True, but people themselves alter so much, sometimes no persuasion is necessary."

"I see. And were any of your friends in Kent much altered? Has Mr. Darcy deigned to add ought of civility to his ordinary style? For I dare not hope that he is improved in essentials."

"Oh no," she replied, eyes flashing. "In essentials, I believe, Mr. Darcy is very much what he ever was. Though I would say, from knowing him better, his disposition is better understood."

Worse and worse! She actually liked the starched bastard. Her dreadful taste notwithstanding, he feared she must now believe whatever version of events Darcy had spun. How to undo her faith in him? "You, who so well know my feelings towards Mr. Darcy," he began, "will readily comprehend how sincerely I must rejoice that he is wise enough to assume even the *appearance* of what is right. His pride in that direction may be of service, if not to himself, to many others, for it must deter him from such foul misconduct as I have suffered by."

That earned him naught but a raised eyebrow. He was growing excessively tired of her sanctimony. "I only fear," he pressed, more loudly for the music had struck up again, "that the sort of cautiousness to which you, I imagine, have been alluding, is merely adopted on his visits to his aunt, of whose good opinion and judgment he stands much in awe. His fear of her has always operated, I know, when they were together; and a good deal is to be imputed to his wish of forwarding the match with Miss De Bourgh, which I am certain he has very much at heart."

She only inclined her head and made to step around him, but with such a glimmer of amusement in her eyes as filled him with alarm. He could not tolerate being at such a disadvantage. If she were privy to information that could ruin his good name, he would discover it. He stepped closer, reaching for her hand. "Madam, we have not finished our conversation. I must insist upon this dance."

"Miss Elizabeth, I believe this dance is mine."

He spun around. "Mr. Bingley!"

"Mr. Wickham," Mr. Bingley replied brusquely, reaching for Miss Elizabeth's hand himself and leading her away.

Wickham turned and leant against the wall, glaring at their departing backs. For all that effort, he was still none the wiser. He knew neither how much she had been told nor how likely she was to repeat any of it. He must now live on tenterhooks, fearing the chit would out him at any moment. Damn Darcy to hell and back! The man blighted everything!

Elizabeth was not sure she had ever seen such a pained expression on her sister's face as when she took to the floor for a second set with Mr. Bingley. It made her slightly nauseous to be the cause of it. She had assured him she was grateful for his intervention and to dance was not necessary, but he had been insistent upon shielding her from Mr. Wickham's attentions. There was nothing to be done but complete the set and make her excuses to Jane afterwards.

She was grateful for the liveliness of the dance and Mr. Bingley's loquaciousness, for both excused her from having to offer much conversation. He chattered on amiably as they came together and whirled apart, apparently content with smiles by way of response. She gave the appropriate felicitations when he mentioned his sister was with child and would soon join him at Netherfield but otherwise said very little. He gained her immediate and full attention, however, when his ramblings touched upon the object of her reflections.

"...and I have yet to hear from Darcy, which is surprising. Still, he was very busy when I left him."

After a moment's consideration, Elizabeth enquired, "Do you correspond with him often?"

"Fairly often, yes."

"I wonder—that is, there is something I would ask of you." She paused, unsure how to proceed with what he might consider a vastly improper request. An explanation seemed the best way to begin. "When Mr. Darcy and I spoke of Jane, we...well, it became something of a debate."

"Was it as fierce as those you enjoyed at Netherfield?"

"Rather more so, I am ashamed to say." They broke apart to perform a figure with several other dancers. When they faced each other once more, she continued quietly. "I wonder, would you be so good as to pass on my apologies in your next letter to him?"

"I should be happy to, but I must say he gave no indication he was affronted by anything you said."

Mr. Darcy's discretion only deepened her remorse. A vicarious apology seemed wholly inadequate, yet it was all that was in her power to offer him. Her later apology to her sister was little better received. Despite Jane's attempts to be gracious, Elizabeth could easily perceive she was dismayed by what must have looked to all their neighbours as Mr. Bingley's marked attentions to the wrong sister. Between Mr. Wickham's persistent lies, Mr. Bingley's overzealous defence, Jane's jealousy, and her mother and younger sisters' improper behaviour, she was ready by the end of the evening to forswear assemblies forever.

Saturday, 16 May 1812: Hertfordshire

Though happy for the opportunity to recommence his courtship, Bingley vastly disliked the hours he was obliged to spend alone at Netherfield each day. In a bid to pass the time more agreeably, he invited his neighbours to fish with him in his pond. Barring the crayfish that made a hole in Mr. Goulding's net and the chill Mr. Philips contracted after falling in the water, however, not a thing was caught. Mr. Bennet's rod was discovered to have woodworm when it split in two, Mr. Hurst's dog absconded with Mr. Greyson's tackle, Mr. Long's best (and only) beaver blew into the lake, and the whole thing was rained off after but half an hour by a sudden storm.

The gentlemen ended ensconced in the comfortable parlour of the Millstream Inn while they waited for the rain to stop. Spirits were high, conversation flowed as freely as the ale, and the fishing party was unanimously declared a raging success.

"It is capital to see you back in our little corner of the world again, Bingley," Sir William said to him over his second or third flagon. "We had worried you meant to quit the neighbourhood entirely."

"As did I, at one point," Bingley replied. "Though I *am* fond of the country, there was some uncertainty as to whether the country returned my regard. Fear not, though. Darcy set it all to rights for me, and here I am!"

"Darcy, you say?"

"The one and only. Assured me the country was completely in love with me."

"Capital, capital! I daresay he is correct, too. Will he be joining you at Netherfield?"

"He said not, but he had praise enough for Meryton when he was convincing me to return, so he may yet decide to visit."

"He is very good," replied Sir William, preening as though any praise for the neighbourhood must necessarily encompass him.

"He sends his regards, of course." Bingley placed his forearm on the table and leant forward, adding in a hushed tone, "He did ask me to convey his regrets for his reserve during his last visit, but I am sure you agree with me it is not necessary."

"Indeed, I do. His manners were faultless—here and in Kent. Capital fellow! Whatever gave him the impression we found him otherwise?"

"I did," Bingley slurred, grinning. "It was quite unintentional. I was teasing him for squabbling with Miss Elizabeth Bennet. He took it altogether the wrong way."

Sir William nodded sagely. "He must not blame himself for that. Miss Elizabeth can be rather pert. A good girl, though."

"No need to convince me of that—or Darcy. He assured me he thinks she is perfectly lovely."

"Did he indeed?"

"He did! Apparently, he finds her very pleasing company."

Sir William's eyebrows began creeping up his forehead. "Indeed! Maria mentioned he called on them often at Hunsford."

"Not often enough for them to say all they needed to say, for I am still passing messages between the pair of them." Bingley briefly wondered whether he ought to have said as much when Sir William's eyebrows all but lost themselves in his hairline, but two more flagons of ale and four rounds of skittles quite put the matter from his mind.

The End of Equanimity

Monday, 18 May 1812: London

Darcy accepted the stack of letters from Godfrey and waited until he was alone before permitting himself a small groan. He was tired and in no humour to attend to correspondence. His mood soured further still when he espied one letter written with Bingley's unmistakable hand. He knew not that he had stomach enough to read what his friend had to say, but he could not ignore it. Steeling himself, he opened the letter and began to read.

Netherfield, Hertfordshire
May 12

Darcy,

I cannot thank you enough for sending me back to Herts! I have called at Longbourn and received a ~~hearty~~ warm welcome. Miss Bennet is somewhat reserved still, but as you predicted, Miss Elizabeth was encouraging. I have some chance with Miss Bennet, I believe, but I proceed with caution. ~~I am not~~ She is as serene as ever, but I would be sure ~~before I make any~~

Are you certain you will not come to Netherfield? I have been fishing with the other gentlemen. Caught nothing. Ding-dong of a head on me the next morning though. ~~Sir William was~~ You could, of course, bring Georgiana. If you come, bring your own rod. Lent my spare to Mr. Bennet.

Any luck discovering an attorney to look over my cousin's proposal? Survey expected within the month—should like to know what to do with it. ~~It was interesting to~~ Great news! The Hursts are expecting a child! They come hither to avoid the London air. Miss Elizabeth was just last evening extolling the benefits of country air, as it happens—hardly surprising to hear she enjoys it, given her fondness for walking. She remains as engaging as ever. Her manner of speaking is delightfully unaffected. She assures me her sister receives my attentions with pleasure, for which I am exceedingly grateful, for I might otherwise begin to think I had no hope. Would that the one conversed as easily as the other! Might have better luck next week. I have decided to put on a picnic for all and sundry. Miss Bennet was anxious it might be too cold, but Miss Elizabeth thought it a fine idea—

Darcy snarled a curse and snapped his gaze away from the page. That it should be Bingley and not him receiving Elizabeth's warm welcome and enjoying Elizabeth's unaffected conversation was simply too much to bear. With no desire to read any more of that which was forever denied him, he wrenched open a desk drawer, threw in the letter, and slammed it closed again before surging from his chair and stalking to the window. He leant heavily against the frame. Did Elizabeth know he had confessed his mistake to Bingley? Did she think any better of him? He pressed his forehead against the cold glass.

"Do you know it has all been for you?" His breath frosted the glass, obscuring his view of the world. Of course she did not know. She thought him devoid of every proper feeling. He straightened, adjusted his coat, and strode from the room. Summoning his man, he informed him that he meant to go out, and he was duly provided with the appropriate attire. Then he quitted the house and did not return for many hours.

Portman Square
May 18

Dear Cousin Fitzwilliam,

I beg you would speak with my brother. We were to go to Gunter's this morning for ices, but he did not come for me as arranged. He sent no note and no messenger. I waited for three hours, then went to Darcy House, only to be told he was from home. I waited another hour there and was about to return home when I heard him in the hall, talking with Godfrey. He had been injured! He had a ghastly cut to his cheek that bled freely ~~and his face was bruised and~~

Forgive me, my hand cannot keep pace with my thoughts. He would not look at me, and Mrs. Annesley drew me back into the parlour before I could speak to him and warned me it would be impertinent to interfere, but I can no longer overlook his malaise, which has been of many months' duration now. Please come, for I know not what else to do.

Georgiana

Tuesday, 19 May 1812: Hertfordshire

"Oh! There are no officers! Why are there no officers?"

"Lydia! Lower your voice." Elizabeth took her sister by the elbow and marched her away from the gathered company.

"But it would be much less dull if Wickham and Denny were here."

"Colonel Forster's regiment is engaged elsewhere today, Miss Lydia," said Mr. Bingley behind them. Elizabeth cringed at having been overheard.

Lydia felt no such contrition. "Oh, pooh! Are there games at least?"

Mr. Bingley graciously directed her to where some of the other ladies were playing shuttlecock. Lydia sighed loudly but nonetheless trudged to join them, leaving Elizabeth to apologise for her impertinence.

"Think nothing of it," Mr. Bingley assured her. "It was a stretch of the truth in any case. I have no idea where Colonel Forster's regiment is today. I did not invite them." He leant slightly closer and lowered his voice. "I did not wish to give Mr. Wickham any occasion to importune you."

"Oh! Why, that is most considerate of you but not necessary."

"Pish posh!" He offered his arm, and they ambled back towards the picturesque array of beribboned tables and chairs where Jane waited. "Besides," he went on, grinning, "I am more than tired of being shone down by a hundred red coats at every gathering."

"Oh, yes! A gentleman ought to be allowed the advantage at his own picnic," she agreed, drawing an undignified snort of laughter from him.

"Lizzy!" Mrs. Bennet cried, bursting forth from the midst of a nearby huddle of matrons. "Mr. Bingley did not invite us here so you could run on at him all afternoon." Grabbing her elbow in much the same manner as Elizabeth had grabbed Lydia's, she tugged her away and hissed loudly, "Leave him alone to speak to Jane."

With an apologetic grimace, Elizabeth excused herself from her host and went in search of the promised games. At the other side of a little folly, she was delighted to discover a quantity of targets had been set up for archery.

"Do you enjoy the sport, Miss Elizabeth?"

She turned. Mr. Greyson had followed her from the seating area. "Very much, though I cannot claim any skill, and I am quite sure those targets are at least twenty yards too far off for me."

"That will never do!" he declared, marching to the nearest and hefting it a good deal nearer. "Will that suffice?"

"It most certainly will not!" Mr. Bingley called, coming around the folly with Jane on his arm and a large grin on his face. "I will stand for none of your nonsense, Greyson." So saying, he walked to another of the targets and brought it level with Mr. Greyson's—and then an additional two feet forward. Thereafter, the pair took turns shuffling their targets ever closer until they were directly in front of the ladies. Elizabeth raised her arm and poked her target with a finger.

"Bulls-eye!" Mr. Greyson shouted.

"Foul play!" Mr. Bingley replied. "I insist on a proper tournament!"

Thus, the targets were returned to a distance agreeable to all, chairs were set out for the gathering spectators, and refreshments were provided for the ladies. Mr. Bingley paired with Jane, of course. Elizabeth supposed it was fitting Mr. Greyson should remain with her since he had instigated the game, though she could not have said why the arrangement made her so uncomfortable.

It was not much of a contest, for neither sister fired well. Elizabeth's first three arrows all landed in the grass, much to the amusement of everyone watching. She gave in to laughter when her next hit the target lengthways and bounced off. "I am even worse than I recall!"

"Allow me."

Mr. Greyson stepped forward and placed a hand around the bow directly below hers, mumbling about how best to grip it. Elizabeth remained very still, intensely aware of his nearness. From the corner of her eye, she regarded his profile. He was a touch taller than she and had straight, light brown hair and elegant features. Indeed, he was not an unattractive man. Neither was he Mr. Darcy, of whom her memory was vivid and in comparison to whom no man fared well.

She flushed hot to have caught herself comparing *any* man to Mr. Darcy. Mr. Greyson further flustered her by turning his head towards the target, all but resting it on her shoulder. Her fingers twitched and the arrow loosed, shooting in a straight line to the bulls-eye—of Jane's target. Whilst everyone else delighted in the happy accident, Elizabeth stepped away from her companion and drained her glass of lemonade dry.

Jane's next arrow flew so far off the mark it was lost in the shrubbery.

"Jane, that was terrible!" Kitty cried. "Even Lizzy does better than you!"

"Yes, so it would seem." To Elizabeth's great surprise and greater disappointment, Jane then handed Kitty her bow and added, "You had better take my place, for I cannot compete."

Mr. Bingley's objection to her withdrawal coincided with Elizabeth's own, but Jane would not be swayed. Claiming fatigue, she begged everyone to play on without her and went to sit with Mrs. Hurst at the end of the row of chairs. Elizabeth thought she looked more piqued than fatigued but could not fathom why that should be—over a lost arrow! Whatever was becoming of her sweet Jane?

Kitty called everyone to attention, impatient for her turn. Yet, with Jane now sitting down, Elizabeth found herself flanked by both Mr. Greyson and Mr. Bingley, both offering advice and both disturbing her equanimity with their closeness.

Mr. Bennet chuckled as Elizabeth's next arrow landed in the same bush as Jane's. The two gentlemen flanking her were evidently more hindrance than help, but then, had Mr. Bingley spent more time watching his own partner rather than Mr. Greyson's, he might not have scared her away, and Elizabeth would not presently be thus encumbered.

"I know not how you can laugh," his wife whispered heatedly. "You must stop Lizzy flirting with Mr. Bingley this instant."

He wrinkled his nose. "Nay, my money is on Mr. Greyson. He at least is consistent. Mr. Bingley seems unable to decide whom he prefers. Be not surprised if he offers for Mary next week, my dear."

"I am in earnest, Mr. Bennet! Mr. Greyson prefers Lizzy and will not have Jane; therefore, Lizzy cannot have Mr. Bingley, for otherwise Jane will have no one!"

"And, um, who will Mary have?"

Mary would have to wait, it seemed. Her mother had stormed away in a cloud of smelling salt vapours without nominating a beau for her.

After her mother's third instruction to leave Mr. Bingley alone, Elizabeth stole away from the main party in search of solitude. She had only spoken to him in an effort to disguise Jane's reluctance to do so—an increasingly difficult endeavour. She comprehended her sister's unwillingness to surrender her heart too easily, but Jane's present guardedness was beginning to look like indifference. At this rate, there was a real danger she would frighten Mr. Bingley off before her mother had the chance.

Elizabeth settled herself beneath a tree and took out the letter she had received that morning from Mrs. Gardiner. She had not long been reading it when Mr. Bingley himself came upon her, breathing heavily and looking excessively hot.

"I beg your pardon," he panted, bending forward with his hands on his knees to catch his breath.

"It is I who must beg your pardon. I did not think anybody would notice if I slipped away for a short time."

"Do not make yourself uneasy. I am not part of a search party." He straightened, put his hands on his hips, and grimaced, no less short of breath. "Well, I am, but you are not the quarry. I am after our cricket ball."

"Oh, you are playing cricket? You were speaking with Jane when I left you."

"I was, but…" He coloured slightly and looked at his feet. "I do not think your sister much cared for my talk of Nova Scotia. Goulding saw me standing idle and press-ganged me into the game."

Elizabeth attempted not to allow her frustration to show. "Pray do not mistake Jane's serenity for indifference, sir. She often prefers to listen to other people's opinions on a subject before forming her own." *At least, that used to be true.*

Several bellows of "OUT!" from beyond the crest of the rise confirmed someone else had found the ball.

"Excellent, that saves me a job," Mr. Bingley said, puffing out his cheeks. He took out his handkerchief and mopped his brow. Then, with a quizzical look, added, "May I be so bold as to enquire what that is?"

Elizabeth followed his gaze to the crayon sketch in her lap. "Oh, 'tis me!" she said, laughing. "My cousin drew it. She is but four years old. I have not seen her for nearly a month. I think it a very good attempt from memory."

He agreed it was, enquiring afterwards whether she saw her relatives in London often.

"Not as often as I should like," she answered, refolding the pages of her letter. "And my aunt writes with news of another delay. I am to accompany her and my uncle on a tour of the northern counties in the summer, but it seems my uncle's business will prevent us leaving as soon as we had planned or staying away as long. We will no longer be able to travel as far as Yorkshire."

"That is a great shame." He perched farther down the same root upon which she was sitting. "I was raised there. It is a wonderful part of the country."

"I hope to still see it one day, but for now, I shall have to content myself with Derbyshire."

"That is no great hardship. Derbyshire is delightful. You will enjoy walking in the Peak, I think. And you could visit Pemberley while you are there."

The mention of Mr. Darcy's home so thoroughly unsettled Elizabeth that she stumbled over her reply but managed to make it known she thought it unlikely he would appreciate her visiting.

"Nonsense! Darcy takes great pleasure in entertaining his friends at Pemberley. I daresay he would be delighted were you to visit."

Something tugged inside her to think of the extent to which she and Mr. Darcy must now be removed from friends. Then she rallied indignantly with the remembrance of his avowed disdain for her connections. He would not be delighted to receive her at Pemberley with her relations from Cheapside in tow.

"You ought to go," Mr. Bingley said, a sly grin overtaking his countenance, "if only to hear Mrs. Reynolds' panegyric on him."

"Mrs. Reynolds?"

"His housekeeper. She is a delightful lady—most amenable, very intelligent—but *excessively* fond of Darcy."

"Does she not have good reason to be so?"

"Oh, certainly. Only she does rather like to boast of his virtues. She has a sort of paean to which all tourists and visitors are subjected." To her vast amusement, he affected a falsetto voice and screeched, "The best landlord, the best master that ever lived! Never had a cross word from him in my life, and I have known him since he was four! He is sweet-tempered, generous-hearted, good-natured!" With each accolade, he flopped his head from side to side. "Affable to the poor, revered by his tenants and servants, the most wonderful brother, and"—he put the heels of his palms together under his chin and splayed his fingers—"I am sure I know none so handsome!"

It was too much. Elizabeth burst into laughter. "I have no need to go there now since you have acted her part so faithfully!"

"As I said, it is quite something."

"It is a very fine account," she observed, for notwithstanding the silliness of his performance, every commendation he attributed to the housekeeper was favourable to Mr. Darcy's character, and what praise could be more valuable than the praise of an intelligent servant?

"And justly given," he assured her.

"You are very good to speak so highly of him."

He shrugged lightly. "It is no effort to speak highly of good friends. Which brings me full circle: Darcy speaks very highly of *you*. He would be very well pleased if you were to visit Pemberley."

Elizabeth scarcely knew what she said in response but nodded gratefully when he suggested they join the other guests.

Great was her confusion! Mr. Bingley had been in company with Mr. Darcy more recently than she. What could possibly have been said—or not said—to make him think his friend still held her in high esteem? And what did it matter? For if, despite everything, Mr. Darcy still felt some lingering regard for her, it only made both their situations more pitiable. No man so savagely rejected could ever concede to rekindling such a disastrous acquaintance. Knowing that did not prevent her from examining endlessly every new morsel of information about him she had gleaned.

It was true. Darcy *did* speak highly of Miss Elizabeth. He wondered that such an endorsement had not occurred to him sooner. Unsure why he did so and deliberately giving it as little thought as possible, Bingley slipped the piece of folded paper she had dropped into his inside coat pocket and went to re-join the cricket.

Tuesday, 19 May 1812: London

Though he had intended to call at a more acceptable hour, a brawl at the barracks had waylaid all his plans. It was, therefore, gone seven in the evening before Colonel Fitzwilliam arrived at Darcy House. A frequent visitor and one of a very few with the privilege of doing so, he declined any attendant and made his way to the study alone. He found his cousin in a chair before a banked fire, coat and cravat discarded, elbows on his knees, staring into the glass he held in his hands.

"Fitzwilliam." It was a cursory greeting, and Darcy did not look up as he gave it though it gave a fair idea of how the interview was to go. If Fitzwilliam was to deal with him in that state, he thought he ought at least to be on a level footing. He went first to the sideboard, filled his glass, drained it, refilled it, and only then claimed the other fireside seat.

"Must I beg?" he enquired after a full ten minutes of silence.

For the first time, Darcy glanced up. He looked awful. Apart from the obvious gash and bruising to his cheek, his pallor was ashen, his expression grim, and it would seem he had not slept for days. He uttered not a word, only sipped his drink and returned to staring at it.

Fitzwilliam leant forward in his chair, mirroring his cousin's pose with his elbows on his knees. "Who did that?" he enquired, gesturing to Darcy's cheek with his glass.

"No idea. I was not taking note of their names."

"You were not taking note of much yesterday, it seems. You completely overlooked Georgiana's distress."

Darcy winced but held his tongue.

"How many did you fight?"

"Not enough."

"And whatever it is that troubles you, has it been put to rights by the addition of a bloody great gash to your face?"

Darcy almost spoke several times before throwing back the remainder of his drink and clamping his lips shut. It was deeply unsettling. Fitzwilliam was not sure he had ever before seen Darcy as discomposed as this. He stood to retrieve the decanter from the sideboard, refilled both their glasses and set it down within arm's reach of his chair. "You know I will assist in any way I can."

Darcy's eyes slid closed, and he grimaced as though pained. "You cannot."

Silence reigned, the daylight ebbed, and the fire dwindled.

"Come, man, you are disconcerting me. This is not at all like you."

Darcy's lip curled. "Thank God for that."

"Bloody hell! Darcy, what has got into you?"

Silence.

"Tell me."

"Go away, Fitzwilliam."

He leant forwards. "*Tell* me."

Darcy snapped his head up, his eyes savage. "What exactly would you have me tell you?"

"Look at you! I would have you tell me what has you sitting in a chair with your face cut up and pissing self-pity into your boots!"

Darcy held his gaze for a moment but then, in a move destined to disturb Fitzwilliam far more than a raised voice or hint of aggression, merely looked away, tilted his head forward, and pinched the bridge of his nose.

Fitzwilliam waited. He watched Darcy's jaw working as he clenched and unclenched it, and still he waited. The clock struck eight, and still he waited. When Darcy finally spoke, his voice was almost inaudible.

"I love her."

A *woman* was the cause of all this? Of all the possible circumstances Fitzwilliam imagined, Darcy fancying himself in love had definitely not been one. If the man had not looked so damned wretched, he might have thought him in jest. "Who?"

"Miss Elizabeth Bennet."

Miss Bennet? Cousin to Lady Catherine's parson? "And you love her, you say?"

Darcy levelled a glare at him. "Since you found your way in, I assume you can find your way out just as easily."

Fitzwilliam held up his hands. "I beg your pardon. It is only, after so patchy an acquaintance, I must admit to some surprise at hearing you speak of love. Are you sure it is not merely a fascination that will pass in time?"

"How long do you propose I wait to find out? A month? Six? Eight months, Fitzwilliam—*eight*—and still I am in as deep as the first day. I have never felt aught akin to this before. It consumes me."

Fitzwilliam knew not what to make of such talk. It was not that either of them had ever explicitly disdained the notion of love, but it had never occurred to him—and he was damned sure it had never occurred to

Darcy—that they would ever be troubled by it. Of course, he knew people who claimed to be in love. Some of them were even married, though none of them to each other. But that Darcy, who never caught a cold but that he planned it in advance, should be thus afflicted was…incredible.

He could not be satisfied until he had an account of how it came about. As he listened to Darcy's rather halting depiction of his association with Miss Bennet, it became clear that there was even more to admire in the lady than he had observed for himself in Kent—aside, that was, from those most fundamental of virtues: connections and fortune. No wonder the old chap was languishing in despair. "Are you distressed, then, because you cannot have her?"

Darcy gave a bark of bitter laughter. "In a nutshell, yes."

"Well, admittedly, there is little to be done about her relations, but you could surely afford the want of fortune."

Darcy exhaled heavily. "I am somewhat comforted to know your assumptions mirror what my own have been."

"Pardon?"

"It is not her circumstances that hamper me."

"What then stands in your way? Marry the girl!"

"She will not have me."

"Pardon?"

"You heard. I offered for her. She refused. Emphatically."

"But why?"

No answer was forthcoming.

"Does she favour another?"

Darcy grimaced and lifted a hand to run over his face, only to catch the slash on his cheek, ripping a harsh curse from his lips.

"Pardon me. That was impolitic."

Darcy dismissed his apology with a grunt. Dabbing blood from his cheek with the back of his hand, he murmured, "She does not love me."

"She does not *what*? *She* turned *you* down—Pemberley, for God's sake—for a want of love?"

"That was the gist of her reasoning."

"Singular. I have not been used to consider love as high on most women's list of criteria for a husband."

Darcy sighed. "Elizabeth is not *most women*."

That much was becoming clear. "But you are friends. Was that not enough for her?"

"We were never friends," he said stiffly. "In that, as in so much else, I was mistaken. She despises me."

"Surely not!" Yet apparently, it was true. Darcy's expression said it all.

"I gave her no reason to like me. I slighted her. I ignored her. I quarrelled with her."

Fitzwilliam raised his eyebrows. "An interesting approach to courtship."

Darcy paused, drank, and sneered. "I all but laid the path for Wickham's damned lies."

In this new light, his insistence upon revealing Georgiana's misadventure with the miscreant back in Kent made eminently more sense. "Devil take the scheming bastard! I ought to have known he could not be in the same town as you without causing some manner of difficulty. Would that I had insisted you lean on him when first we learnt he was there!"

"It would have made no difference, Fitzwilliam. Her sympathy for him only made for a more heated rejection. She made it perfectly clear she would have refused me anyway."

"Your manner offended her that much?"

Darcy returned to staring at his drink, shadows once more obscuring his downcast face. "You may as well know the whole of it. Last year I took steps to discourage an alliance between Bingley and Elizabeth's eldest sister. She somehow got wind of it. As you might imagine, she took a dim view."

Fitzwilliam's stomach dropped like a stone. "Gads, Darcy, I think that might have been my doing." His cousin looked up sharply. "Well it came up in conversation, you see—the whole Bingley fix. I could not be more sorry. Had I but known it was her sister, I—"

Darcy shook his head. "What's done is done. In any case, it *was* wrong of me to intervene as I did. Elizabeth had every right to be angry."

"But it is easily rectified. Surely, you could—"

"I have already spoken to Bingley. He returned to Hertfordshire a fortnight ago."

"Well, then, I do not see that you could not also."

"He has the advantage of not having proposed as I did."

"Granted, but now that you have corrected Miss Elizabeth's misapprehensions about Wickham and sent Bingley back to her sister, she might be willing to reconsider."

"No, I mean, he has not offended her as I did with my proposal."

"Upon my life, how did she contrive to take offence from a proposal of marriage?"

"Because, in the course of *my* address, I catalogued the countless reasons why I should *not* marry her," he said, his voice dripping with bitterness. "I scorned her situation—waxed eloquent on the degradation such a connection would afford me." He gestured wildly as he spoke, heedless of the drink splashing from his glass, his voice rapidly gaining volume. "I made damned sure she understood how hard I had fought to repress my feelings and accused *her* of pride when she took offence. I might, at one point, have mentioned that I loved her, but only to exemplify my generosity, because regardless of the diminution of my fortune, society's contempt, and my family's abhorrence, I would take her *anyway* because I am *that gracious*!" He bellowed the last and pounded his fist on the arm of the chair. Then, all was still but for the sound of him breathing heavily through his nose.

"Good God," Fitzwilliam said quietly. "What the devil possessed you to express yourself thusly?"

"Would that I knew!" He threw back the contents of his glass and thrust it out for more, which Fitzwilliam moved hastily to provide. "I am the greatest fool that ever was. It never even occurred to me that she might say no!"

"I really think that is the part you ought *least* to regret! It is not unnatural that you should expect a lady of lesser consequence to accept your offer of marriage."

"That does not excuse the way I vilified her family's condition in life. I cannot think on it without abhorrence. It is insupportable that I have occasioned her such pain—*any* pain! She wept, Fitzwilliam. I brought her to tears."

"Women cry all the time."

"Not by *my* hand." He leant forward to stare into his drink again. "What have I become?"

"There is naught wrong with what you have become! One poorly handled courtship does not make you a bad sort of person."

"Would that were the extent of my mistakes," he mumbled, his words now distinctly slurred. "But she held a mirror to me, and I did not know myself. She has properly humbled me."

"That she most certainly has, my friend."

Darcy discarded his glass carelessly on the table and put his head in his hands. "I am so in love with her. What am I to do?"

There was nothing to be done and nothing more to be said. All Fitzwilliam could offer was a strong arm to haul Darcy to his bedchamber and a word to his valet to have a tincture ready for the morning that would ease his sore head, if not his bruised heart.

Knightsbridge
May 20

Georgiana,

Distress yourself no longer. Have duly admonished your brother for conceding injury to anyone other than yours truly and threatened matching slash on opposing cheek should he attempt it again.

Be assured—naught ails him that time will not mend.

Fitzwilliam

Wednesday, 20 May 1812: Hertfordshire

Jane started when the parlour door was flung open and her mother swept in.

"Ah, good, you are both here," said Mrs. Bennet, dropping into her favourite armchair. "Come closer, girls. I would speak with you."

Jane looked enquiringly at Elizabeth, who looked back at her with equal bemusement. Both set their work aside and moved to sit on the sofa.

"It is clear after yesterday," began Mrs. Bennet, "that you are both in dire need of some direction. Jane, I shall begin with you. Mr. Bingley arranged that picnic in your honour, yet you spent most of the afternoon sitting out of games and refusing to speak to him. He will think you are not interested if you continue to be so unforthcoming."

Her mother could not have made a more distressing observation, for Jane was all too conscious that the easy and treasured friendship she and Mr. Bingley once enjoyed had been eclipsed by awkwardness and reserve.

"You like him, do you not?"

"I *love* him!"

"Then you must show it, or he will never offer for you."

Jane gasped.

"I think what Mama is trying to say," Elizabeth interjected, reaching for Jane's hand, "is that perhaps Mr. Bingley needs a little encouragement. If you only spoke to him a little more—"

"Oh, as you do?" Jane had not meant to say the words aloud, and she was sorry when Elizabeth recoiled. Yet, now it was said, she found she could not regret it. All day at the picnic, whilst she had struggled to think of a thing to say, her sister had delighted the guests—and, more particularly, the host—with her easy conversation and clever wit. Watching Mr. Bingley watch her at archery had been deeply troubling, akin to watching the entire neighbourhood watch them dance together at the assembly. Both incidents had kindled a wholly unfamiliar yet potent sentiment in her mind: envy.

"She is quite right, Lizzy," Mrs. Bennet said. "You must desist from flirting with Mr. Bingley."

Elizabeth's expression of pained disbelief was nothing to Jane's dismay. Surely, her dearest sister would never usurp Mr. Bingley's attentions by design. Yet, if her mother believed it…

"I assure you, ma'am," Elizabeth said tightly, "I flirted with nobody yesterday, and certainly not Mr. Bingley. Indeed, it grieves me that you consider me capable of it."

Mrs. Bennet clicked her tongue impatiently. "Do not get on at me, girl. I did not say your manner was at fault—only your focus. Leave Mr. Bingley alone and—"

"You speak as though I am Lydia, pestering the poor man for attention! If Mr. Bingley and I have become better acquainted, it is only through my attempts to help you, Jane, when you have been too shy to speak to him."

"You have no business being friends with Mr. Bingley!" her mother objected, negating the necessity of Jane saying the same thing. "No, *you* must direct your efforts towards Mr. Greyson."

Elizabeth's eyes widened. "Mr. Greyson?"

"Why, yes! He likes you very well. You could secure him in an instant if you would only use the same charm on him you have done with Mr. Bingley."

"Madam, I have used no charm! And I do not wish to persuade Mr. Greyson of anything."

Mrs. Bennet's expression grew pinched. "You will do as you are told. If you had done your duty and married Mr. Collins, none of this would matter. Then, you could have flirted with whomever you chose!"

Elizabeth surged from her chair with an angry growl and stormed to the door. Mrs. Bennet followed her, screeching at her even after she quitted the room about wilful ways and ingratitude. Elizabeth's only reply was to close the front door with excessive force. Mrs. Bennet turned back into the parlour, her lips pursed and her face and neck suffused with a deep flush. "Obstinate, headstrong girl!"

Jane was unused, but not entirely averse, to the sense of vindication that overcame her. "Not quite so charming now, Lizzy," she muttered. Her complacency was not to last. In the next moment, her mother rounded on her.

"You could learn a good deal from your sister. She has gentlemen eating from the palm of her hand. You would do well to take a leaf from her book before Mr. Bingley changes his mind again and disappears off to this Nova Scotia place he keeps wittering on about forevermore!" She stomped from the room shouting for Hill, and Jane was left to all the satisfaction of having forced her to say what gave no one any pain but herself.

Thursday, 21 May 1812: London

The air was damp and the sky overcast, yet the day was not cold, and birdsong filled the park. Had Darcy not been burdened with the prospect of a most disagreeable conversation, he would have taken a good deal more pleasure in the early morning ride.

As soon as he was certain no passers-by were near enough to overhear, he turned to his sister riding beside him. "I am sorry if my appearance on Monday gave you cause for alarm. It was naught serious, but I ought to have told you that sooner."

"There is no need to apologise."

"Yes, there is. It was selfish of me not to consider how seeing me thus might distress you. I have been careless with your feelings too often of late, and I apologise. I shall endeavour to be more attentive in future and to cancel no more engagements."

"I do not need you to be more attentive," Georgiana replied, her voice quiet but her tone uncommonly severe. "I can live very well without ices at Gunter's or *Romeo and Juliet*. You must truly think me a child yet if you believe my only concern is for my own entertainment."

Darcy returned his gaze to the distant trees, frowning in consternation. "It was not my intention to cause further offence."

"You misunderstand me. I am not offended or feeling neglected. I am concerned—for *you*."

He tugged his horse's reins, needlessly adjusting its heading. Was there a woman alive he did not misunderstand? "I see. Thank you."

She had bowed her head, he noticed, and her cheeks were pinked where they had not been before. There was every possibility he was wrong, but she seemed distressed. Again. "I comprehend," she said with a quiet sigh.

"Would you care to enlighten me? Because I do not."

That earned him a sad smile. "It grieves me to see you unhappy, Fitzwilliam. I wish it were in my power to relieve your pain, yet I am too young to be of any use as a sister, too old to be your daughter, and too much a woman to be your friend. I fear the years that separate us will forever be an obstacle."

It was a poignant summation of their relationship. Compared to Elizabeth's intimacy with Miss Bennet, Darcy's attachment to his sister was markedly patriarchal. What can a young man do with a baby sister, after all, but dote on her? Yet, he was no longer so very young, and she was assuredly no longer an infant. Perchance they had at last reached an age where they might enjoy a more equal friendship. After all, a full eight years separated him from Elizabeth, and he craved her companionship like nothing else.

"Not as much as they have been, I think," he offered with a gentle smile.

A mix of hope and delight overspread her countenance as she enquired whether that meant he would now tell her what troubled him. He baulked at the prospect. Then, just as quickly, he imagined Elizabeth laughing at him for it. She would no doubt accuse him of being unsocial and draw from him more than he intended to reveal, as she had done on so many occasions. There was no doubt she would have better understood—better respected him—had he been less reserved.

"I have," he began, his eyes fixed on the trees ahead, "through my mistaken pride, lost the chance to wed a lady whom I greatly admire. It has been difficult to accept both my mistakes and my loss."

Georgiana gasped softly. "I had no idea you liked her so very well."

"Of whom do you speak?" he demanded, looking at her sharply.

"Why, Miss Elizabeth Bennet."

He looked back at the trees, hoping his mortification was not obvious. "How did you know?"

"You spoke well of her in your letters, and Mr. Bingley said you enjoyed her company."

He pressed his lips together in vexation. Bingley—indiscretion personified.

"What did you mean," Georgiana went on, "when you said your mistaken pride had lost you the chance to wed?"

"I would not dwell on this, Georgiana. Suffice to say that her opinion of me is not as great as my own has been, and my arrogance gave her reason to believe other, less favourable reports of my character."

"What reports? Who does she know that would speak ill of you?"

His instinct was to shield Georgiana from the painful truth, yet his pledge to treat her more equally forbade it. It was nonetheless with great caution that he informed her of Wickham's part in his present misery. Her response surprised him, being more furious than distraught.

"Has he not done us enough harm? He is entirely unrepentant!" Her horse skittered sideways, startled by her outburst. Darcy grabbed for its reins, easing the beast closer to his own.

"Unfortunately, yes, he is. I doubt he will ever improve."

"Then I pity the next person he importunes, for it is too much to hope he will not impose upon anybody else."

A horrible foreboding blossomed in the pit of Darcy's stomach. Elizabeth had never sought Fitzwilliam's corroboration of the account of Wickham's character he gave in his letter. He knew not whether she had even read it. Part of him hoped she had not, for it was full of bitterness and resentment. Yet, if she had not and she was still enamoured of the fiend… Repugnant visions of Wickham's filthy hands on her and her reputation in tatters filled his head.

"Good day, Mr. Darcy, Miss Darcy!"

He started and looked up. Two gentlemen from the fringes of his set were walking by. "Mr. Temple, Mr. Vaughan," he said, slowing his horse and tipping his hat.

"'Tis true then?" Mr. Temple said, staring brazenly at Darcy's cheek. "You did get a beating at Jackson's?"

Darcy glared balefully at the man and said not a word. He had taken countless punches at Jackson's, none of them having the desired effect of beating off his heartache, but to mention it in the presence of his sister was unpardonable. Mr. Temple paled. Mr. Vaughan babbled an apology for his friend's impertinence and both men scurried hastily away. Darcy shook his head and nudged his horse into motion.

"One day you will meet somebody who fails to be intimidated by that stare of yours," his sister reprimanded him gently.

"Believe me, I have met her already, and she is far more than a match for me."

Georgiana only smiled sympathetically, and they left the park in companionable silence.

Darcy House, London
May 21

Colonel Forster,

I hope this letter finds you well. I write in regard to one of your officers, Lt. Wickham, in whose character I fear you have been most unhappily deceived.

It has recently come to my attention that he has given the people of Meryton an account of his prior acquaintance with me that bears so little resemblance to the truth as to place any who believe it in substantial danger. Allow me to give you a more truthful report. (Supporting documentation and addresses of referees are enclosed.)

Mr. Wickham is the son of my late father's steward and godson to my father. He was bequeathed an amount of money upon my father's death, which he was granted as well as the promise of a living, which he rejected in favour of mutually agreed remuneration. This he squandered in its entirety within months and soon returned with a request for more, which was denied. Nonetheless, I have been obliged on more than one occasion to clear considerable debts in his name.

He is also a known philanderer and has not scrupled to prey upon young ladies—particularly those in possession of any significant fortune. I would ask that you be particularly vigilant of his activities in this quarter.

In acknowledgement of the harm the delay in divulging this information may have caused, I shall settle any debts Lt. Wickham has accrued that he is unable to pay himself up to the date of receipt of this letter. Thereafter, I relinquish all responsibility for the man to you, his commanding officer.

Yours sincerely,
Mr. Fitzwilliam Darcy

Saturday, 23 May 1812: Hertfordshire

Elizabeth strained for composure as she walked, angrily divesting the twig in her hands of its leaves, one forceful tug at a time. The Bennets, along with many of their neighbours, had dined at Lucas Lodge the night before. This morning, as all five sisters strolled into Meryton, Jane had once again begun bemoaning Elizabeth's familiarity with Mr. Bingley.

"I comprehend you feel conscious in Mr. Bingley's presence," she said to her, "but surely you would not have me slight him simply to make your diffidence less obvious."

"Of course not, Lizzy, but it *is* possible to constrain yourself to mere civilities. You need not monopolize every conversation."

"I was not aware that I had."

"So you have said, but your manners—well, there must be *something* in your manners, Lizzy, for you are forever the centre of the gentlemen's attention."

"Is that not proof you ought to make more effort to converse if that is what gentlemen admire?"

"I have no doubt, but not everybody has wit and self-assurance in infinite measure. Besides, Mr. Bingley was perfectly satisfied with my manner last autumn whilst you were busy sparring with his friend. All I ask is that you be mindful not to out-vie me simply because you no longer have Mr. Darcy to occupy you."

The remark took Elizabeth aback. She had thought herself terribly clever last autumn, never speaking to Mr. Darcy unless it was to demonstrate how much wiser and more perceptive she was than he. Yet something in her manner had misled him into believing she liked him— even loved him. Her twig snapped in two. She threw it aside.

Had she flirted with him? Certainly not consciously, yet her sister and mother's charges of wanton coquetry and her aunt's tease not to make men love her were all suggestive that her manner was not beyond reproof. The possibility that Mr. Darcy's attachment to her (and therefore, too, his disappointment and humiliation) was of *her* doing was inexpressibly painful.

She dared not voice her regrets lest it excite her sister's misgivings, but she could, and did, promise to stay out of sight whenever Mr. Bingley called so as not to obtrude upon their time together.

"Lizzy," Lydia called from behind them, where she walked with her other sisters. "Kitty says you refused to tell Aunt Gardiner in your letter that I am to go to Brighton with the Forsters!"

"Kitty is right," she replied.

"But I asked you to put my news in your letter! I would have written to her myself had I known you would not! You are only jealous that *you* have not been invited to spend the summer with Wickham!"

"I did not tell her, Lydia, because it is not true. Mrs. Forster merely said it would be pleasant if you were to go."

"Aye," said Kitty, "and even she admitted Colonel Forster was unlikely to agree to it."

"And Papa would forbid you from going even if she did invite you," Mary added.

"Mama would never allow him to do that," Lydia scoffed petulantly. Her gaze flicked past them all briefly, then back, and in a challenging tone she said to Elizabeth, "Let us see who is right about my being invited." So saying, she stepped out into the thoroughfare, waving and calling, "Denny! Sanderson! Wickham!"

Elizabeth turned to see a disorderly group of militiamen spilling from the Red Lion on the far corner, all evidently in their cups. She and Jane called for their sister to come back, but to no avail. With a defiant look, Lydia hitched up her skirts and ran across the road. There was little else the rest of them could do but follow her to the throng of officers.

Wickham squinted at the approaching figure. When it materialised into Miss Lydia Bennet, he attempted to hide behind Denny. Denny promptly fell over, and Wickham tripped over him and stumbled to the left, shoving Brichard into Sanderson. When he righted himself, he found he was no longer facing one Bennet woman, but five—Miss Elizabeth, with her potentially damning information, amongst them. He groaned.

"Wickham!" the youngest screeched, and he winced as the sound lanced through his head. "You will never guess what! Mrs. Forster wishes me to come to Brighton for the summer!"

This news left Wickham utterly unmoved but for the hope she might learn to temper her voice somewhat before she arrived.

"Only, she does not think Colonel Forster will agree. But you could persuade him, Wickham, I know you could."

Miss Elizabeth appeared by her sister's side. "Mr. Wickham is the last person you should expect to help you, Lydia. You lack the only inducement that might persuade him you are worth the trouble."

"Are you calling me plain?" she objected, resisting her sister's attempts to drag her away.

"No," Miss Elizabeth said under her breath. "I am calling you poor."

Panic assaulted him. Did she know it all then? His reduced circumstances? His less than honest schemes to acquire whatever money he could get his hands on? If she revealed his shot at Miss Darcy's fortune or Miss King's or any of the others in between, it would almost certainly spell the end of his career in the militia. And God forbid that his dalliance with Forster's wife should be discovered. "On the contrary, Miss Elizabeth!" he blurted. "Your sister boasts many inducements that might tempt a man."

A gasp from Miss Bennet and the look of horror on Miss Elizabeth's face convinced him that those might not have been the most well considered words with which to defend his honour. He stepped backwards, attempting to meld into the safety of his regiment, only to discover the bastards had all deserted him and were halfway down the street. His head began to pound.

"I would not have thought you imprudent enough to attempt it," said Miss Elizabeth as she turned to leave, ushering her sister before her.

Seized with the conviction the wench was threatening to expose him, Wickham's panic swelled into indignation. "What is your meaning, madam?" he called, walking after her, but he stumbled over his own drunken feet and staggered towards her, grabbing for something with which to steady himself. That something was her upper arm. His grip spun her around to face him.

"Unhand me at once, sir!"

He made to let go but thought better of it when a wave of nauseating dizziness assailed him and he almost fell atop her. "I hope you did not mean to threaten me just now, Miss Elizabeth."

"Mr. Wickham, I beg you would release me," she replied, looking about in alarm.

"I should not like to think you so cruel as to reveal whatever tales Darcy has filled your pretty little head with. It is not kind to gossip."

"Are you preaching to me, Mr. Wickham?" she said angrily. "I had been given to understand that making sermons was not always so palatable to you."

"I would really rather you kept Darcy's charges to yourself." His head was thumping mercilessly, and he felt perilously close to vomiting.

"And so I shall, but *my* charges are my own to make. You have lied to me from the very beginning of our acquaintance—"

"Lower your voice, madam!"

"Unhand me!"

She tugged her arm away, pulling him off balance. His feet scuffed forward, his head spun, and he held on all the tighter, for there were now black spots at the periphery of his vision. "Stand still!"

"You have whispered vengeful falsehoods in my ear," she said more loudly, trying to pry his fingers from her arm. "You have defamed a good man for your own promotion."

"Enough!"

"You have ingratiated yourself into this neighbo—"

He heard his name called and swung his head up. People were emerging from shops the length of the street. His fellow officers were running back towards him. "Look what you've done, you infuriating tart!"

"Release me!" the wench squealed then stamped hard on his foot. "Mr. Darcy was right about you!"

"Hold your tongue!" he snarled in her face. Half the town was bearing down upon him, and she was about to spill all his secrets at the top of her lungs. His pulse thundered in his ears.

"You are vicious and unprinci—"

"I said, *hold your tongue!*" Addled by alcohol and fear alike, Wickham was unable to think of aught but silencing her before she exposed him to the world as a fraud. His fist connected with her temple, and she crumpled into an insensible heap at his feet.

The other four Bennet women reminded him of their presence with a collective scream. He looked up. People were yelling and running—and very close. He did the only thing he could do. Without a backward glance, he ran as fast as his drunken legs would carry him to the nearest tethering post, purloined the first horse he came upon, and ran the beast until it went lame.

Many hours later as he cowered in the back room of a pounding house in Edmonton, Wickham cursed Darcy for probably the thousandth time that day. It was all his bloody fault.

The Beginning of Despair

Thursday, 28 May 1812: London

Darcy was midway through a meeting with his housekeeper when Godfrey brought him the morning's post. Atop the pile sat a new missive from Bingley, bringing an abrupt end to his interlude without thoughts of Elizabeth, which on this occasion had lasted almost an entire hour.

He was in no humour to subject himself to Bingley's raptures on all matters pertaining to the Bennets and particularly unwilling to learn, as he feared he might, that Elizabeth would now be sister to one of his closest friends. He opened a desk drawer, tossed the letter in, and slammed it closed again. The rest of the post he put aside to read later and returned to reviewing the ledger before him.

It was not until later in the day, upon addressing the outstanding correspondence, that his niggling guilt was assuaged. A reply from Colonel Forster assured him that Bingley had not written with news of his engagement after all; thus, his letter could be ignored with impunity. Regrettably, the news with which Colonel Forster—and, he presumed, Bingley—had written was far less agreeable.

Meryton, Hertfordshire
May 25

Mr. Darcy,

My sincere thanks for your recent communication. It grieves me to report, however, that your warning has come too late. On Saturday last, whilst in his cups, Wickham seriously injured a young woman and left the scene without being apprehended. By all accounts, her condition is considered to be very grave and recovery becomes increasingly unlikely. Thus, the charges against him look set to be for considerably more than assault alone.

My men have traced him as far as Edmonton but no farther. If you have any information that might help locate him, I should be grateful to hear from you, or you can pass details directly to Col. Dempsey of the Eighth Regiment of the City Militia.

Lastly, I enclose a list of debts accrued in the area by Wickham up to and including Friday, May 22, the total of which I have offset with his last month's salary. I pass on the profound thanks of all the local merchants for your generosity.

Yours sincerely
Colonel Forster

Friday, 28 May 1812: Kent

"MR. COLLINS, MA'AM," ANNOUNCED THE AGED BUTLER.

Mr. Collins ducked past him and scuttled over to Lady Catherine de Bourgh, bowing as deeply as his corset allowed.

"This is most inconvenient," she said with a sniff. "I was not expecting you until tomorrow."

"My humblest apologies, your ladyship, but I come bearing news of a most distressing nature, which I felt my duty to impart without delay, for it is imperative in circumstances such as these, and in particular when such cherished and venerable personages and their futures are involved, that no time is wasted that could be better spent putting into place measures that will prevent events progressing to a point at which they cannot be undone."

"To what events and which personages do you refer?"

He thought he had just told her that. Perhaps he had couched the news in too gentle terms. "I have received word that your nephew Mr. Darcy has expressed serious intentions towards a young lady other than your most illustrious daughter—that he intends to affiance himself to another!"

"That is impossible."

"It ought to be, your ladyship, but my wife has received a letter this morning from her father. The whole of Hertfordshire is apparently alive with the news that—"

"Hertfordshire? Who is there for my nephew in *Hertfordshire*?"

"Miss Elizabeth Bennet."

An angry flush overspread her ladyship's countenance, and she gripped the arms of her chair with both hands. "*Your* cousin?"

He nodded. "I suspect they formed an attachment at Easter and now—"

The wisdom of coming to share his news shrivelled to a distant memory when Lady Catherine reared up from her seat and pointed a shaking finger at him. "*You* have done this! *You* brought her here! *You* allowed her, a member of your own family, to come into my home and wilfully enthral my nephew under my very nose!" Her pique reached such a pitch as brought on a fit of coughing for which Mr. Collins was immeasurably grateful, for he knew not when or, indeed, whether her wrath would otherwise have exhausted itself.

"Pray forgive me! Had I known this would be the result of her visit, I should never have allowed her to come."

"I do not forgive you!" she croaked, hauling herself to her feet. "You have no idea what you have done. But it will not be borne, not while I live to prevent it."

Mr. Collins cowered out of her path as she hobbled furiously from the room, bellowing between coughs for her trunks to be packed. The silence left in her wake was as a vacuum, sucking the sound from his ears and the breath from his lungs. He fumbled for a hold on the back of the sofa and, by placing hand-over-hand, dragged himself on unsteady legs towards the door, then all but ran back to the parsonage.

Friday, 29 May 1812: London

Knightsbridge
May 29

Darcy,

Received your note. So it comes to this! Your father must be turning in his grave. Thank God this violent streak did not reveal itself around Georgiana. Not that I am not sorry for the girl in Herts, but still, she is not dear to us.

Rest assured, Wickham will be found. You did well to put Jameson on the hunt. He is a good man for the job. Needless to say, my boys enjoy a good chase—have allowed a few to take up the scent. Between both our men and Forster's, the bastard will be in irons in no time. I should not bother with the Runners. They will not touch this while the army and the militia are involved—nothing in it for them.

Not at all surprised you have managed to assume culpability for the whole affair. I shall not waste His Majesty's ink attempting to persuade you otherwise, though I trust you can guess my opinion.

Keep me informed. I shall do the same for you.

Fitzwilliam

Darcy put the letter aside. Regardless of his cousin's opinion, he knew no one would have been harmed had he only deigned to warn people of Wickham's depravity sooner. It pained him to think Elizabeth must know this also and despise him for it.

The sound of voices in the hall brought a welcome interruption to such wretched reflections. He pushed himself out of his chair, happy for the reprieve of a visitor—and a familiar one, given the absence of a calling card. His surprise was great indeed when Lady Catherine de Bourgh swept into the room.

"I am relieved to find you at home, Nephew," said she, enthroning herself in an armchair. "A report of an alarming nature has reached my ears. I could not rest until I had your word it was without foundation."

Darcy suppressed a sigh. "Good afternoon, madam."

She blinked at him, her countenance reddening slightly. "Yes, yes, good afternoon."

"And what is this report you would have me refute?"

She bristled. "A vile rumour has spread all the way from Hertfordshire…"

The mention of that place set Darcy's heart to racing. He ignored it. Hertfordshire was a large county, and reason would have it that not every piece of news to travel thence must pertain to Elizabeth.

"…that you are very soon to become engaged to Miss Elizabeth Bennet!"

Reason was overrated. "Where have you heard this?"

"From Mr. Collins. His wife's family would have it that in Hertfordshire it is widely expected you will soon make your addresses."

He glanced heavenward. "You have met Mrs. Collins's family. Can you truly credit any report from Sir William as being grounded in truth?"

"I can credit him with knowing every rumour there is to be known."

"What that man imagines he knows and what the rest of the world believes are highly unlikely ever to coincide. I have not been in Hertfordshire for many months. Why should this particular rumour be circulating now?"

"Do not be obtuse. Miss Bennet clearly set her cap at you after her Easter visit and has begun the rumour herself in an attempt to entrap you from afar."

Darcy almost laughed. Little did his aunt know how willingly he would submit to any such entrapment. "I assure you, there is no possibility Miss Bennet might invent such a tale. This report is nothing more than fanciful conjecture, likely spurred by my friend's return to the area."

She peered at him for a moment, as though deciding whether to believe him or not, then sighed overly loudly. "Thank heavens! Such an alliance would have been a disgrace! But then I knew it could not be true. You would never connect yourself to a woman of such inferior birth, of no importance in the world. You know your place."

Darcy clenched his teeth against rising indignation. "I am very sensible of my place. Do you know yours, though, I wonder?" Her eyes widened in outrage, but he pressed his point. "Do not presume to instruct me on whom I may or may not wed."

She seemed torn between fury and alarm. "Surely, you cannot mean to tell me you *do* have intentions towards this girl?"

"You are mistaken if you believe you are in any way entitled to know my private concerns."

"But she is *nobody!* She has nothing to recommend her! She is a tradesman's niece, a parson's cousin—"

"Lady Catherine, I have said nothing of my intentions, but whatever they may be, Miss Bennet is a gentleman's daughter and an exceptional woman whom I hold in very high esteem. I will not hear you disparage her."

She looked at him aghast. "Have you lost the use of your reason?"

"Quite the contrary, I am more master of myself than I have ever been."

"Her arts and allurements have drawn you in!"

"I believe I made clear my wish for you not to speak ill of her. She is quite without art and deserves no censure of yours."

"You cannot be serious!"

He only glowered silently at her.

"You are infatuated then."

When still he gave no answer, she threw a hand in the air and cried, "Heaven and earth, can you not find a half decent incognita to relieve you of your fascination?"

"You forget yourself, madam!"

"No, Nephew, it is *you* who forgets yourself!" she cried, slapping the arm of the chair. "Need I remind you that you are engaged to my daughter?"

A vein pulsed in Darcy's temple. "I am bound to your daughter by neither honour nor inclination."

"You deny the arrangement? You refuse to obey the claims of duty, honour, and—"

"A tacit agreement made between four parties, three of whom are now dead, eight-and-twenty years ago can have no possible claim upon me. No principles of duty or honour would be violated should I not marry your daughter."

"Not marry?" Her ladyship clutched at her chest, air wheezing in and out as she rasped breath after furious breath. "This is not to be borne! I am not used to brooking disappointment!"

"Then I suggest you adjust your hopes accordingly."

She let out an inarticulate cry and heaved herself to her feet. "You are then resolved to have this…this Bennet creature?"

"Regardless of your determination to know them, my private affairs will remain so."

"What of your family and what you owe all of us?"

"Your performance today has quite convinced me of the limits of my obligations there."

"You would then see us all ridiculed for a whim to marry a buxom pauper?"

Darcy could not recall ever being thus enraged. "I will countenance no further censure of Miss Bennet, either in this house or abroad. If you can say nothing civil, I strongly recommend you refrain from speaking at all."

"I came to you, hoping you would discredit Mr. Collins's report, and you have all but confirmed it!"

"I have confirmed nothing. You have drawn your own conclusions."

"Indeed I have, and I am most seriously displeased. Depend upon it: I shall carry my point. Do not imagine Miss Bennet will *ever* be your wife!"

Darcy turned his back on his aunt and rang for the butler. He closed his eyes and pressed his clenched fist to his lips 'til the sting from that blow passed but, after a very short while, squared his shoulders and turned back to the room. "There is nothing left to say on the matter. Godfrey will show you to your carriage. Good day, madam."

Lady Catherine gave a wheezy splutter of indignation. Darcy gave a curt nod and left the room.

Lord Matlock eased slowly into his chair, unsure which creaked more loudly, the furniture or his knees. His man handed him his tincture, which he swallowed greedily. It had been a long and tedious day, and all he presently desired was to spend his evening in quiet reverie with a book, a cigar, and some port. He had taken up none of these before the door was flung open, and to his great surprise and immeasurable displeasure, his sister swept into the room.

"Reginald! We must act immediately! Darcy has lost his wits!"

The improbability of any such thing convinced him no action was required at all.

"He will not marry Anne! He will not have her! Obstinate, selfish boy! He would hear no reason! He refuses to honour the agreement of his mother, his father…" On she raged until Matlock began to wonder whether he might enjoy the whole of his book ere she exhausted her ire. Perchance if he lit his cigar, he might smoke the shrew from the room. Alas, the door was then opened a second time, and all hope of a peaceful evening was lost.

"What is this frightful commotion?" enquired his mother-in-law, coming into the room.

"My sister waits upon us."

"Is that all? I thought the French had arrived."

"Oh," Catherine said with undisguised loathing. "Mrs. Sinclair is here."

"Pray, continue," the older lady said, settling herself on the sofa and propping both hands atop her cane as though awaiting a performance. "I shall be in nobody's way here."

"My brother and I are discussing a *family* matter."

"How fortunate then that I am here."

Regardless of his desperate wish otherwise, Matlock could not deny that Mrs. Sinclair was family. Eager to have the vexatious ménage à trois done, he waved away his sister's protests and instructed her to speak, which—after several rancorous glares and some unpleasantly noisy clearing of her throat—she eventually did.

"Mr. Darcy has reneged on his engagement to my daughter."

"Gracious me!" Mrs. Sinclair interrupted immediately. "When I saw Mr. Darcy a little over a fortnight ago, he was quite unshackled. If he has indeed offered for and forsaken your daughter since *then*, I think your displeasure perfectly reasonable."

"The engagement has obviously not come about in the last fortnight."

"How then has he reneged?"

Catherine hesitated for a moment before replying. "The engagement between them is of a peculiar kind. From their infancy, they have been intended for each other. It was the favourite wish of his mother as well as of hers. While in their cradles, we planned the union."

"Yes, and that is certainly the best time to forge an alliance—when the man and woman are insensible of each other. But now this! Has he recently come to know her better and changed his mind?"

"Mr. Darcy and Miss de Bourgh have been well acquainted all their lives. My sister and I made sure of it!"

"So he has had ample time to find reasons to object to her?"

"Upon my word, I have not been accustomed to such language as this!"

Mrs. Sinclair shrugged. "I was only trying to help."

Matlock wondered whether, if he were to sneak from the room and lock it behind him, one or both of the feuding harridans might soon end up dead. He looked longingly at the door but concluded his chances of escaping without notice were regrettably slim.

"You must have other suitors in line," Mrs. Sinclair said. "What makes it imperative that she marry her cousin over and above some other poor rich soul?"

"Anne is of a delicate constitution! She will not suffer being auctioned off to the rest of society."

"For God's sake, perhaps it is best that she not marry at all!" Matlock growled. "Her health has ever been fragile. If it continues so, she may not even survive the childbed."

"I think it likely she would not survive the begetting," mumbled Mrs. Sinclair.

"*I beg your pardon*?" Catherine squawked.

"Well, let us be truthful. You could squash Miss de Bourgh in a money clip. I shudder to think what a man like Mr. Darcy would do to the girl."

"Yes, thank you!" cried Matlock, anticipating his sister's paroxysms. "My niece and nephew's carnal compatibility notwithstanding, Darcy would never have wed her in any case. Sister, you must be aware what the detriment to Pemberley would be if the estate were forced to subsidise Rosings' losses."

"I did not come here to discuss Rosings. I came to compel you to make Darcy marry my daughter."

Matlock snorted. "I could no more make Darcy *laugh* than I could make him do aught he is decided against. I should only end up looking a fool."

"He must listen to you! He cannot be so far beyond family honour that—"

"I do not suggest his family honour is wanting."

"Is that so? Then how do you account for his decision to forsake us all in favour of the impudent and penniless niece of a tradesman?"

"There is no accounting for taste," said Mrs. Sinclair. "I should not attempt it."

"I do not have the pleasure of understanding you, Catherine," Matlock said.

"I have received a report that he is expected to make his addresses to a ghastly little upstart from Hertfordshire."

"And what does Darcy have to say of this report?"

"That it was without foundation."

"Then why the devil are we even discussing it?"

"Because his violent defence of her was more than adequate proof of his attachment. Never before have I heard such language from him."

"You do seem to struggle with other people's dialogue, do you not?" said Mrs. Sinclair.

"Darcy defends all his acquaintances loyally," Matlock replied. "If you were fool enough to storm in there as you stormed in here, hurling insults about one of his circle, you cannot be surprised you received short shrift!"

"She is not one of his circle! She is a nobody with no connections save being cousin to my parson, no consequence save that with which she credits herself, no respect for her betters, and a wickedly impertinent tongue in her head."

"She sounds wonderful!" opined Mrs. Sinclair.

"I am sorry, Sister, I have no interest in spurious rumours and even less in interfering in Darcy's affairs. He is a sensible man. He will act as he sees fit."

"He is utterly lost to reason! He will bring derision and contempt upon us all."

"People may think him a fool, aye, but few would be fool enough to admit they think it. And it would not be the first time I have been labelled as possessing foolish relatives."

"This is your real opinion? Very well! *Somebody* must prevent him from making a mistake he will regret all his life, and since you will not, it must fall to me to act!"

"You will not make him choose Anne."

Catherine coughed, as though he had literally knocked the wind from her sails, but strode from the room without further word—her demonstration of pique somewhat diluted by her return moments later, to request that a room be made available to her for the evening.

After she quitted the room a second time, Mrs. Sinclair tutted and shook her head. "People with more money than sense must be very careful that, when their fortune diminishes, their reason does not dwindle with it."

With slow deliberation, Matlock picked up his cigar and lit it. Then he picked up his port and drank it. Then he picked up his book and began to read it. He was assured that Mrs. Sinclair, with her overabundance of sense, could not mistake his meaning. Indeed, he was much gratified when at length he heard the swish of skirts, the tap of her cane, the click of the closing door, and the blessed sound of silence.

Tuesday, 9 June 1812: London

His aunt's philippic had done nothing to diminish Darcy's regard for Elizabeth. He knew she was not faultless. She had neither fortune nor connections, but that was long since any concern of his. Her looks may not be considered classic, but her beautiful dark eyes and comely figure afforded her a staggering allure. Her courage rendered her impetuous and her loyalty gullible, but her compassion and sanguinity only made those qualities more endearing. She cared less than she ought for social conventions but flouted them with such éclat that no one much cared. Elizabeth made her own rules, only for the pleasure of breaking them. She was not perfect, but to Darcy, she was perfection. Being without her felt like drowning.

Days, weeks, months had not lessened her grip on his heart. He knew now that what he felt for her was not in the common way. Elizabeth had all but broken him—shattered his misplaced reserve, unravelled his mistaken principles, and revealed a man in desperate need of redemption. Then she had entwined herself about his heart, reformed him by her design, and made a true gentleman of him. She was not merely the woman he loved; she was the architect of his soul. He could no more stop loving her now than he could stop breathing.

Yet, time cared for no man's pain; thus, he persevered without her, reasoning that perhaps, if he kept moving, his heart would have no choice but to keep beating. In that vein, he expended a good deal of energy on the hunt for Wickham. He coordinated every aspect of the search and paid every bribe until he was found. The temptation to deliver the news of his capture in person was compelling, yet Elizabeth would not wish it; thus, he stayed away.

Indeed, now that Wickham was in custody, and for as long as Bingley tarried over securing himself a wife, Darcy could claim no further connection to Meryton or Elizabeth whatsoever. His life marched inexorably farther away from that juncture when she had almost been his, and there was naught he could do but march with it, hoping the pain would eventually ease. Hence, this afternoon, with no expectation that his anguish would be in any way alleviated by the endeavour, he was off to his club to do whatever it was gentlemen were supposed to do in such places.

"I say, Darcy! What a pleasant surprise!"

Darcy looked up from his paper. "Montgomery! I had not realised you were back in England."

He called for more drinks, and his friend joined him at his table, regaling him with tales of his recent travels, the small fortune he had amassed while he was at it, the sad business of his wife's passing, and the vexing business of hiring a decent nanny for his young son.

"Are you enjoying being returned?" Darcy enquired.

"Tolerably so, I suppose, though London still brims with immoderation and staggers under the weight of its own pretension. I cannot say I have missed it overmuch."

Darcy smiled, having found little pleasure in Town himself of late.

"That reminds me," Montgomery added. "Did you ever hear of the debacle with that turd Wrenshaw at Covent Garden?"

"I have heard nothing of Wrenshaw in weeks."

"No, no—this happened in April, but a day or two after I arrived home."

"I was away for much of April."

"Ah! Then you must allow me to tell you the story."

Darcy listened indignantly to Montgomery's account of Wrenshaw's calumny, tired of worthless men maligning his good name. "Was he overheard?"

"There were a fair few eager ears, I shall not lie. But that night, my friend," he jabbed Darcy affably on the arm, "you had a champion. She reduced all Wrenshaw's claims to a bag of moonshine. Damned fun to watch, too."

"She? It was not Miss Bingley, was it?"

"Ha! God forbid! No, this was an altogether different sort of creature. I did not catch the introductions, but she was quite magnificent."

Darcy's thoughts were drawn immediately to the only magnificent woman of his acquaintance, and despite knowing it to be absurd, his insides jumped at the thought of Elizabeth having said anything in his favour. Frustrated by the foolishness of such a notion, he informed Montgomery more curtly than was necessary that he knew not of whom he spoke.

"That is a shame, for I intended to ask for an introduction. She was quite something. I know not how, for it was subtly done, but with just a few remarks, she had Wrenshaw tied in knots and unable to speak unless it was to accede to his own depravity. It was extraordinary. I do not think I have ever seen a woman so deftly turn a conversation to her advantage."

Darcy had. His heart pounded so loudly he wondered that Montgomery could not hear it.

"Well, whoever she was," his friend concluded, "I believe you are very much in her debt."

Darcy sat perfectly still, fighting prodigiously against a swell of false hope. Elizabeth was as likely to defend him as to marry him—and yet…"You say you did not hear her name?"

"I said I did not hear the introductions," Montgomery replied, looking as though he was enjoying the suspense far too much. "But I was close enough to hear her tell her friend she was 'very wrong about you' and that you are 'not a bad man.'" He paused to sip his drink, his eyes twinkling at Darcy over the rim. "And to hear her companion call her Lizzy."

It was all Darcy could do to keep his tone even. "What did she look like?"

"Ah, yes! For who has use of an ill-favoured heroine?" Montgomery replied with great amusement. "You are in luck, though. Yours was really rather handsome—about yay high with dark hair and the most exquisite eyes. Do you think you know her, after all?"

Darcy felt winded. "I believe so." God, he hoped so.

"Then you shall have to introduce me. I should dearly like to make her acquaintance."

"If the opportunity arises, I should be delighted."

DARCY WAS ALMOST RUN DOWN AS HE HASTENED ACROSS THE BUSY THOROUGHFARE, but he scarcely noticed the driver's angry shouts above the clamour of his own thoughts. If it *had* been Elizabeth, if she truly now thought him a good man, then there was a chance—a small one, it was true, but a chance nonetheless—that he might yet make her love him.

His mouth twitched, attempting to smile, but he fought it, for he could not be sure. When last he saw her, she had thought unspeakably ill of him. Well, not unspeakably—she had articulated her dislike rather eloquently in fact. He laughed aloud then clamped his lips together in consternation. Was he to break into song next? His conjectures were tenuous at best, his giddiness unwarranted.

The thought of Elizabeth now defending his honour was outside of sublime, yet he could not imagine what might have affected such a change of heart. Surely not his letter, as bitter and remorseless as he knew it had been. Reason compelled him to doubt, yet "… *the most exquisite eyes.*" Who else could it be? Longing increased his pace to one just shy of a run as he raced home to retrieve the letter that had lain ignored in his desk drawer for weeks. Fool that he was, he had eschewed reading Bingley's mentions of Elizabeth, yet presently he was desperate for any news that might substantiate his hopes.

Godfrey attempted to address him as he burst through the front door and strode across the hall, but he barked an impatient "Later!" and dived inside his study, slamming the door shut behind him. He rifled through three drawers before he found it. With great trepidation, he lowered himself into his chair and began, meticulously, to re-read it.

Bingley extended another invitation to Netherfield, said something of a fishing party, touched briefly on his sister's increase and his venture in Nova Scotia. Darcy sat up straighter. Bingley wrote that Elizabeth encouraged his suit, Elizabeth was as engaging as ever, Elizabeth still enjoyed walking. Then there was something of a picnic, a mention of Bingley's boots…and in a scrawled postscript at the foot of the page, his salvation.

P.S. Almost forgot. I have a message for you from Miss Elizabeth. Your quarrel in Kent troubles her. She asked that I tell you she is sorry. Tried to assure her it was unnecessary, but she insisted.

Early evening found Darcy bathed in the last mellow rays of sunlight at the library window, looking out across the gardens. All arrangements for travel had been set in motion. He could not avoid a meeting with Myers on Thursday, but he would wait no longer than that. Friday would see him in Hertfordshire.

Anticipation thrummed in his chest. He had no idea what reception he might expect from Elizabeth, but her message of apology had taught him to hope as he had scarcely ever allowed himself to hope before. He was not fool enough to think she meant to apologise for refusing him, but she had forgiven him, and that was enough to have liberated every passionate feeling he had been battling these long weeks to repress. He felt nigh on delirious with happiness and restless with impatience to see her.

Long evening shadows crept across the gardens, and the library ebbed into darkness. His lips curled into a slow smile as he basked in the warmth of her long-coveted and fierce loyalty, for he was now certain it had been Elizabeth at the theatre. He could just imagine the arch of her eyebrow as she engaged Wrenshaw, the small, dangerous smile as she set her trap, the flash of her eyes as she cut him down, and the dazzling smile that obliterated all affront and left her opponent dumbfounded. It made him wild to hold her, to tell her how he adored the liveliness of her mind. How he had survived this long without her was suddenly impossible to comprehend.

It galled him to think of the weeks he had wasted wallowing in despair. He longed to know all he had missed and tortured himself envisaging every smile and witticism he had not seen. As the sun dipped below the horizon and he was plunged into gloom, that longing materialised into a recollection. Bingley had sent two letters. Without a moment's hesitation, he went to his study, anxious for any and all news of Elizabeth he could find.

This letter took longer to locate, but he eventually found it at the back of a drawer beneath the household ledger. He moved closer to the only lit candle in the room, broke the seal and began to read. And as he read, all the blood drained from his face, all breath left him. His world cracked, began to crumble, and then shattered into dust. His heart, he was quite sure, stopped dead in his chest.

She was gone.

Netherfield, Hertfordshire
May 25

Darcy

Pray, come—

~~*There has been an atta a dreadful incident. Something has happened that has caused me such—caused me much anguish*~~

I beg you to come. Your acquaintance, Wickham has attacked Miss Elizabeth.

He had been ~~harass~~ pestering her for some time. She disliked his ~~fawni~~ attentions. It was even necessary for me to intervene on one occasion. Would that I had done more! I shall never forgive myself for not preventing this. I saw him grab her and I swear I ran but I could not reach her in time and he hit her so damned hard. Dear God, she just crumpled! I cannot bear to think on it, yet I see it over and again. He was ape-drunk. I held her in my arms all the way to Longbourn, but she never awoke. Her family's distress is difficult to behold for had I but done more ~~to~~—

I can write no more, 'tis too distressing. Pray come, Darcy. I need you, my friend.

Bingley

For a long time, nothing moved. Not the air. Not him. Not his heart. Then, as though mired in treacle, he reached for the stack of papers containing his correspondence from Colonel Forster. With his vision blackening at the edges, he unfolded the uppermost letter, though he knew very well what it said.

"Condition very grave. Recovery increasingly unlikely."

He lifted Bingley's letter and re-read that also.

"...she never awoke."

He let both letters slide from his grasp and watched them flutter innocuously to the ground. Until that moment, Darcy had never known the true meaning of despair. The pain of Elizabeth's rejection was rendered insignificant in comparison to the staggering, devastating grief that overpowered him. He grunted as though he had received a blow to the gut. Nausea engulfed him. He sucked in a desperate, ragged breath, then his anguish tore from him in a single, hoarse cry that resounded like a death knell around the chamber.

Everything was lost. Elizabeth was gone.

There came a knock at the door—unearthly loud. He did not think he gave any instruction to enter, but the door opened nonetheless. Godfrey stepped cautiously around it, his candle casting horrible deathly shadows across his face. "Mr. Darcy, sir. Forgive me; I heard a shout. Is aught amiss?"

Darcy's mind writhed in agony, unable to settle upon a single coherent thought. He attempted to speak but stopped when his voice caught.

"Sir, is there anything at all I can do to be of assistance?"

He gave a brief shake of his head. It was all he could do. The butler hesitated, his eyes darting about the room as though searching for the cause of his master's distress before reluctantly taking his leave. The door clicked closed. Darcy pressed his fist to his mouth in a vain attempt to stifle the agonised groan that burst forth. His knees threatened to buckle. He sank into the nearest chair and dropped his head into his hands. His eyes closed, and an influx of images assaulted him: her beautiful smile, her dancing eyes, her joyous laugh. His fingers clawed his scalp. His chest constricted.

"Oh, God, not her. I beg you. Not my Elizabeth."

He knew not for how long he sat there. Only the coolness of the room and the guttering candle recalled him to his surroundings. Ignoring the excruciating hollowness in his chest, he rose to pull the bell cord. At some point, Godfrey arrived. Darcy rasped out his instructions, his dry lips cracking. Godfrey assured him all would be in place by first light and left.

Before quitting the room himself, Darcy penned a brief note and set it out for delivery on the morrow. Then, he drifted through the dark halls to his bedchamber, where he slumped into the chair beside the fire and returned his head to his hands. He could see naught in the obsidian abyss of night, but in the deathly hush, he heard the first of his tears drop to the floor with a dull thud. It was followed by many, many more, as he surrendered to his soul-shattering desolation and wept.

Wednesday, 10 June 1812: London

GEORGIANA HAD BEEN DELIGHTED WITH HER BROTHER'S INVITATION TO spend the entire day visiting galleries and museums together, perceiving it as testament to their recent advancement in understanding. She arrived in time for breakfast in anticipation of an agreeable day, only to find him gone and the house in a state of muted alarm.

"Mr. Darcy left early this morning for Netherfield," Godfrey informed her. His expression convinced her there was naught auspicious about the destination.

"Has something happened to Mr. Bingley?"

"Not Bingley, Cuz."

She started and turned. Her cousin Fitzwilliam was coming through the front door, his expression grim. He held out a letter. "He sent me this."

Fitzwilliam, it was Elizabeth whom Wickham assaulted. Bingley wrote with news of it weeks ago, but I have only today read his letter. He wrote that she never awoke. She is gone.

Georgiana's stomach turned over. "Mr. *Wickham*? How could he?"

"Never mind that. It is your brother who concerns me now."

With the efficiency of one used to command, her cousin soon gleaned from the staff all they knew of Darcy's mysterious behaviour the previous day. Georgiana was particularly alarmed by Godfrey's account of her brother's excessive anguish, for not even when her father passed away had he revealed such an excess of emotion.

It was his journey to Hertfordshire that baffled her cousin. "She has been dead a fortnight. There does not seem any point in going, unless he means to…" He frowned but seemed to think better of finishing the thought. Instead, he simply concluded, "I think I must go there also."

"Ought I to come?"

"No, I think it best if I go alone."

"Look after him," Georgiana pleaded, gripping her cousin's forearm. "This will grieve him deeply."

"I know," he replied gravely. Then he patted her hand. "But try not to worry. He is an obstinate old ox. He will weather it in time." Promising to send word as soon as he was able, Fitzwilliam left in search of the groom and directions to Netherfield.

Georgiana declined Godfrey's offer of breakfast, but too agitated to go home directly, she requested some tea in the morning room instead. She was distraught for her beloved brother, unable to cease agonizing over what he must be suffering. She had privately hoped he might find a way to resolve matters with Miss Bennet, but now, unthinkably, the man with whom she had once fancied herself in love had dashed all such dreams.

Godfrey cleared his throat from the doorway. "Pray excuse the intrusion, Miss Darcy. A letter has just arrived for Mr. Darcy. Given the circumstances, I thought you might like to know it is from Hertfordshire."

The letter was addressed in an unfamiliar and shockingly untidy hand. Georgiana took it instinctively although there was no question she would open it. That did not prevent her from dwelling on the wretched news it must contain. What all Miss Bennet's poor family and friends must have endured! What her own family might have endured had not Darcy intervened last summer.

It did not bear thinking about. She set down her tea and stood to leave. Before quitting the house, she slipped into her brother's study to put the letter where he would find it upon his return. As she crossed the room, she saw another, lying crumpled and forgotten on the floor, and upon crouching to retrieve it, yet another, tucked beneath his desk.

She had no wish to read either yet could not help but notice, as she folded them away, that one was in the same hand as the unopened letter arrived that morning, and both were sent from Hertfordshire. She shivered, for they evidently bore the news of Miss Bennet's passing and immediately brought to mind the vision of her brother reading them and then dropping them in despair. She hastily placed all three letters atop a stack of other correspondence on the desk and left the house to wait impatiently at home for news.

Wednesday, 10 June 1812: Hertfordshire

"You!" Fitzwilliam yelled, leaping from the carriage before the horses came to a halt. "Where can I find your commanding officer?"

The soldier turned, his lips already forming a cuss, but upon espying Fitzwilliam's own scarlet coat and vast array of decorations, he instead drew up into a salute and gave a hasty direction to Colonel Forster's establishment. Fitzwilliam went directly to the specified building, hoping to God he had made better time than Darcy. He could conceive of no other reason for his cousin to travel here than to exact some form of revenge on Wickham, and he was resolved to prevent him, lest the wrong man ended up swinging.

Colonel Forster's assurance that Darcy had never set foot in his establishment was not only a relief; it presented Fitzwilliam with a unique opportunity. Bringing to bear the full weight of his rank, he quickly secured permission for an audience with the sorry pox-crust of a man in Forster's gaol.

Wickham scrabbled back against the wall when Fitzwilliam stepped into his cell. "What do *you* want?" he said, looking frantically about as though there might be a door he had somehow previously failed to notice, which might now afford him escape. "Is it not enough for you or your bastard of a cousin that I shall be flogged?"

"Wait outside," Fitzwilliam ordered the accompanying soldier, glaring at him until he complied. Turning back to Wickham, he crossed his arms and watched him bluster and flap and attempt to justify his crime.

"What is so special about the mort? 'Tis not as though I lay finger on your precious little cousin."

Fitzwilliam never ceased to be amazed by the man's foolhardiness. He shook his head and removed his gloves, one finger at a time.

Wickham watched his movements with wide eyes. "It was an accident!"

Fitzwilliam put his gloves in his pocket and patted them flat.

"She provoked me to it!"

Then he rolled his shoulders, laced his fingers, and cracked his knuckles.

Wickham recommenced his backward scramble. "I wished only to silence her!"

That was as good a cue as any. Fitzwilliam exploded across the room and rammed his fist down violently into the cowering runt's sternum. There was a loud crack and a forceful wheeze as Wickham's chest emptied of air. His head snapped forwards, then back again, banging against the wall. His eyes glazed and blood trickled from his mouth where he had presumably bitten his tongue. Fitzwilliam held him upright until his focus cleared somewhat, delivered two further punches to his cheek for good measure, then leant into his face. "I will see you swing for this, you bastard."

Wickham managed only a weak gurgle before slumping sideways, insensate. That much achieved, Fitzwilliam left the gaol with but one thing on his mind.

Where the hell was Darcy?

Caroline Bingley turned away from the window in disgust as Netherfield's chimneys came into view across the detestable Hertfordshire landscape. There was nowhere in the country she wished less to be than here, yet her sister's summons had obliged her to forego all her engagements and endure half a day in a jolting, ill-cushioned post chaise—all to prevent her hapless brother embroiling himself with the wretched Bennets. *Again.*

The sisters' horror at the prospect of such a union was not without foundation. Miss Deverall had been visiting when Louisa's summons arrived, and in her consternation, Caroline had let slip those details which prudence might have counselled her to conceal—namely her brother's imminent alliance with the Bennets of Longbourn. Miss Deverall's response, "*Who?*" had been the first nail in her social coffin—the lady's hasty departure thereafter, the second. Mrs. Blacknell's subsequent and unexplained cancellation of their trip to Bond Street later that afternoon had been the third, and she knew very well that, unless she prevented her brother from making his addresses, all hope for the Bingleys would soon be lost.

Snapping at her slumbering maid to awaken, she stepped down from the carriage and trudged towards the house, enquiring of the awaiting butler as to her sister's whereabouts.

"She is from home, Miss Bingley," he replied.

Caroline stopped walking and took a deep breath before repeating her enquiry.

"I understand Mr. Hurst had business with the McAllisters in St Albans, ma'am. They are expected to return on the morrow."

Having sacrificed all her arrangements, Caroline was less than impressed to discover Louisa off gallivanting with friends. "And my brother?"

"Is from home also."

She bit back an unseemly retort. "Do you know where he has gone?"

"He is at Longbourn, ma'am."

"Oh yes, of course! He would be, would he not! How completely marvellous!"

Such was her pique that it was a moment before she noticed the carriage rolling through the gates at the head of the drive. When she did, her insides performed a little summersault, for there was no mistaking the Matlock crest emblazoned upon the doors. "For heaven's sake, get that contraption out of sight!" she barked at the driver of the post chaise.

No sooner had she straightened her attire and pinched some colour into her cheeks than the ornate carriage drew to a halt, and out stepped Darcy's cousin. They were well enough acquainted that the salutations were swiftly observed, and the colonel barely waited that long before announcing he had come in search of his cousin.

"I am sorry to disappoint you, Colonel. Mr. Darcy has not been here since la—"

"He was here this morning, sir. His trunks are within, but he left again directly."

Caroline turned to look at the cretinous butler. "Is that so, Peabody?"

"Oh, yes, ma'am, quite so."

"And do you know where he went?" Colonel Fitzwilliam enquired.

"To Longbourn, sir."

At last, some welcome news! Darcy had persuaded Charles against marrying a Bennet before, there was every reason to expect he would do so again. The Bingley name was secure for another day.

"Why would he go there?" Colonel Fitzwilliam muttered, shaking his head.

"Indeed, why would *anybody*?" Caroline agreed. With a delicate chuckle she added, "I believe he will be safe, though, for my brother is there with him."

"I see," the colonel replied, looking no less uneasy. "I shall not trouble him while he is with his friend. Might I impose upon your hospitality and await his return here?"

"But of course!" Caroline instructed Peabody to have a room readied, and once he had left to arrange it, she turned back to her guest. "You are wise to steer clear of Longbourn. It is the home of the Bennet family, and while they fancy themselves one of the leading families in the area, in truth—"

"I know of the Bennets."

"You do? But, of course, Mr. Darcy has mentioned them to you. I assure you, they are every bit as dreadful as I know he must have described them. Regrettably, my brother fancies himself in love with one of them. I live in hope that your cousin will persuade him against…offering…for…" She faltered as Colonel Fitzwilliam's expression grew ever more indignant.

"If Bingley has not yet made his addresses," he clipped, "he will not be able to for the foreseeable future."

"He will not?" Matters were taking a decidedly more favourable turn.

"No. The Bennets are in mourning."

"Oh, thank God!" There were occasions when Caroline wished her sense would make a more determined effort to precede her sensibility. Nonetheless, Colonel Fitzwilliam's evident displeasure vexed her, for what were the Bennets to him? "That is quite shocking news," she continued tartly. "Was it Mrs. Bennet who passed? That must be a great loss to her family, though I daresay she will be impossible to forget."

"Your compassion astounds me, madam, but it is Miss Elizabeth who has died."

This time Caroline was more successful in keeping her thoughts to herself, which was fortunate, for they were not significantly less unfeeling than the last. Though she would not wish an early death upon anyone, if there must be one less Bennet in the world, she was quite sure she could not have chosen a better candidate. She expressed the customary dismay with what she considered laudable verisimilitude, but the colonel was apparently not fooled.

"You are right not to trouble yourself too much with grief, Miss Bingley. It is an irrational sentiment, best left to those with a susceptibility to the inconvenience of feeling."

She gritted her teeth. It was not every day the son of an earl graced one's home, yet his consequence notwithstanding, his ill humour was making an already exasperating day worse still. "I assure you, sir, I am *vastly* grieved.

I merely prefer to refrain from exhibition. We may console ourselves with the knowledge that a family as demonstrative as the Bennets can have little need for anybody to feel aught further on their behalf."

Into the silence of his incredulity, she bade him make himself at home and excused herself. Colonel The Honourable Richard Fitzwilliam, third son of the Earl of Matlock, could entertain himself with his own righteous anger until Charles and Darcy returned. She had lost the will to be civil.

Darcy saw little and cared less as he rode the familiar path between Netherfield and Longbourn. Bingley was there already, the butler had informed him, "mourning the loss of Miss Eliza." That remark had almost toppled Darcy into the chasm of grief awaiting him. Only his resolve to pay his final respects before submitting to his despair lent him the fortitude to continue. He journeyed to bid farewell to his love.

"Excusing me, sir," said a groom when Darcy arrived at Longbourn's stables, "but none of the family are at 'ome. Was it the master you was after?"

"I understood Mr. Bingley was here."

"Oh, yes, 'e be visiting up at the churchyard with the other Miss Bennets."

Of course—mourning the loss. Mumbling his thanks, Darcy walked in the direction of the church, and as he walked, memories of Elizabeth fell upon him, threatening to crumble the fragile walls that shored up his anguish.

They had sat at table together—she avoiding the ragout but taking extra salmon. They had read together—she humming quietly, eyes downcast, long lashes resting on her cheeks. They had danced together—she with obstinacy fully engaged and eyes aflame. They had walked together at Rosings—she with her dusky pink dress pressed full against her form by the breeze. They had almost walked together at Netherfield, but she had run away, nymph-like and laughing. In his dreams, he ran after her. Now she was forever beyond his reach.

He came to the towering oak that grew in the lane beside the churchyard and steadied himself against it with one hand, running the other over his face. After a deep breath, he forced himself to look over the wall into the sea of gravestones.

And there she was.

Pain lanced through him as her perfect, beauteous spirit, wreathed in radiant sunlight, pierced him anew with its ethereal splendour. Her head was bowed and her hands clasped in prayer, but he would know her from a thousand miles afar. He felt his heart, motionless in his aching chest, break all over again. "Elizabeth."

The apparition snapped its head up, fixed its beautiful dark eyes directly upon him, and gasped. Darcy's heart leapt into his mouth. His breath came too fast, his legs felt not his own. "Elizabeth?"

Her face showed confusion and surprise, her hand came up to her chest and she stepped towards him—and tripped. Events unfolded protractedly, as though in a dream, yet too quickly for Darcy to act upon any of them. With mounting horror, he watched Elizabeth stumble forward and cry out. Somebody—Bingley—appeared and called her name. Not Miss Bennet, nor even Miss Elizabeth, but *Lizzy*. Darcy's heart screamed its protest as Bingley gathered her to him, and she looked up at him and smiled.

He had been mistaken. Elizabeth was alive—and in Bingley's arms.

Whims and Inconsistencies

Saturday, 23 May 1812: Hertfordshire

The room was still at last. The apothecary was gone, the maid sent for more firewood. Her younger sisters were downstairs, her mother abed. Her father was closeted in his library with Colonel Forster, the magistrate, and Mr. Bingley. Elizabeth lay unmoving on the bed, her eyes not quite closed, and the whites visible between her lashes. The ugly welt on her cheek darkened along with the receding daylight.

"Oh, Lizzy!" Jane whispered. "How could he do this to you?"

Silence was the only answer. Tears came and would not stop. She held her sister's hand and spoke of childhood memories and nonsense. Things that would commonly have made Elizabeth laugh now roused not a murmur. She attempted to spoon some water into Elizabeth's mouth, but she would not swallow. She sang, half the words replaced with sobs, but she sang nonetheless for the sister she loved so dearly. Nothing worked. Elizabeth did not awaken.

"Pray, Lizzy, wake up," she begged. "Lizzy? Lizzy!"

The name sounded loud in the quiet of the room. Just as it had when Mr. Bingley shouted it upon falling to his knees beside Elizabeth in the middle of Meryton's High Street. Jane squeezed her eyes shut against the memory, ashamed to have even noticed at such a moment. Yet closing her eyes only recalled to her the image of Mr. Bingley tenderly cradling Elizabeth in his arms as he bore her home and the distress etched upon his countenance as he laid her reverently upon the bed.

Her eyes flew open, and she blinked furiously, struggling to suppress a surge of resentment. His concern was reasonable. He would have to be the most unfeeling of creatures not to be distressed by such a circumstance. She would have to be the most unfeeling of creatures to begrudge her sister anyone's compassion as she lay wounded and unconscious. Try as she might, however, Jane could not dismiss the voice that whispered that was precisely the problem. If, even when unconscious, Elizabeth had more power to attract Mr. Bingley's notice than she, how was she ever to compete?

Monday, 25 May 1812: Hertfordshire

None of the Bennets attended church on Sunday, and Bingley passed the day in a harrowing state of suspense awaiting news from Longbourn that never arrived. Over and again, his mind's eye showed him Wickham seizing Elizabeth by the arm, shouting in her face, driving his fist into her temple 'til she collapsed to the ground, all before he was able to reach her. Over and again, he agonised over the memory of Wickham importuning her at the last assembly. Why had he not done more *then* to protect her? It was as a result of his inaction that Elizabeth was suffering thus, and guilt threatened to overwhelm him.

He called at Longbourn at a barely respectable hour on Monday, desperate for better news, but such relief was not to be had. Miss Bennet was tending to Elizabeth, thus Mr. Bennet received him in his library. His haggard countenance told Bingley all he needed to know of Elizabeth's condition even before it was confirmed that she had not yet awoken. They spent some time in discussion of events, joined after half an hour by Colonel Forster, who brought the rather unhelpful news that Wickham remained at large.

"Who is it?" Mr. Bennet grumbled curtly when there came a second knock at the door.

"Papa, Mr. Jones wishes to see you," Miss Bennet answered.

Bingley's insides jumped. He had not spoken to her properly since Saturday's unpleasantness and found himself suddenly eager for a measure of her sweet serenity. He stood, as did they all, when she came in. Her lovely countenance lit up with tired but happy surprise upon seeing him, easing his disquiet considerably. He returned her smile, but the moment was broken when the apothecary came in behind her, his expression severe.

"What news?" Mr. Bennet enquired.

"The swelling appears reduced, sir," Mr. Jones replied. "But that is no longer my primary concern." He paused, glancing hesitantly at the other occupants of the room.

"Never mind them," said Mr. Bennet. "Let us hear it."

"As you wish. Sir, your daughter has taken little or no fluids for above six-and-thirty hours. Unless she awakens and drinks something soon, she cannot survive."

"Good God!"

Bingley assumed Mr. Bennet had spoken the words until he noticed everybody peering in his direction. Miss Bennet let out a small sob and ran from the room. With all colour drained from his countenance, Mr. Bennet muttered an invitation for Bingley and Colonel Forster to stay and finish their coffee then went after his daughter, nodding for the apothecary to follow.

"Wickham might well hang if she dies," Colonel Forster said once they were gone.

Bingley's guts twisted upon themselves. He sat heavily back in his chair. Elizabeth could not die!

"If they ever catch him," the colonel added.

"I ought to have gone after him," Bingley said apologetically. "Only my first thought was for Miss Elizabeth."

"I understand entirely. It cannot have been a pretty thing to witness."

Indeed not. Bingley would never forget the sight of Elizabeth lying prone on the ground. Or the feel of her in his arms—so fragile, so delicate.

"Speaking of Wickham's crimes," Forster went on, "I received a letter from your friend, Mr. Darcy, this morning. He wrote to warn me about Wickham. All too late, of course, but we cannot blame the gentleman for that."

"Darcy wrote to you about Wickham?"

"Aye. Offered to pay his debts. Think you he would object to my asking for assistance with the search for Wickham?"

"Gads, no! I cannot imagine why I did not suggest it." Why had he not thought to contact Darcy himself? Resolving that instant to write to him, Bingley fared Forster well and rode post-haste for home. He would write and beg Darcy to come, for never had he needed him more.

Barely able to look at the frightful bruise marring her sister's cheek, Mary chose to walk about the room as she read. She knew not what passages she chose, only that Elizabeth showed no sign of hearing any of it. When tears blurred the words on the page, she dropped her hands and succumbed to her sorrow.

With her head bowed thus, her eyes were drawn to the corner of a letter obtruding from beneath the dresser. Further inspection revealed it to be addressed to her Aunt Gardiner in Elizabeth's hand. How it came to be there mattered not a whit to Mary. She could think only that her beloved sister might be about to die, and this letter seemed the closest she might ever again come to speaking to her. Without further thought, she broke the seal.

Yet, reading it only made her cry harder, for the letter was more wretched than Mary would ever have imagined possible. Elizabeth was lonely—grieved by the change in her relationship with Jane, mortified by accusations of flirtatious behaviour and struggling to suppress her natural inclination to playfulness. She was wary of appearing too familiar with Mr. Bingley, terrified of being forced to marry Mr. Greyson, and most surprising of all, she held a tender regard for Mr. Darcy!

"*The worst of it,*" Mary read aloud, giving voice to her incredulity, "*is my contrary and treacherous heart. I have come to understand Mr. Darcy so much better and deeply regret my unjust behaviour towards him. What pain I must have inflicted with my accusations! And now my heart seems attuned to the very mention of him and races at the thought of him. Though I have tried and tried again, I cannot laugh myself out of it. If I am honest, I do not think I wish to, though it would be for the best, for I shall never see him again. I have lost the only chance to allow this little skip, upon which my heart insists, to run into a full reel. I regret him, Aunt. There, I have written it. I regret Mr. Darcy. Would that he could forgive me and come back, but—*"

At that moment the letter was forgotten, for Elizabeth abruptly groaned and opened her eyes, thus proving that indeed she was attuned to the very mention of Mr. Darcy.

Longbourn
May 25

Mr. Bingley,

Elizabeth awoke at a little after four. She is vastly weakened and in pain, but compos mentis.

Yours,
Mr. Bennet.

Friday, 29 May 1812: Hertfordshire

"MR. BINGLEY AND MR. GREYSON, MA'AM," THE HOUSEKEEPER ANNOUNCED.

Feeling a little thrill for Mr. Bingley's fifth visit in as many days, Jane looked up from her embroidery in time to see Elizabeth close her eyes and sigh. She felt a pang of guilt. It was only the second day her sister had felt well enough to come downstairs, and she likely did not feel equal to callers.

"Shall we walk about the lanes?" she asked Mr. Bingley, already on her feet, more than happy to relieve Elizabeth of this particular visitor's company.

"Had we not better remain?" he replied. "I do not think your sister ought to be left unattended."

"What am I, Bingley—a candlestick?" Mr. Greyson said, smiling—a little thinly in Jane's opinion. "I believe I shall be company enough for Miss Elizabeth."

"And I," Mary said from the window seat.

"You could be the most charming candlestick ever to grace a parlour, Greyson," Mr. Bingley replied, "It would not persuade me to desert a wounded friend."

"Nonsense! Off you go," Mr. Greyson insisted, seating himself. "If Miss Elizabeth is content with my company, you can have no objection to leaving us alone."

"You will not be alone," Mary said indignantly. "I am here."

Bingley promptly sat down. "There, it is decided. Miss Mary cannot be in two places at once, and it would be unthinkable for either of us to go unchaperoned. Let us all stay and keep Miss Elizabeth company together."

Jane lowered herself back into her chair. Mr. Bingley's good humour was one of the things she most loved about him. Indeed, she would not wish him to behave in any less of a gentlemanlike manner. She told herself firmly, therefore, that she had no just cause to be alarmed by his gallantry towards Elizabeth.

"I received a letter from my cousin this morning," Mr. Bingley said, a short while into the visit. "He begs me again to go to Nova Scotia."

Jane felt as unequal to discussing foreign places today as she had at the picnic and had no notion how she ought to respond. She glanced at Elizabeth, but she had returned to pressing her compress to her temple and did not answer.

"Nova Scotia?" Mr. Greyson said dubiously. "Why does he wish you to go there?"

"Well, his most recent idea is that I should build him a colliery."

Mr. Greyson looked intrigued. Jane attempted to mimic his expression. Elizabeth had closed her eyes.

"I shall have to pester Darcy for his insight on the matter," Bingley mused. "He is the expert."

"On the place or the industry?" Elizabeth enquired, at last roused to participate.

"Oh, the industry. He is quite *au fait* on the subject of mines, his half of Derbyshire being quite overrun with the things. Though my cousin has provided me with a wealth of information about the place. He is eager for me to build my home and settle there."

"And pray, are *you*?" Elizabeth enquired.

"Lord, no!" he replied, to Jane's profound relief. "Though he assures me it is a truly beautiful country and seems delighted with the society. He is braver than I. I should find it a good deal more daunting to be so far from home."

"The unfamiliar is always daunting," Elizabeth replied. "It does not follow that it cannot be agreeable. Indeed, it makes it more exciting."

"I ought to have expected you would not be intimidated by moving half way across the world."

"But the opportunity to go somewhere new, to see so many different things—is not that an appealing prospect?"

"Are you sure you are not working for my cousin?"

Despite all her efforts to be reasonable, Jane was vastly relieved when her father appeared to interrupt this cosy exchange.

"Lizzy, an express has arrived for you from Kent," he announced, coming into the room and handing it to Elizabeth, who immediately paled.

"Is it aught serious?"

"No," Elizabeth replied after a cursory read. "Charlotte writes to see if I am well. Sir William has sent her news of my injury." Despite this, she did not regain her colour and asked Mr. Bennet to escort her upstairs, claiming her headache had worsened.

"Is she much troubled by these headaches?" Mr. Greyson wished to know after she had gone.

"Is Mr. Jones aware she suffers thus?" Mr. Bingley enquired. "He ought to be informed."

Jane patiently assured them that Mr. Jones was pleased with Elizabeth's improvement. Then she less patiently assured herself that it would have been impolite for Mr. Bingley *not* to express his concern, given Mr. Greyson's alarm. It was more difficult to explain his departure moments later, mere minutes after Mr. Greyson took his leave, though the intimacy of their farewell was sufficient to allay almost all of her anxiety.

Hunsford, Kent
May 29

My dear Eliza,

I have urgent news, but first allow me to express my sincerest condolences for what you have suffered and my vast relief you have not taken lasting injury. I pray your convalescence is swift and beg you to take care.

Now to business. I received two letters from my father this morning. One contained news of your injury; the other was posted last week and made mention of a recent conversation with Mr. Bingley. That gentleman apparently claims his friend from Derbyshire has come to hold you in very high regard. This, of course, is proof enough for my father that your engagement must be imminent. Perceiving my amusement as I read this, Mr. Collins insisted I tell him what diverted me. Regrettably, he took the report rather more seriously and, before I could prevent him, left to relate the whole of it to Lady Catherine. By his account, she was furious with the news and declared it would not be borne, though until now I thought that little more than bluster.

But Lizzy, I have just heard from Mrs. Jenkinson that her ladyship left Rosings this morning in a frightful temper. I know not where she travels, but I know it cannot bode well that she has gone at all. I fear you must prepare yourself for a visit. If that is the case, I pray this letter reaches you first, that you may at least be prepared. I hope, however, that my worry is without cause and you are left in peace. Pray write in either case and assure me you are well.

With the greatest affection,
Charlotte Collins

Saturday, 30 May 1812: Hertfordshire

Mr. Bennet went to Sawbridgeworth on Saturday and Mrs. Bennet to Netherfield with all but one of her daughters. Still too unwell to tolerate a jolting carriage ride, Elizabeth remained at home, taking advantage of the empty house to play the pianoforte in her preferred style—with all the passion (and mistakes) an audience would bid her restrain. Her fingers swept over the keys, chasing away some of her more unpleasant reflections, tripping over others.

Jane's exasperating diffidence added considerable fervour to her playing. Though she had been constrained to an armchair with a pounding head all week, her sister had still thought it necessary to remind her of her pledge to be unobtrusive in Mr. Bingley's presence. She had made the promise to do so in earnest but hardly thought she could be accused of coquetry at such a time as this. She banged out the next few arpeggios excessively loudly in protest then winced as pain lanced through the bruise on her temple.

She sighed, displeased to have been reminded of the injury, for she did not like to dwell upon Mr. Wickham's attack. She recalled very little of it though her sisters had told her enough to make her glad of that. It was not Mr. Wickham's brutality that distressed her most, however. She was more concerned with just how profoundly she had misunderstood his character, for only now that she knew him capable of this did she comprehend how prodigiously foolish Mr. Darcy must have thought her when she stood before him, defending the blackguard's character. She vented her consternation on the keys, missing most of the notes in the next phrase.

It pained her deeply to consider how ill Mr. Darcy must think of her. Before yesterday and despite Mr. Bingley's various mistaken claims, she had not thought his opinion could diminish any further. Yet, if Charlotte was correct, Lady Catherine might be about to change that. Elizabeth did not believe her ladyship would condescend to come to Longbourn, but she did fear she might visit her nephew, for Mr. Darcy would then learn of the spurious rumours her friends and family had been circulating, vindicating all his accusations of the impropriety of her sphere. A series of discordant notes followed as she lost and retraced her place in the score.

Her greatest vexation was that, in contrast to how much Mr. Darcy must now hate her, she had begun to miss him. She was weary of her family's immodesty, wary of the militia, forbidden from engaging with Mr. Bingley lest Jane call it flirtation, and afraid to sigh within one hundred yards of Mr. Greyson lest her mother call it love. She felt desperately alone and fancied that some time spent with the astute, worldly, gentlemanly Mr. Darcy would suit her very well indeed. She began to comprehend that he was exactly the man who, in disposition and talents, would most suit her. His understanding and temper, though unlike her own, would have answered all her wishes. His arms wrapped around her would have soothed away all her ills. Her fingers played an entirely erroneous chord, dissonant and grating.

"Your playing has not improved at all I see, Miss Bennet."

Elizabeth gave a squeak of surprise and jumped an inch off her seat. How long Lady Catherine de Bourgh had stood in the doorway, regarding her with a disapproving sneer, she dared not suppose.

"Forgive me, Miss Elizabeth!" Hill called from the passageway beyond. "I could not persuade her ladyship to wait in the parlour."

"I quite understand," Elizabeth assured her, coming to her feet. "Be so good as to bring us some refreshments in there now, would you?"

"I do not care for refreshments," Lady Catherine stated imperiously.

"Very well. I hope you will not begrudge me some. I have been practicing very diligently." Indicating that her visitor should follow, Elizabeth walked the short distance between the rooms and chose the seat farthest from any other in the room.

Lady Catherine's lips thinned almost to the point of disappearing, but she nonetheless chose a seat and sat on it. "You can be at no loss, Miss Bennet, to understand the reason for my journey hither. Your own heart, your own conscience, must tell you why I come."

"Indeed you are mistaken, madam. I am quite unable to account for the honour of seeing you here," Elizabeth lied.

"You ought to know that I am not to be trifled with," replied her ladyship in an angry tone. "A report of a most alarming nature reached me yesterday morning. I was told that you, that Miss Elizabeth Bennet, would be, in all likelihood, soon united to my nephew, Mr. Darcy. I went immediately to London to have it confirmed as a scandalous falsehood. He was adamant there must have been some mistake, that no such rumour could possibly exist, but I instantly resolved on setting off for this place to have your word that you would never accept an offer of marriage from him."

Elizabeth's heart sank. She had visited him already! "If Mr. Darcy has said no such rumour could exist, I wonder you took the trouble of coming so far."

"He may have denied the existence of the rumour," she replied with narrowed eyes, "but he would not—nay, he *could* not deny the foundation for it. I perfectly comprehended his feelings. He is infatuated. Your arts and allurements have drawn him in."

"If that were the case, you could hardly expect me to refuse an offer, having gone to so much trouble to extort it from him."

Lady Catherine sucked in a breath, coughed sharply, and grew even more vexed. "Miss Bennet, do you know who I am? I have not been accustomed to such impertinence as this. I am almost the nearest relation Mr. Darcy has in the world and am entitled to know all his dearest concerns."

"But you are not entitled to know mine."

"When your concerns begin to obtrude upon mine, then I most certainly am entitled to know them!" She leant forwards in her chair, piercing Elizabeth with an icy glare. "Because of his fascination with you, Mr. Darcy has reneged on his engagement to my daughter. Now what have you to say?"

Elizabeth scarcely knew what to think but schooled herself to composure, for she would not satisfy Lady Catherine's hope of intimidating her. "A decision not to marry Miss de Bourgh, if indeed such a decision has been made, is by no means proof that he will offer for me."

"Do not be deliberately obtuse. Of course it is! Do you imagine me ignorant of the attention he showed you in Kent? He and his cousin have been intended for each other from their infancy, yet you, a woman of inferior birth and wholly unallied to the family, have caught his fancy, and now my daughter has been forsaken!"

"That cannot be blamed on me! I have no control over Mr. Darcy's whims!"

"Regrettably, that is precisely what you do have, and I mean to see that you use it as duty and honour prescribe. I would have you promise me never to enter into an engagement with him or act in any way that will prevent his marrying my daughter."

Elizabeth's head throbbed. "I am neither honour nor duty bound to do your bidding and can only pity Miss de Bourgh for being so. I shudder at what mortification will be hers when she is forced upon a man disinclined to the union. Have you no regard for sensibility?"

Lady Catherine scoffed disdainfully. "Frankly, I am more concerned with her security. My daughter requires a husband who will be considerate of her delicate constitution, who has consequence enough to elevate her reputation despite her absence from Town, who will manage her estate properly in the interests of her heirs. Do you suppose the world brims over with such men? Good, conscientious, distinguished men? It does not!" Her ladyship's voice became more hoarse the louder it grew. "Equally, my nephew requires a wife who will bring credit to his name, not ostracise him from the sphere in which he was raised. Do you not consider that a connection with you must discredit him in the eyes of everybody? The alliance would be a disgrace, and you must be the one to prevent it since he is so bewitched by you he will hear no reason on the subject from anybody else."

Elizabeth's heart pounded in consonance with her head. "I do not see that you have given me good reason to do so. So far, you have catalogued Mr. Darcy's virtues, informed me that he has denounced all other engagements, and impressed upon me the depth of his regard. It seems to me your ladyship has rather come to commend the union."

"This is not to be borne!" Lady Catherine struggled out of her chair and sucked in great wheezy breaths of outrage as she stalked to stand before her. "Do not deceive yourself into a belief that I will ever recede. I shall not..." Her tirade faltered. She frowned and peered more closely at Elizabeth's countenance. "Heaven and earth, what is that?"

Elizabeth sighed quietly, surprised it had gone unnoticed this long, notwithstanding her artfully arranged hair. "A bruise, ma'am."

Lady Catherine recoiled. "On your *face*? Wherever does a person obtain such an injury?"

"I acquired this one in Meryton."

"And you claim to be a gentlewoman? Never in all my days have I seen the like!"

"I believe it is yet to become fashionable in London. Perhaps next Season?"

Lady Catherine's eyes grew flinty. "Your impudence has lost all its charm, Miss Bennet. I insist you tell me how you came to be wounded thus."

"I was struck."

"You have been *brawling?*"

"I hardly think brawling is—"

"And this behaviour is what my nephew plans to inflict upon us! Are the shades of Pemberley to be thus polluted?"

Elizabeth stood up. "Lady Catherine, I have nothing more to say, and my head pains me. I beg to be importuned no further."

"You have yet to give me your word."

"True, and behaviour such as this will never induce me to give it. You had much better go, for you are wasting your time with me." She strode to the door, leant upon it for a moment while a wave of dizziness passed, then continued to the front of the house.

Lady Catherine followed, barking demands and invectives all the way. "I take no leave of you, Miss Bennet," she concluded as she swept past and climbed into her awaiting carriage. "I send no compliments to your family. You deserve no such attention."

Elizabeth did not trouble herself to reply and returned hastily to the house. The walls swam about her, and she clutched the back of a chair with one hand and her head with the other. She was inordinately grateful when Hill came to her aid, helping her to bed, giving her a measure of the tincture prescribed by Mr. Jones and mercifully agreeing to conceal the extraordinary visit from the rest of the family.

Left alone, Elizabeth almost immediately succumbed to sleep, unable to reflect clearly on any of what had been said whilst her head throbbed thus. Lucid or not, however, thoughts of Mr. Darcy were still foremost in her mind as she drifted off, and though that was not an unusual occurrence, this was the first occasion such thoughts had ever been accompanied by hope.

Monday, 1 June 1812: Hertfordshire

PEABODY LIT ONE OF MR. BINGLEY'S FINEST CIGARS AND LEANT BACK IN his chair. "She'll be one of old man Bennet's."

"Hush your tongue before the walls hear you!" warned Mrs. Arbuthnot.

Peabody shrugged and blew out a smoke ring. "What say you, Mr. Banbury?"

"I noticed a resemblance, I'll grant you," answered Mr. Bingley's manservant from behind his newspaper.

"The master's noticed it, too."

"How do you know that, then?" jeered Mrs. Arbuthnot, "Tell you himself, did he?"

Peabody smirked, tapping his ash on the flagstones. "He caught her scrubbing the grate in the library. Near buttered his breeches when he saw that face. I tell you, he's noticed the replica, just as he's noticed the original."

Banbury lowered his paper. "Indeed?"

"Aye," Peabody assured him with a sage nod. "And no person can look so much like another without being from the same seed. If Amelia's not old man Bennet's by-blow, I'll eat my hat."

"I care not who her father is," groused Mrs. Arbuthnot, "so long as she keeps the brass shiny. If it keeps the master happy to have her looking like his fancy woman, then more's the better. Might be as he don't forget my tip this quarter."

"The resemblance is not so very marked," Banbury opined. "Miss Eliza has a smaller nose and less pointy chin. And much prettier eyes."

Peabody did not reply. His attention was now on the glass of Mr. Bingley's best port in his hand.

Thursday, 4 June 1812: Hertfordshire

ELIZABETH PEERED LONGINGLY INTO THE GARDEN. IT HAD BEEN A LONG week confined to the house, first by faint spells and then, when those receded, the weather. She yearned for air and exercise to banish the confusion Lady Catherine's visit had occasioned. Denied any such relief this day, she sat in the window seat in the parlour, paying scant attention to her mother, sisters, or book, tracing raindrops as they slithered down the glass and thinking about Mr. Darcy.

As recently as last week, he had convinced his aunt of his enduring regard. The possibility of his loving her still was more gratifying than she could have imagined possible a few short weeks ago, yet it was scarcely to be believed.

Indeed, it was impossible to believe. Lady Catherine could not know of her nephew's previous offer or indeed how very much he must now be repulsed by the notion of a second. She must be mistaken.

A flash of movement drew Elizabeth's eye to the paddock; a rider was coming towards the house. For one horrid moment, she thought it might be Mr. Greyson. Mr. Greyson who had pressed his thigh against hers throughout last night's dinner and afterwards insisted she play the pianoforte, only to repeatedly brush his hand the length of her arm as he turned the pages for her. Mr. Greyson, who mistook her mother's encouragement for permission and with whom she had no desire whatever to be in company.

The dread of that encounter was soon replaced with a greater terror as she caught sight of the rider's red coat. She quite unintentionally cried out.

"What is it, Lizzy?" Jane enquired, all concern.

Lydia and Kitty rushed to the window, leaning over her in their rage to see. "La, 'tis only Colonel Forster!" cried Kitty.

"I thought the pigs had got out," Elizabeth said feebly, too shocked to admit how much the sight of a red coat had frightened her.

Colonel Forster presently arrived at the house and expressed his dismay at finding Mr. Bennet from home, for he had important news.

"There is nothing you can have to say that we cannot hear, sir," Mrs. Bennet assured him. "We have grown quite accustomed to being astonished these past weeks." She proved quite insistent, and Colonel Forster eventually relented, conveying the news that Mr. Wickham had been apprehended. Elizabeth could not comprehend why that intelligence should make her hands shake.

"My dear Colonel Forster, what wonderful news!" her mother exclaimed. "We shall be able to sleep peacefully in our beds at last. How shall we ever thank you?"

"I cannot justly accept your thanks, madam. Though my men did assist in the search, it was Mr. Darcy who had him found and arrested."

Despite her mother's assurances, Elizabeth was not prepared to be quite *that* astonished. "Mr. Darcy? But, I—"

"Yes, it was rather a strange turn of events," the colonel agreed. "He had written to warn me about Wickham. Unfortunately, his letter arrived too late, thus I was obliged to reply not with thanks but with an account of Wickham's violence and desertion. Thereafter, nothing was to be done in the search that he did not arrange himself."

This prompted Mrs. Bennet to declare him a fine young man, adding, "I knew nobody could really be that disagreeable! Would that half the young men these days were as good!"

"He truly *is* good," Colonel Forster replied, "for he has also settled the majority of Wickham's debts in Meryton—more than a thousand pounds."

"A thousand pounds!" Mrs. Bennet screeched. "Heaven and earth, his fortune must be vast to afford such a sum!"

Elizabeth shared a glance with Jane, and together they redirected their mother's raptures from Mr. Darcy's wealth to the somewhat less vulgar subject of his generosity with it.

Elizabeth hardly dared suppose the wish of protecting her had added force to whatever other inducements led Mr. Darcy to take so much trouble. She could not even be sure whether he knew it was Wickham who had injured her. She did think it possible that his decision to write to Colonel Forster might be a result of her reproofs, and she respected him all the more for the graciousness and humility he had shown in doing so. It was yet another thing to admire. Indeed, there was nothing she had learnt about him in the weeks since his proposal that had not deepened her regard. She would not be whimsical enough to say she loved him, but never had she felt so certain she could.

Nevertheless, the greater swelled her affection, the heavier grew her heart, for naught spoke more eloquently of the improbability of his renewing his addresses than his continued absence. His aunt's claims notwithstanding, he stayed away, and whatever he might feel was moot.

Friday, 5 June 1812: Hertfordshire

BINGLEY WAS FOXED. HE KNEW THIS, BECAUSE EACH OF THE TANKARDS ON the table before him overlapped the other by several inches. He wished he knew which one of them held his ale.

"Speaking of women," somebody said, slapping him heavily on the shoulder and sitting down next to him, "how goes your courtship?"

Had they been speaking of women? Bingley barely recalled to whom he had been talking, let alone what they had been discussing. "Terribly!" he slurred. Then his forehead thumped onto the table, and laughter erupted all around him.

"That bad, eh, old boy? Come, tell us all about it."

Would that he could explain it, but he was tied in such knots, he knew not how to begin. He had come back to Hertfordshire to court Miss Bennet, the handsomest woman ever to have walked the earth and for whom he had pined all winter. Yet, it was not she who trespassed his dreams at night. That honour was reserved for Elizabeth, possessor of the most provocative smile, penetrating eyes, and extraordinary, tempting figure of any woman of his acquaintance. Elizabeth whom he had carried in his arms, broken and beautiful. Elizabeth with a marked resemblance to the maid he had squeezed past in the narrow passage to Peabody's pantry earlier… He lifted his head and propped an elbow on the table, pointing his forefinger at the sea of expectant faces. "'Tis the wrong one!"

"Ah ha! He is wavering!" another voice cried, banging the table triumphantly.

"I told you he would. They all do. Only took him a little longer than most."

"Damn it, Bingley, you've cost me a florin!"

Bingley squinted at them all. "What are you blathering about?"

"Miss Bennet, man," Henry Lucas, sitting opposite him, said with a grin. "The enthralment wears off after a while, does it not?"

Guilt sent a hot flush up Bingley's neck. "It does?"

"Invariably, my friend. Trust me, I have known the Bennets all my life. I have watched more than a few men follow the same course." Addressing the entire table, he said loudly, "Boys, shall we? Attend, Bingley—*the Bennet Ballad*!"

Bingley almost fell off the bench when, without warning, the man on his right gave forth a booming note, from which several others took up their harmonies then burst into a rowdy tavern song.

Take the fifth for a wife only if ye dare,
For a man tied to her will needs must share.

A ripple of sniggers and snorts rolled around the table, and more voices joined in the evidently well-known song.

Wed the fourth if you value not common sense,
For asinine prattle will deafen you hence.
Take the third for a wife to atone for your sins,
She'll preach you to death but yield not her quim.

He had lapsed into a drunken stupor. It was the only explanation.

Marry the first and be every man's envy,
'Til ennui strikes and witless rends ye.

Every man in the tavern seemed to join the refrain as the volume swelled loud.

But hail the man who weds the second,
For she is the jewel, alluring and fecund,
She'll fill your days with laughter and wit,
And by night, beguile ye with that arse and those tits!

Someone raised his tankard in a toast, and the final note promptly dissolved into a roar of hearty laughter that filled the parlour.

Bingley was speechless. He ought to call every one of them out! He ought to rid Lucas of his smirk. At the very least, he ought to denounce the bloody song. Yet, he did so like it when others made decisions for him, and so in the end, all he did was sit still and allow a stupid grin to spread across his face.

Saturday, 6 June 1812: Hertfordshire

PEABODY SHOWED MRS. BENNET AND HER ELDEST DAUGHTER INTO THE saloon, informed them they would be attended directly, and went to fetch the master.

He knew precisely where he would find him. Some hours earlier, as dawn broke across the sky, Mr. Bingley had staggered through Netherfield's front doors and fallen into his study. Peabody had followed to ensure his well-being, only to have a piece of paper shoved under his nose. Pointing at it, Mr. Bingley had exclaimed, "Is not she the most beautiful creature you ever beheld? Is not she an *angel*?" After a moment's consideration, Peabody had agreed that the crayon scribble of a purple and orange potato was indeed remarkable. Seemingly satisfied, the master had announced his intention to marry the gaudy vegetable. Peabody had left him settling down to write to his friend with the joyous news.

When Mrs. Hurst had enquired at breakfast as to her brother's whereabouts, Peabody had led her to the study where, as per his expectations, they found Mr. Bingley sprawled insensible across his desk, his slumped form not adequately arranged to conceal the letter beneath him from his sister's view. The Bennet ladies' call had curtailed Peabody's enjoyment of the supervening cataclysm, thus it was with no little relish that he now tripped back to the study to announce their arrival.

"I will not allow you to do this! You will ruin us all!" Mrs. Hurst screeched as he sidled into the room.

Mr. Bingley winced and rubbed his eyes. "Do not be absurd. I will ruin nothing."

"I have not endured the indignity of being married to a bloated dandy for these past two years, only to have you announce that you will marry where you will! Do my sacrifices mean so little to you? You selfish, selfish man!"

"What is wrong with Hurst? I like him!"

"Must you be so tiresome, Charles? This is not about my husband. I rather think that situation is beyond salvation." She looked pointedly at her rounded belly. "But I will not see it all made meaningless because you are in a rage to secure your own fancy!"

Mr. Bingley backed away from her, tripped on an undetectable hazard of the variety to which only drunk people are susceptible, and fell against his desk, where he then remained, leant at a precarious angle. "I have heard it all before, Louisa, but you shall not dissuade me again. I *shall* marry Miss Elizabeth, *you* will be her sister, and that is *all* there is to it."

In Peabody's humble opinion, Miss Elizabeth Bennet was considerably prettier than the garish tuber he had been shown a few hours earlier, but Mrs. Hurst seemed less convinced of her merits.

"Why her? She is the most impertinent, undignified, unfashionable woman I have ever met! At least her sister is beautiful! If you must marry one of them, marry her. Her looks might halfway excuse your absurd choice to the rest of the world."

"I cannot marry Miss Bennet."

"You certainly cannot marry her sister. I would sooner you marry her mother!"

Peabody cleared his throat. "Miss Bennet and her mother wait upon you in the saloon."

Both siblings started. Mr. Bingley looked terrified, his sister, furious.

"Go to her, then!" Mrs. Hurst fumed. "Choose the sister least likely to disgrace us with her savage country manners!"

"I shall not! Attend them yourself. I am for bed." Shakily but determinedly, Mr. Bingley snatched the letter from his desk, folded it roughly and shoved it at Peabody's chest with the instruction to see that it was posted. Then he stormed unsteadily from the room.

"If you do not choose Miss Bennet, mark my words, you shall have neither of them!" Mrs. Hurst called after him, growling in exasperation when he did not answer. "Inform my guests I shall join them presently," she ordered; then she too swept from the room.

Left alone, Peabody took a moment to peek at the contents of the letter, smirked a little, then refolded and sealed it. He exited the room in time to see Mrs. Bennet scurrying away down the corridor like a startled vole along a riverbank. Diverted further still, he pocketed Mr. Bingley's letter to add to the others set aside for posting, sure Mr. Darcy would find it fascinating reading.

Sunday, 7 June 1812: Hertfordshire

"Slow your pace, Jane. I would speak with you."

Jane turned, surprised to see her mother hurrying to catch up with her, for she had left her still speaking to Mrs. Philips at the church. She duly fell into step alongside her, observing that her lips were pressed tightly together in a telltale sign of vexation. "Have I displeased you, Mama?"

"Yes!" Mrs. Bennet replied in an angry whisper. "You and all your sisters! I know not what any of you is about. Colonel Forster's regiment are removing to Brighton on Monday, and not one of them has shown an interest in marrying any of you. Lizzy has allowed Mr. Greyson to go off on business without making her an offer. And you!" She threw Jane an angry look and shook her head. "If you do not secure Mr. Bingley soon, he will have none of us, and we shall all be ruined!"

Tears sprang to Jane's eyes. "Mama, I should like nothing more than for Mr. Bingley to offer for me, but I cannot make him love me."

"Of course you can! That is what I wished to speak to you about." She looked over her shoulder and all about before continuing. "Men are essentially very easy to work on once you know how. They can be persuaded to almost anything by—that is, all it takes is—well, the heart of the matter is, the prospect of becoming intimately acquainted ought to induce Mr. Bingley to hasten proceedings. And you and he are so close to an engagement, I cannot see that it would do any harm at all to give him a little encouragement of that sort."

"I have tried conversing with him more, and I thought he seemed pleased by it."

Her mother gave her a strange look. "You must know I was not referring to small talk."

Jane shook her head.

"Oh, for heaven's sake, child, do you not read novels? And you, the eldest of all my girls! I am speaking of the intimacies between a husband and wife."

Jane's eyes widened. Heat suffused her cheeks. "Why?"

"Have you not listened to a word I have said? It is simple enough. Men find great pleasure in it, and the promise of it ought to encourage Mr. Bingley to cease dallying. Lower your lace, tighten your stays, and show him what he may look forward to!"

Jane stared at her, aghast.

"Do not look at me that way, Miss Jane. You would not be the first girl ever to use her womanly assets to convince a man he loved her. Only consider how low Miss Bingley's necklines were cut—a good three inches lower than her married sister's—though I must say it did her no favours. You have a good deal more of which to boast in that area if only you would make the most of it."

"I have no wish to draw Mr. Bingley in with arts and allurements."

"Indeed, you would not be drawing him in, for he is already in love with you! If he were a stranger, I should never suggest it, but you are already so close to being married, I am convinced it will do no harm."

"But I am not! What would he think of me?"

"Precisely what you require him to think! Really, Jane, if you will not be helped, do not run to me when it all comes to nothing."

"Forgive me, ma'am, I know you mean well, but this is hardly helpful! I have neither the confidence nor the inclination to behave in such a manner. You will not convince me that this is the only way to let Mr. Bingley know his addresses would be welcomed."

"No, indeed! I suppose if all else fails, a well-aimed swoon ought to do it."

"Mother!"

"Oh, proceed as you will, child—only make certain you do so with haste before it is too late and you end up an old maid!" That comment saw them to the front door, and her mother disappeared inside, leaving Jane alone but for a miserable sense of urgency.

6
Mixed Blessings

Monday, 8 June 1812: Hertfordshire

The sight of his wife eavesdropping at the door to the little parlour presented a temptation too great to overlook. Rather than lead the recently arrived Sir William into the library, Mr. Bennet directed him thither.

Upon noticing his approach, Mrs. Bennet began frantically flapping her hands at him and alternately shaking her head and twitching it towards the parlour door. Fortunately, after many years of marriage, Mr. Bennet had become accustomed to his wife's delicate subtlety: she did not wish him to go into the parlour. Thus assured of sport of some variety, he was less inclined than ever to leave. "Shall we take our coffee with a view of the pond for a change?" he proposed to his guest.

"Why not!" Sir William replied amiably, following him along the passageway and bidding Mrs. Bennet good morning.

She graced him with a perfunctory curtsy. "What do you mean by bringing poor Sir William to this cold, unpleasant little room, Mr. Bennet? He would be much more comfortable in the front parlour."

"Nonsense, my dear, this is the best room in the house," he replied, reaching for the handle.

"No!" she hissed, thrusting herself across the door. "Mr. Bingley is within! He requested a private audience with our daughter!"

Mr. Bennet leant back on his heels and smiled. "Indeed? And pray, which one have you sent him?" His curiosity was partially satisfied by the appearance of one of the five contenders through the front door. "Not Lizzy, then."

"What is not me, Papa?" Elizabeth enquired, removing her bonnet and coming down the hall to join them.

"Shall we see?" He gestured to his wife to step aside. "Apparently, Lizzy, Mr. Bingley has made one of your sisters an offer your mother cannot refuse!"

It occurred to Bingley too late that he had not specified to Mrs. Bennet *which* of her daughters he wished to see—and it was not this one. Miss Jane Bennet entered the room in high colour, unable to meet his eye. They exchanged an awkward greeting and spoke briefly of the weather but then lapsed into silence as she no doubt awaited his addresses, and he tried in vain to think of a polite way not to make them.

"Please do be seated," she said at length.

He declined, not wishing to give the impression of wanting to be there.

"Should you like some refreshments?"

He repeated his refusal but then felt compelled by her disappointed expression to say something more obliging. "This is a delightful room. I do not believe I have seen it before."

"Thank you. My mother likes to keep it for special occasions." She stopped, looking as embarrassed as he felt by the allusion to everyone's expectations.

Her blush, he could not help but notice, spread down her neck and beyond, drawing his attention with it. He was quite sure he had never seen her wear that gown before, and it looked remarkably well on her. "I see," he said distractedly. "I wonder that she was good enough to let us use it then."

She let out a little gasp. Bingley made a silent imprecation. He had not meant to so bluntly announce what his intentions were *not*. He had not the time to apologise, for in the next moment, Miss Bennet unexpectedly swooned towards him. He threw his arms out to catch her but was unbalanced and fell heavily on the nearest sofa with her somehow sprawled, supine, across his lap.

He was instantly returned to a fortnight earlier when it had been Elizabeth he held lifeless in his arms. There his mind lingered, for with her head reclined thus, both of Miss Bennet's eyebrows were arched, her cheekbones were accentuated and her lips slightly parted—and she looked more like her sister than ever.

Had she not looked so much the picture of the woman he wished he were embracing, he would likely never have remained bent over her as long as he did. Then, she would never have observed him looking at her in such a manner when her eyes fluttered open, might never have mistaken his ardour as meant for her, and might never have been emboldened to lift her head and kiss him. Had he not been consumed with unfulfilled yearning for Elizabeth, he might have pulled away sooner.

He registered the click and creak of the door too late and was still engaged thusly when Mrs. Bennet's shriek fractured the quiet of the room, followed immediately by Mr. Bennet's voice.

"And there my money was on Mary."

Bingley almost tipped Miss Bennet to the floor in his haste to detach himself.

"Young love, eh?"

His stomach sank, for he knew that voice. Sir William, of all people, had observed his transgression!

"I always knew how it would be!" Mrs. Bennet all but sang.

Bingley turned to face his audience and froze—Elizabeth! Her expression was one of pure surprise, sending remorse knifing through his gut. His mind turned over, searching desperately for a way to explain, to apologise, to salvage what had meant to be *their* union.

"Capital! Capital!" Sir William went on. "What congratulations will now flow in!"

"Indeed," said Mr. Bennet coldly. "I may be forced to overlook the prematurity of your celebrations, Mr. Bingley, once those of my neighbours begin." He glanced meaningfully at Sir William.

Bingley broke into a sweat. Mr. Bennet was correct. Between Sir William and Mrs. Bennet, news of his amorous clinch and presumed betrothal would be all over Meryton before supper. How could the alliance possibly be avoided? He looked at Elizabeth in desperation.

"I am very happy for you both," said she.

Bingley almost whimpered. She was utterly lost to him. He briefly considered running from the house and not coming back, but the notion only made his despair greater, for he could not countenance the prospect of never seeing her again. Then she smiled, and the matter was settled. He could not leave her, but if he stayed, he must marry her sister.

He turned to Miss Bennet. She returned his look with a tentative smile, seeming better pleased with the turn of events than he, which was rather too little relief too late, for he had come to doubt whether she welcomed his attentions at all. Louisa was correct, however. She was decorous and sweet and uncommonly pretty. A union with her could hardly be considered a punishment.

He looked back at Mr. Bennet. "My apologies, sir. I meant to come to you directly of course."

Mr. Bennet grunted. "I shall await you in my library, then. Jane, I shall speak to you afterwards," he said as he quitted the room.

Miss Bennet rose hastily from the sofa and came to stand before Bingley. "I beg you, take no offense," she whispered. "I am sure he will be happy for us once the surprise passes."

"He has every right to be angry. It was ill done."

"I daresay there are worse ways of declaring oneself," she whispered shyly.

Bingley refrained from actually kicking himself. Surely to God, there was no worse way to declare oneself than to do it to the wrong woman! "You are quite sure this is what you wish?" he enquired as quietly as humanly possible. Her expression of heartfelt delight as she nodded her acceptance rendered her even more handsome than usual, vaguely disposing him to be more hopeful. "And are you well? You swooned very suddenly. Ought we not to call for the apothecary?"

"Oh, no! Pray do not! I should be mortified. I was only a little too warm."

"As you wish. I—I ought to go to your father now."

She smiled and stepped away from him, and she was immediately engulfed in her mother and Sir William's rapturous celebrations. Elizabeth came to Bingley, shaking his hands with cordiality he did not deserve. He opened his mouth to beg her forgiveness, but she spoke first.

"You have been very good to me these past few weeks. I could not have wished for a better brother or a better husband for Jane."

God in heaven, how was he ever to be brother to her? He gripped her warm hands tighter still to prevent himself dipping his head to kiss her, but she was gone to her sister before he could do more than thank her. Thus, with very startling rapidity, the affair that had given him so much suspense and vexation was finally settled, and in the most perverse manner possible. With one last rueful glance, he left the room and Elizabeth behind.

Wednesday, 10 June 1812: Hertfordshire

ELIZABETH CROUCHED TO LAY HER FLOWERS ON THE GRAVE AS SHE DID ON this day every year. Mrs. Lincoln had been the wife of one of Longbourn's tenants, and she was survived by her husband and two children. Four years after her passing, Elizabeth still vividly recalled teaching her little boy to read, his grief as he struggled to follow her instructions weighing particularly heavy on her this year, for what right had she, compared to such loss, to mourn that which she had willingly thrown away?

Endlessly, she tortured herself with thoughts of Mr. Darcy—his subtle smile, burning gaze, absorbing conversation, and unassuming generosity. His impassioned declaration of love. Regardless of how she told herself a person ought not to form a design on a memory, her heart would not be dissuaded. She could think of him in no other terms than of being in love, for no other sentiment came close to expressing the depth of her present feelings towards him. Observing Jane's happiness had taught her how utterly foolish she had been to refuse him.

"Do you visit her grave often?" Bingley enquired behind her. She almost toppled over in surprise and stood hastily to prevent it, making her head reel as it had not done in days.

"Forgive me, I meant not to startle you," he said.

"You are forgiven. I thought you would be longer with the curate."

"He is not yet here, but we found Mrs. Goulding in the church. Jane is speaking to her about flowers for the wedding. Speaking of flowers..." He crouched unexpectedly and reached to gather up those Elizabeth had just laid, which she only then noticed had been strewn untidily over the grave when he startled her.

She was glad of his distraction. It meant he did not witness the blush that any and all mention of his and Jane's wedding brought to her cheeks. Arrangements for the occasion were now a source of constant deliberation at Longbourn—and constant anxiety for her as she fretted over Mr. Darcy's attendance. She dreaded feeling his enmity should he come but dared not ask after him lest she learn he meant not to, for the prospect of never seeing him again grew ever more difficult to bear—which was perhaps the reason that the unmistakable sound of his voice affected her so.

"Elizabeth."

She whipped her head up—but too quickly. Her temple throbbed, and her vision swam. Nevertheless, she saw him, standing motionless beyond the wall, his eyes fixed upon her. She gasped at the familiar intensity of his stare. He was come! Pressing a hand to her thundering heart, she took a step towards him but no more, for faintness encroached, and her knees buckled.

"Lizzy!" cried Bingley, lurching to his feet to arrest her fall.

The wave of dizziness receded as quickly as it arrived, and barely an instant passed before Elizabeth twisted from his grip to look for Mr. Darcy. She almost cried out to discover he was no longer there.

"What is going on?"

Reluctantly, Elizabeth gave up peering around the perimeter of the churchyard and turned back to see Jane approaching them along the path from the church.

"Your sister is unwell," Bingley informed her. "She almost fainted."

"I am not unwell," Elizabeth assured them. "I only felt a little light-headed. It has passed now."

"Indeed. How fortunate that Mr. Bingley was here to catch you," Jane replied coolly. Taking Mr. Bingley's arm, she said to him, "The curate will see us now."

"But your sister—"

"Go, go, I am perfectly well, I assure you," Elizabeth insisted, though she began to wonder whether she might actually be hallucinating, for Mr. Darcy was nowhere to be seen. Resolved on searching for him beyond the churchyard, she added, "Indeed, I believe I shall continue on to Oakham Mount and join you again at Longbourn."

Jane took her at her word and left, pulling Bingley with her. No sooner had they disappeared inside the church than Elizabeth whirled about in the direction of the lane—and gasped in surprise. Mr. Darcy, more striking, more imposing, more *real* than any memory she had conjured in his absence, stood directly before her. The world stilled.

"You awoke," he whispered, staring at her as though she were an apparition.

"I, oh, I—pardon?"

"You awoke. You are alive." His accent had none of its usual sedateness; his voice was hoarse and urgent.

"I do not—"

"Bingley sent word that you never awoke." His eyes darted across her face, settling on her bruised temple. To her astonishment, he raised his hand as though to cup her face. "After this."

She held her breath, but rather than touch her, he lowered his hand to his side and pressed it in a tightly clenched fist against his thigh.

"I thought you dead."

"Heavens, no! I suffered from a concussion for a few days, but I am recovered now. But for the odd spell of faintness," she added, indicating the spot behind her where she had swooned moments before.

"Then Bingley—"

"Caught me."

Elizabeth fancied she saw a greater contrariety of emotion in his look at that moment than in the whole of their previous acquaintance. His manner bemused her. He was as discomposed as she had ever seen him, apparently stunned to see her, with an urgency about him of which she could make no sense but that her heart yearned to understand.

"Pardon me—if you thought me dead, why are you come?"

He was shaking slightly as though from some great emotion or the effort to constrain it, but when he spoke, his voice was steady and impossibly deep. "I have yet to find a way to live without you by my side. When I thought I should have to live without you alive in the world at all, I could not bear it. I came to say goodbye. I knew not what else to do."

Hope overturned her heart. "Then I am very glad to be alive, for I should have been sorry to miss the opportunity of seeing you again—very sorry indeed."

Mr. Darcy blinked several times and frowned but was otherwise motionless. She watched, hoping dearly that he would take her meaning, and drank in the sight of him as she waited. He was every inch as handsome as she recalled, though with one addition to his countenance.

Quite without forethought, she raised her fingers to touch the vivid red line beneath his left eye. "This is new."

His eyes widened, and his hand flew to cover hers, bringing her mortifying awareness of her presumption, but he would not surrender it for all her efforts to withdraw.

"Have I any hope?" His voice was strained with emotion.

She let out a breathy, nervous laugh and nodded. "I think you may never be more assured of anything."

His breath caught. His eyes darkened to a fathomless ebon hue. His palm, warm and sure, came at last to rest upon her cheek. "Marry me. I am so in love with you. Marry me, I beg you."

All her wishes were answered. He loved her still! With nary a moment's hesitation, she assured him of her jubilant acceptance, and she was at once pulled into his fervent, desperate embrace. Encircling her completely in his arms, he whispered her name like a promise and held her to him as though he would never let her go. Barely crediting her own boldness, she snaked her arms about his waist beneath his coat. He stiffened and drew back far enough to look at her. She did not think she would ever forget his expression.

"I have not the words to describe what I feel for you, dearest, loveliest Elizabeth."

He leant down and slowly, reverently, pressed his lips to hers. She shivered. Her skin veritably crackled at being so tenderly touched. At once, every feeling of futility was banished, all hope vindicated, and every expectation exceeded. She was lost to him.

She kept her eyes closed for a moment or two after he ceased his caress, daring not to break the spell. When she did open them, she found him watching her, piercing her with his gaze and thrilling her with the most enigmatic smile she had ever beheld.

"I do not give you leave to *ever* die again, Elizabeth Bennet."

Darcy's happiness was such as he had never felt before. Elizabeth, who only weeks earlier had fractured his world with her avowals of disgust and until moments before he had believed dead, had agreed to marry him, had allowed him to kiss her, and was standing in his embrace, laughing with unaffected delight. It was nothing, however, compared to the joy her next deed produced. He watched, enthralled, as she placed her hands flat upon his chest and fixed him with the same exquisite dark eyes that had haunted him since the first moment of their acquaintance.

"I love you."

He stilled, astonishment and exultation paralysing him as readily as had his utter despair the previous day.

"I see you doubt it," she said softly, smiling a small but magnificent smile. "I shall say it again and again, 'til you believe me. I love, I love, I *love* you, Fitzwilliam Darcy."

Such elation as this declaration produced could not be constrained to speech. He kissed her again—possessively, as a man kisses a woman he means to bind to him. His heart, his soul, his world were bound up in this one woman, and here she was in his arms at last. His.

Regardless of his disinclination ever to relinquish his hold upon her, they could not continue thus indefinitely. He drew a short distance away, feeling instantly bereft. He knew he ought to speak but could no more order his turbulent mind to form a coherent thought than he could bestill his racing heart that, in contrast to its notable silence over the last day, was near deafening him with its present thundering. He caught the familiar expression in her eyes. She, without doubt, was laughing at him, and his heart soared. That decided him. He stepped back and held out his arm. "Shall we?"

She gave him a quizzical look, wrinkling her nose charmingly, but nevertheless wrapped both hands about his arm. He clasped his hand over hers, drew her tightly to his side and set off along the path.

"What are you about, sir?"

"I am taking you to that church."

"That is as I thought. May I ask why?"

"I am done waiting for you, Elizabeth. I would marry you. I daresay this church will do as well as any other."

Her laughter lifted his soul. To his complete joy, she rested her head against his arm and gave him a playful nudge.

"I would not object, but we must wait our turn. Jane and Mr. Bingley are within—oh! Does Mr. Bingley know you are here? I do not think he saw you before."

Darcy immediately reversed their path, overtaken with an irrational surge of resentment at the memory of Elizabeth in Bingley's arms. "Not as yet, and I would keep it that way for a while longer, for I am in no haste to share you. Would you do me the honour of walking with me? I have much I would say."

Thus, together they passed beneath the lychgate, and though he had expected to leave his heart behind in the churchyard, Darcy left with not only his but also Elizabeth's.

Bingley could have sworn he heard Elizabeth laughing, but when he and Miss Bennet exited the church, she was nowhere to be seen. He could not help but be disappointed.

"Is something the matter?" Miss Bennet enquired.

"I was only thinking how very ill your sister looked earlier. I am not at all sure she ought to have walked on by herself."

"You are good to be concerned," she replied stiffly, "but Lizzy would not have gone if she felt unwell. She is very sensible."

"Aye," he conceded with a wry smile. "As are you, Miss Bennet."

"Jane."

"Pardon?"

"I thought you might like to call me Jane now that we are betrothed."

"Well, yes, if you like."

"I would like it very much." She smiled brightly, always a pleasant surprise.

"Then, yes, of course. *Jane*."

"Thank you. It seems only right after all that, since you have dispensed with propriety when addressing Lizzy, you ought to do the same for your wife."

Elizabeth glanced up at Darcy. He looked happier than she had ever seen him, his eyes burning intensely and his lips curled slightly at the corners as though a laugh might come as easily as a smile—or a kiss.

She felt a thrill at the thought of his tender caresses. It had felt necessary, after their painful journey, to seal their union in such a way, and she was determined to waste not a moment in consideration of their impropriety. It was for them to forge their path, and this intimacy was theirs alone to know. She smiled to herself; after so long wishing for his embrace, she was more than happy to discover it such an agreeable place to be.

"You are happy?"

She started a little but was not surprised to find him watching her. It was what he did. "Never more so. You?"

"More than I have the words to express. I fear I will awaken at any moment to discover this but a dream."

"If it is, then it is an uncommonly authentic one."

"As are all my dreams of you."

He held her gaze, unabashed, and though she felt herself colour, she delighted in his characteristic frankness. Having once accused him of speaking only to amaze the whole room, she better understood now that he spoke only when he could do so with conviction. If the whole room took it upon itself to be amazed, that was up to them. She chose not to be.

"If my actions so far today have not convinced you I am real, I am afraid you will have to wait until we are wed and apply to me then for further proof." His eyes widened, and she smiled at his surprise, though with so much regret weighing upon her, she soon sobered. "I hope your dreams of me were not all nightmares. I have treated you very ill."

"There is nothing to reproach in your behaviour to me."

"We both know that is untrue!"

"I do not."

"Nay, you cannot deny I have been hateful. Certainly, I cannot forgive myself for the things of which I have accused you or the way I have spoken to and about you. In fact, I cannot fathom how you came to love me at all."

"Fortunately for you, your obstinacy is one of many reasons." The smile with which he said this faded, and in a more strained voice, he added, "I think it more reasonable that I should wonder how you have come to love me."

Remorse twisted her stomach, for despite his demurrals, here was proof of how deeply she had wounded him. "I have come to better comprehend you, and there is very little I have discovered that has *not* brought me to loving you." His brow furrowed endearingly, but he spoke not, and she determined to erase his every doubt. "Your letter did much to improve my opinion."

He groaned. "You cannot know how I regret ever having presented you with material proof of my resentfulness."

"I may not have liked it very well at first," Elizabeth admitted with a smile. "But I have since come to treasure it. It has been a comfort to me."

"For that alone I am glad to have written it, but you may burn the wretched thing now. I intend henceforth to provide all the comfort you require."

Elizabeth was rather diverted by the fluttering this produced in her stomach. "Then there was Mr. Bingley's return." He looked a little abashed, which was proof enough for her of his part in it. "It was more comfort than you can know to see Jane's heart mended. They are engaged, did you know?"

"I did not. That is happy news indeed."

She squeezed his arm. "Thank you."

"Pray, of all things, do not *thank* me! They would be wed by now if not for my interference."

"Nevertheless, I do thank you. It must have taken great courage to speak to him."

"Not as much courage as it took to hear what he said in response."

"I can imagine."

"You mistake my meaning. Bingley was not angry. It was his observations of my behaviour to *you* that were most painful to hear."

"Well, then I must thank him, for now you and I may quarrel about whose behaviour was worse, and that will give you a fine opportunity to admire my obstinacy."

He stopped walking and turned her to face him, his eyes so focused that she could see flecks of gold glinting in his brown irises. "I cannot laugh about it. I am so in love with you. Knowing I have pained you has been unbearable."

Before she could think how to reply, he wrapped his arms around her, cradling her shoulders and head as he whispered a heartfelt apology. With her ear to his broad, solid chest, she heard his heart beating, powerfully and much too fast.

"I forgave you all your mistakes long ago, Fitzwilliam. Pray, I would hear you say that you have forgiven me mine."

He tightened his hold on her. "Every one." She did not expect him to continue and was surprised when he added, "Even your decimation of Mozart's Eleventh Sona—"

She poked him in the ribs before he could finish, laughter bursting from her lips. "Teasing man! Will you always know so easily when I need a laugh?"

"I hope so." He took her hand and placed it on his arm. When they had walked a short distance, he said, "It is to be 'Fitzwilliam,' is it?"

"'Tis your name, is it not?"

"It is, though I am little in the habit of answering to it."

"I have read the adieu in your letter every day since you gave it to me. I am afraid you cannot be aught else now but my Fitzwilliam Darcy."

Clearly moved, he lifted her hand to his lips. "God, I love you, woman."

They walked on, Elizabeth with a lightness in her heart she had begun to fear forever lost. As they often did, her emotions bubbled over into action, and she reached up to snatch a leaf from the overhanging canopy—which the tree refused to yield. The resulting flick of the branch showered them both with debris from on high. She shrieked in surprise and hopped backwards, laughing as she brushed bits of foliage from her dress. Turning with an apology on her lips, she was utterly undone to discover the illustrious Mr. Darcy, bespattered with flora, now reaching to pluck a leaf from the canopy.

"You cannot know the pleasure I find in pleasing you," he said as he presented her with it. "I had long despaired of ever having the privilege."

"How fortunate for me that your happiness is dependent upon my own," she replied, accepting it.

He pointed to the leaf. "Had I known pleasing you was so easily done, I should have given you a tree the day we met."

Oh, how she adored his unexpected teasing! "Do you recall," she said, turning them back to the path, "when I said at Netherfield there is something new to be observed in people forever?"

"I do."

"That is what falling in love with you has been like. With every mention of you, every memory or thought, I have found more to love."

"Such as?"

"Such as learning it was you who saw to Mr. Wickham's arrest."

He instantly stiffened. "Had I but known it was you he hurt, I should have come directly, but I discovered it only yesterday and then…you…it was—"

"Put it from your mind," she said softly. "I am yours now."

He exhaled heavily. "Thank God for that."

At Elizabeth's request, Darcy stumbled through an explanation of the events that had led him to believe she had died. It was evident she found the entire situation diverting, but she checked her laugh.

"Would that I had known your opinion of me was so soon improved," he said. "I would have returned in an instant."

"I daresay you saved yourself considerable effort by staying away. I was not consciously in love with you when I spoke to Mr. Wrenshaw or when I asked Mr. Bingley to send my apologies. But I have since courted myself quite effectively on your behalf with memories and hopes and dreams."

Darcy smiled but begged that she allow him to take up the office of lover henceforth. Her mumbled, breathless acquiescence pleased him very well indeed. God, but she was beautiful! Again and again, he looked at her, each time falling further under her spell. Watching her thus, he soon noticed when her pace slowed and her head rested more heavily against his arm. "Are you well?"

"My head is beginning to ache a little. Perhaps I have walked too far today."

"Forgive me, I did not think." Ignoring her protests, Darcy led her to the low stone wall bordering the lane, spread his coat atop it, and insisted she sit down to rest. For all her bravado, she sank heavily onto the improvised seat and closed her eyes.

He lowered himself to sit next to her and tenderly nudged her bonnet and curls aside that he might examine her injury more closely. It was an ugly wound, still somewhat swollen and yellowing at the edges. His chest tightened painfully at the sight. He cupped her face and placed a feather-light kiss upon her cheek.

She let out a shuddering breath. "How I wished you were there to hold me."

His arms were about her instantly, pulling her in one deft move onto his lap and making her squeal with surprise. "I shall never forgive myself for not being there, but I am here now and shall never allow anybody to hurt you again."

She left him in no doubt of her gratitude but, after that, refused to dwell on the matter. Instead, they far better employed their time discussing every detail of each other's lives since Easter. She remained in his lap while they talked, he tracing patterns on her lower back with his right hand, she toying with the fingers of his left. In that attitude, they remained until she enquired about the scar on his cheek. He gave explanation, she kissed it, he kissed her, and shortly thereafter, the arrangement was abandoned before too much adoration could be expressed.

"Are you recovered enough to return? I have a great inclination to speak with your father."

She assured him she was, and they set off in the direction of Longbourn.

"Does it give you much pain?"

"Not very often now. Aside from the odd headache and a little giddiness and this ghastly bruise, I am perfectly well."

"I never saw a bruise worn more handsomely."

She laughed. "That is not what your aunt said."

"My aunt? Lady Catherine?"

She pulled a wry face and nodded.

"And when did she have occasion to comment on it?" he enquired warily.

"When she called on me to forbid me from ever marrying you."

"When she *what?*"

Mr. Darcy was the kind of man to whom Mr. Bennet should never dare refuse anything he condescended to ask, and he gave his consent at once. That he should ask *this* was somewhat bewildering, but since Elizabeth had come to him first, assuring him of her wishes, he felt not unduly concerned. He cared for only three things: Elizabeth would be well looked after, she would be able to respect her partner in life, and he need lose no more sleep over his *other* soon-to-be son.

He remained entirely unconvinced that Bingley had secured his preferred choice of sister, and he had not been able to dispel the concern that he might yet abandon Jane. He had infinitely more faith in Mr. Darcy's ability to direct his friend's romantic interests, and his appearance was vastly reassuring.

"Would that you had asked her sooner," Mr. Bennet said, reaching to shake hands. "You might have saved your friend weeks of indecision." He regretted the jest when he saw Mr. Darcy's frown and hastily suggested they collect Elizabeth and announce the news to the family.

He led the couple into the parlour, but before he could draw breath to speak, Bingley was on his feet.

"Lizzy! Thank heavens—I say, *Darcy!* What the deuce are you doing here?"

Having already been denied the privilege of announcing Jane's engagement, Mr. Bennet was unwilling to forfeit his due a second time and answered before Mr. Darcy. "He is a single man in possession of a good fortune. For what other purpose could he have possibly come but to secure himself a wife? It is my very great pleasure to inform you all that Lizzy and Mr. Darcy are engaged."

It was much to his consternation that the announcement he ultimately made should be met with stony silence. Mrs. Bennet sat perfectly still, seemingly unable to breathe, let alone speak. The irony of his lamenting her want of theatricals on the sole occasion upon which she had been shocked into quiescence was not lost on him. His younger daughters all stared aimlessly between him, their mother, and Elizabeth. Jane looked by turns amazed, relieved, and then vexed—for none of which he could account. Bingley stood unmoving before him, open-mouthed and ashen.

"Well," he said into the deafening silence, "if you are all quite done with your celebrations, I think I shall return to the quiet of my library. I can scarcely bear all the commotion."

Turning to leave, he laid a hand on Elizabeth's arm, intending to counsel her not to be dismayed by their surprise. Upon observing her, however, he decided she needed no such assurance. Had his wife suffered a fit of apoplexy and died right there on the carpet, he thought it unlikely the pair should have noticed. Elizabeth and Mr. Darcy had eyes only for each other. He smiled to himself as he left the room, satisfied she truly would be happy.

To hell with waiting for Darcy to speak with his friend! Fitzwilliam resolved to ride to Longbourn directly unless the wayward pair appeared within the next ten minutes. He stalked to the sideboard to refill his glass then back to the window to look for any sign of their return. There was none.

He was excessively concerned for his cousin, certain Miss Bennet's death would affect him deeply, and he could not account for every other bugger's apparent indifference to the tragedy. Colonel Forster had seemed flabbergasted that a man of his rank should show any interest in, as he put it, *"the transgressions of a mere parish lieutenant."*

"Transgressions, my arse!" he grunted and sipped his drink.

Indeed, Wickham had seemed no less surprised by his interest in the affair, but if the dullard thought a flogging was all the punishment he would receive, he was due a harsh shock. Nor could he fathom why Bingley had failed to inform his own sister of Elizabeth's passing or why none of the staff had mentioned it…

Slamming his drink on a table, he strode across the room and yanked open the door, looking for a servant.

"Ho, man!" he called to a footman by the front door, marching there as he spoke. "Do you know the Bennets of Longbourn?"

"Yes, sir," the rather startled man replied.

"Have any of them died recently?"

"Er…not to the best of my knowledge, sir."

"Thank God's celestial ballocks for that!"

At which moment, Darcy stepped through the front door. "Fitzwilliam! What on earth are you doing here?"

All possible answers to his question were rendered absurd by the revelation that Miss Bennet was alive and well. "I paid Wickham a little visit," he admitted with a grin.

Darcy pulled an odd face—half frown, half smirk. "And how did that go off?"

"Well, nothing actually *came* off, so I daresay it could have gone worse for him."

Darcy's lips twitched, threatening a laugh, and Fitzwilliam knew all would be well. "She is not dead, is she?"

"No," his cousin replied, his eyes burning with startling vehemence. "She is very much alive—and very much mine."

They were interrupted by a low groan from Bingley, who came trudging over the threshold behind his friend. "You are very welcome, Fitzwilliam, but I hope you will forgive me if I postpone a proper greeting until tomorrow. I have the devil of a headache. I think I shall retire directly. Feel free to use my study, Darcy. I am sure you two have much to discuss."

"There is no need to make yourself scarce in your own home, Bingley," Darcy assured him.

"You give me false credit. I had no such noble intentions. I only wish to be spared your raptures."

Fitzwilliam scoffed. In eight and twenty years, he had never heard Darcy rhapsodise.

"Help yourselves to brandy," Bingley offered. Then, eyeing Fitzwilliam, he added, "If there is any left."

"We shall make do! Snap to it, old boy!" he said as he passed Darcy. "I cannot bear to be kept in suspense any longer!"

Thus the cousins retreated to Bingley's study to enjoy a second evening of drink-fuelled discourse on the subject of Elizabeth Bennet—this one far pleasanter than the last.

Bingley hauled his tired body up the stairs, alarmingly close to vomiting. Darcy and he had passed the journey home explaining to each other how their relative betrothals came about. He had been largely unmoved by his friend's allusions to various disappointments and struggles, for Darcy had Elizabeth and, therefore, no cause to repine.

His own story had been necessarily abridged, for he could hardly own that he had meant to offer for Darcy's future wife.

Darcy's last declaration, *"She is very much mine,"* was simply outside of enough. Ravaged by the thought of Elizabeth in any other man's arms, Bingley had not the fortitude to listen to Darcy rave about it or hear his cousin congratulate him for it. Instead, he gathered his regrets and took himself off to bed.

Thursday, 11 June 1812: Hertfordshire

It had been arranged the previous evening, after a dinner taken up predominantly with Mrs. Bennet's vociferous musings on the perquisites of her daughters' advantageous alliances, that the newly affianced couples would breakfast at Netherfield.

Elizabeth sighed as the carriage juddered into motion. "I thought we might never find the opportunity to speak privately again."

Jane regarded her sister's radiant smile sullenly. They might have spoken last night had she not pretended to be asleep. Wounded that Elizabeth had concealed all hint of her dealings with Mr. Darcy from her and devastated by Bingley's apparent dismay, her envy had left her disinclined to celebrate. "I was not aware you wished to speak to me. You seem to have kept much *unsaid* of late."

Elizabeth's smile died instantly. "Are you angry with me?"

Jane turned to peer out of the window. "I am more hurt than angry." She felt her hands taken up and reluctantly looked back.

"I did not set out to exclude you," Elizabeth began, "but in London you were still so very low, and at the time, I was convinced everything that happened in Kent would soon be forgotten anyway. I saw no advantage to burdening you with any of it. And then..." She looked down at their clasped hands, and her voice became unexpectedly tremulous. "Once I ceased being a fool and acknowledged to myself that I loved Mr. Darcy, I was too embarrassed to mention it, for I was sure he would never return for me. It was easiest to say nothing."

Jane understood better than most how much easier it was to deny heart-ache than suffer everyone's remarks. Hearing it explained thus disposed her to be more understanding. "You must love him very much."

"I do, Jane! So very dearly." Her eyes sparkled as they had always used to whenever she disclosed some great mischief as a child.

Jane felt a flush of shame. This was Elizabeth—ever her dearest friend and closest ally. From whence had such unjust bitterness sprung? "Well then," she said gently, "we have most of our journey remaining. Will you not tell me more about my new brother?"

By the time they arrived at Netherfield, Elizabeth's brief wretchedness had passed, and she once again bubbled over with jubilation. Jane's own equanimity was less assured. Though delighted to have regained her sister's confidence, she was, by the same token, returned mercilessly to her earlier envy as every part of Elizabeth's quixotic tale gave stark contrast to her own less than zealous courtship.

Caroline Bingley awoke in a much-improved humour on Thursday morning. Louisa had said in her letter that Charles was immovably decided for Eliza Bennet, whom Colonel Fitzwilliam assured her was dead. She had sought and received confirmation of that from Peabody, who had shaken his head gravely and agreed that no party could have wished for matters to end as they had. Though she would not rejoice in any person's death, one played the cards one was dealt. Miss Eliza was deceased, Charles was unshackled, and her own future in society was secured.

With a decided spring to her step, she made her way to the breakfast room. To her satisfaction, it was Darcy, discomposingly handsome in all his sartorial splendour, whom she first espied upon entering. He halted in his path from the sideboard to bow. She smiled warmly and expressed her sincere pleasure to see him. That was as long as her satisfaction lasted. Darcy continued on his way, revealing a wider view of the room—in the midst of which sat Miss Eliza Bennet. All visions of dancing at Lady du Grallier's next ball evaporated in the blink of an eye.

"Oh, you are *not* dead."

Several objections went up about the table, though the lady herself looked only amused.

"You see, Miss Bingley? I am not without accomplishments, after all."

Caroline had forgotten, in the months she had been away, how very much she detested this woman. "Forgive me, madam. I was informed yesterday you had passed away." She threw Colonel Fitzwilliam a withering glance, but he only shrugged. "I am vastly relieved to discover that is not the case. I trust you are well?"

"Very well, I thank you." She smiled at Darcy, and he, to Caroline's disgust, returned it. With a burgeoning sense of foreboding, she turned to her brother for explanation—and was startled a second time to see Miss Eliza's sister.

"Miss Bennet! What a surprise! Are you well also?"

The terminally insipid bore replied that she was, her smile revealing no hint of discomfort to be breakfasting with her erstwhile suitor and his new paramour, her sister. Beginning to suspect she was overlooking some salient information, Caroline edged into her seat and turned an enquiring look upon her brother.

"Louisa wrote to me of your decision, Charles." He blanched, deepening her suspicion. "I came as soon as I was able. I naturally assumed matters had been forestalled when I heard of Miss Eliza's passing, but…well, thankfully, I was misinformed about that. May I assume congratulations are in order after all?"

Charles had progressed from looking pale to looking positively unwell. "Yes," he replied then swallowed. "I am engaged to Miss Bennet."

Caroline held her smile fixed in place, her eyes locked with her brother's beseeching ones. "Miss Jane Bennet," she replied, attempting to keep the enquiry from her tone but raising an eyebrow slightly in question.

"Yes," he repeated, this time reaching for Jane's hand and patting it as though to prove a point.

While Caroline could not deny her preference for the meek and tractable Jane Bennet as a sister over the insufferable younger alternative, an alliance with either of them would inevitably mean the sinking of the Bingley name in the eyes of the world. She offered perfunctory congratulations and turned her attention to Darcy in the hope he might yet be able prevent the union. "What think you of Charles's news, Mr. Darcy?"

"I am very happy for him."

He seemed in earnest, which vexed her further still. "Perhaps, when Charles next visits Pemberley, he will bring his new relations with him. His mother, mayhap, or his aunt and uncle from Cheapside."

"They would be very welcome. It would not do, I am sure you agree, for me to begin excluding Bingley's relations from Pemberley."

"Certainly not." She selected a muffin and concentrated on buttering it.

"Oh!" Miss Eliza exclaimed. "I shall no longer be able to travel with my aunt and uncle!"

"You were due to travel?" Darcy enquired.

"Yes, in a few weeks. To Derbyshire, as it happens."

"Think you they would accept an invitation to suspend their travels for a few days to visit with us?"

Caroline's muffin abruptly wedged itself in her craw, and she suffered several exceedingly uncomfortable moments attempting to repress the consequent sputtering cough.

"I think they would be delighted if all our plans allow. I should dearly love to receive them."

Caroline placed her trembling hands in her lap, out of sight. "Miss Eliza, are you planning to travel to Pemberley with my brother and Miss Bennet?"

"No, Miss Bingley," Darcy answered for her, unequivocally extinguishing all Caroline's aspirations to distinction with his next dozen words. "Miss Elizabeth will be travelling to Pemberley with me after we wed."

How utterly marvellous! She glared askance at her brother. This, then, was the reason for his earlier discomfiture. How on earth the tragic buffoon had ended betrothed to the wrong sister she dared not suppose.

"What simply *wonderful* news," she offered as graciously as she was able. Oh, how she reviled the pity overspreading Miss Eliza's countenance—so much so, it quite overshadowed her reason for a moment. "Your catalogue of accomplishments certainly increases, Miss Eliza. Not yet dead *and* betrothed to a man of great fortune. You will be quite the envy of society."

She heard someone, Colonel Fitzwilliam perchance, suck in his breath, but she only continued eating her muffin. What had she to lose now?

"I could not agree more, Miss Bingley," Darcy said. "Being alive and being mine are presently my favourite of all Miss Elizabeth's accomplishments."

Caroline barely managed to suppress a scream but could not prevent her foot's incessant tapping on the floor. "May we presume it was her *fine eyes* that drew you in?"

"No. It was most definitely the certain something in her manner of walking that tempted me. I thank you for bringing it to my attention. Bingley, I see Fitzwilliam's carriage awaits him. Do not trouble yourself. We shall see him off."

After a hasty farewell between Charles and the colonel, the trio left the room. In the supervening silence, Caroline had, of all things, a tray of smoked fish shoved under her nose. She looked up into Peabody's bored countenance.

"Herring, ma'am?"

Her plate cleaved in two when she threw her knife down upon it, though the noise was drowned when the howl of frustration that had been building since she first met Eliza Bennet at last found its release.

Longbourn, Hertfordshire
June 13

To Miss Georgiana Darcy,

I hope this letter finds you well.

Your brother tells me he has received a letter from you with your congratulations. I may say your blessing pleased him very well, and I thank you for myself for your heartfelt acceptance of our betrothal.

Pray, be not angry with him when I tell you he also relayed some other of your sentiments. I should not like to wait until we meet to allay those anxieties, and thus I have determined to write to you that you may know me a little better and see why you have absolutely no cause to be apprehensive.

Forget at once everything your brother has told you. His account of me is grossly inaccurate. He may have said my playing gives him great pleasure, but he neglected to mention that is only because there is such teasing to be made of my clumsy recitals. Much though I enjoy the pianoforte, I practice too little to play well. I have no superior talent for dancing, other than being practiced at compensating for heavy-footed partners—your brother excepted. My style of dress, which he has proclaimed elegant, is in truth my eldest sister Jane's outmoded style from last season, unpicked and remade with a little embellishment. My beauty I shall not decry. I am quite content to remain the most beautiful woman in the world for the short time until you meet me and see for yourself how your brother has exaggerated that fact.

As to any comparison between you and my sisters, allow me to put your mind at rest. I have four. One is lively and obstreperous, one is silly and inconstant, one is serious and exacting and one is impressionable and diffident. I love them all dearly. I myself tend towards obstinacy and impertinence, but the least said of that the better. I am quite sure that, whatever your nature, it will neither shock nor displease me. Your brother has made me so blissfully happy, there is but one thing that could add to my joy, and that is becoming acquainted with his beloved sister.

I will only add, thank you for looking after him these past weeks. We made a fudge of coming to an understanding, and it lightens my heart to know he has not been without comfort. That alone endears you to me more than any of the accomplishments lauded by your brother, aunt, cousin, or friends, which you are too modest to own. We have in common our affection for a wonderful man, and that is enough to convince me we shall be the very closest of sisters and the very best of friends. I wait impatiently—another of my vices—until we meet.

Yours in anticipation,
Miss Elizabeth (Lizzy) Bennet

Sunday, 14 June 1812: Hertfordshire

A FLURRY OF LETTERS HAD BEEN SENT OUT IN THE DAYS FOLLOWING ELIZAbeth and Darcy's engagement, most of them from Mrs. Bennet to every person in the country with whom she could claim a connection, though one or two were from the happy couple themselves. Elizabeth knew not what Darcy had said in his letter to Lady Catherine, but he had finished it long before she finished hers to Mrs. Gardiner, thus she assumed his message was to the purpose. His letter to Lord Matlock took a little longer, but that to his sister must have been more effusive, for four sides of paper were insufficient to contain all her delight when she replied.

Elizabeth's letter to Miss Darcy was the last to be delivered, and whilst everyone else milled about outside the church after the service, she pulled Darcy aside to give it to him. He stood close with his head tilted down, ostensibly that they could speak confidentially, but she wondered whether he were tempted to kiss her. She hoped so.

"This is for your sister. I do not have the address. Pray, would you send it for me?"

"Gladly. She will be delighted."

"'Tis nothing. She is very sweet to be so anxious to please me. I rather think it ought to be the reverse."

"She will not be displeased with you. I have assured her of as much."

"That is precisely what has made her nervous. You have painted me with Aphrodite's looks, the queen's wardrobe, and accomplishments to make even Miss Bingley jealous."

Darcy slipped the letter into his coat and looked at her intently. "You make me nervous for all those reasons. I do not see why I should suffer alone."

She scoffed at the notion, recalling the countless occasions she had been discomfited by his penetrating stare. "I do not make you nervous, Fitzwilliam."

His gaze darkened. "Oh, you do."

She blushed but nonetheless enjoyed the compliment. "Very well. I suppose my good qualities are under your protection now. I give you leave to exaggerate them as much as possible—only not to your poor sister."

Darcy conceded with a small nod and indulgent smile.

"Shall I meet her before the wedding?"

"I should like that very much. I have long desired that you be introduced. Would you like to go to London?"

"Never mind whether she would like it—she *must* go," came a strident interruption.

With an apologetic look at Darcy, Elizabeth turned to her mother, whose conversation with Mrs. Philips had evidently not precluded her eavesdropping on everyone else's.

"And Jane must go too," Mrs. Bennet added, "for you must both have trousseaus and new gowns and—"

"There are plenty of shops nearby where we can purchase what we need," Jane said, disrupted from her own conversation with Bingley by her mother's vociferous decree.

"Not of the quality that—"

"Actually, the reason for my visit was to meet Miss Darcy," Elizabeth interrupted before her mother could embarrass them further.

"If you wish to purchase some new gowns while you are there, it can certainly be arranged," Darcy offered.

"Let us all go!" Bingley blurted.

"Lizzy and Mr. Darcy wish to spend time with his sister," Jane demurred. "Might we not do well to remain here and spend some time with yours?"

"Well, yes…although I do need to find an attorney to draw up the articles for the wedding."

"My Uncle Philips could do that."

"Oh, certainly, he would be honoured!" Mrs. Philips agreed.

"Right, then. We had better stay here," Bingley conceded, a little disappointedly, Elizabeth thought.

"He had better work more quickly than he usually does," Mrs. Bennet said to her sister, "for Mr. Darcy has told Mr. Bennet he wishes to wed before his cousin's ball in July, and if Jane and Mr. Bingley are not ready, he may very well like to be married first."

"I would not steal Bingley's place at the altar, madam," Darcy said with strained forbearance.

"Why not all stand up together?" said Bingley. "After all, we are invited to Lord Ashby's ball as well," he explained, indicating Jane and himself. "It makes sense that we should all be married beforehand. And Darcy and I planned to stand up for each other in any case."

"What think you, Jane?" Elizabeth enquired, delighted by the prospect of sharing such a wondrous occasion with her dearest sister. She worried, for a fleeting moment, that Jane looked a little distressed, but then her mother pounced upon the idea with gusto, informing everyone how it would be; after that, no one else's opinion mattered.

Elizabeth turned to Darcy. "Do you mind?"

"I care not where or how we are married as long as we *are* married—and soon." He looked away briefly, as though searching for something, then reached to pluck a leaf from the rosebush growing near the church wall. He pressed it into her palm and brought her hand to his lips to kiss the backs of her fingers.

"Thank you," she whispered.

"I am so in love with you, Elizabeth. I made a poor job of showing it before. I shall not make the same mistake again."

"No, indeed," she said, lifting her closed fist and her leaf with it to her heart. "You are proving yourself to be quite the romantic."

He chuckled slightly. "I see you intend to exaggerate my good qualities also."

"I thought I would attempt it," she replied, grinning, "since exaggerating your bad ones proved so disastrous."

Tuesday, 16 June 1812: Kent

Charlotte Collins had only just read the letter informing her of Elizabeth's engagement when she looked up to espy Lady Catherine de Bourgh storming down the lane towards the parsonage at a startling rate for one her age, her cane spraying gravel in all directions each time it struck the ground. She leapt to her feet, stumbling over a chair in her haste.

"Mr. Collins! Mr. Collins!"

"What is the matter?" he enquired testily as he came into the room.

"Eliza and Mr. Darcy are engaged! And look!" She pointed to the window.

He looked then let out an inarticulate wail that Charlotte thought might denote the shrivelling of his manhood. Moments later, her ladyship burst into the parlour, wheezing with the effort of her march there and coming to a halt only when nose-to-nose with her parson.

"YOU!"

"Phnar!" Mr. Collins replied, cringing.

"This is *your* fault! Had you married her at the off, this never could have happened!" She slammed her cane on the floor, igniting sparks on the flagstones.

Mr. Collins's face had lost all colour, and Charlotte wondered whether his grimace were a precursor to imminent tears.

"Instead," her ladyship continued, "you left her unbound and untamed to wreak havoc upon my family!" Her voice cracked under the strain of her displeasure, and she coughed.

"Lady Catherine, you are upset," said Charlotte. "Can I fetch you a glass of wine?"

Her ladyship rounded on Charlotte. "You dare speak to me? I have welcomed you, shown you endless condescension, made this house comfortable for you, furnished the closets with the very shelves upon which you lay your clothes! Was I shown any gratitude for my forbearance and charity? I was not! Instead, you invited the same ungoverned, ungrateful girl who refused all this to visit! Then you allowed her to inveigle herself into my good favour and enthral my nephew under my very nose. It shall not be borne!"

"Your ladyship, my friend gave no hint of any designs on Mr. Darcy whilst staying h—"

Lady Catherine swiped at the air between them with her cane—which was rash, considering how little of it there was. "Your friend is a scheming little upstart, but she will learn I am not to be trifled with."

"Pray, Eliza is by no means artful—"

"Indeed she is! She has beguiled my nephew, to whom I have been almost a mother since his own died, into severing all communication with me unless I condone their union! When it is my own daughter who has been jilted!" She spun theatrically to leave, but turned before quitting the parlour to deliver her coup de grace. "I am not so easily gainsaid. If *he* will not hear me, mark my words: *she* will."

She left, the room stilled, and Mr. Collins abruptly fainted. After a few deep breaths to compose herself, Charlotte stepped over her prostrate husband and walked to the door, where she found a petrified maid in the hall.

"Some tea if you would and perhaps a dash of something stronger. And, Harriett, would you arrange for our trunks to be packed? I believe we shall be visiting my family in Hertfordshire for a while."

In Love and War

Wednesday, 17 June 1812: Hertfordshire

84 Gracechurch Street, London
Monday, June 15

My dear Lizzy,

You have amazed us all, but we could not be more delighted for you. You have been very sly, very reserved with me though. How little did you reveal of what passed at Hunsford! I confess I suspected something when you were here, but my imagination did not run beyond a slight partiality. I ought to have known you had made him love you!

Your uncle and I should be delighted to attend your wedding. Do let us know the date as soon as may be, for we will likely depart on our northern tour directly from Longbourn. I have written separately to Mary, inviting her to travel with us, and though I know she will bring her own delights to our party, we shall miss your company sorely. Visiting you at Pemberley, however, will be fine compensation for our disappointment.

Pemberley, Lizzy! Would that I could see your face when first you lay eyes upon your new home. Its grandeur notwithstanding, the grounds are simply delightful, and the estate boasts some of the finest woods in the country. You will be perfectly spoilt.

The children want me, so I must end here. In closing, I shall say that you and Jane must congratulate yourselves. As a result of your achievements, your mother will now die happy.

Yours very sincerely,
M. Gardiner

The smile this letter produced had not faded from Elizabeth's face before her mother burst into the room, wafting another in her direction.

"This is for you, Lizzy. It was in amongst my correspondence. 'Tis from Kent. Look at the seal. My poor eyes cannot make it out properly, but it seems very fancy—too fancy for the Collinses. It must be from Lady Catherine. She has written to congratulate you. Oh, Lizzy, what an honour! Open it up, child. Let us see what she has to say."

A quick glance confirmed her mother's suspicions, driving away Elizabeth's high spirits. Darcy had confided that his letter to Lady Catherine had forbidden any further communication with him unless it was an apology. Whatever this missive contained, be it grudging contrition or something else, it would certainly not be congratulations, and she had no wish to excite her mother's nerves with its contents. "I think it is only from Charlotte, Mama," she lied.

"Oh, that is a shame. Though I daresay her ladyship will write soon. Well? What news from the Collinses?"

"I beg you would excuse me. I have been indoors reading for too long. My head is beginning to ache. I would take some air."

Elizabeth escaped the house directly, pleased to pass Kitty returning from the garden on her way, for it assured her privacy. Tearing the letter open, she stomped onto the lawn, growing more indignant with every step at being written to against Darcy's particular wishes.

Even twelve hours separation was too much for Darcy's liking. Not for one moment since taking his leave of her yesterday had Elizabeth left his thoughts, and he was too impatient to see her this morning to wait for Bingley to finish his meeting with Mr. Philips. Leaving a message with the butler that he had gone ahead, he set out for Longbourn as early as good manners allowed.

Before he even reached the house, he caught sight of Elizabeth walking towards the hermitage at the far end of the garden. His heart leapt—then began to pound with the immediate recognition that something was terribly wrong. He dismounted, threw the reins to the nearest stable boy and hastened across the lawn after her. He found her pacing the full width of the retreat, her countenance stained with high emotion and her eyes flashing fire.

"Elizabeth, what is amiss?"

She whirled to face him, whispering his name in apparent dismay. Her eyes darted to a letter held in her hand.

"Who has written to you?"

In answer, she only sighed and let her shoulders drop. He moved to stand directly before her and reached for the hand that held the letter. His anger flared when he felt the tremble in her fingers. "May I?"

She nodded, relinquishing it to his grip. He had meant to keep hold of her hand, but the moment he espied the letter's seal, all good intentions were forgotten.

Rosings Park, Kent
June 16

To Miss Elizabeth Bennet,

You probably think yourself terribly clever, persuading my nephew to refuse any communication from me. You ought to know that I am not in the habit of submitting to any person's whims, least of all those of presumptuous upstarts such as yourself. I shall make my sentiments known after all, for my nephew did not forbid me from writing to you.

Never have I met a more reckless, unreasonable creature. Your schemes have won you my nephew's hand, but at what cost? Either you do not truly comprehend the consequences of your actions, in which case you are ignorant and obtuse, or you do, in which case you are an unprincipled self-seeker. Neither much recommends you to me.

Consider this if you are able. In acting so wilfully against the inclinations of his family, you disgrace not only Mr. Darcy but all of us. All his relations, everyone associated with him, must be discredited by such a connection. My daughter and I shall be ridiculed as a result of his defection. Miss Darcy's chances of finding a suitable match are ruined, for with such a sister, it is doubtful she will ever marry. Even his relatives long-deceased are not immune from your inflictions. Regardless of his mother's wishes, you have obstinately pursued your goal, and in so doing, sullied her memory.

As to my nephew, he will be universally despised for having such a wife. Everything he has worked for, everything he represents—his noble and ancient heritage, his triumphant achievements at Pemberley, his unblemished reputation in the very highest circles—will all be reduced to nothing when he marries you. If the objectionable situation of your mother's family and your own wild, ungoverned upbringing were not proof enough, your impudent, wilful comportment announces to everybody your unsuitability for polished society. Your alliance will be a disgrace. You are a disgrace. I do not recognise you at all.

Lady C. de Bourgh.

Elizabeth could only imagine Darcy's pain to be thus abused by his own relation and did not blame him for his fury. "Do try not to let it distress you, Fitzwilliam. 'Tis but one person's opinion. It does not matter."

"Of course it matters!" he replied with glacial severity. "I was a fool to think we might elude such censure."

She stilled. "It would not concern me if our marrying excited the censure of the whole world. I thought you had decided it would not concern you, either."

He regarded her incredulously. "You well comprehend my feelings. You *must* understand I will tolerate reproach from no quarter."

His pride was not all gone then. "I see, but I suppose what you and I consider *tolerable* has ever been at odds."

Displeasure gathered like a storm over Darcy's countenance, and she began to feel its force as the tenor of his voice sharpened. "Do you expect me to stand by and permit derision because you are able to tolerate it? I assure you I shall not! It is my responsibility—my *right*—to act however is necessary to protect my family."

Elizabeth's chest emptied of air. "You would forsake me now?"

Darcy stepped backwards as though she had struck him. "*Forsake* you? I would *protect* you!"

"No, sir, you would protect yourself! Nothing has changed. You are still ashamed of me!"

Darcy stared at her in evident, mortified confusion. "Elizabeth," he said very gravely, "never in the whole course of our acquaintance have I been ashamed of you. I beg you would explain what on earth I have said that has made you believe I am."

The necessity of fighting her tears stoked Elizabeth's indignation, and she responded heatedly. "You have just informed me that you consider yourself a fool for believing you could avoid censure for marrying me, declared that I ought to understand your intolerance for it, and impressed upon me the importance of protecting your family from it—from me! Pray tell me what, in all that, would *not* make me believe you are ashamed of me?"

"Nay, you have mistaken me entirely!" he exclaimed, aghast. "My concern is not for myself but for you! I was a fool not to have foreseen Lady Catherine's determination to have her say or shielded you from her insults. I will tolerate no censure of you. My God, you know what I feel for you! How could you ever think I meant to say I was ashamed of you?"

Overcome with relief yet paralysed by the ugliness of their quarrel, Elizabeth struggled to find her voice. "It would not be the first time you have said as much," she whispered. Then, against her every inclination, she burst into tears.

She was in his arms in a heartbeat. "Would that I could erase from your memory every reprehensible word I said to you in Kent." He pressed his lips to her temple, speaking against her skin between softly bestowed kisses. "I beg you would understand. I am no longer that man. You have made me a better one." He pulled away slightly and wiped away her tears with his thumbs. "I am so in love with you. If you think I could forsake you now, you have taken leave of your senses, woman."

"Forgive me. I did not wish to think it of you—only, when you said you would act to protect your family, I—"

"*You* are my family now. I meant *you.*"

With indescribable tenderness, he cradled her face and kissed her without any urgency but in just such a way as left her in no doubt of his devotion. She curled her hands about his forearms and leant into him, covetous of the intimacy after her brief but awful moment of doubt. For one heavenly moment, the kiss deepened before he gently pulled away, straightened to his full height and once again enfolded her in his embrace.

"That was more in keeping with the greeting I had in mind," he said gruffly.

She grinned into his waistcoat. "Shall we resolve all our quarrels in a similar fashion?"

"We should be in very great danger of doing nothing *but* quarrelling in that case." He leant back and regarded her with a decidedly devilish glint in his eye. "I can be very disagreeable, you know."

"Yes, I do know! Fortunately for you, my character is equally objectionable."

"Then I look forward to many a pleasurable reconciliation. Cruellest, fiercest, Elizabeth."

"Are you seeking inspiration amongst the flora, sir, or are you hoping to avoid more talk of wedding frippery?"

Bingley spun around. "Mr. Bennet! I…um…" He ceased stammering as he became aware that his efforts to hear what was being said beyond the hermitage wall had led him to step into the flowerbed. He stepped out again, flapping at the thorns snagging his coat.

"Be not embarrassed, Mr. Bingley; I comprehend. I, too, would rather hide in the hedgerows than hear another word on lace."

Bingley would rather be anywhere than listen to another word on his wedding. Next to offering for the wrong woman, he could not conceive of anything more ill advised than standing at the altar with the right one, watching her exchange vows with somebody else. He had spent the last three days cursing Darcy's mention of stealing people's places at the altar, which prompted him to suggest it.

"But surely your own shrubbery would have been more convenient for the purpose?" Mr. Bennet concluded.

"Pardon me?"

"You could have concealed yourself just as well in Netherfield's bushes," he explained, turning away and walking towards the house.

"I had no wish to hide in my bushes," Bingley answered, trailing after him.

"I suppose I ought to be flattered by your preference for mine, then!" Mr. Bennet ushered him through the hall and into the parlour, announcing, "Mr. Bingley! Freshly plucked from the rose bushes."

Bingley was made welcome with refreshments and conversation, to which he made a concerted effort to attend despite his preoccupation with the events unfolding in the garden. After a short while in discourse with Jane, however, she observed that he seemed somewhat distracted.

"I confess I am. Darcy is here, you see. I overheard him with Lizzy in the garden as I exited the stables. They are arguing." He could not tell from her expression what she thought of this; thus, he added, "They seemed to be at variance over the likelihood of her being scorned by Darcy's circle."

"I am not overly surprised to hear it. Lizzy can be very dismissive of rank. Mr. Darcy will not like it if she does not respect his station or that of his friends."

That was precisely the sort of thing that would offend Darcy, but Bingley had not the opportunity to say as much, for Jane then went off on a bit of a tangent, questioning him about his own circle. He answered as best he could, though his mind returned frequently to the thought that, were he engaged to Elizabeth, an argument would not be the method he would choose to pass any moments of privacy in the garden.

Darcy forced himself to look away from Elizabeth's face and consider what else he must add to his picture. The discovery of Miss Catherine's abandoned drawing apparatus beside the bench had prompted Elizabeth to request that he sketch Pemberley. He was more than happy to oblige in principle, but their present attitude, opposite each other with their feet interwoven on the ground between them, made it impossible to concentrate on the task—that and the desire to kiss her again.

She entertained herself while he drew by proposing myriad reasons they might squabble in future. He was deeply dismayed to have quarrelled with her at all, but she, in her inimitable way, would be diverted, and she teased them both for their folly.

"It has been said that I give my opinion too decidedly for so young a person," she said with a grin. "If only you had taken heed, you would not have ended up shackled to so impertinent a wife."

"I have a very great fondness for the liveliness of your mind," he replied, utterly enthralled and not a little aroused by the mischief flashing in her eyes. "Do I wish to know who said as much?"

His outline of the roof suffered somewhat when she leant towards him and placed a hand on—no, *above*—his knee and squeezed.

"I care for nobody's opinion but yours, so it is of little matter who said it."

Darcy doubted she intended to be so overtly provocative. Unlike him, Elizabeth was insensible to the potency of her charms. God help him the day she learnt to wield them by design. He stoically set about drawing some more columns, and after a last devastating squeeze, she withdrew her hand.

"Speaking of your relations," she said with excessive archness.

It had been Lady Catherine, then! He looked up. She quirked an eyebrow, and the east wing lost its chimney. He cleared his throat and dashed off a few more windows. "What of them?"

"Shall I meet any more of them while I am in Town?"

"I am sure Fitzwilliam will want to see you. I regret I cannot vouch for my uncle. Though he is typically less belligerent, in this instance, he may prove as inimical as his sister."

"Oh, I have great hopes of finding him absolutely insufferable. So far, you only have one awkward relation to my half a dozen. I might feel their impropriety less keenly if you could produce somebody half as embarrassing as Mrs. Philips." She grinned wickedly, and Darcy's charcoal snapped.

"Enough talk of family! I am done." He detached his sketch from the board and passed it to her. "Elizabeth Bennet, I give you Pemberley."

Though he had come to enjoy Elizabeth's singular manner of teasing, he would be the first to admit he had not yet learnt to be openly laughed at, and he knew not quite what to do when she took one wide-eyed look at the drawing and erupted into unreserved peals of laughter. "You are displeased with the house?"

She sucked in a vast breath and said in a slightly more sedate tone, "It is not quite what I was expecting, no."

Her entire countenance was contorted with the effort of suppressing her laughter, and in spite of himself, Darcy felt his own lips begin to twitch. "Am I to be included in your joke, madam?"

"'Tis only that I must be sure to inform Miss Bingley that I have found a fault in you after all."

"I hardly think Miss Bingley would agree that Pemberley is a failing."

"And neither would I, but honestly, Fitzwilliam, who taught you to draw?" She turned the sketch, holding it up so only her eyes were visible above the page—and a perfectly arched, perfectly derisive eyebrow.

He tore his gaze away from her to look at what he had drawn. "Oh."

She began laughing again. "Please tell me our apartments are not in this wing," she begged, pointing to the part of his sketch where he had apparently seen fit to squash some nine or ten exceedingly irregular windows into a space not large enough for six. "I do not think we shall both fit."

He smiled wryly and shook his head, revelling in her teasing once more.

"Though the other wing is little better with the roof pitched as it is. Perhaps we could put the nursery there. The children would have no need to stoop."

He bit the insides of his cheeks, determined not to laugh and thereby allow her a complete triumph, but she was not done.

"However does one see out between all these columns? And is that a ghost on the roof? Is the house haunted? Or is it on fire because this chimney has fallen over?"

"In my defence, you have been distracting me since we sat down."

"You cannot talk and draw at the same time?"

"Elizabeth, I can barely *think* in your presence. You must know this. I have been afflicted thus since first I laid eyes on you."

"I think not. I distinctly recall your being decidedly unimpressed on that occasion."

She spoke in jest, but Darcy was at once all seriousness. "I beg you would forget the things you overheard me say that evening. I was determined to be displeased with everything, and so I was, and I have paid a heavy price for it. You must know you are so much more than tolerable."

She looked wholly unconvinced. He reached for her hands, setting the sketch aside. "I have not the talent to compose you a poem to convince you of your loveliness, but I can tell you that I forget to breath when you smile, that my heart races when I hold you, that I am at my least gentlemanly when this eyebrow arches just so." He ran a thumb along her eyebrow, pressing it upwards at the centre with the slightest pressure. "And I can tell you that kissing you is both the greatest pleasure and the greatest torture I have ever known."

A gentle blush suffused her countenance, but she shied not from his gaze. "I am mindful that I have said much worse of you than you said of me that evening. I am afraid I owe you quite the panegyric now." She broke into a broad smile. "But you shall not rush me. Mr. Collins assures me that superior flattery cannot proceed from the impulse of the moment, and so you must allow me time to arrange a suitable compliment."

God, but this woman made him happy! "By all means, take as long as you need," he told her. "I would wait a lifetime for you."

Netherfield, Hertfordshire
June 17

To Lady Catherine de Bourgh,

In view of your violent objections to your future niece, I have taken steps to relieve you of the indignity of accepting subsistence from her future husband's estate. You may expect to receive articles from my attorney in due course with particulars.

As to my mother, she is dead and her memory, such as it was by the end, buried with her. My memory of her is perfectly intact and wholly unsullied, thus your concern is without foundation.

Fitzwilliam Darcy

Tuesday, 23 June 1812: London

Darcy exchanged one last private smile with Elizabeth and left the shop, surrendering his betrothed and his sister to the safekeeping of his most reliable footman and the redoubtable modiste. His happiness as his carriage set off across London verged on the preposterous.

Both he and Elizabeth were relieved to be away from the cloying and intrusive society in Meryton, and they had enjoyed more private conversation on their journey here yesterday than in the nearly two weeks since they became engaged.

It had been agreed between the ladies that Elizabeth would stay with Georgiana, and he had delivered her there with the greatest of trepidation, for never had he been more anxious for two people to get along. He need not have concerned himself. Though his sister had been shy and Elizabeth reservedly polite at first, by the end of dinner they had seemed to be far more at ease, and when he returned to collect them this morning, both had been in observably fine humour.

The unparalleled pleasure of showing Elizabeth around Darcy House and her delight in it had been greater even that he had hoped. Her admission of impatience for it to be her home pleased him so well that not even the audience to which he now travelled could dampen his spirits.

Upon arriving at Matlock House, he was announced into the drawing room where sat his uncle and Mrs. Sinclair in pointed silence at opposing ends of the room. He gave a single bow to the space between them and wished them both good day.

Matlock grunted. "Good of you to call, Darcy. I began to think you would not bother."

"Pardon me. I have been rather busy of late."

"So I have heard."

Darcy did not doubt it. He had written to his uncle with his news, of course, but with fewer details than Lady Catherine was sure to have provided. He crossed the room and took the nearest seat to his uncle. Mrs. Sinclair materialized in the adjacent one and sat regarding him with an expectant expression so presumptuous it was diverting.

Matlock hauled himself upright in his chair. "Now you are here, you can do me the honour of explaining what the devil has transpired between you and your aunt this time, for her last letter was so full of ravings, I could make neither head nor tail of the matter."

Darcy duly summarised Lady Catherine's letter to Elizabeth.

Matlock sucked in his breath. "That was impolitic."

Darcy answered the gross understatement with a slight inclination of his head.

"For a woman who hardly ever leaves Kent, your sister manages to afford the rest of the world an inordinate amount of bother," Mrs. Sinclair said to Matlock, who ignored her entirely.

"How have you responded?"

"I have withdrawn all pecuniary support."

His uncle looked truly shocked. "I had no idea you were subsidising the estate. What effect will your withdrawal have?"

"My assistance has merely eased her present solvency. She will require a much larger investment to prevent its eventual dissolution."

"Such she had deluded herself into thinking you would provide, of course," Mrs. Sinclair said.

Matlock puffed out his cheeks and rubbed his eyebrow with his forefinger. "She would push the matter, the stubborn harpy. Now this is a fine mess."

"It need not be," Darcy pointed out. "She need only apologise for her threats and accept my choice, and all will be resolved."

"Only!" Matlock scoffed. "You ask much of her, Darcy."

"Aye," agreed Mrs. Sinclair. "You cannot expect her holyship to bless the union that will impoverish her coffers."

"You are mistaken, madam," Matlock said. "Catherine is many things, but she is not mercenary. She is concerned for Anne's future."

"With good cause," Mrs. Sinclair replied, "for who else will have the scrawny little thing?"

"And she is worried about the family's reputation." He turned to Darcy. "She is convinced this marriage will be a great mistake."

"Upon my word," Mrs. Sinclair exclaimed, "Mr. Darcy's reputation would do much better if she was not in such a rage to discredit him to everybody who would listen. I have heard more whisperings about his choice of wife that have originated from her acquaintances than any other source."

"Naming a horse lame does not oblige it to limp," Matlock objected.

"No, but it guarantees no one will bet on it," Mrs. Sinclair replied tartly.

"To what whisperings are you referring?" Darcy enquired.

"Your aunt is industriously circulating the rumour that you have been thoroughly worked on. I heard it directly from Lady Metcalfe and vicariously from several other of her friends. Presumably, it is the only way she feels she can justify the alliance."

Darcy felt no fury towards his aunt. It seemed all his anger was spent. Instead, he felt a very great disappointment. He had once believed her to be a sensible woman whose officiousness could be excused as ill-applied interest, but the discovery and dismantling of his own conceit had exposed hers as equally indefensible. "She may circulate whatever rumours she desires. It will not change my mind."

"It might change your lady's mind," Matlock warned.

Darcy smiled slightly. "Elizabeth would not be intimidated by something as transient as society's indignation."

Mrs. Sinclair banged her cane on the floor triumphantly. "I was always assured of liking her since I am predisposed to like most things in opposition to Lady Catherine, but it seems Miss Bennet is going to make it easy for me."

"Much though I should hate to deny you the pleasure of vexing my aunt, I hope you learn to like Elizabeth for her own merits."

"Have no fear; you shall not deny me that pleasure. I live to vex the vexatious. But I also detest being wrong; thus, I shall have to like Miss Bennet now regardless. For heaven's sake, do not tell her, though, or she will feel no obligation to please me, and at my age, other than gin, deference and flattery are the only palatable forms of sustenance."

"Then I must advise you to keep the gin well stocked," Darcy replied. "For there is every chance you may starve otherwise."

"I am not that fortunate," Matlock grumbled under his breath. For the remainder of the visit, he showed no further interest in Elizabeth and made no request for an introduction.

Before he left, Darcy invited them both to dine with him on Friday when Elizabeth, Georgiana, Fitzwilliam, and the Gardiners were also to join him. Mrs. Sinclair accepted with alacrity. His uncle declined, citing the usual excuse of his sore bones. Darcy knew not, and frankly cared less, whether in truth Matlock disapproved of Elizabeth. She was, with good reason, beloved by all who knew her. Those who disdained the privilege of her acquaintance would be the only ones disadvantaged.

Thursday, 25 June 1812: Hertfordshire

On clear summer nights when the windows were open and the rest of the house was quiet, Jane could sometimes hear the noise from the kitchen as she lay in her bed. This was such a night, and it was a sound that filled her with happiness, for the supper that was being cleared away had been one of the most enjoyable of her life.

Her mother had invited as many of their neighbours as Longbourn could accommodate, and every one of them had congratulated Bingley and her at some stage. Though modesty prevented her from admitting it, Jane delighted in their enthusiasm. Bingley was just what a young man ought to be—sensible, good-humoured, and lively—and she never saw such happy manners, so much ease, with such perfect good breeding. She loved him dearly and was very happy for the chance to show him off without the constant distraction of her more obtrusive sister and her more illustrious lover.

He was also good looking, which added to the giddiness she felt when she recalled their twilight stroll in the garden and their stolen kiss beneath the willow tree. For all its brevity, it had brought colour rushing to her cheeks and hope rushing to her heart. There had been times of late when she distrusted his affections, but no one could have doubted his attachment this evening.

Bingley haphazardly refilled his glass, dropped the decanter back down on his desk and gulped another mouthful of port. His evening had been pleasant enough. Mrs. Bennet had ensured dinner included as many of his favourite dishes as the season allowed, and supper had been almost as grand. Jane's sisters had entertained him all evening with lively music and dancing. Caroline and Louisa had grimaced their way through the whole thing, managing to offend no one.

Another larger gulp. Jane had bestowed upon him more smiles tonight than in the whole two months since his return to Hertfordshire. He wished they had found more time together, for their solitary kiss had been disappointingly brief and all their attempts at conversation curtailed by one or other of their neighbours. Indeed, every person there had seemed covetous of their attention, and Jane determined to please them all.

He tipped the remainder of his drink down his throat, poured another, splashing liquor everywhere, quaffed half of that, and returned to staring at the sheet of paper in his hand. The blue and orange crayon sketch blurred before his eyes. His head fell back, and the room swam out of focus.

"Mr. Bingley? Mr. Bingley, are ya dead?"

His eyes flew open, and they were greeted by the same sight as that upon which they had closed. "Lizzy!"

"Amelia, sir," Elizabeth replied, which was confusing to say the least.

He sat up and shook his head—and immediately regretted it. "What are you doing here?"

"Cleaning."

"Cleaning? What? Oh!" *Blast it, the maid!*

"Beggin' your pardon, Mr. Bingley, sir. I wouldn't 'ave woken you, only I thought you'd taken ill. I think you've been 'ere all night."

"Not at all, Liz—Eliz—Emil—"

"Amelia."

"Quite." He ran a hand through his hair, mortified. "It is very good of you to be concerned."

The maid blushed and bit her lip prettily. "'Tis very good o' you not to be angry with me, sir." She curtsied but then seemed to hesitate, regarding him with eyes that felt too familiar for comfort.

"Thank you," he mumbled then dismissed her before confusion and his pounding head overwhelmed him. The moment the study door closed behind her, his forehead hit the desk. Elizabeth's crayon eyes stared up at him, one blue eyebrow quirked as though waiting for him to explain himself. He could not and, instead, surrendered once more to oblivion.

Friday, 26 June 1812: London

At precisely seven o'clock on Friday evening, Darcy's carriage arrived in Portman Square to collect Elizabeth and Georgiana. It then continued on towards Mr. and Mrs. Gardiner's establishment in Cheapside, whereupon the postilion promptly lost his way, having never once ventured into that part of the city. It was, therefore, somewhat later than anticipated that the party of four was delivered to Darcy House.

As their conveyance drew into the gated driveway, Elizabeth stole a glance at her aunt and uncle. They had yet to meet her intended or see her new London home, and she privately suspected their determined reasonableness on the subject of both to be a mote affected. She turned away to conceal a smile when Mrs. Gardiner's mouth dropped open, and Mr. Gardiner pursed his lips in a silent whistle. She had no intention of becoming proud of her new situation, but there was some satisfaction to be had in astonishing her typically phlegmatic relatives.

Darcy met them himself at the door, expressing his relief to see them safely arrived. She introduced him to the Gardiners, whom he greeted with a humility she comprehended as being recompense for his previous censure. She was only grateful that he should know she had relations for whom there was no need to blush. Divertingly, it could not be said the reverse was true, for Mrs. Gardiner had been in high colour since first setting eyes on Darcy. Not wishing to embarrass either of them, Elizabeth said nothing of it, though she could not help but triumph at having a husband for whom there was every need to blush.

"About time!" exclaimed an elderly lady almost before they set foot through the door of the parlour to which Darcy led them. "I was beginning to despair of having any conversation worth the while. Between Mr. Darcy's incessant brooding over your tardiness and Thirson's incessant teasing over Mr. Darcy's broodiness, my evening thus far has been distinctly underwhelming."

Darcy's countenance darkened, and Georgiana was visibly shocked, but a close connection with Mrs. Bennet inured one to brash behaviour, making Elizabeth and the Gardiners far more disposed to be diverted. All three of them laughed.

"May I introduce my grandmother, Mrs. Tabitha Sinclair," said Colonel Fitzwilliam, seeming equally amused. "If I may, Darcy? Grandmother, this is Miss Elizabeth Bennet."

"Pray, call me Lizzy," Elizabeth offered.

"Call me anything you choose, dear, as long as you are sitting on my right," Mrs. Sinclair replied. "I am deaf as a post in that ear."

Mr. Gardiner chuckled, Darcy interceded to perform the remaining introductions, and Elizabeth drew a smile from Mrs. Sinclair by choosing the seat on her left. That put her on the colonel's right, and she fixed him with a suspicious grin. "Thirson?"

"It is an abbreviation of Third Son," Mrs. Sinclair answered for him. "His eldest brother was christened 'Albert', nicknamed 'Alby' within the year, and styled 'Ashby' before his second birthday when his father was awarded the viscountcy. I resorted to numbering the rest of them."

"You are the third son of three?" Elizabeth asked him.

He confirmed he was and took some time sketching his eldest brother's character and that of his *ghastly* future sister, the soon-to-be Lady Ashby.

"And your second brother?"

"Was lost at sea."

"Oh, I beg your pardon!" she exclaimed, mortified to have brought up such a painful subject, even though he was splaying his hands and smiling with the evident intent of reassuring her.

"He was fairly lost when he was on land. He never stood a chance on a boat," said Mrs. Sinclair. "I always said he should have gone into the Church."

Thus, the tone for the evening was set, and a vastly enjoyable evening it transpired to be. Darcy was as unreserved as she had ever seen him in company. Despite having come to understand him better, to see him thus amazed her still. It may have been the glass of sherry in which she indulged after dinner, but she rather thought the warm feeling that suffused her as she watched him speaking with her uncle later that evening was her falling further in love with him. He happened to look at her as she thought it, and the intensity of her affection made her suddenly breathless. She held his gaze and mouthed, *I love you.* His countenance barely moved, but she perfectly comprehended the sentiment behind the small, private smile he sent her.

"Lizzy was wonderful," Georgiana said to Mrs. Gardiner beside her. "I should have been terrified to be asked so many questions by so many strangers."

"Miss Darcy is telling me about your trip to the theatre on Wednesday, Lizzy," her aunt explained. "You were well received, I hear?"

"Well enough. Nobody was uncivil at least. No doubt, I disappointed them all by not being dressed in rags. Oh, but there was one gentleman there whose acquaintance I was particularly happy to make—Darcy's friend, Mr. Montgomery. He is very amiable."

"And exceptionally useful, so I understand from Darcy?" Fitzwilliam said.

"Aye!" she agreed, briefly explaining for everyone else Mr. Montgomery's part in uniting her with Darcy.

"It is so sad that he should be a widower at such a young age, though," said Georgiana.

"Is he?" Fitzwilliam cried.

"He is," Darcy confirmed. "His wife died the year after they arrived in India. The man is in an unenviable state of limbo. He has returned to England in possession of a young son with no mother and a considerable fortune with no estate."

"No estate?" Mrs. Sinclair enquired. "I understood the Montgomerys owned Stortley Castle?"

"His father gambled away every brick," said Fitzwilliam. "And then died."

"Not quite as useful as his son, then?"

Fitzwilliam snorted. "Perhaps if Montgomery is in possession of both fortune and heir but wants for land and a wife, *he* could marry Anne and save me the bother."

"His uses multiply!" Mrs. Sinclair exclaimed.

"What is this?" Darcy enquired.

"Lady Catherine has set her sights on Thirson now that her preferred suitor has made himself unavailable."

Other than pressing his lips together very slightly, Elizabeth thought Darcy did an admirable job of concealing his amusement.

"Matlock would never consent to it," he said.

"I do not know," his cousin replied. "My aunt likes to have her way very well."

"True, but Montgomery has had misfortune enough. Pray find another dupe to saddle with such a mother."

The subject was pursued no further, and the evening then took a musical turn with performances at the pianoforte by Mrs. Gardiner, Georgiana, and Elizabeth. After that, Fitzwilliam and Mr. Gardiner proved a hilarious pairing as they read scenes from *Tristram Shandy*. Eventually, Mrs. Gardiner begged her husband to take her home before she fell asleep on the sofa, and the exceedingly agreeable evening drew to an end.

Whilst everyone else donned their hats and coats and expressed their anticipation to be reunited at Longbourn for the wedding, Darcy pulled Elizabeth to one side for a private goodbye.

"Before you go, I have something for you."

He produced a small box, lifted the lid and held the contents towards her. Elizabeth's chest squeezed with emotion. Within lay a silver and diamond leaf-shaped brooch.

"I preferred you to have one I could be sure would not wither and die." He lifted her chin with a finger. "For I shall never cease loving you, Elizabeth."

"Oh, Fitzwilliam, it is exquisite! Thank you."

"Thank *you*. Darcy House has never felt more my home than with you here with me. The day I do not have to watch you leave cannot come soon enough."

The look he gave her branded itself upon her mind and stayed with her the entire journey back to Portman Square and farther—to her bed and, ultimately, her dreams.

Wednesday, 8 July 1812: Hertfordshire

It seemed every man and his dog had decided to call at Longbourn that afternoon and had subsequently been trapped there on account of the imminent thunderstorm threatening to drench anyone who ventured to leave. Mr. Bennet would not have been the least bit troubled if they all got wet, but his wife was adamant they should stay, browbeating them all with reminders of Jane's fever the previous autumn. Still, not one to miss an opportunity for sport, he observed the simmering discontent in his parlour with some amusement.

Mr. Collins stood as far away from Elizabeth and Darcy as the walls would allow, regaling anyone who would listen with the pitiful tale of his patroness's wrath, having been chased by it all the way here from Kent. Miss Darcy sat with her hands in her lap and her shoulders folded in, as though trying to make herself small enough to be invisible. Lydia and Mr. Hurst wore divertingly similar expressions of ennui. Miss Bingley and Mrs. Hurst looked as they always did—pained. Mrs. Bennet seemed to be attempting to manoeuvre Kitty into Colonel Fitzwilliam's field of view—or possibly his lap—it was difficult to discern from where he was sitting. Jane was glancing suspiciously at Bingley, Bingley was stealing furtive glances at Elizabeth, and Elizabeth was directing frequent apologetic grimaces at Darcy. Darcy stood glowering from the window, possibly attempting to scare away the encroaching clouds that they might all be allowed to escape their hellish captivity. Mary very kindly set the entire scene to music as she banged out a discordant lament from the adjoining room.

"Are all your parties this successful?" Mrs. Sinclair enquired from the seat next to Mr. Bennet.

"Sadly, no. I might be tempted to entertain more often if they were."

"Be sure to give me warning next time. I shall endeavour to have a previous engagement."

Bingley ran a hand around the back of his neck, cursing the insufferable midsummer heat. He would be perfectly glad of a ride in the rain if only he was allowed. Indeed, he fancied he was not alone, for there was nary a person in the room who did not look overheated and irritable—except Elizabeth. She sat calm, composed, and lovely in the midst of the hurly-burly: the very eye of the storm. Mrs. Bennet's flapping and fretting was not relieving the general malaise in the slightest, and Jane's strenuous efforts to mitigate her mother's improprieties were having little to no effect. At last, a sudden and stupendous clap of thunder, which rattled the windows and made Mrs. Bennet wail, heralded the arrival of the storm.

"Oh! My book!" Elizabeth cried. She rose hastily from the sofa, declaring her intention to retrieve it from the garden before the heavens opened.

"Sit down, Lizzy," her mother said impatiently. "We have plenty of books within doors if you wish to read. There is no need for you to be running about in the rain. Send Sarah to fetch it if you must."

Elizabeth only laughed. "Mama, it would take me longer to explain where I left it than it would to fetch it myself. I will be but a moment." With a quick smile to Darcy that sent shards of envy slicing through Bingley's gut, she left the room.

The parlour returned to its previous state of tedium. Jane drifted to sit with Caroline and Louisa, Darcy glared at Fitzwilliam as he flirted with Miss Catherine, and Hurst looked to have fallen asleep. With a loud sigh, Bingley crossed his legs at the ankle and stared at his feet, listening as the patter of raindrops began pinging off the windows. The pall was fractured when Darcy, quite without warning, reared up to the window and braced the frame with both hands, his nose almost pressed to the pane. In a blink, he had slammed his palm violently against the jamb, pivoted on his heel and flown wordlessly from the room, leaving it in brittle, stunned silence.

Bingley leapt to the window, as did Fitzwilliam. The scene unfolding in the garden was all too familiar: Elizabeth being manhandled, yet too far away for him to save.

"Come!" Fitzwilliam ordered, charging from the room.

Nauseated by the remembrance of Elizabeth lying broken on the ground, Bingley turned and ran after him.

The air outside was scarcely cooler than within; nonetheless, Elizabeth was relieved to have escaped the crowded parlour. She tipped her head back and breathed deeply of air redolent with the promise of rain before crossing the lawn to the hermitage. She pitied poor Darcy his continued captivity. After their blissful week in London, the confines of Hertfordshire society were testing his patience, and today's unfortunate entrapment with half the neighbourhood was evidently vexing him greatly. It was for his sake as much as the imminent rain that she did not dally longer.

She had just recovered her book from beneath the stone bench when a familiar voice wished her good day, bringing her spinning around in surprise.

"Mr. Greyson!"

"Forgive me for startling you," he said, bowing. "I am just arrived and saw you enter here from the stables. I could not pass up the opportunity of speaking to you privately." He took several steps towards her. "I have missed you."

Elizabeth started. He had left on business above a month ago, and so much had transpired in the meantime that she had quite forgotten him—and his unwelcome attentions. Another rumble of thunder rolled over the garden, smothering her sigh and providing her with an excellent reason to hear none of what he wished to say. She set out for the stone archway, taking a wide path around him.

"I fear this rain is almost upon us. Let us return indoors and speak there."

"No, wait! I would speak to you alone about a matter of some delicacy."

Her stomach sank. He meant to propose! "Mr. Greyson, please, there is nothing to be said between us that requires privacy."

His brow contracted, and his air became more cautious. "You are angry with me for being gone so long."

"No, not at all—"

"Forgive me. It took longer than anticipated to set my affairs in order. I ought to have written, but I dared not risk your reputation."

A few spots of rain hit her face. "I must insist we go in." She turned and walked determinedly away.

"Why will you not hear me?"

"I would get out of the rain!" she called over her shoulder.

"Then I shall speak hastily!" he insisted. "I love you!"

She stopped just short of the archway and turned back to him, determined to reject him civilly. Let it not be said she had learnt nothing.

"Sir, I beg you would not speak at all in that case."

"What?"

"I am excessively flattered, but I must inform you I am promised to another."

"What?" he repeated more heatedly. "To whom?"

"Mr. Darcy."

"*Mr. Darcy*? I understood him to be gone from the neighbourhood." He recoiled. "Oh, I see how it is! You have used me grievously ill, madam."

Elizabeth shivered as more rain fell on her bare arms. "I have not used you in any way at all!"

"It is clear to me now. It was his hand you coveted from the beginning. But he was not here, was he? You settled for accepting my attentions until he returned!"

"I did not accept your attentions! I afforded you the same civility I do all my acquaintances." *Must all men be so insufferably conceited?*

"We walked in this very garden the day I left, discussing my plans to ready my affairs to take a wife!"

"We discussed nothing but your intention to leave for a while on business. Any other intentions on your part were not apparent!"

He stepped towards her, his expression fierce. "I do not think you comprehend the trouble I have gone to in order to make this possible. It is no small undertaking to wed a woman with no fortune. I have spent weeks rearranging my interests to ensure I can afford the injury to my estate." He sneered unpleasantly. "And do not be fooled into thinking my family welcome this alliance. I have worked hard to convince them of your worth, and you would have it be all for naught!"

Elizabeth let out a great huff of consternation. "I am well aware of what other families think of their stock marrying me! I wonder that everybody is still in such a rage to do it!"

"You would taunt me at such a moment?"

"No, sir! I am sorry you have been inconvenienced, truly, but I cannot marry you, and I gave you no indication that was my wish."

"Your mother certainly did!"

Elizabeth threw her hands in the air, almost losing her book to the shrubbery. "Then I must insist you take issue with her. There is nothing more for me to say on the matter!" She pirouetted away from him and stormed onto the lawn. Lightning flashed overhead and rain pricked her face, plastering her hair to her cheeks.

"You cannot seriously mean to refuse me?" he called, striding after her.

"Yes, I can!"

"Miss Bennet! Miss *Bennet*! *Elizabeth!*"

She found herself suddenly spun around as he seized her arm, sending her book tumbling to the wet ground. His face was close to hers, and he looked to be pleading with her, but she could not hear his words. She was too overcome with a memory she had until that moment been blissfully unaware she possessed—that of Mr. Wickham similarly restraining her, his fist raised to strike. Pain shot through her temple in remembrance of his blow, and she cowered, covered her face with her free arm and screamed.

Then Darcy was there. He appeared from nowhere, propelling Mr. Greyson away with monstrous force and pinning Elizabeth to his side. She buried her face in his coat and felt his guttural command reverberating through her more ferociously than the overhead thunder.

"Unhand my wife!"

Mr. Greyson made a noise, but Darcy cut him off, his voice cold and hard. "Leave now. Never come back. Do not test my resolve not to kill you."

Elizabeth felt him shift and peered around him to see Colonel Fitzwilliam had arrived and was forcefully leading her ashen assailant away. She saw nothing more, for she was then enveloped in Darcy's embrace so completely that not even the rain could penetrate his hold.

"My God, Elizabeth! Are you hurt?"

She felt more than a little foolish for screaming. "No. Only a little shaken. And very damp."

Reverently, he turned her towards the house, keeping his arm wrapped tightly around her. When he paused to retrieve her book, wiping it clean on his pristine trousers before handing it back to her without comment but with a tender kiss to her temple, she thought her heart might burst.

Explaining the matter to her father and changing into dry clothes took Elizabeth more or less the same time as it did for the storm to pass. Her return downstairs, therefore, coincided with the departure of most of Longbourn's callers. Only Darcy, Bingley, and Colonel Fitzwilliam stayed, all eager to join Elizabeth and her sisters on a walk after having been trapped within doors all afternoon.

Elizabeth and Darcy soon outstripped the others, though they walked in silence, her every attempt at conversation falling flat. He was not uncivil. Indeed, he was overly solicitous, enquiring frequently whether her head ached and needlessly helping her over every twig and pebble in their path, yet his distraction was obvious.

"Truly, Fitzwilliam, you must not worry. I was not hurt in the slightest." He nodded once but said not a word. She frowned in consternation. "And you must think no more on Mr. Greyson. I see you are distressed, but you ought to know I should have refused him even were I not promised to you."

"I assure you, I am not thinking of Mr. Greyson."

She puffed out her cheeks. Darcy saw it and, in an impatient tone, added, "It is your well-being that concerns me, Elizabeth, not my own." He clamped his mouth closed and stared directly ahead, his jaw clenched and his countenance severe.

Elizabeth smirked. If one was going to be an awful object, one may as well be an awfully handsome one. She ceased walking, put her hands on her hips and attempted in vain to conceal the grin on her lips. "If you do not divulge what is the matter, I shall be forced to conclude 'tis I who have vexed you."

He turned to face her, his eyes widened, his nostrils flared, and he winced as though pained. "It *is* you, woman!" The look he gave her belied his claim, however. "You would push me?" he enquired softly. "Very well. Though it would be more accurate to say *torture*, than vex."

Her heart began to pound as he took up her hands and tenderly but surely removed her gloves.

"All day I have watched these hands toying with your hair, pouring tea, playing the pianoforte." One after the other, he lifted them to his lips and kissed them. "All day I have watched those eyes sparkle and laugh at the world." His gaze fell to her mouth. "All day, I have watched these lips talk, smile, hum." He slid a hand around the back of her neck. "To see another man's hands upon you was insufferable." He leant closer until their mouths were a mere hair's breadth apart. "I would make you mine. The wait is torture."

His kiss was barely gentle, his struggle for restraint unmistakable. Elizabeth's heart was thundering too loudly to be discouraged by so trifling a thing as temperance, however. They were to be married within the week, and given the day's objectionable events, she was sure a little less restraint would be entirely forgiveable. She lifted onto her toes to press herself against him and held his face with both hands, encouraging him to kiss her more deeply.

With an inarticulate groan, he thrust both arms around her and pulled her closer than ever before. His hands ran a path up and down her back, settling finally upon her hips. His mouth left hers and rained kisses along her jaw, down to her collarbone and farther, to the swell of her breasts at her neckline, making her gasp. Driven by a passion altogether unknown to her, she drew her hands down over his chest and without overmuch consideration, unbuttoned his waistcoat. He seemed not to notice until she slid her hands around his broad back and gripped his shirt in her fists, tugging him roughly against her.

He brought his mouth back to hers with a kiss that felt as hard and unyielding as had his previous restraint; yet, just as she thought she might abandon herself to his passion, he withdrew it. With a groan that clearly evinced his reluctance, he ceased his ardent kiss. Cradling her face, he peppered her lips with light chaste touches until, finally, he dropped his hands to her shoulders and pushed her gently away.

"Marry me," he said gruffly.

She laughed breathlessly, noting that his hat, at some point, had been lost. "I shall have to now. That was rather a damning embrace."

He smiled faintly but shook his head. "Now. Marry me now. I cannot survive until Tuesday."

She smiled broadly and began buttoning his waistcoat. "If it is any consolation, you have at least succeeded in making my anticipation as great as your own."

"Good *God*, would you desist your torture, woman!" Before she could reply, however, he kissed her again—one last, passionate kiss that devastated her equanimity and proved beyond a doubt he was not without the talent for torture himself.

"The ladies are in the drawing room, sir," Peabody informed Bingley when he, Darcy, and Fitzwilliam arrived home later that evening.

"Then be a fellow and bring us some supper to the library, would you?" he replied. It was late, his day had been atrocious, and he was in no humour to make small talk with his sisters.

His failure to save Elizabeth weighed heavily upon him. He had wanted to desperately, but the rug in the hall had hindered his flight from the house, and by the time he recovered his footing, Fitzwilliam had escorted Greyson off the premises, and Darcy had led Elizabeth back inside. He had been too late to help her. Again.

"Is there any brandy in the library?" Fitzwilliam enquired.

"You drank me dry the last time you were h—" He gave a muffled grunt as he bumped headlong into Elizabeth, who was coming out of the library. She stumbled backwards, landing heavily on the floor.

"Good Lord!" he exclaimed, partly in apology, partly in chagrin as he belatedly recognised her as the maid with Elizabeth's eyes.

"Beggin' your pardon, Mr. Bingley, sir. I was lightin' the candles."

"No, no," he replied, leaning down to assist her to her feet. "That is neither here nor there. Are you hurt?"

"Strike me!" Fitzwilliam exclaimed. "I thought for a moment you had smuggled Elizabeth back here with you, Darcy."

Amelia took the opportunity to give a quick curtsy and dart away into the shadows.

"She looks nothing like Elizabeth," Darcy remarked airily, walking past Bingley into the library.

"Not a mirror image, I grant you," Fitzwilliam replied, following him in. "But an uncommon likeness, you must admit. Wherever did she come from, Bingley?"

He shrugged. "I have nothing to do with hiring the housemaids."

That settled the matter, but Bingley was too uneasy to attend to the conversation thereafter. Such was his discomfiture that, after only a few minutes, he invented a spurious pretext and made his excuses. His surprise could not have been greater when he opened his study door to discover Amelia now lighting the candles in there.

She jumped. "Oh no! I'm sorry, sir! Mrs. Arbuthnot told me to light candles in all the rooms."

The flickering light of the taper she held cast a shadow beneath her cheeks, making her appear more like Elizabeth than ever. Bingley stepped farther into the room. "There is no need to apologise. Pray, tell me I did not hurt you when I knocked you over."

She lost some of her servility and smiled as she assured him he had not. Bingley nodded his relief and stepped closer, and when his approach did not seem to perturb her, closer still. "I am glad to hear it."

"It were very kind o' you come to my rescue."

He triumphed to have succeeded, at last, in rescuing *someone*. "It was nothing," he assured her. "Anybody would have done the same."

"No," she replied softly. "There's many a master'd be less gen'rous to 'ave caught a maid at 'er work. You're very kind." She smiled coquettishly. "Quite my 'ero, in fact."

A short while later, Bingley stared at the canopy above his bed, reflecting upon his brief and ill-advised kiss. Shame had rapidly obtruded upon his ardour, prompting an abrupt end to their clinch. That shame persisted. Alone in his bedchamber with only his thoughts for company, however, it was so very tempting to imagine it had been Elizabeth he had taken in his arms and Elizabeth's willing lips to which he had pressed his own.

8

Wilful Misunderstandings

Monday, 13 July 1812: Hertfordshire

Darcy set his book aside, for he had not the concentration to read. He closed his eyes but could not sleep. He used to be a far more sensible man, but impatience for his wedding on the morrow had rendered him distracted and restless.

He rather thought he had good cause to be in a hurry. Theirs had not been an easy courtship. From their devastating quarrel in Kent to Greyson's unpardonable transgression, they had suffered more than their share of misfortunes. He was done waiting to be Elizabeth's husband—to protect her, to love her. By God, he was impatient to love her. After his brief glimpse of her nascent passion last Wednesday, he downright ached for her. An absurd number of vexatious social obligations meant they had been rarely together since then—and not for one moment alone. Tomorrow could not come soon enough.

This day was apparently not quite done, however. His door abruptly banged twice, flew open, bounced on its hinges, and swung back to hit his visitor in the face.

"Blast and bugger it!" came Bingley's muffled voice from the passage beyond.

With a wry smile, Darcy crossed the room to hold the door open.

"Thought I would take you up on that offer of a drink," Bingley mumbled, rubbing his forehead.

"You might have waited for me in that case," he replied after watching his friend sway across the room and slump onto the foot of the bed.

"Eh? Oh, yes. I might have had one or two already."

Darcy pulled the bell for his man. "Have you forgotten you are to be wed at nine in the morning?"

"Not quite. Another couple of measures ought to do it, though."

Wetherby arrived, and Darcy gave a quiet instruction for him to bring some coffee then turned back to his friend. "Is this merely nerves, Bingley, or is there something you wish to tell me?"

"What? No! I meant not to give the impression that I—I meant not to say anything at all. Blast! I cannot speak of this with you!"

That stung, though Darcy knew it was deserved. "My previous interference in your relationship was indefensible, I know. But if you have need of me now, I beg you would not be discouraged from asking."

"No, you mistake my meaning." Bingley gave him a rather pained look. "Dash it, Darcy, what if…what if a person does not feel what they ought to when they marry?"

"You doubt Jane's affections still?"

"No, I doubt my own."

"Your own?"

Bingley appeared to immediately regret admitting as much and began shaking his head violently in denial, but Wetherby's arrival with the coffee interrupted his frantic attempts to explain himself.

"Do not be concerned that I shall judge you," Darcy assured him when his man had gone. "I comprehend why you might expect me to, but I have been taught better. Speak frankly, my friend."

Bingley's shoulders slumped, and he ran a hand dejectedly through his hair. "I meant only that…well, so much has transpired. Jane is not the same as she was, and I certainly am not."

Darcy filled a cup and settled himself in the armchair by the fire. "I think it is safe to say none of us are. People change, Bingley. As a wise woman once said, 'There is something different to be seen in them forever.' Naturally, your affections will change accordingly, but it does not follow that the change must make them insufficient." His friend looked pensive, an expression Darcy saw on him but rarely, and it struck a chord. "I believe I comprehend your problem."

Bingley flinched. "You do?"

"You have been given entirely too much time to think. Had I not interfered, you would have wed Jane after three weeks and been happily married for above eight months by now. I daresay this will all seem a good deal better after tomorrow."

This and the coffee lightened Bingley's mood sufficiently that, by the time he retired to his own room, Darcy was assured he would neither arrive at the church still addled nor forgo attending at all. He smiled to himself as he climbed into his own bed, thinking his friend would probably enjoy a far better night's sleep than he. The morrow was still too many hours away, and coffee had robbed him of all hope of sleep just as anticipation had robbed him of his last vestiges of patience.

Tuesday, 14 July 1812: Hertfordshire

"And after they leave London, they will go to Derbyshire. I suggested they go to Brighton for the summer, but they preferred not to, though I suspect he would have gone willingly had Lizzy wished it, for I begin to think there is nothing he would not do for her. Just look at the way he gazes at her."

Jane did as she was bid, as did everyone else to whom her mother had been extolling the Darcys' virtues for the last ten minutes. Mr. Darcy was, indeed, watching his new bride intently as she spoke to their little group. It was very romantic.

"It is obvious how greatly he admires her, for he does not object at all to her running on at everybody in that way," Mrs. Bennet continued. "Ah, what a fine thing to see my girls so well loved."

The others all agreed. Jane smiled and said not a word, feeling distinctly less well loved than her sister at that moment. Whereas Elizabeth's husband pinned her possessively to his side and hung on her every word, her own tarried on the other side of the room, speaking to anyone and everyone but her. She endeavoured to think nothing of it. Bingley was naturally sociable, certainly not the sort to remain in one spot at a gathering. And there had been nothing else in his behaviour today that could be construed as cause for doubt. He had greeted her at the church in excellent humour, enthusiastically praised her appearance, kissed her affectionately after the ceremony, and proudly paraded her through the village to Longbourn as his wife. He was, in any case, a vastly different creature to his friend, and Jane supposed she ought not expect him to behave similarly.

It was not long before she began to feel altogether less sanguine. The small group of people to whom Elizabeth had been speaking had swollen to include most of the guests. Hers had diminished to just one, Mr. Collins, whose determination to be heard had overcome all her best attempts to escape his company. Perhaps this was what Louisa and Caroline had been speaking of when they advised her that ladies who were too meek did not do well in society. If she could but harness a whit of her sister's assurance, she might become a woman worthy of the world's notice—and perchance her husband's also.

She looked for Bingley, her one consolation being that he was not part of the group surrounding her sister. He was by the window, nodding at whatever Mr. Philips was saying and staring so brazenly at Elizabeth, it was a wonder the whole room had not noticed. She turned back to Mr. Collins and pretended to listen, a headache burgeoning between her temples.

At length, Mr. Darcy announced he and Elizabeth would depart, which prompted something of an exodus as the Gardiners, Collinses, Lucases and all Mr. Darcy's relations called for their carriages as well. Jane watched unhappily as everyone filed out of the parlour. Of course, they would all go now. Why would anybody wish to stay once Elizabeth left?

Longbourn's drive was soon overtaken with milling guests. Elizabeth and Mr. Darcy bade them all goodbye, coming to Jane and Bingley last.

"Thank goodness we need not say our goodbyes yet. I believe I shall survive the three days until I see you at Lord Ashby's ball," Elizabeth said, taking Jane's hands. "Something tells me our farewell in London will not be so easy."

"I do not think you will ever be forgiven for stealing Lizzy away, Darcy," Bingley interrupted.

Jane would forgive her new brother a great deal if he would only hasten and do precisely that.

"You are welcome to visit Pemberley as often as you please," Mr. Darcy said, looking at her.

"Then I daresay you will be seeing much of us," Bingley answered in her stead.

The effort of keeping her smile fixed in place began to tax Jane such that it was a relief when the leave-taking was done and Darcy handed Elizabeth into their carriage.

"Are you well?" enquired Mrs. Gardiner, stepping to her side to wave them off. "You look a little piqued."

"It is difficult to see Lizzy go, is it not?" Mary said, appearing beside her aunt. "If it were not that I shall see her at Pemberley in a few weeks, I should be miserable too. I know you will miss her terribly."

Jane's uncharitable thoughts to the contrary were interrupted when Mrs. Sinclair bustled past to her carriage.

"Fear not, Mrs. Bingley, your husband has employed your sister's twin as a maid, so you will have her to remind you in Lizzy's absence."

Tuesday, 14 July 1812: London

Baker, the young girl appointed as Elizabeth's lady's maid, moved about in the dressing room, emptying the bath. Elizabeth came to perch on the dressing table stool in her bedroom, rubbing her hair dry with a towel, not quite believing she was here at last. Her wedding day had been perfect but with a good deal too many people to speak to before she and Darcy were able to leave and a good deal too many miles to travel before they were able to arrive here, everyone and everything seemingly indifferent to her impatience to begin her life as Mrs. Darcy.

In recent weeks, she had derived the distinct impression she was expected to be nervous for her wedding night, but she was not. She could never be nervous of a man who took such prodigious care of her, who looked at her as though she were a work of art, who held her as though she were made of glass, and who responded to her as though she were a seductress. On the contrary, she had great hopes of his recreating the same wonderful sensations he had on their walk the previous week.

"Should you like me to brush your hair, Mrs. Darcy?" enquired the maid, coming into the room.

Elizabeth declined and waited only long enough for Baker to lay out a nightgown on the bed before dismissing her for the evening. She reached for her brush but froze when she caught sight of the most enormous house spider on which she had ever laid eyes, not a yard from her bare feet. She did next what any well-bred young lady of good sense would upon discovering such a beast in her presence: she screamed and clambered up on the stool. The spider scurried for the nearest cover, which happened to be said stool. She jumped off it, screaming again and laughing all at once. The stool clattered back against the dresser and fell to the floor. She stumbled over her bathrobe and lunged towards the bed, laughing at her own ineptitude as she leapt onto the mattress and clutched at a post to steady herself.

The door from the sitting room adjoining the master and mistress's bedchambers flew open and banged against the wall with enough force to rattle the pictures and make every candle gutter.

"Elizabeth! What is the matter?"

Darcy wore only a bathrobe tied loosely at the waist, which accentuated the broadness of his shoulders most agreeably. His hair was dripping wet. Rivulets of bath water ran down his face and dropped onto his exposed chest, as though Neptune himself had risen from the sea to defend his bride. Under any other circumstances, the sight might have weakened Elizabeth's knees. As it was, she was somewhat distracted by the gargantuan creature darting towards his feet.

She pointed at it. "Spider!" It was all she could manage. His incredulity rendered her incoherent with hilarity thereafter.

"For God's sake, woman, I feared something serious had befallen you! Again!" He looked in the direction she pointed with obvious disdain, though upon espying the long-legged colossus, ceded some ground, his eyebrows raised in surprise.

Elizabeth's sides hurt. "'Tis a monster! Kill it!"

"With what?" he cried, now laughing also.

"Stamp on it!"

"Not likely! I have bare feet!"

Elizabeth scrambled across the bed, grabbed an empty candlestick from her nightstand and threw it at the spider. It hit Darcy soundly on the leg, and she was reduced to making such gasping, snorting noises as only a person in the grip of hysterical laughter can make, somewhat ruining the credibility of her sputtered apology. Her mirth turned to a surprised shriek as Darcy abruptly launched himself over the monstrous beast and onto the bed, wrapping his arms around her as he landed, bringing them both crashing onto the mattress.

His laughter stilled first, though once Elizabeth observed his expression, hers ebbed also. Flickering candlelight threw every angle of his face into striking contrast with magnificent effect. It made her slightly breathless. "*Bonsoir*," she whispered.

His mouth twitched. "*Bonsoir, mon amour*." He brought his hand to caress her face, running his fingertips in a feather-light touch over her lips, her eyebrows, her cheeks. Then he gently pushed her hair behind her ear.

"I have not brushed it," she said softly, wrinkling her nose in chagrin. "I expect I look wild."

He nodded and held her gaze as his fingers blazed a trail down her neck to the edge of her robe. Nudging it open, he leant over her and kissed the bare skin of her shoulder. His touch, his warmth, his weight pressing her into the bed, ignited a now-familiar ache for which she had no name but for which she had long since surmised the remedy. She moaned, though it came out more like a purr.

"What great deed have I ever done to deserve you?" Darcy whispered, his voice rumbling deep and low in her ear.

"I know not." She slid her arms around his shoulders. "Perhaps you ought to do another? Then we might both be certain that you do."

He drew back and looked down at her. The intensity of his desire afforded him a severe mien. Her pulse quickened to be the object of it. He let go of her shoulder and took hold of her waist, his large, hot hand pulling her tightly against him. "Oh, I intend to make very, *very* certain."

Tuesday, 14 July 1812: Hertfordshire

Truly, Providence was set on persecuting Jane this day. By the time the Bingley party left Longbourn, *hours* after the Darcys thanks to her mother's flutterings over the loss of two daughters in one day, she had begun to feel a very insistent discomfort in her abdomen. To her utter dismay upon arriving at Netherfield, she was forced to retire immediately to her new bedchamber to deal with the onset of her monthly courses.

She sat at the little writing desk between the windows to pen a note of apology to Bingley—scarcely the letter she had envisioned first composing there.

"Excuse me, Mrs. Bingley," her new lady's maid enquired from the doorway. "The water is ready. Should you like your bath now?"

"Yes, thank you, Lacey."

At the young woman's direction, two housemaids trudged into the room, lugging pails of steaming water to the bathtub. One was a young red-haired girl with freckles, the other the very ghost of Elizabeth. Jane's mortification was complete. Refusing to succumb to tears in front of the staff, she folded her note and handed it to Lacey. "Pray, see this is given to Mr. Bingley." Then, simply to get her out of sight, she pointed at the second housemaid and added, "Send her. I would rather you stayed."

After that, she submitted to Lacey's ministrations in silence though her thoughts were far from quiet as they railed against the injustice of her predicament. Here she was, mistress of Netherfield and wife to Mr. Bingley yet unable to enjoy being either. One moment she cringed to consider what her new husband must be thinking of her, the next she recalled him staring at Elizabeth and decided she did not care. If she shed a few tears, it was only as her hair was rinsed and her face was awash with water anyway.

When she was dressed and her hair brushed, she sent Lacey to fetch her some supper. The maid returned with a tray of food and an answering note from Bingley. Jane thanked her for both and dismissed her then stared at the missive for a good ten minutes before summoning the courage to read it.

Dearest Jane,

I would not have you distress yourself any further about such a trifling matter. I have grown up with sisters, and I am not insensible to the inconveniences they often suffer.

I am sorry—truly sorry—that you have been aggrieved on this of all days, but rest assured I shall endeavour to put all to rights, to cheer you by every possible method as soon as you feel well enough to leave your room. In the meantime, anything you require for your comfort shall be yours. Pray do not hesitate to request whatever you wish of the staff.

You looked beautiful today, Jane. I deeply regret we have been apart for most of it. What say you we forget this day and have our beginning on the morrow?

Charles

She did weep in earnest then. It was not the message she had been expecting, but she ought to have expected it, for Bingley was nothing if not kind-hearted. It brought everything into question. Had he truly avoided her all day or merely been waylaid by the excessive number of guests? Had he really be staring at Elizabeth, merely looking at his friend, or indeed, merely looking? When had she become so captious?

She could not easily forget her doubts, profuse as they were, yet here was proof he did at least *care* for her. Surely, with Elizabeth gone, she had every reason to be hopeful for a new beginning? Of course, Elizabeth would need to actually be gone. She stood up and pulled the bell for Lacey, who was sent directly away again to inform the housekeeper the new mistress wished to speak to her.

Half an hour later, Jane was alone again and indeed feeling eminently more hopeful. By nightfall, Netherfield would be short of a maid, but she would be free to commence her new beginning without the impediment of suspicion.

Friday, 17 July 1812: London

To his new sister's credit, Fitzwilliam could not deny she put on a lavish ball. Derwent House had been transformed into a sort of enchanted forest, every cornice, mantel, and mirror festooned with greenery.

His grandmother harrumphed, stepping away from a trailing spray of ivy that brushed her shoulder. "If you had such a burning desire to be out of doors, I wonder you did not host a picnic rather than a ball, Lady Ashby."

Fitzwilliam stifled a snort.

"Philippa has done admirably," objected Lady Catherine, the stupendous feather in her headdress bobbing indignantly. "At least one of the additions to this family is sure to make a favourable impression."

"Sister!" Matlock groaned.

"Do not 'sister' me, Reginald. And do not say I did not warn you when Darcy's scandalous alliance brings shame upon us all."

"The scandal of which you speak seems to me largely of your own making, Lady Catherine," Mrs. Sinclair opined. "Perhaps if you refrained from advertising Mrs. Darcy's purported insufficiencies to the world, you might better survive the ignominy of being her aunt."

"I sincerely hope she does not exhibit any of her insufficiencies this evening," Lady Ashby clipped. "This is my inaugural ball as Lady Ashby. I will have no scandals!"

"I am inclined to agree with Grandmother," Ashby said apathetically. "Nothing is drawing more attention to Darcy's marriage than all of us standing about discussing it. Besides, she cannot be wholly deficient, else Darcy would not have married her. He is not in the habit of brooking mediocrity."

"Here is your chance to judge," Matlock said, signalling the Darcys' arrival with a nod.

They all ceased arguing and turned to observe the approaching couple. Fitzwilliam mouthed a silent oath. He had ever considered Elizabeth handsome, but this evening, in a gown unlike any he had seen her wear before, her hair arranged exquisitely and in her countenance something…*different*, she was resplendent.

"What the devil has he done to her?" he murmured.

"Naught I would not have done had I got to her first! Bloody hell!" Ashby whispered back.

Never had Jane seen such opulence. Lord and Lady Ashby's ballroom looked like a tableau from a staging of *A Midsummer Night's Dream*. The quiet purr of refined music suffused the chamber, and sumptuously adorned guests made elegant the art of flirtation. A far cry from Meryton's crude and disorderly assemblies, it filled her with pride to behold the world into which she had arrived.

Into that world then obtruded her sister, appearing on a crest of silence succeeded by a wave of urgent whispers, bringing an abrupt end to her complacency.

Despite the first three days of her marriage having turned out to be extremely agreeable and Bingley nary raising an eyebrow at her dismissal of the maid, Jane yet dreaded seeing any symptom of regard when he was reunited with Elizabeth. To her chagrin, her sister arrived looking astonishingly well, in a gown and jewels that would have seen Mrs. Bennet calling for her smelling salts. Jane continued to watch until the Darcys had spoken to their relations and moved to the refreshment table, only then daring to look at Bingley to judge how he had been affected. Alas, the dimness of the ballroom's periphery made his features indistinct, and she was unable to determine aught but the unwavering direction of his gaze.

"You look exceedingly well, Jane," Mr. Darcy said, turning from the refreshment table to hand her a glass of wine.

"Thank you," she replied, as pleased by Bingley's silence on the matter of Elizabeth's appearance as by Mr. Darcy's compliment on hers.

"May I have the honour of dancing with you this evening?"

"Of course. I should be delighted."

"You have anticipated me, Darcy," said Colonel Fitzwilliam, arriving to join them. "Might I, too, claim a dance, Mrs. Bingley?"

"Why, yes, of course."

"It is *my* ball," Lord Ashby announced, appearing with his wife beside the colonel. "I shall have my share of the dancing." Then, quite mistaking where the conversation had been tending, he turned to Elizabeth and asked her for the next set. Jane did not miss the manner in which Lady Ashby glowered at him. She quite sympathised.

"The next is mine, Ashby," Mr. Darcy said, quietly but firmly.

"You have had this stunning creature all to yourself for three days, man. I think you could be a little more generous."

"The next is mine," Mr. Darcy repeated.

"Then I shall have them play a jig!"

"I should be happy to dance a different set with you," Elizabeth said.

"'Tis my turn after Darcy's, though," the colonel said, grinning.

"I beg to differ, old boy," Bingley objected. "'Tis mine!"

"Either way, Ashby, you will have to wait your turn."

The four men continued to argue over who would next dance with Elizabeth while she grinned brazenly between them, basking unashamedly in the attention.

Lady Ashby glared with alarming venom at them all. "Really, Ashby," she said coldly. "There are many single ladies in attendance yet to bring off a coup as great as Mrs. Darcy's, who do not have a wealthy husband with whom to dance. You cannot believe she is so deficient in good breeding that she would slight every one of them by stealing all the dances."

Elizabeth bore the remark with civility though Jane did not think for one moment that her sister would pay the reproach any heed.

Darcy paid only the vaguest attention to the conversation, unable to think on aught but that, surely to God, Elizabeth's dress had been designed to bring men to their knees. It celebrated every curve, accentuated her slender waist, and drew his eye again and again to the generous swell of her bosom—and he was damned if he could refrain from envisaging how its gauzy layers had pooled about her hips as he loved her not an hour ago.

The woman had ruined him! After but three days of marriage, he could no longer hold a rational conversation for want of a thought in his head that did not centre upon loving her. Hearing the music start, he made his excuses and led her to join the line, never in his life so desirous of dancing or so enamoured of his partner.

"Say what else you will, Philippa, you cannot deny her dress is exquisite."

"Yes," Lady Ashby said with a strained smile. "Thank you for bringing it to our attention *again*, Daphne."

"Be not jealous of our praise," said another of the little coterie of ladies, a Miss Valerie Floyd. "A fine dress is a fine dress, regardless of who wears it. Do you know where she had it made?"

"I have no idea. Do you know?" Lady Ashby enquired, glancing at Jane.

Miss Floyd turned to her also. "Does this lady know Mrs. Darcy?"

"Oh, for heaven's sake, Valerie, this is Mrs. Darcy's sister. Do keep up."

"We were introduced earlier, madam," Jane said quietly. "I am Mrs. Bingley."

"Oh, well you never said you were Mrs. Darcy's sister. I should have remembered that. But, now that I know who you are, you simply must tell me how your sister met Mr. Darcy. I have heard such varying reports that I know not what to believe, and I cannot stand to be in ignorance of such things."

"Why, yes, of course," Jane replied. "My husband leases an estate near my father's and—"

"Your father has an estate?"

"Yes. Longbourn."

"Then Mrs. Darcy is a gentleman's daughter?"

"Yes. We both are."

"Well, that is quite the revelation. I was led to believe her family was in trade!"

Undesirous of inviting derision, Jane made no mention of her aunts or uncles. Lady Ashby was either unaware of Elizabeth's connections or similarly disinclined to divulge them, for she also said naught. "Um…well, in any event, Mr. Darcy stayed with my husband last autumn. We all met at an assembly in the local town."

"An assembly?" Miss Floyd cried, her expression an unflattering mix of amusement and disgust. "Oh, that is wonderful! Philippa, had you any idea Mr. Darcy was so liberal?"

"None at all."

"I am not surprised to hear he took a fancy to her at a dance, though," said Lady Daphne, "for she treads uncommonly well. Did you see their dance, Philippa?"

"*Everybody* saw it, Daphne, because *everybody* was watching," Lady Ashby replied indignantly.

"Let it not make you uneasy. People are only intrigued."

"If the Darcys wish to intrigue people, let them hold their own ball for the purpose!"

"I doubt they have time to arrange one this late in the Season. Oh, but I should like to go to a ball at Pemberley. Do you think they will hold one there before next spring?"

Jane held her tongue as the ladies' curiosity flowed long—as did Lady Ashby, who stared vindictively in Elizabeth's direction.

"Ugh! See how brazenly she makes love to them all!" her ladyship muttered to no one in particular.

Jane looked and saw, with no great surprise, that Bingley had been waylaid amongst the throng of gentlemen surrounding Elizabeth. His desertion prompted a painful surge of resentment. "My sister wields her charms liberally and indiscriminately."

Lady Ashby looked at her sharply. "Well, would that she not wield them at *my* ball!"

Elizabeth and Bingley both laughed loudly at some shared joke.

"She is well versed in stealing thunder," Jane mumbled.

"I pity you, Mrs. Bingley. I have been her cousin for less than a week, and already I am grown weary of her brilliancy. You have borne being shone down by her for a lifetime." With a disdainful snort, she turned her back on both Elizabeth and the gaggle of women yet engrossed in discussing her. "Fie! Let us cheer ourselves by examining those parts of her that do not shine so brightly."

Overcome with a violent sense of vindication, Jane did naught to discourage Lady Ashby from cataloguing Elizabeth's faults. Her form lacked symmetry. Her smile revealed too many teeth. Her voice was too deep, her wit too keen, and in her manner was such shameful coquetry as would surely invite disaster.

"Her manners have already invited disaster," Jane admitted. "Only a few days ago, Mr. Darcy was obliged to rescue her from the clutches of a man who claimed she had willingly received his addresses."

"Is that so? Do tell me who."

"His name is Mr. Greyson."

Lady Ashby beamed. Encouraged to have finally pleased *someone* this evening, Jane continued. "And earlier this year she was knocked insensible by an officer with whom she had previously been on very friendly terms after they quarrelled in the street."

"Well, well," her ladyship replied. "How delicious! I am indeed vastly cheered." She peered closely at Jane for a moment, apparently deep in thought, then abruptly delivered a most welcome elixir to her bedevilled spirits. "You must call me Philippa, Jane. I should dearly like us to be friends."

Matlock took one look at his supper companions and sent a man to fetch him another glass of punch, of a mind that his fortitude required fortifying. He was imprisoned between his sister on his right, her ever-loyal playfellow Lady Metcalfe on his left, and opposite him, Mr. and Mrs. Darcy and his own omnipresent demon, Mrs. Sinclair. There passed some minutes of barely civil conversation, seasoned with enough sour glares to curdle every reserve of the cook's white soup—and then proceedings took a turn for the worse.

"I must say, Mrs. Darcy," said Lady Metcalfe, "I was excessively diverted to hear you never had a governess."

Matlock glared at his sister, whence that nugget had undoubtedly sprung.

"I am very happy for you," Mrs. Darcy answered, seeming not in the least perturbed. "I, too, dearly love a laugh."

Mrs. Sinclair cackled gleefully into her soup. Catherine harrumphed into hers.

Lady Metcalfe sallied forth more determinedly. "And now, I understand, you have taken to schooling tenants on your father's estate. You feel an affinity for them, I suppose?"

Matlock winced at his nephew's flare of anger, but was intrigued to observe how easily his new niece quelled her husband's rage with a discreet touch of her hand to what he hoped was only Darcy's leg.

"It is quite an absurd notion," Lady Metcalfe continued, oblivious. "People of that class have not the wit to be properly schooled. You must not expect to have any success in the scheme."

"Entrenched ignorance will always be exceedingly difficult to overcome," Mrs. Darcy replied.

Her ladyship gave a firm nod. "Quite so. Good breeding is essential if one is to achieve true erudition."

"You were not so resolute in *your* opinion on the matter though, were you, Lady Catherine?"

Matlock raised his eyebrows. She meant to draw his sister into the fray as her advocate? Interesting.

"Of what are you speaking?" Catherine demanded, her brow creased in affront.

"Why, when you and I spoke on the matter, you conceded in the end that a person's intellect might not be dictated by their descent."

"I acknowledged your success in teaching a boy to read. Nothing more."

"You see?" Lady Metcalfe announced airily. "Our minds will never be moved on this subject."

Thus, the trap was sprung, and Matlock received his first, exceedingly satisfying taste of the cleverness that had caught his nephew's notice.

"That is precisely as I would have expected, madam," Mrs. Darcy said drily.

Boasting a broad smile, Mrs. Sinclair signalled to the nearest footman. "Have you any gin? I feel a thirst coming on."

"You achieve nothing with this shameless sauce but prove your own want of good breeding," Catherine snarled at Mrs. Darcy in a harsh whisper. "I am not in the habit of being toyed with. Do you still not comprehend who I am?"

"By your own admission, you are one of my husband's nearest relations and, hence, mine also."

Her ladyship sucked in a breath, instigating a virulent fit of coughing. Shaking her head and waving her hand to indicate she was not done, she choked out, "Being my relation does not qualify you to bandy words with me!"

Mrs. Darcy's eyes flashed. "My point exactly."

"Oh, for the love of God, Catherine, desist!" Matlock hissed. "You are making a fool of yourself."

"*She* is making a fool of me!" her ladyship spat back.

"No, she is merely holding doors open. You are striding unhindered through them."

"Am I to be betrayed by my brother as well as my nephew?" she replied in a rasping whisper. She reached for her drink only to discover her glass was empty.

"Where is the disloyalty in saving you from humiliation?"

"If that was your design, why did you do nothing to prevent Darcy marrying her?" She coughed again, more strongly than before.

"Enough!" Darcy hissed furiously. His expression was thunderous. "This will not do." He motioned for a footman to fill Catherine's wine glass. "You are not well, madam. Pray leave off squabbling over unalterable particulars and recover yourself." With that, he stood, held out his hand for Elizabeth and left the table.

Chagrined that Darcy's unfailing restraint had made him look a fool by comparison, Matlock shook his head at his sister. "He does not deserve this from you. He is a fine young man."

"Of that I am fully aware, Reginald! Why in heaven's name do you think I am so angry? Who will care for Anne now?"

He had to assume the question was rhetorical, for she then left the table, taking Lady Metcalfe with her and abandoning him to the company of four empty seats and one Mrs. Tabitha Sinclair. He gritted his teeth and waited for her inevitable acerbic commentary. Some ten minutes later, he was cursing the vexing old baggage's ability to wield complete silence and an infuriating, self-satisfied smirk to infinitely greater effect than any of her usual persiflage.

There was not enough air in the room for so many candles *and* Elizabeth to burn so hot. Her chest heaved with the effort of claiming her share as she spun through the figures of the *La Boulangere.* Over and again, Darcy reclaimed her from the tangle of dancers in the centre of the circle to swirl her vis-à-vis, his grip emblazoning her skin as though she wore no gloves at all and the brand of his touch eclipsing the feel of every other man's as she danced away again.

The circle of dancers skipped wildly to the left and then all the way back to the right. Bingley lurched along with them, chasing Elizabeth in one direction then Jane in the other. The weight of each of their hands naught to that of the turmoil in his heart.

Though he had struggled, after his calamitous proposal, to resign himself to his fate, he had thought his endeavours to be content with Jane as a wife and Elizabeth as a sister largely successful. Only as the sun set on his ill-fated wedding day had he acknowledged how spectacularly he had failed.

The circle slowed to a halt. His heart cavorted in time with his feet as he performed a turn with Elizabeth in the centre, but too soon, she spiralled away from him, spinning about with the other dancers in the ring. He accepted Jane's hand once more, assumed third position, and fought a losing battle against his guilt.

Entering his study uninvited late on Tuesday evening, his sisters had left him in no doubt of his offences. Why, Caroline had railed, had he thought it politic to neglect his own bride at his wedding breakfast?

Another of the ladies swept him into a frenzied turn before moving on to the next man. He resumed his place beside Jane.

How, Louisa had demanded, were they to convince the world of Jane's worth in the face of his flagrant disesteem?

Heat erupted across his palm as Elizabeth reclaimed his hand. He looked about. Everyone was returned to his and her positions in the circle. They all set off again, prancing leftwards in a vast sweeping arc, and he found himself once more chasing Elizabeth in circles.

What possible reason, Louisa had wanted to know, had Jane for dismissing the maid with a marked resemblance to Elizabeth? When, Caroline had demanded, would he overcome his reckless fascination with Mrs. Darcy?

The circle changed direction. It was now Jane who pulled him onwards and Elizabeth's scorching presence chasing him relentlessly back to his place.

Again and again, he had denied any misconduct to his sisters, his shame deepening with every reiteration of the lie.

It was his turn to lead Jane through the complicated figure in the centre. They forged headlong into the fray, moving in good time if not perfect unison.

At what point had he ceased concerning himself with her feelings?

He was swept into a dizzying turn with another of the ladies then flung back to his wife.

He knew full well his regard for Jane had been neglected once his feelings for Elizabeth emerged.

He staggered about in a disorientating pirouette with the next lady before being returned to Jane's more steady presence, falling more quickly into step with her this time.

He had made no attempt to discover why she dismissed Amelia, grateful only that the woman was gone and more resolved than ever to conquer his feelings for Elizabeth.

He lost Jane to Lord Vale, who whisked her off into a turn in the centre. Bingley watched her dance. The candlelight afforded her countenance, which was already glowing prettily from her exertions, a soft, delicate sheen. She truly was an astoundingly handsome woman.

Vale spun past, delivering her back to him. Bingley took hold of her hand and smiled, earning himself a look of hopeful surprise.

Was not this rectifiable? Given time to nurture his regard—away from the distraction of either Elizabeth or Amelia—had he not every reason to hope that his feelings for Jane would grow to surpass all other desires? He raised her hand to his lips and kissed her fingers. Perchance she might be ready to receive him this evening. Then they might begin their journey to felicity in earnest.

He set off into the next round ahead of tempo, willing the set to end that he could escape the place and return home into the arms of his beautiful, serene, uncomplicated wife—away from the terrifying, fierce, and insuperable passion of her sister.

Elizabeth grew giddy from Darcy's affect upon her senses as they wheeled feverishly towards the end of the set. He drew her closer, held her tighter, and released her later with every glancing convergence. The feel of him so close behind, as he pursued her through the dance's closing steps, set her heart to racing, emboldening her to stop two steps early and wait—heart thundering, eyes closed, and all anticipation for that moment he would, inevitably, capture her.

They came together with too much force, toppling onto the bed in a tangle of limbs and lust to enact a dance all their own, the tempo fierce and the steps urgent. They moved fervently, Darcy incandescent with desire. No other woman had ever roused in him such ferocious lust. Elizabeth was sublime, her skin flushed in the candlelight and exquisite gasps of pleasure on her lips as he loved her. He welcomed the familiar coil of tension when it began and increased his pace, pursuing his bliss. Elizabeth's passion rose to meet his. Her hands tangled in his hair, and she bucked against him muttering incoherent half-formed words 'til, without warning, she cried his name, and Darcy was sent reeling violently into the rapturous denouement of the most exhilarating dance he had ever performed.

He lay still, unmoving but for his heart thundering in his chest, and fought to catch his breath. Into the stunned hush came Elizabeth's sultry, passion-drenched voice.

"Fitzwilliam Darcy, had I known you could do that, I should have said yes the first time."

Saturday, 18 July 1812: London

On the afternoon following *The Evening Before,* Jane sat in her parlour, her hands idle and her mind engaged in reflections answerable for the blush overspreading her cheeks. *The evening before*, she and Bingley had at last consummated their union, binding themselves eternally in body where she was certain their hearts must soon unite. Such reveries rendered her already somewhat discomposed—and therefore apt to become even more so—when none other than Lady Ashby came calling.

Her ladyship blew into the room in an eddy of hauteur and installed herself ceremoniously upon the chaise longue.

"I did not expect to see you so soon, Lady Ashby," Jane began nervously.

"Come now, did we not agree you would call me Philippa?"

"Oh, yes. Forgive me."

"Never apologise, Jane; it is unbecoming."

A footman delivered some refreshments, and Jane proceeded to pour tea for her visitor, glad of some activity to steady her hands.

Lady Ashby accepted her cup with a wide, close-lipped smile. "Now tell me, how did you enjoy my ball? Did you approve of the decoration? You seem the sort of woman to appreciate finery."

This began a discussion on all things refined and admirable, from Miss Christopherson's exquisite performance at the pianoforte to the divine shade of Lady Frances's gown.

"You, too, were quite sublime, my dear," her ladyship added, much to Jane's delight. "I believe I must be allowed to detest you just a little for your looks. You were universally admired. And you acquitted yourself admirably given your recent elevation to your husband's sphere. Everybody to whom I introduced you was well pleased. But then, there is nothing better, I find, than to have one's expectations exceeded. It disposes one to be satisfied."

"Why, thank you."

"Such a shame your sister saw fit to prove correct all our prepossessions. In her every action there was something of which to be ashamed. One can hardly blame your husband for his enthralment, for what man's interest would not be piqued by such a flagrant exhibition of feminine charms?"

Jane gasped and coughed, and hot tea burnt the back of her nose. Throughout their intimacy the previous evening, Bingley had showered her with such assurances of his regard and promises for their future as made her forget, momentarily, Elizabeth's claim on his affections. "Pardon?" she whispered.

"Oh, I have an eye for these things, Jane. And believe me, your husband was not alone in being drawn in. It was precisely as you said: Mrs. Darcy teases and flirts at will with no adherence to the practices of the sphere into which she has imposed herself. That a few weak-minded individuals should fall prey to such a widely cast net is wholly unsurprising."

"Yes, I suppose…"

"No matter. Your husband, indeed the whole of society, will soon tire of her when they realise she has naught to offer but coquetry and satire."

"They will?"

"Indeed, it cannot be otherwise. One wonders when Mr. Darcy will tire of her…but in any case, *your* husband will certainly lose interest soon." She leant forward and patted Jane's hand. "Understand, my dear, that while men's heads are easily turned by women's charms, their hearts are governed by pride. They have a great need to feel respected. Your eminently more sensible marriage has allowed you to achieve that which your sister never will—the very ne plus ultra of your rightful sphere. Of course, a connection with me will recommend you further still. Mr. Bingley cannot long remain unmoved by such distinction." She gave her hand a parting pat and leant back, smirking as she withdrew. "You observed, I presume, how his interest in her waned once you began dancing with the likes of Lord Vale?"

"I had not—though, yes, I suppose it did."

"There, you see? It is perfectly within your power to harness his esteem if only you can learn to become the sort of wife of whom he can be proud."

Thus, the ember of hope that flickered so erratically in Jane's heart was rekindled. "Yes, I believe I do see."

Lady Ashby smiled. "Good. So! Do not allow your sister's selfish behaviour to distress you a moment longer. No good will come of a rift between the pair of you. Suffer her as best you can, and take comfort instead in *our* friendship. And the next time her manners or actions grieve you, bring your vexations to me. Mine will ever be a willing and sympathetic ear."

When the visit drew to an end a few minutes later and her new friend departed with the warmest of adieus, Jane felt vastly comforted to have secured the friendship of such a shrewd and obliging woman—and a good deal of satisfaction to have proved herself, on this occasion at least, better admired than her sister.

"Have I called at an inconvenient time, Jane?"

"What do you mean?"

"You seem determined to be displeased with me today."

Elizabeth had called at Grosvenor Street with the hope of exchanging tales of newly wedded bliss with her dearest sister but had been there for little more than five minutes before comprehending there would be no sharing of confidences this day. Jane was uncommonly ill-tempered, inclined to take offense at most everything and find fault with all the rest.

"Forgive me, I am a little fatigued," Jane replied. "Last night was…taxing."

"It was? I hope nobody was uncivil to you."

Jane's cheeks pinked a little. "I believe it was unintentional."

"Then you *were* slighted by somebody?"

Jane shrugged slightly. "I was merely ill-prepared for the want of consideration I was shown in some quarters."

This caught Elizabeth by surprise, though she was instantly angry with herself for being surprised. The nature of her acquaintance with Darcy had afforded her an invaluable understanding of his sphere and its inherent intolerances. Moreover, he had warned her what to expect at the ball since it was his family and his acquaintances to whom she was being introduced. Poor Jane had been given no such advantage. Even Mr. Bingley possessed only a passing acquaintance with the majority of Lady Ashby's guests. Elizabeth was ashamed to acknowledge she had done naught to prepare her unsuspecting sister for the contempt of those whom she herself must now call family.

"I beg you would forgive me, Jane. I was too engrossed in my own world to consider how you must have felt. It was selfish of me."

Her sister did not smile. "I shall not say you are wrong."

Elizabeth blinked away her surprise, for she supposed, having claimed the offence, she could hardly blame Jane for agreeing with it. "But did you manage to enjoy yourself at all? Not every person was uncivil, I hope."

"By no means. There were a number of very charming people there. I found Lady Ashby particularly agreeable."

"You did?" Elizabeth said with a little laugh, wondering not for the first time at Jane's ability to form attachments to the most insincere of people.

"Yes, Lizzy, I did! I see you think it diverting. And, of course, *I* must be the one at fault because *nobody* is as good a judge of character as you."

Though she continued to be taken aback by her sister's ill-will, the barb served its purpose. She was duly humbled. "I beg your pardon. You are quite right. Lady Ashby showed me no great courtesy, but I do not doubt you were able to see some good in her that I was not."

"Perhaps it was because I was more respectful of her that she showed me more courtesy than she did you."

"Do you accuse me of being disrespectful to her?"

"Not by design, I am sure, but your teasing ran as unchecked last night as ever it did in Hertfordshire, and such irreverence could never be considered respectful. Your new family will never like you if you make no effort to please them."

"How fortunate, then, that I do not require their approbation."

"Do you not? You are not concerned that Mr. Darcy will grow weary of the schism you have caused—that he will tire of you?"

"Are you worried Mr. Bingley will tire of you?" Elizabeth threw back, incredulous at the very suggestion.

A stony veil fell across Jane's countenance. Too late, Elizabeth realised the imprudence of using Mr. Bingley's constancy as a case in point. "Forgive me, I meant not to allude to past troubles, only to demonstrate my faith in Darcy's affections. I have every reason to believe his esteem will endure regardless of his family's opinion of me."

Jane unfurled from her rigid pose and turned away to take up her embroidery. "I am sure you are right."

An oppressive silence fell over them. Jane, her expression pinched, worked doggedly on her stitches. Elizabeth sat motionless and wretched, wondering whether their friendship might be forever changed. They had been sheltered, she recognised, growing up at Longbourn. Harmony and contentment had been easy to nurture when the greatest tribulations they faced were Mrs. Bennet's nerves and the occasional uncertainty of which gown ought to be worn to this or that dance. Exposed for but a few months to the influences of the wider world, they had both been irrevocably altered and seemed unable to rediscover an equal footing.

"Jane," she said softly, "we are about to be separated for an indeterminate length of time. Let us not part on bad terms. Shall we not speak of something else? What of your time left in London? What are your plans?"

They talked of happier things after that, and Jane even showed Elizabeth the house. The visit was too overshadowed by their quarrel for there to be hope of a complete recovery, however, and they parted soon after. Elizabeth spent the remainder of the day in a fog of indignant disappointment, unable to fathom how the argument had come about. Not until many hours later did she feel calm enough to relay the exchange to Darcy.

They lay entwined in the dimly lit cocoon of his bedchamber. His eyes were closed, but his mouth was curled into Elizabeth's favourite half-smile, and he held her tightly to his side. The arrangement made her wish to forget the outside world—but she could not.

"I called on Jane this afternoon," she said quietly.

"Was she well?"

"Yes, only…" She sighed deeply. "We quarrelled."

He looked down at her. "About what?"

"Everything! There was little I said that did not seem to displease her in some way." She rolled onto her back and looked up into the darkness of the canopy. "She apparently found the ball quite trying. I believe she felt a little out of her depth."

"Why should that make her angry with you?"

"Because I did not notice or do anything to alleviate it."

"It is not your responsibility to play nursemaid to your sister, Elizabeth."

"No, but it would have taken but a moment to warn her that she might encounter some disdain."

"Was she openly disdained? I must say I saw nothing of it."

Elizabeth shrugged. "I know not. She said only that she disliked the want of consideration some people showed her."

"Perhaps she was jealous of your greater notoriety."

His voice dripped with sarcasm, but Elizabeth did not blame him. Though she had been tolerably well received at the ball, Lady Catherine's industrious calumny and the general prejudice of Darcy's set had ensured that hers was a conspicuous and somewhat perilous entrance into society. Jane's presence had been of comparatively little interest to anyone. Had her complaint been the lacklustre nature of her own reception? Elizabeth chafed at the notion. If Jane begrudged her greater share of attention, she was most welcome to it!

Darcy pulled her back against him and placed a gentle kiss atop her head. "I have offended you. Forgive me."

"No, not at all. She was certainly severe on me." She wrapped her arm about him and nestled closer. After a moment's consideration, she enquired, "Was I uncivil to Lady Ashby?"

"Indeed not! Quite the reverse. Why?"

"Jane thought I was."

He made no response though he adjusted his shoulders restlessly. His silent agitation spoke volumes.

"Pray, be not angry with her. I believe—I *hope*—it was only concern that made her speak thus. She is anxious I should not be disliked by my new family." She thought it unwise to add that Jane feared for the longevity of his affections in the face of any prolonged antagonism.

He gave a sardonic huff. "I should not like it if my sister married and suffered the same disdain from her new family as you have suffered from mine, but if she did, I should not blame *her*."

Elizabeth raised herself onto her elbow and looked down at him. "I can tolerate your family's disdain with perfect indifference, but I am less willing to see them despise you because they cannot like me. Have no fear that I mean to turn into Mr. Collins and fawn and toady after all your relations, but clearly, I cannot remain obstinately indifferent forever. I must make some effort." She kissed him lightly on the tip of his nose. "And you never know—in ten or twenty years, I might even persuade a few of them to like me."

He lifted her hand from where it lay on his chest and kissed her fingers. "Lady Catherine already likes you. It is why she despises you so violently. It is exceedingly inconvenient to her that she should esteem the person responsible for ruining all her plans. And I wish you would not waste a moment more of your time on my cousin's ridiculous wife. We can very well live without Lady Ashby's good opinion."

Elizabeth let out a long sigh. "Both our families seem determined to make us pay for our happiness. How long ere we leave? I would go home!"

In answer, he wrapped his arms around her and rolled her onto her back, gazing at her fiercely with eyes cast jet-black by shadows—or fervour, she knew not which.

"God, I love you, woman." Then he stretched over her to the nightstand and snubbed out the candle, surrendering them to the intimate secrets of the darkness.

Wednesday, 22 July 1812: London

It took Bingley a moment to realise Godfrey did not mean to show him into Darcy's study. He almost tripped over his own feet as he trotted to catch up.

"Mr. Darcy is not at his desk?" Darcy always passed the hours before breakfast attending to business in his study.

"No, sir. He and Mrs. Darcy will receive you in the morning room."

Bingley groaned. In adherence with his resolve to overcome his fascination, he had determined to avoid Elizabeth completely until they all removed from Town and, until now, had been successful. He had evaded calls, committed Jane and himself to engagements that conflicted with any to which the Darcys had invited them, and generally exhausted himself keeping far busier than he usually preferred in order that he could truthfully claim to have been too busy to see either of them.

The Darcys were leaving for Pemberley on the morrow, however, and he had not wished to insult his friend by not even saying goodbye. Persuaded by his confidence in Darcy's unswerving routine and the perfectly reasonable assumption that Elizabeth would rise as late as the women in his own household, he had elected to call at an hour scarcely past dawn so they would be assured of their privacy. Yet, here was Darcy, dallying in the morning room. With his wife.

Godfrey slowed before the door, and Bingley's insides lurched at the prospect of seeing Elizabeth again and then twisted with guilt and vexation for being still so hopelessly affected by her. The door swung open, and husband and wife stood to greet him.

"Has Jane not come with you?" Elizabeth enquired.

"Er, no, she is still abed."

"Oh."

She sounded horribly disappointed, and he scrambled to preserve her feelings. "But she does not know I have called. We did not return home until very late last night, and I did not wish to wake her so early."

"Early? 'Tis nearly ten o'clock!"

"That is early for Bingley," Darcy stated, resuming his seat and motioning for a footman to clear the table at which they sat. Only then did Bingley notice it was laid out for breakfast.

"Forgive me, I would not wish to interrupt your meal. I did not expect to find you eating."

"That is my doing," Elizabeth admitted. "Your poor friend—I am imposing my will at every turn. His life will be unrecognisable within a twelvemonth."

"What else remains for you to alter that you have not already?" Darcy replied seriously. How the man could be so advantageously wed, yet remain perpetually dissatisfied, Bingley knew not.

At Elizabeth's insistence, he accepted a cup of coffee and sat down. He consciously chose a seat facing Darcy, which afforded him naught but a stiff neck since she proceeded to do all the talking and Darcy barely any, requiring him to twist awkwardly towards her for most of the visit.

"How did you like all Darcy's other friends?" Bingley enquired when it came to discussing the dinner he had declined to attend.

"I thought them universally charming," she replied. "I got on particularly well with Mr. Ferguson and his wife, and Mr. Montgomery was his usual, gentle self."

"Montgomery is liked wherever he goes," Darcy agreed.

"More so now he has made his fortune, I imagine," Bingley quipped. "Perhaps I ought to introduce him to Caroline."

"You must act quickly then, for I do not think he will remain available for long," Elizabeth said. "Not now that Mrs. Sinclair has set her sights on him."

Bingley almost choked. "I do not think even Montgomery is that amenable."

"Not for herself!" Elizabeth protested, laughing. "For Miss de Bourgh! In lieu of Colonel Fitzwilliam, who has been Lady Catherine's preferred suitor ever since a certain other gentleman married elsewhere."

Bingley turned to Darcy, ready to share a laugh at Fitzwilliam's expense, but he was deterred from commenting by his friend's fierce glower.

"This again?" Darcy clipped. "I have told them Montgomery deserves better. Would that Mrs. Sinclair cease pushing the match."

"I am not sure the acquaintance can be avoided now. I understand she has invited him to dine at Matlock House this evening with the particular purpose of introducing him to your aunt."

"Then it is fortunate that my aunt will not be there."

"Oh?" Elizabeth smiled wryly. "Is it safe to assume that is because I shall be?"

That lost Darcy his ire. His mouth worked to find words that seemed stubbornly to evade him.

"Lady Catherine and I, you see, are not the best of friends," Elizabeth said to Bingley. "But given my beginning with her nephew, I shall not be discouraged. I have high hopes we shall be inseparable by next Christmas." She grinned. Darcy only shook his head.

"Er…are you looking forward to seeing Pemberley?" Bingley enquired, feeling rather awkward.

"I am thoroughly impatient to see it. I have grown weary of hearing strangers eulogise about my own home and being unable to join in their raptures."

"I imagine so," Bingley replied. "You will enjoy the journey almost as much as the destination. There is some uncommonly pretty countryside to be seen en route. I have not been north of Hertfordshire in months. I am quite jealous."

"Will you not soon be travelling north yourself?" Darcy enquired. "I presumed you would take Jane on a wedding tour."

"You are not taking Lizzy on one," he answered, feeling rather petulant at having his oversight called out.

"Elizabeth has met all my relations. *You* have enough to fill half of Yorkshire. I imagine some of them would like to meet your wife."

"Oh, do bring Jane north!" Elizabeth appealed. "You could visit us at Pemberley."

"No!" His heart was not yet resilient enough for that manner of test! "No, I would not dream of invading your privacy so soon after you arrived home."

"Nonsense! Darcy will have had quite enough of me by then. And you can be sure we will have no other visitors, for I am persona non grata with all his family."

Bingley looked at Darcy, but he only rolled his eyes and said nothing at all to contradict her. It was as though he saw nothing wrong in his relations' disdain for his wife.

"Well then," Bingley said defiantly, resolved to offer her the comfort Darcy seemed unwilling to provide. "I shall not countenance being the cause of any further distress of yours. Leave it with me. I shall see what I can arrange."

Saturday, 25 July 1812: Derbyshire

At the sight of Pemberley's home farm from the carriage window, Darcy grew taut with anticipation. Another few minutes' travel would bring them within view of the house, a moment of which he had dreamt more often than he would like to admit.

"Elizabeth?" he whispered, gently rubbing her arm to rouse her. With Georgiana and Mrs. Annesley dozing in the opposite seat, she had dared to lean against him, where she too had then been lulled to sleep by the carriage's steady sway. She did not awaken, but nestled deeper into his embrace, broadening the smile he already wore. "Elizabeth, we are almost there."

She peeled herself reluctantly from his side and rubbed her eyes then squinted at him. How she could sleep so soundly in a moving coach he knew not, but he found her drowsy confusion tremendously endearing. Wordlessly, he placed his hands upon her shoulders and turned her towards the window. After a quick glance to determine that the others still slept, he snaked one arm about her middle and rested his chin on her shoulder that he might perceive the unfolding panorama as she did.

She said naught, only pulled his arm more tightly about her, raised her free hand to rest against his cheek and waited. Together they held their silent vigil as the carriage crested a final rise, and Pemberley at long last came into view. The hand that cupped his face fell away and Elizabeth sat forward. "Oh my," were her only words, exhaled on a breath of wonder.

When several moments passed without further comment, Darcy leant sideways to gauge her expression, and for the first time in the whole of their acquaintance, saw her altogether stripped of courage. He could not deny the gratification of her being thus affected by the place he loved so well. Nonetheless, he would banish all her trepidation for good ere they reached the house. He touched her chin and turned her gently to face him.

"I have wrestled senselessly with many mistaken scruples in the past, love, but I never doubted you. I have always known you belonged here."

The day was by no means glorious. Clouds concealed every inch of blue sky, and rain earlier in the day had tramped down much of the surrounding flora. Yet, the affection to be seen in Elizabeth's eyes at that moment rendered it a picture Darcy would never forget.

She kissed his cheek. "Thank you, my darling man."

"Oh, we are here! Lizzy, how do you like it?"

At his sister's pronouncement, Darcy withdrew his arm and sat back a little from Elizabeth, not missing the look she wore, which satisfied him her courage had returned. He watched her, anticipating mischief of some kind, and was not disappointed. She withdrew from her reticule a rather scruffy piece of paper, which she unfolded and held up to the window, looking repeatedly from it to the house.

"I must say, I am rather disappointed, Georgiana. It is not at all what I was promised. All the windows are symmetrical, there are no crooked columns—and I had quite set my heart on there being a haunted chimney, but it is very clearly not there." She lowered his sketch to her lap and sighed loudly. "At least the roof is level."

Mrs. Reynolds waited in a vanguard of staff in front of the house and watched the approaching carriage with trepidation. She had been employed at Pemberley for four-and-twenty years and had never been given cause for complaint. Yet, whomever Mr. Darcy had chosen as his wife had the potential to significantly affect her own life and work, and she wished, at her age, that neither would be too grievously disrupted.

On either side of her were Mr. Barnaby and Mr. Maltravers, neither of whose thoughts on the master's marriage were known to her. As steward and butler respectively, both men were of such assiduous loyalty as all but prevented either of them having an opinion on the matter, which left her alone in her trepidation.

Fortunately, her first impressions were favourable. Though very young, Mrs. Darcy seemed friendly, unaffected, and quaintly handsome. The master certainly appeared vastly taken with her, his manner well pleased as he introduced her to the household. In short order, the presentation was complete, the majority of the staff dismissed, and their party removed within doors.

"Would it please you if dinner was served at six, Mrs. Darcy?" Mrs. Reynolds enquired.

"It would please me better if it were served at five," Mr. Darcy replied. "Our breakfast was abysmal."

Mrs. Darcy regarded her husband with obvious amusement, but he either did not notice or chose to ignore it, turning instead to speak to Mr. Barnaby and Mr. Maltravers. Miss Darcy excused herself to change, and Mrs. Annesley went with her, leaving Mrs. Reynolds alone with the new mistress.

"We have been here but a few minutes, and already we are making more work for you," said the latter. "You will wish us gone again by morning."

"Oh, no, ma'am. We are all hopeful Mr. Darcy will choose to be here more often now. Pemberley is never quite the same when he is away from home."

"He is well liked, then?"

"Oh, yes! The best landlord, the best master that ever lived."

Mrs. Darcy's eyes flashed with something Mrs. Reynolds did not recognise, but it rendered the young lady uncommonly pretty.

"I understand you have known him for many years."

"Aye, ma'am, since he was four."

"And never had a cross word from him in your life, I imagine?"

"Never!" she answered proudly. "But then, I have always observed that they who are good-natured when children are good-natured when they grow up."

This further animated Mrs. Darcy's countenance. "Was he good-natured as a boy?"

Mr. Darcy cast his wife a rather suspicious look then, but he continued in his conversation with the men, so Mrs. Reynolds continued hers with the mistress. "He was, ma'am. The sweetest-tempered, most generous-hearted boy in the world."

Mrs. Darcy broke into a dazzling smile and even laughed a little. "It is as much to your credit as his that you speak so highly of him, Mrs. Reynolds."

"I say no more than the truth," she demurred, feeling suddenly foolish to be recommending the lady's own husband to her.

"Indeed, and the truth often bears repeating," Mrs. Darcy replied with an enigmatic smile.

"If you are ready, then?"

The housekeeper jumped slightly at the master's interruption though the mistress seemed not in the least startled and answered very equably that she was. She took his arm, and as one, they turned to ascend the grand staircase, so easy together that they looked for all the world as though they had done it every day of their lives thus far.

"Slow down! You are going too fast for me to see anything!" Elizabeth said, laughing as Darcy all but dragged her through a maze of rooms.

He did not reply. She began to think he might be displeased in some way when he abruptly pulled her sideways through a door. She had barely time to deduce the room must be his bedchamber before he had torn off his coat, plucked her from her feet, thrown her onto his bed, and planted himself firmly atop her.

"What are you about?" she cried.

"I could ask the same of you," he replied, leaning to kiss her neck. "You cannot pretend ignorance with me, wife. I well know how you look when you are being sly." He peppered kisses across her breastbone. "What mischief were you up to just now?"

Elizabeth bit her lip, chagrined to have been discovered teasing the housekeeper and too distracted by Darcy's wandering tongue to think of how she might explain it in a favourable light.

He lifted his head to look at her. "You will not tell me?"

His eyes danced with a playfulness she had never seen there before, and the slight curl of his lips gave him such an appearance of rakishness she wondered with some relish how he intended to extract her secret from her. She gave him a smirk of her own. "I think not."

He raised an eyebrow. Unhurriedly, he lifted her arms above her head and pinned them there with one hand then smoothed the other down her side. His head he lowered until their lips almost touched—then he took her utterly and completely by surprise by digging his fingers into her side and mercilessly tickling her. She shrieked and bucked beneath him, laughing in astonishment. The illustrious and stately Mr. Darcy surely did not *tickle* people! She implored him to stop.

"Not until you share your joke." He moved his excruciating touch to under her arm, provoking her to squeal and writhe anew.

"Very well! I yield! It was Mr. Bingley's fault! Pray desist!"

He did and squinted at her dubiously. "Bingley?"

"Aye! He was telling me about Mrs. Reynolds and did a little impersonation of her. It transpires it was an uncommonly good one."

"And wherefore were you discussing my housekeeper with Bingley?"

She wrinkled her nose, feeling a little embarrassed. "Because we were speaking of you."

He looked momentarily surprised then insufferably smug. She attempted to tug her hands from his grasp that she might tickle him, but he was having none of it. Still pinning her arms in place, he wrapped his other hand beneath her and brought his lips to hers for a blistering kiss, banishing all thoughts of retribution from her mind. She signalled her surrender with a groan of pleasure, and he promptly tickled her other side, making her yelp against his lips.

"What has come over you?"

He pulled away and smirked at her, his countenance, if possible, even more handsome than usual for his present liveliness. "I am home," he said simply, as though informing her of nothing less obvious than that day broke when the sun rose.

Noises from beyond a door caught both their attention. He rolled his eyes, kissed her forehead, and removed from the bed, tugging his attire straight, then strode purposefully to the door to speak with whoever was without. She watched enthralled as her adoring and playful husband of moments before reverted effortlessly to the commanding, dignified, and extraordinarily alluring master of Pemberley.

"As am I," she whispered, full in the belief she was the most fortunate woman alive.

Wednesday, 29 July 1812: Derbyshire

Elizabeth's delight with her new home knew no bounds, though perhaps most precious to her was the fondness with which Darcy introduced her to every part of it. Three days had not been enough for her to learn all its passageways and rooms, but the orangery and the woods around the lake had already been settled as two of her favourite places in all of Pemberley. This morning, at her request, breakfast had been laid out on the veranda outside one and overlooking the other.

"What news from Grosvenor Street?"

Darcy ceased scowling at his letter and looked up. "I *believe* Bingley is proposing a visit, but it is high Dutch for the most part." He dropped it onto the table. "The man is useless."

"I shall send an invitation directly to Jane. It seems safest."

"Are you certain you wish to receive them? You were upset after your last visit."

Since they parted ways, Elizabeth's feelings towards her sister had vacillated constantly between indignation to the deepest concern. Yet, on one thing she was decided: they would not resolve the matter whilst five counties apart. "I was, but we have quarrelled before. I am sure it will all be forgotten. Besides, I did not have the opportunity to show her our London home. I should dearly love for her to see Pemberley."

That much agreed, Darcy turned his attention to his breakfast, and she turned hers to her correspondence, opening a letter from her friend in Kent. She read and relayed the happy news that Charlotte Collins was with child, though Darcy was far more animated by the next report—that Mr. Montgomery was presently at Rosings, paying court to Anne. Much to Elizabeth's surprise, he threw his unfinished toast onto his plate and grabbed up his napkin, managing to make the innocuous act of dabbing the corners of his mouth appear the most resentful thing in the world.

"Are you truly so violently opposed to the match?"

"I am. Montgomery is an excellent man and the means of uniting us, for which I owe him more than I can ever give. He deserves better than a joyless marriage with a malicious harpy as a mother."

"There is nothing to say it will be a joyless marriage, and I daresay that, since you are able to put up with my mother, Mr. Montgomery will find a way to tolerate Anne's."

"*Your* mother is neither malicious nor disloyal. She may be a total stranger to propriety, but everything she does is done in what she believes to be the best interests of her family."

Elizabeth bit her lip and gazed at him tenderly. "Thank you. But...do you not suppose it possible that Lady Catherine also believes she has been acting in the best interests of her family?"

"I am her family. How has she acted in my best interests?" he said with startling emotion. Never had he appeared so young, so vulnerable as in that rare unguarded moment, and Elizabeth thought her heart might break when his meaning struck her. Lady Catherine had been the one to proclaim herself almost his nearest relation, and she had been correct. It could surely only have been worse had Lady Anne Darcy herself scorned his choice of wife and industriously maligned him to the whole world.

She reached to gently squeeze his hand. "Well, I am your family now. And I love you enough to out-vie a thousand ignoble aunts."

Darcy stared at her silently for a moment, his gaze swimming with sentiment. Then his lips quirked and he shook his head slightly. Reaching sideways, he plucked a leaf from a nearby potted plant and presented it to her with a look so intense it made her shiver. "You fell me, Elizabeth. I have no words."

She beamed at him. "Good, for I have another letter to read, and your chatter would make the task impossible."

She withstood his smouldering gaze very well as she read Mrs. Gardiner's note confirming their expected arrival on Saturday morning, by now more than comfortable being the object of his adoration.

Pemberley, Derbyshire
July 29

Dearest Jane,

I hope this letter finds you well. Mr. Bingley has written with the news that you are travelling north, but it was not clear from his letter whether or not you intend to visit Pemberley. I beg you would. I know we parted on an unhappier note than either of us would have liked, but we have never let a quarrel keep us long divided, and I hope this one may be soon forgotten also. Pray, write to say you will stay with us for a little while at least, or if you cannot, send addresses where I may write to you while you are on your travels.

Oh, Jane, Pemberley is wonderful! Such a home I never saw—so filled with light and elegance and surrounded by a stunning park. The house is large, but Darcy is determined to show me every corner, thus little by little I am discovering its secrets. I have met his parents at last of a fashion: I have seen their portraits in the gallery. Lady Anne looked to be a very fine woman with a marked resemblance to her sister, though less severe and, of course, much younger. The late Mr. Darcy sports a wig and seems very sombre in his portrait, though he has kind eyes. More than that it is difficult to impart from two paintings, but you will be pleased to hear they made no objections whatever to our marriage.

All the servants have been exceedingly patient as I fudge my way through household tasks that must seem elementary to them. I think it will take some time to become accustomed to it all. Darcy is adamant that everybody should fit in with me rather than the other way around, but I cannot agree. Pemberley has run perfectly well without a mistress for years. It seems nonsensical to adjust perfectly good practices simply to save me the bother of learning them. Still, until I am proficient, the entire staff and my poor beleaguered husband must make allowances for my mistakes!

Georgiana, too, has been a dear. We spend much time together, particularly when Darcy is occupied with estate matters, and we are growing very fond of each other. She seems so very young compared to Kitty and Lydia, mostly because of her shyness, I think, yet I do believe I have detected a small streak of playfulness that wants only a little encouragement to blossom into a very fine wit. I have added her edification to my list of duties.

I will end, for I could write another eight or ten sides and not impart half of what I have to tell. I will save it all for subsequent letters or, better yet, for your visit. I await your response impatiently and hope to hear of all your adventures in London and plans for travelling north.

With the warmest affection,
Lizzy

Sunday, 2 August 1812: Derbyshire

It was a moment after Miss Darcy played the last chord of her aria before Mary recollected herself and applauded. Rarely had she heard the pianoforte performed with such proficiency and elegance of expression. So great was her awe that she was unusually unwilling to accede to Mrs. Gardiner's suggestion that she play next.

"I cannot but think the comparison would show me to great disadvantage."

"That is easily resolved," Elizabeth announced, standing up. "I shall play first; then all subsequent comparisons will be favourable to you."

Mary felt a swell of gratitude then a twinge of sadness that her sister was forever gone from Longbourn. As all eyes followed Elizabeth to the instrument, she took a deep breath to compose herself. She had arrived with her aunt and uncle, as planned, the previous afternoon. It had been an unnerving day, for her new brother was a formidable man and Pemberley vast. This afternoon, the gentlemen had left the women on their own and gone fishing. Two hours of feminine conversation had returned Mary to some semblance of equanimity, but it did not require much to remind her how far removed she was from her usual sphere. She marvelled that her sister showed no sign of being similarly daunted. To all appearances, she was as well settled as though she had lived her entire life in such grandeur.

Elizabeth fudged and faltered her way through a minuet before calling upon Mary and Miss Darcy to join her in playing a trio. After but three bars and thrice as many mistakes, however, she threw her hands in the air.

"'Tis no good! You two had much better play without me."

"You did not play so very ill, Lizzy," Miss Darcy hastened to assure her.

Mary said naught. Her earlier gratitude notwithstanding, she had dearly wished to impress Miss Darcy and would have made no mistakes at all had Elizabeth not forced several upon her. She would have thought, with an instrument as fine as this to play and a husband as grand as Mr. Darcy to please, her sister might trouble herself to practice more often.

"Mary does not agree," Elizabeth said with a wink as she stood to rummage through the sheets of music atop the piano. "What say I find a reel that we might all dance a little?"

"A reel, Lizzy?" Mrs. Gardiner said with a raised eyebrow and a smirk. "Hardly a dance befitting the mistress of Pemberley."

"I daresay nobody will be surprised," Elizabeth replied. "Very little of what I have done thus far befits the mistress of Pemberley."

"I have seen you do nothing unbefitting of your situation," Miss Darcy said. She sounded more than a little alarmed, reminding Mary how unaccustomed she must be to Elizabeth's teasing.

"I agree," she added, more for Miss Darcy's sake than Elizabeth's. "You seem remarkably capable to me."

"You are both invaluable as sisters, discerning none of my mistakes, but I assure you the servants have noticed."

Mrs. Annesley, Mary observed, had picked up her hoop and was too busy attending to her stitches to contradict Elizabeth as she described the butler's horror the first time she returned home from a walk, caked in countryside.

"Though I believe it was my attempt to come into the house via the kitchens that most horrified him. I would have been better advised to trample the clean carpets than his sensibilities."

"Oh, is that why Cook was in a lather on Wednesday?" Miss Darcy enquired.

"No. That was due to my trespassing in her domain to hang some flowers to dry."

"You are not supposed to go below stairs at all?" Mary queried.

"I only think I need to announce myself in future. I had on an apron, cap, and old walking dress, and the poor woman mistook me for a maid. She served me the sharp edge of her tongue before she recognised me."

"Oh my! What did you do?" Miss Darcy exclaimed fretfully.

Mary was unsurprised to hear her sister say she had only laughed.

"Might I suggest you make an effort not to shock your poor staff with such regularity? You would not like to sink any further in their esteem," Mrs. Gardiner ventured. Her tone, which verged on admonishing, caused a fluttering in Mary's stomach, for it made her wonder whether Elizabeth had not been teasing when she decried her performance as mistress.

"No, indeed! I have mortified them all enough," Elizabeth agreed. "I thought my lady's maid would faint when she caught me mending my own chemise. Still," she added, looking up from her search and grinning at them all, "if my husband can tolerate my unfashionable independence, I am sure the staff will grow accustomed to it in time."

Mary knew not whether to be diverted or dismayed. That her sister should be struggling to adapt to her new life would have been vastly distressing but for the fact that Elizabeth did not seem in the least perturbed by her professed insufficiencies. She had no time to do aught more than frown over it. Having found the piece of music for which she had been looking, Elizabeth announced her intention to have the staff move the furniture aside. Rather than walking around the piano to the bell pull, however, she squeezed between the stool and a nearby pedestal, sending the very expensive-looking miniature bust atop the latter sailing to its demise.

No one spoke as all five women congregated around the shattered figurine, each gazing down upon it with various degrees of alarm.

"Whose likeness was that, Georgiana?" Elizabeth said quietly.

"I am not sure. Nobody I knew."

Elizabeth breathed a sigh of relief. "Well, then, do any of you think Darcy will notice?"

"My dear girl," said Mrs. Gardiner, "your husband is apparently blind to just about everything where you are concerned! I daresay you could string the pieces together and hang them as bunting, and he would not blame you for it."

This comment, after a short, shocked silence, set them all off into the peals of laughter that consumed them still when Mr. Darcy and Mr. Gardiner entered the room. Having the most direct view of the door, Mary noticed them first and watched with considerable trepidation as Mr. Darcy took in the scene.

It was her uncle who first spoke. "It seems we need not have been concerned for their entertainment after all, Darcy. They appear to have been amusing themselves perfectly well without us."

All four of the other women started and spun around.

"So it would seem," Mr. Darcy said, his gaze fixed upon Elizabeth as he crossed the room and came around the piano to discover the source of their amusement.

Mary fought the absurd impulse to whimper.

Elizabeth only grimaced contritely—and barely so. "Forgive me. I was a little too eager to begin dancing."

"You intended to dance?" he enquired gravely, adding, when she nodded, "Without me?"

Elizabeth broke into an exceptionally mischievous smile. "Yes, I felt a great inclination to seize the opportunity to dance a reel."

Miss Darcy sucked in her breath. Mary quite agreed with her apprehension. She thought she might cry when Mr. Darcy turned his piercing gaze upon her—until he smiled. Then she thought she might swoon.

"Mary, would you be so kind as to play for us?"

She nodded mutely, but he could not have seen, for his eyes were already upon Elizabeth again.

"I am suddenly tempted to dance myself."

Mary watched, incredulous, as Elizabeth accepted his proffered hand and stepped clear of the broken bust.

"Yes, mind not old Tobias," Mr. Darcy said, so dryly it almost belied the glint in his eye. "He only built the place."

Elizabeth was yet smiling over that remark when all the chairs had been pushed aside and her husband whisked her with improbable dignity into the first figure of a most undignified reel.

Thursday, 6 August 1812: Derbyshire

Elizabeth returned to her bedchamber to find her aunt as she had left her, wandering the room, peering curiously at everything. She closed the door behind her. "There, he knows you are here and will not disturb us or wander into the room in his undress."

Mrs. Gardiner looked at her in mild surprise. "He does not knock before entering?"

"Not usually," she answered, sitting on the bed and curling her feet beneath her.

Her aunt turned fully towards her, her surprise transformed into alarm. "He ought to! Do not be afraid to ask it of him."

"I have no wish for him to knock first. We are very easy with each other. We come and go as we please between all our rooms."

Her aunt looked decidedly sceptical. "Familiarity is one thing; privacy is quite another. What if you are…you know…"

"I have a separate room for my toilette."

"No, no—well, yes, that is bad enough, but what if you are unclothed?"

Elizabeth laughed. "Well, forgive me, but that is often the point of his coming in."

Her aunt's eyebrows shot up divertingly. "Indeed! I did mean to enquire whether you were yet comfortable with the intimacies of married life, but I take it you have overcome any trepidation in that quarter?"

She nodded, unable to keep from grinning.

"Lizzy, you look unpardonably smug."

"Do I?"

"You know you do. And let us not be shy about it: you have good reason. Your husband is an uncommonly handsome man—with something particularly pleasing about his mouth when he speaks."

Elizabeth wondered whether her aunt knew she was blushing and if that was why she changed the subject.

"Tell me: Is Jane as contented with Mr. Bingley?"

The question caught Elizabeth by surprise. She pulled a pillow from behind her and hugged it to her chest. "Truly, I could not tell you. She was not happy with *me* when I saw her last. How happy she is with her husband was not something she wished to discuss."

Mrs. Gardiner came to join her, perching on the edge of the bed. "Why was she unhappy with you?"

"She was upset that I neglected her at Lady Ashby's ball."

"I do not take your meaning. In what way did you neglect her?"

"She felt I cared only for my own reception and paid no heed to how she was treated—which, by her account, was with a marked want of respect."

"Well, what on earth did she expect? Fanfares? She is not of the same sphere."

Elizabeth shrugged. "Neither am I."

"But you are now, Lizzy. If Jane imagined she would be received with the same deference as Mrs. Darcy of Pemberley, she was dreaming. She ought to be careful. She will make people think she is jealous."

"Darcy said something very similar. I do not wish to believe it of her though."

"Neither do I, but we are none of us without faults."

"True, but why should Jane be jealous? She is five times as pretty as I and ten times as good."

Mrs. Gardiner leant back against the bedpost, rearranging her skirts around her. "Mayhap, therein lies the rub. How often have you lauded Jane's goodness? How often does your mother boast of her beauty?"

"Often, I suppose. Why?"

"I can conceive that being told constantly she is superior to all her sisters and friends might have instilled in her a propensity to resent anything—or anyone—who makes her feel inferior." There was a pause. "I suspect, presently, that anyone is you."

"Yes, I gathered you were heading in that direction," Elizabeth replied miserably. "But Jane has never coveted greater consequence. I cannot comprehend why she should suddenly be envious of my having a superior situation."

"Perhaps not of your better situation, per se, but that your situation means you are better admired."

"Hardly!" Elizabeth exclaimed, with a bitter bark of laughter. "Half of society despises me, and the rest is completely indifferent to me!"

Mrs. Gardiner raised an eyebrow. "Truly? Because Jane's grievances, as you have related them, rather suggest it was she to whom society was indifferent and you whom they admired."

Elizabeth shook her head, wondering vaguely when it had begun to ache. "Jane may have been less admired than she felt she deserved, but I assure you she was under no illusion that I fared any better. Indeed, she went to great lengths to ensure I understood just how ill my new family thought of me." She picked unhappily at the pillow's trim. "They will never like me, apparently, if I do not learn to respect them properly."

When she received no answer, she looked up and was taken aback to discover Mrs. Gardiner's lips pressed together into a tight line and her countenance stained an angry red. "What is it?"

"I am loath to say too much more, for I would not stir ill-feeling between the pair of you, but I regret it sounds very much as though Jane has maligned your success merely to lessen her own disillusionment."

Elizabeth recoiled. That Jane should feel some jealousy for their altered situations was, perhaps, only natural. That she should blame her for it, consciously set out to punish her for it, was inexpressibly painful. "Think you that was her design?"

"I sincerely hope it was not her design, but it may well have been unconsciously done."

Elizabeth felt quite nauseous with dismay, yet a friendship such as hers and Jane's was too important to be forsaken over such a nasty little thing as jealousy, and she was nothing if not obstinate. "Then I shall just have to convince her she has nothing of which to be jealous, shall I not?"

Her aunt smiled warmly. "And I have every faith you will put it all to rights, Lizzy, but you look tired. Let us speak no more of it this evening." After a fond goodnight, she left to find her own apartments.

Mere moments after Elizabeth closed the door to the hall behind her aunt, the one from the sitting room opened, and Darcy, after a quick glance to ensure she was alone, stalked in.

"Forgive me, Elizabeth, I know I said I would wait, but truly, what can you possibly have been discussing with your aunt for so long that you have not already spoken of this past week?"

She meant to tease him for his disgruntlement, but instead surprised herself by feeling suddenly tearful. "We were talking about Jane."

His countenance was overcome with alarm, and he strode across the room to embrace her. "What in God's name has been said?"

"Oh, nothing new. Only what passed between us in London. Forgive me. I know not why I am allowing it to upset me so. I am only tired, I think."

She promptly found herself whisked off her feet and carried directly to her bed. He joined her, lying on his side with his head propped on one hand, and wiped away her tears with his thumb.

"I shall write to Bingley and tell him not to come," he said so very gently.

"No," Elizabeth answered sleepily. "Pray, do not. I should like to see Jane. To set matters aright."

She was sunk too far into sleep to discern what he said in response. She knew only, as she drifted off, that his assurances were whispered so tenderly and his caresses so gentle, she could not have remained awake had she tried.

Friday, 7 August 1812: Derbyshire

Darcy caught his breath when he espied her. She stood at the top of the steps just beyond the main door, half-illuminated by the sunlight cascading around her, humming quietly as she awaited the rest of the party.

Her distress and fatigue the previous evening had alarmed him greatly, for though little in the world compared to the contentment of watching her sleep in his arms, he was unused to seeing aught akin to fragility in her. To see her now banished all his concern. She was breathtaking—radiant of complexion, comely of figure, assured of carriage—and *his.* He moved to stand directly behind her and put his lips to her ear. "I swear you grow more tempting by the day."

She jumped, gasping and laughing, though she made no attempt to move away. Indeed, she arched her back slightly to press her temple to his cheek. Whether it was also intentional that her buttocks pressed against him he could not be sure, but he thought it probable. He made a small, strangled noise, and his hands flew to her hips to stay her motion ere she rendered him indecent. "My God, woman, I am on my knees for you."

She turned to face him and raised one delicious eyebrow. "Now *that* is an intriguing prospect."

Dear Lord, would she slay him here in the hall? "Pray, torture me not! I am only human, Elizabeth, and you are divine."

She gave no response. With naught but a saucy smirk, she was gone, walking around him to greet her aunt, uncle and sister, just arriving downstairs with Georgiana. He had married the Devil in a siren's guise! Biting the inside of his cheek to suppress an exultant smile, he straightened his attire, that he might at least appear outwardly composed, and turned to escort their guests to the awaiting carriage.

"We have thoroughly enjoyed our visit, Darcy," Mr. Gardiner said as they walked outside. "Pemberley is without equal, and you and Lizzy have been delightful hosts. I cannot thank you enough for making us so welcome."

"It has been our pleasure," Darcy replied. "We are delighted you have agreed to come back at Christmas. Pemberley is an enchanting place for young children. I hope yours will enjoy it."

"I have no doubt they will, sir, though whether Pemberley will like them quite as well in return by the end of the visit remains to be seen."

"It has weathered worse in its time, I am sure."

"And will again, I should not wonder, for if they are aught like their mother, then any children of Lizzy's are unlikely to be particularly tractable, I am sorry to say."

Darcy agreed with a small smile that did not come close to expressing his eagerness to begin a family with Elizabeth. The prospect of establishing his own legacy at Pemberley—of its being Elizabeth with whom he did so, of seeing her make a child in her image and in her body—was one he anticipated with absurd impatience.

At the foot of the stairs, Mr. Gardiner paused to say goodbye to his niece, and Darcy turned to bid farewell to the ladies. His happy reflections having put him in an exceedingly good humour, he was moved to kiss each of their hands as he helped them into the carriage. Mary smiled and wished him well. Mrs. Gardiner audibly sucked in her breath and stumbled on the steps.

Keeping hold of her hand to steady her, Darcy leant to better see her face around the rim of her bonnet, enquiring gently after her well-being. Her eyes, when they met his, widened ever so slightly, and she promptly flushed bright red, skewering him squarely betwixt amusement and mortification. For though humility demanded he admit it to no one, he was not unconscious of his looks, and hers was not an unprecedented reaction.

"Silly me, I missed the step," she said, all but leaping into the carriage.

"Oh, I shall miss you, Lizzy!" Mary said, leaning back out of the door to squeeze her sister's hands, as close to high emotion as Darcy had ever seen her. "Pray write often and visit us at Longbourn as soon as may be."

"There, there now, child," Mr. Gardiner said, shooing her back into her seat as he climbed in. "You have been away as long as your sister has. It is time we took you home." He indicated that the driver should set off then raised his hat cordially. "Thank you again, Lizzy, Darcy, Miss Darcy. Until Christmas!"

A chorus of goodbyes arose between them all as the carriage pulled away. Darcy observed Elizabeth from the corner of his eye, hopeful that her relations' departure would not distress her overmuch. On the contrary, she showed every sign of being greatly diverted.

"What amuses you?"

She made a poor attempt to conceal her mirth and shrugged. "Nothing."

"You are determined to exclude me from *all* your jokes?"

"No, only some of them."

"Have I not demonstrated my capacity for extracting information?"

"Yes, very well, but I am wise to your methods now."

God, he wanted to kiss her. He wished his sister were not there, staring at them aghast as though they were hurling oaths at each other. Keeping his expression perfectly blank, he looked back to the disappearing carriage.

"You have no respect for me whatsoever, wife. I ought to have invited your aunt to stay. *She* is not so impervious to my charms."

He vastly enjoyed Elizabeth's surprise, by now of the firm opinion he must take his victories whenever he could with her.

"You know full well what diverted me!" she cried, laughing.

It was his turn to shrug. If he had noticed Mrs. Gardiner's discomposure, it was no great surprise her niece might have.

"Which is a shame," she continued, "for I was thinking, had you got down on your knees, I might have been persuaded to tell you."

Thus, she effortlessly reclaimed the victory and ran off gaily, leaving brother and sister staring after her in astonishment—the former wondering how on earth he was to reassure the latter that his wife did not truly expect him to beg, despite that being precisely what he meant to do.

Scarisbrick, Hampshire
August 8

Dearest Jane,

I thank you for your letter and good wishes. You are too kind. We are indeed having a wonderful time. This year's gathering is even better than last since the Countess of Paignton is among the party. Of course, you could not know her reputation for fun, so you must take my word that we are all having a lark. And my, my! Your sojourns about London seem to have kept you busy! I myself frequent the places you describe but rarely, but I am delighted to hear they pleased you so well.

Now, as to your reluctance to visit E. I entreat you not to refuse her invitation. Have I not counselled that a breach would be ill advised? Besides, if B's letter to D did indeed make no mention of visiting them, it seems I was correct, and his interest has already run its course; thus, there can be little to fear on that score. I say go, enjoy the many delights of P, and should E's teasing and flirting prove no better, you may commiserate with me at your leisure.

Indeed, pray write to me anyway with news of how she gets on, for I should be vastly comforted to know D does not regret his choice. Your mention of her struggles with her new role is a cause for great alarm in that regard, though little surprise. I can only hope the mistakes to which she alluded in her letter to you are neither too many nor too egregious. Mayhap when you visit, you might show her by your example how a woman ought to be sensible of her station?

I wish you a happy wedding trip and look forward with relish to your next letter.

Lady Ashby

9

Of Revelations and Resentment

Friday, 14 August 1812: Derbyshire

One month of marriage had not diminished Elizabeth's happiness in any way, and familiarity had not dampened her bliss. She still woke each morning as surprised as the last to find herself a woman married, still delighted every day in discovering more to love in her husband, and still marvelled constantly at her new situation.

Much of what there was to marvel could be seen from her bedroom windows as she idled at her dressing table, quietly humming the tune she had been practicing that afternoon and brushing her freshly washed hair. It was into this bubble of utopian contentment that Darcy stormed with a quantity of papers in his hand, an angry imprecation on his lips and a savage scowl upon his countenance.

"Of all the vexing, ill-timed mishaps!" He strode back and forth across the floor. "I never heard such a catalogue of poor excuses and incompetence! He ought to have put Ennings to the job in the first place. A leg will not mend before the harvest. Magnus will have to journey from Kympton! Blast it, Barnaby!"

"Fitzwilliam, is there some way in which I can help?"

"What? No. No." He shook his head and continued pacing for a moment then whirled back to her. "I must postpone our trip tomorrow."

This news brought Elizabeth nothing but relief. They had visited several local towns that week already and dined with neighbours twice, and she was exceedingly tired. A long jostling carriage ride to Buxton had lost all its appeal. She opened her mouth to tell him she had no objection to the delay when he abruptly set off about the room again, fuming about the as-yet-unspecified calamity. Her third attempt to regain his attention silenced him at last.

"Fitzwilliam, what exactly has Mr. Barnaby done?"

His countenance darkened further still, and his answer, when he gave it, took her by surprise, for it had naught to do with legs, harvests, or trips to Buxton. "He has asked me to be godfather to his new son."

The cogs of her mind laboured to fathom why on earth that might have distressed him. Her heart squeezed when she comprehended the answer, but once again, before she had the chance to speak, he took to pacing and bemoaning Mr. Barnaby's ineptitude.

Despite his pique, Elizabeth found herself smiling fondly at him, for it was becoming ever clearer that he had come to her seeking neither advice nor answers but only to vent his spleen. After all her regrets to have left him broken-hearted and comfortless following their quarrel in Kent, she rejoiced at being able to provide him such consolation. She returned to brushing her hair and simply watched him, content to let him rail until his ire ran cool—and rail he did.

"There is not room enough for Magnus to board with Powell or Craig. I shall have to reopen the long barn and have it fitted out for all the extra hands."

He paused to send her an exasperated glance, and she smiled sympathetically.

"Ennings will have to stand in for Donaghue—no! There is the north gable to be seen to this autumn, so he cannot be spared, either."

She thought he might be biting off an oath when he snapped his mouth shut and threw her another irate scowl. She smiled again.

"Somebody else will have to be found," he resumed. "God alone knows who will replace Donaghue permanently if his leg does not heal! How Barnaby thinks to arrange it all before he leaves for York is the devil's own guess. And this—*this*—is the day the man thinks it prudent to ask me to be godfather to his child! Would that he ask his brother, or cousin, or one of the damned *sheep*, for I want no part of it, and for the love of God, would you *cease your infernal humming, woman!*"

They both froze, staring at each other, dumbstruck. Darcy looked horrified. Elizabeth was immobilised with the near-insurmountable urge to guffaw. Persuaded by his vast dismay that now would be the most inappropriate time to do so, she turned away to hide her smirk.

"Dear Lord, I beg you would forgive me, Elizabeth. That was unpardonable."

Would that he be less contrite, that her amusement might seem less unfeeling! Her shoulders began to shake with silent laughter.

He was at her side in an instant. "Love, pray do not cry. I am sorry."

Oh, good heavens, he thought she was weeping! A snort of laughter burst from her lips, and she clamped a hand over her mouth, shaking her head for him to cease apologising, but he would not desist. He reached for her hand and turned her gently but insistently to face him. His expression was one of mortified concern—briefly. It was soon overtaken with confusion then affront.

"You are not crying."

"No." She sniggered despite herself and pressed her lips closed.

He stepped away from her. "You are laughing."

"Yes, a little."

"Elizabeth, I just bellowed at you."

"I noticed."

"I fail to see the humour in that! I have never shouted at a person in such a manner in my life! That I should have done so at you is insupportable!"

"Ah, but you have never had a *me* before to cut up your peace and turn your world upside down. Besides, you would not be the first person to be irritated by my humming."

"Your humming does not irritate me, not usually."

She supposed growing up almost as an only child meant he was unaccustomed to the compromises and vexations of living with another person. She felt a little teasing was in order to compensate for his deprivation. "'Tis well, Fitzwilliam, I am not offended. Your pacing does not usually irritate me, either."

He frowned at her. "My pacing?"

"You pace, more so when you are agitated. But it is not as vexing as your teeth grinding."

"What teeth grinding?"

Elizabeth thought he was doing an admirable job of maintaining his dudgeon, given her own broadening grin. How she adored him and his silly pride! "When you are concentrating, you grind your teeth."

"I do not."

"And you sneeze too loudly."

"I beg your pardon?"

"When you sneeze, you do so exceptionally loudly."

"What sort of objection is that? One cannot regulate the volume of one's sneezes."

She shrugged her shoulders. "It makes me jump."

At last his lips quirked. "Is there aught else?"

"That will do for now."

He reached for her hands and pulled her up off the stool and into his embrace, his mouth upon hers ere she was on her feet. It was over too soon, yet for all its brevity, his kiss left her breathless and flushed.

"I am so in love with you, Elizabeth."

"Despite my humming?"

"Your humming is Mozart to mine ears."

She giggled, but her smile faded as her thoughts sobered. She placed a hand upon his chest and looked up at him earnestly. "You know, Fitzwilliam, you are not your father. And Mr. Barnaby's son is not George Wickham. You are not destined to repeat their mistakes."

He sighed heavily. "I know, but I cannot abide the thought of imposing the same blight upon my own children."

"It will not go the same. We shall make sure of it. Do not let your resentment for a bad man lead you to offend a good one."

"You are right, of course." He kissed her once more and released her, turning to retrieve his papers from the table. "I am sorry we can no longer go to Buxton tomorrow," he said, holding up a letter from the pile and peering at it as though noticing it for the first time. "I am certain you will like the place very well."

"I am sure I shall." She returned to her stool and picked up her brush once more. "But it will still be there next week. We need not explore the whole of Derbyshire in my first month here."

He did not answer, for he had begun reading the letter, and his countenance, so recently relieved of its angry glower, was very rapidly being overspread with an even stormier expression. "God in Heaven, what is the man thinking?" He threw the sheaf of papers back on the table and turned away in disgust, one hand planted firmly on his hip, the other rubbing his jaw.

"Whatever is the matter now?"

"Montgomery has offered for Anne."

Elizabeth winced. "Well, you knew it was probable. You will just have to accept it."

"That is precisely what he expects me to do," he said, turning to face her. "He wishes me to stand up with him at his wedding. To set aside all my grievances with Lady Catherine as though our estrangement were nothing more than a trifling squabble! But I cannot forgive her; thus, I must disappoint him."

Elizabeth set her brush down. "Will you not even consider reconciliation?" she said cautiously. "For your friend's sake and your cousin's if not your own."

"How can you even entertain the notion after the way she has treated you? She has been insufferable throughout this whole affair."

"She has always been insufferable. She is hardly likely to change at this late stage."

He gestured widely with his hands. "And so I told Montgomery, yet he has chosen to ignore my warning and offer for Anne anyway!"

Elizabeth sat back in surprise. "Did you advise Mr. Montgomery against marrying Anne?"

"I did not," he said firmly. When she raised an eyebrow in challenge, his gaze hardened. "I gave him no unsolicited advice. He sought my opinion of the match."

Her surprise ceded to dismay and then anger. "And you clearly expected your reply to put him off! What did you say?"

"The truth! That Lady Catherine is poisonous and disloyal."

"He is not marrying Lady Catherine!" Elizabeth cried, coming to her feet. "I am beginning to think this has less to do with Mr. Montgomery's happiness than it does your resentfulness."

"I beg your pardon?"

"Your poor friend came to you for your opinion—nay, I daresay your approval of the match. You did him a disservice if you thought only of your own objections in answering him."

"I resent that!" he replied icily. "I said nothing that was not true of the woman who would be his mother were he to enter into the union. Do not underestimate with what caution a man must consider that encumbrance!"

Nothing was as likely to provoke Elizabeth's ire as a reminder of his previous disdain for her family. "You may have been honest about that, but did you consider what comfort it might be to Anne to have a husband or what consolation she might afford his motherless son? Did you mention that his investment would save Rosings or that you should like to be his cousin? Or did you omit all these facts in favour of persisting with your grudge?"

Darcy hesitated, but righteous indignation rapidly overtook any remorse he might have been about to express. "I have been used to consider that a wife will support her husband in such matters."

"Forgive me if I do not agree with your every utterance, Fitzwilliam, but I shall not feel obliged to if you are wrong!"

"No! You are still determined to be more concerned with the misfortunes of the rest of the world than you are with mine!"

The injustice of that charge drew a wordless exclamation from Elizabeth's lips. "On the contrary! I am entirely concerned with my husband's propensity to impose his implacable resentment on the affairs of perfectly undeserving individuals!" She knew then she had said too much. Her stomach lurched hideously to see his expression turn to ice.

"I thank you for expressing your opinion so eloquently, madam." He left without another word, slamming the door behind him. One or two heartbeats of silent anguish followed then Elizabeth sank onto the foot of the bed, one hand to her mouth, and stared in dismay at the closed door.

Oh, she had made him angry! And wherefore? Granted, it was disappointing that he had not given Mr. Montgomery fair counsel, but what did it matter to her whom that man wed? Why, oh why, had she argued the point when she knew how deeply he felt Lady Catherine's betrayal? She, who had promised to love him better than his ignoble aunt and, not ten minutes ago, congratulated herself on being able to console him in his distress!

Resolving immediately to find him that she might hold him and comfort him as he deserved, she set about making herself presentable to leave her room. She paused on her way out to collect the papers he had left behind. As she put the pages of Mr. Montgomery's letter back in order, her eye was drawn to a particular word on the second page that threw all thoughts of their disagreement from her mind. Not wishing to be mistaken about such a thing, she read further and was dismayed to discover her fears founded. Carefully, she refolded the letter and left in search of her husband, steeling herself for a far greater test of her ability to comfort him than either of them would wish.

Darcy stared unseeing from his study window, his jaw clenched and his grip on his tumbler fierce. He was angry—furious, in fact. At whom, was a point on which he vacillated by the moment. His feelings towards his aunt remained inimical in every respect. She had maligned his honour, contested his authority, scorned his happiness, conveniently forgotten his lifelong loyalty, and dared to insult and intimidate his wife. His feelings towards the man who would have him overlook all that and reinstate the connection merely for his own convenience were presently not much better and quite at war with the established regard and gratitude he held for him.

Then there was his wife. Not since he was a boy had he been required to justify himself to another person, yet here he was at almost thirty years of age, somehow accountable to a woman who questioned his integrity at every turn. And damn it if she was not always bloody right!

He threw back a mouthful of brandy. Evidently, he had learnt nothing from the manifold lessons in compassion, tolerance and forgiveness he had received in recent months. Elizabeth knew it and thought ill of him for it, and that made him excessively angry with himself.

The door clicked open and the reflection in the window showed his judge and juror stepping into the room. He wished she had stayed away longer, that he might have regained some measure of equanimity before being required to account for his behaviour. "Have you come to carry your point, madam?"

"No, Fitzwilliam."

He was not familiar with her expression. It made him excessively uneasy. "What then?"

She came to stand in front of him and held out what looked to be the papers he had left in her bedroom. "Darling, you need to finish Mr. Montgomery's letter." She bit her bottom lip and said no more, but continued to regard him anxiously.

He set his drink down on his desk and took the letter from her, skipping directly to the part he had not yet read. Moments later, he lowered himself into his chair, propped his elbow on the armrest and covered his face with his hand. "Damn."

Here, then, was the motivation for his aunt's recent behaviour—her anger at his refusal to marry Anne, her furious objections when he withdrew his resources from Rosings. Lady Catherine was dying.

Elizabeth came to him, cradling his head against her stomach and whispering tender words of comfort. He wrapped his arms about her hips and held onto her.

"I ought to have seen it," he whispered gruffly. "She has been unwell, coughing for months."

"None of us suspected. Not me, not your uncle, not Fitzwilliam. You could not have known. Montgomery says it took the word of two physicians to make her admit it."

He was momentarily rendered mute by the passing thought that his mother would have been devastated by this news. He leant further into Elizabeth's embrace. "Why did she not tell me?"

"I do not know. Perhaps she did not realise. Or perhaps she did, and once she comprehended your resolve not to have Anne, she did not wish to force your hand."

He looked up at her incredulously. "Why then did she go to such lengths to prevent me from marrying you?"

"Not compelling you to marry her daughter is a far cry from condoning your marriage to somebody like me. It is possible she believed she had your best interests in mind in both cases."

"But why persist now we are wed? She has only driven me farther away when she needs me most."

Elizabeth smiled sadly. "Resentment is rarely reasonable."

Darcy stared, dismayed. To all this, his damned, stupid resentment had blinded him! That same bitterness of spirit Elizabeth plagued him constantly to forswear. Pray that she never ceased plaguing him, for she would make him a better man than he could ever hope to be without her. He tugged her down into his lap, rested his forehead on her shoulder and entrusted his sorrow to her embrace. "Thank God for you."

Tuesday, 18 August 1812: Yorkshire

"The weather looks to be clearing at last," Charles announced.

Caroline looked up from her needlework and peered dubiously at what little of the day she could see from the minuscule sash window opposite. The sky looked to her much the same as it had all day: dull.

"Yes, it is brightening a little, I think," agreed Jane, predictably.

Frowning, Caroline turned to look through the marginally larger casement behind her, unsurprised to discover the sky every bit as dreary in that direction as the other—which fairly well epitomised the entire trip thus far. She returned to her work without comment.

"I thought it might begin to before long," Charles persisted. "The clouds were not so dark this morning as yesterday."

"Aye, nor the air so frigid."

"I must say, I had forgotten quite how unsettled the weather in the north could be. Still, the wind has dropped, and it is no longer raining. Shall we all walk out? We could take up Cousin Helena's invitation to join them for tea."

"Oh, yes—" Jane began.

Oh, pray, no! "Surely, we have visited enough relations to justify the trip now, Charles?" Caroline interrupted. "How many more afternoons of drinking revolting tea in cramped, unfashionable parlours must we endure in order to satisfy your notion of a wedding tour? May we not enjoy some more refined entertainment for the remainder of our travels?"

"Caroline!"

"Well really, Charles! Is it imperative that you make claim to every distant relative of ours who is still in trade? Are we to journey to Nova Scotia next for a tour of the hole you have sponsored my cousin to dig?"

"Our family's condition in life is neither here nor there. I wished to introduce my wife."

It vexed Caroline to observe Jane visibly preen at this. The woman was as obtuse as her husband. "Very quixotic, I am sure, but goodness knows Jane has enough unfortunate relations of her own to consider without ferreting out every one of yours as well. God forbid any of my friends should learn I passed my summer traipsing through the dockyards and woollen mills of the north. Or yours, Jane! What would Lady Ashby say?"

Jane's eyes widened. "Would she disapprove?"

"Of course she would!" How this could surprise her, Caroline knew not, yet clearly it did, for she paled and addressed her husband in alarm.

"Perhaps it would be wiser not to advance these acquaintances if it will injure our reputation."

That only made Charles pout. "There is no reason to think the injury to my reputation will be any different presently than it has been these past three-and-twenty years."

"Precisely," said Caroline, maddened by his stupidity.

"I am sure they are all respectable people," Jane pressed, "but is it quite proper that we should visit their homes?"

"If Lizzy did not consider it improper to receive your relations at Pemberley, I daresay you shall survive the degradation of visiting mine, for you cannot believe you are superior to your own sister!"

Jane flushed livid red. Caroline sighed inwardly. She had never ascertained what Jane knew of Charles's *tendre* for Eliza Darcy, though her dismissal of the facsimile maid made it probable she harboured suspicions. In any case, she required no further cause to suspect, for it was foolish to hope that, if Jane discovered the truth, she would not tell her sister and inconceivable that, if Mrs. Darcy discovered it, then her husband would not. Caroline shuddered to think what Darcy would then do. A hasty recovery was required.

"Yes, well, Jane is in possession of a little more sophistication than her sister. You ought to be grateful for her attempts to save you the same indignities Darcy is suffering."

"What reason have you to suspect Darcy is suffering indignities? I cannot imagine Lizzy is giving him cause to repine."

Caroline closed her eyes. You could lead a horse to water, but her brother would always be an incurable idiot.

"And yet she is," Jane said coldly. "Only this morning I received a letter from her in which she owned to quarrelling with him already."

"What? Why? What about?" Charles jabbered.

"By her own admission, she is driving him distracted. Which I can well believe, for she does the same to me! Excuse me, I would write to my friend." With that, Jane stood and flounced from the room.

Caroline glared at her brother, shaking her head. "I had thought your foolish infatuation with Mrs. Darcy was done."

"It is! I was only concerned that she and Darcy have been arguing."

"Married couples do!"

"Jane and I do not."

"True, but then what is there about which to disagree when all you ever discuss is the weather? The Darcys' marriage is none of your business, and you must not attempt to make it so!"

He had no answer to that. After a few minutes of frowning and folding and unfolding his arms and legs, Caroline suggested he be the one to call on their cousin Helena and begged him to inform her that both she and Jane were indisposed. With no reasonable cause to refuse, he reluctantly yielded to her persuasion and left.

Caroline persisted with her embroidery until frustration began to spoil her stitches, at which point she threw her hoop aside and crossed her arms with an angry growl. She had been so looking forward to arriving at Pemberley! Despite the injustice of having been overlooked for its mistress in favour of the objectionable hellcat Darcy had married, it was still one of her favourite places to visit and a far cry from the hovel in which they presently lodged. Now, with the threat of her brother's wayward affections being exposed, the visit held all the appeal of a holiday in Cádiz.

Wednesday, 2 September 1812: Derbyshire

The day of her sister's visit arrived, and Elizabeth awoke feeling entirely unrested with an aching head and a distinctly unsettled stomach. She lay motionless on her back, breathing deeply in the hope the feeling would ease but smiling at a burgeoning sense of excitement.

Though it might be only anxiety for her reunion with Jane, she had reason to hope there was another, happier explanation for her biliousness. She had awoken in a similar state on several mornings of late, but only yesterday begun to suspect the cause. Then it had been poor Georgiana's fractious tears and pimpled skin that roused the suspicion in her mind. For whilst sympathising with her sister over the bane of monthly courses, it occurred to her that, since marrying, she herself had not been thus afflicted.

"Elizabeth, are you unwell?"

She had thought Darcy asleep. Her heart leapt at the prospect of revealing to him her suspicions. "A little unsettled," she admitted.

"You slept very ill," he said gently, rolling to face her with a concerned frown. "Would that you had let me put them off. I do not like that you are this ill at ease."

She likewise rolled towards him and then regretted doing so as a wave of nausea assailed her. "I am not convinced that would have helped in this instance."

"Should you feel better if you ate something?"

The prospect was surprisingly appealing. "Yes, I think I might."

Darcy rose immediately to summon Wetherby. Elizabeth rued her missed opportunity but supposed it would be better to share her momentous hopes in a less dishevelled state in any case. She removed to her own room to attend to her toilette, tidy her hair, and don a shawl. By the time she was done, breakfast had been laid out in the sitting room, and Darcy had prepared her a plate.

"Thank you," she said, sitting down and reaching for it, though she stopped short of actually taking it. First, the odour and then the sight of the insipid, sweaty heap of congealed buttered eggs piled on the plate turned her stomach so violently she thought she would be ill where she sat. Covering her mouth, she surged to her feet, sending her chair thudding to the floor, and was relieved to reach her washstand before vomiting.

"Elizabeth!"

"A moment!" she gasped, urgently waving him away, having no wish for him to see her thus. He heeded her only until her nausea was passed, then he was at her side, easing her into the chair he had brought from the sitting room. He crouched in front of her, holding her hand in his and peering at her with the greatest alarm.

"Forgive me," she whispered, wrinkling her nose with chagrin. So much for announcing her news in a more dignified manner!

"No, no," he assured her. "Can I get you anything? Would a glass of wine give you some relief?"

"No, I thank you."

"Nothing at all? You are very ill."

She shook her head and could not help but smile. "I think not." He frowned as she knew he would. "Fitzwilliam, I believe I am with child."

He sat back on his heels and stared at her, fixed in astonishment. "Truly?"

"'Tis not certain," she said hastily. "It will be some time before I can be sure."

"But you suspect?"

She nodded, her smile broadening, and that seemed to be enough for him. He gave a triumphant little crow and reared up onto his knees to embrace her, showering her with endearments and telling her of feelings that, in proving of what importance the child was to him, made her even more anxious that her hopes be warranted. He leant back and, with the utmost tenderness, placed a hand on her abdomen. "Dearest Elizabeth! Just as I thought I could not possibly love you more!"

"I hope you will not love me any less if my suspicions come to nothing."

"I shall not dignify that with an answer."

She placed both her hands over his. "I dearly hope I am not mistaken, for I should be the happiest creature alive if it were true."

His smile was wonderful. "When will you know without doubt?"

"When I feel the quickening, I suppose, but that could be many weeks from now, for I have only recently begun to suspect. Pray, let our hopes remain private until they are proved. It is yet very early and…well, nothing is guaranteed."

The turn of his countenance assured her he had taken her meaning. "Will you be able to keep it from your sister?"

"That depends very much on her. I never would have used to think so, but we have shared very few confidences of late."

His smile faded, and his frown returned. He stood up. "I shall not have you distressed, Elizabeth. I shall put them off coming."

"There is no need for that! Besides, 'tis too late. They will be here in a matter of hours."

He was evidently uneasy with the arrangement but conceded there was nothing to be done about it. She mollified him somewhat by agreeing to see the apothecary before their guests arrived.

"You summon him while I eat my breakfast," she suggested.

"Breakfast? You have just been violently ill!"

She stood up and shrugged. "I feel better now. And rather hungry."

He shook his head, smiling with incredulity. "It grieves me that you must suffer in this way, but if you mean to carry it off with such éclat, I think I shall bear it almost as well as you."

A burst of laughter erupted from her lips. Oh, how she loved him!

He left to make the necessary arrangements, though not before placing the most tender of kisses upon her forehead and reiterating how very precious she was to him. She sat down to a breakfast sans eggs, reflecting that, after such a happy beginning, she felt eminently more sanguine about the day ahead.

"There it is!" Caroline exclaimed.

Jane opened her eyes and looked out of the window. What she saw, by contrast, lent the lodgings from which she had departed hours earlier all the proportions of a doll's house. She had considered Elizabeth's mentions of Pemberley in her letters somewhat boastful, but it would seem her sister, in fact, had been rather circumspect in her descriptions. The house was palatial.

"Now that is a welcome sight," Caroline continued. "What an improvement to coaching inns and hotels."

"Is there anything about this trip that you have actually enjoyed, Caroline?" Bingley enquired with uncommon asperity. "I wonder that you agreed to come at all."

"My apologies, Charles," she replied with negligible contrition. "But I confess I have had my fill of inferior lodgings and unappetising food."

"The sooner we arrive, the better then for all our sakes!"

They traversed the rest of the implausibly long drive in silence. Jane assiduously avoided all thoughts of her husband's eagerness to get to the house and concentrated instead on Lady Ashby's counsel to enjoy Pemberley and avoid any contention.

The Darcys awaited them at the foot of a grand set of stairs at the front of the house. Elizabeth had a hand raised to shield her eyes from the sun and was peering towards the carriage. Jane waved, and her sister broke into her customary, broad smile that was all the more welcome for the three weeks Jane had spent visiting strangers. For a moment, Elizabeth was Lizzy again and nothing else mattered—'til the horses stopped and Bingley sprang from the carriage, issuing typically effusive greetings and leaving a footman to hand Jane and Caroline down.

"I am very glad you are come, Jane," Elizabeth said to her after they had embraced. "It is wonderful to see you."

Her feelings in disarray, it was all Jane could do to smile at her.

"Welcome to Pemberley," came Mr. Darcy's sonorous greeting.

Jane felt a small frisson of alarm upon meeting his gaze. He regarded her with peculiar intensity, his expression not cold precisely but with little of the welcome his words professed.

"Thank you," she replied, thoroughly disconcerted.

"I trust your journey was agreeable?"

"Perfectly so, I thank you."

"You say so only because you were able to nap, Jane dearest," Caroline interrupted. "I shall not be so obedient, Mr. Darcy, but shall declare that it was a perfectly horrid journey, too hot and too long by half. We are all excessively fatigued."

"I am sorry to hear that, Miss Bingley."

Elizabeth assured them there was plenty of time to rest before dinner and ushered them all into the house. The hall into which they walked was magnificent and as large as Longbourn. Jane could not help but gape at the grandeur.

"How do you like Pemberley then, Jane?" Bingley enquired, loudly enough that everyone was included in awaiting her answer.

"It is a very fine house, though I have not seen much of it yet."

"Should you like a tour before dinner?" Elizabeth enquired. "I shall endeavour not to get us lost."

"An excellent idea!" Bingley answered for them all. "May I join you?"

"Of course! Though I cannot imagine I will be able to tell you any more than you have already heard from Mrs. Reynolds."

"Sshh!" Bingley implored dramatically. "Say no more, lest my impertinence be found out!"

Oh, my sister and husband have a private joke. How wonderful.

"Too late, Bingley, you are already discovered," Mr. Darcy said.

Bingley clutched at his heart with both hands. "Lizzy! You have betrayed me! How could you?"

"It could not be avoided, I am afraid. I am allowed no secrets," Elizabeth replied, glancing coyly at her husband before indicating they should all follow her upstairs.

Bingley frowned between them both but nonetheless came towards Jane. "Shall we?"

Jane smiled wearily and took his proffered arm.

"Here we are then," he said, quietly this time. "It is impressive, is it not?"

"It certainly is."

"You will like it here, I think. I hope. It is much more comfortable, much grander than…well—that is, I know Caroline has disdained our accommodation on this trip. I apologise if you have been disappointed. I procured the finest lodgings available with your comfort in mind."

"Oh, that is very thoughtful. And they were! Fine, that is. Thank you."

"Of course! Nothing but the best for Mrs. Bingley."

Such solicitude was of vast comfort to Jane's distrustful heart. When he leant closer, it fluttered in anticipation of what further assurances of his esteem he might bestow.

"Do you think your sister looks a little pale?"

It was extremely fortunate Caroline had made such a show of declaring them all fatigued, for it excused Jane from any curiosity as to the peculiarly lengthy amount of time she took to overcome her pique at this remark. She eventually left her room so late there was time enough for only a truncated tour of the principal rooms before dinner. Through seven courses, she then listened to everyone's raptures for the proposed round of picnics, phaeton rides, fishing, hunting, luncheons, cards, music, and more that Elizabeth had planned. None of it persuaded Jane that the week ahead would not feel an eternity to her.

Saturday, 5 September 1812: Derbyshire

Elizabeth was true to her word. There was scarcely a moment over the next three days that was not taken up with some entertainment or other. Saturday heralded the first idle morning of Jane's visit, and she and Caroline were enjoying the balmy summer air in a room whose French windows opened onto a pretty lawn.

The gentlemen had left for a spot of shooting, and later that afternoon, the ladies, joined by some others from the neighbourhood, planned to picnic by the lake. Ever somewhat anxious of meeting new people, Jane enquired of her sister whether she was acquainted with any of those due to attend. Caroline replied she had met Mrs. Castleton but not her daughter, whom she did not believe was yet out.

"Yes, that is as Lizzy said. She hopes Miss Castleton and Miss Darcy will become better acquainted now they have both finished school and will be in the country more often."

"It must be a relief to know there are some families in the neighbourhood willing to overlook how far beneath his sphere Mr. Darcy has married," Caroline replied.

At that moment, the door opened, and Elizabeth herself joined them. Jane glanced at Caroline in alarm lest they had been overheard, but Elizabeth exhibited no sign of it. She was occupied ushering someone into the room—a young girl in scruffy apparel with a mane of unkempt hair around her unwashed face. The child's expression was one of utter disbelief as she looked about the room. Caroline's countenance, Jane noticed, was not much different as she looked at the child.

"This is my sister, Mrs. Bingley. And this is Miss Bingley," Elizabeth said, pointing to each of them in turn. "Bess is one of our tenants. She got separated from her brothers coming back from Lambton this morning. I found her wandering near the kitchen gardens, quite lost."

"So...you brought her *inside*?" Caroline said incredulously.

Elizabeth pressed her lips together and remained silent for a moment longer than was polite. "She is but five years old, Miss Bingley, and frightened. And since it was my ambushing her from behind the lavender that reduced the poor girl to tears, it was the least I could do to offer her some comfort." To Bess, she added, "We are to have some chocolate to cheer you up, are we not?"

The little girl nodded but still did not smile. Indeed, to Jane's eye, she looked veritably terrified, no doubt as undesirous of being above stairs as Caroline was to have her there.

"Lizzy, I see that you mean well, but might it not be better to have Bess attended to in the servant's quarters?"

Elizabeth looked at her sharply.

"Allow me to recommend you heed your sister's advice," Caroline cut in. "Your...generosity, far from being viewed with the appreciation for which I am sure you are striving, will much more likely scandalise the entire household."

"You must not concern yourself for my household, madam," Elizabeth replied and looked as though she might have said more had not the entrance of servants with refreshments forestalled it.

The little girl's eyes could not have opened any wider when she beheld the selection of cakes set before her. Jane found the length of time she took to choose one, assessing each with close scrutiny, remarkably endearing. At Elizabeth's request, the child gabbled an animated account of how she had come to be lost, spraying crumbs every-whither as she spoke. Jane could not help but smile despite Caroline's indignant disgust. Before very long, however, Elizabeth remarked that the child's family must be worried and that it was time for her to return home.

"But I don't know the way from 'ere," the girl whimpered.

"I shall not send you off alone," Elizabeth assured her. After peering briefly from the window, she added, "Indeed, I shall see you back myself. A walk would be delightful in this weather. Will either of you join us?" she enquired, looking at Jane and Caroline.

There was a pause; then Caroline answered very slowly as though speaking to a simpleton. "You wish us to accompany you *on foot* to what I can only presume is a farmyard?"

"Pardon me," Elizabeth replied, her tone even but her eyes flinty. "I recall now you are not fond of walking. Of course you must not feel obliged. Jane, will you come? Bullscroft is but a few miles away."

"Well…" Jane faltered when Caroline rolled her eyes. "Think you it is quite proper, Lizzy? Ought you not send her with a footman?"

"I assume your answer is no," Elizabeth replied coldly.

Jane could think of nothing to say that would not displease one of her sisters; thus, she said nothing. Elizabeth stood and beckoned for the child to do likewise. "Then I shall leave you both in peace."

"I suppose we ought to be grateful she did not decide to bring the little wretch to the picnic," Caroline said after they were gone. "I doubt Mr. Darcy's neighbours would be quite that forbearing."

Jane shivered, though whether from the gust of wind that blew in from the garden or the vague and unwelcome sense of guilt, she could not be sure. She asked a servant to close the French doors and excused herself from further conversation to read a book. After four chapters, she began to wish she had joined Elizabeth on her walk, but she was saved from her ennui when Miss Darcy arrived, looking for her sister.

"She walked out," Miss Bingley informed her. "She ought to be back soon, for she must have left an hour ago, and we all know what an excellent walker she is."

Miss Darcy appeared troubled by this, and the reason soon became clear. It was raining and had apparently been raining for above quarter of an hour. As though to mock Jane for not noticing, the heavens then lit up, and an almighty clap of thunder filled the air, a detonation that was further punctuated by the banging of the saloon door against the wall as it was thrown open to admit the gentlemen, returned precipitately from their sport.

"We have been rained off!" Bingley cried, shaking droplets from his hair. "Deuced storm blew in from nowhere!"

"And Lizzy is out in it!" Miss Darcy cried.

Mr. Darcy halted mid-stride, his entire carriage stiffening in alarm. "Why? Where has she gone?"

After sending Jane a fleeting look of triumph, Caroline relayed to him the events of the morning. Jane glanced at Bingley, then away again, ere the picture of his distress could lodge in her mind. To her consternation, when Mr. Darcy announced his intention to ride out and escort Elizabeth home, Bingley offered to join him.

"No, I thank you, that is not necessary," his friend replied. "She will be almost home by now. I beg you would entertain the ladies in my absence. I shall not be long."

Then, he was gone, and there was no more argument to be had on the matter. Miss Darcy also excused herself to arrange for a hot bath to be drawn for her sister. Thus, in no time at all, only Bingleys remained in the saloon, the male of which drifted to the window to stare at the rain. "I sincerely hope she is almost home. It would be most unfortunate were she to take ill."

Jane told herself good manners made his concern necessary. Such she had been telling herself for most of the visit. Whenever he laughed at one of Elizabeth's jokes, showed interest in any of her pursuits, or expressed gratitude for her hospitality, it was all attributable to common courtesy. That did not stop her wishing Elizabeth would tell less diverting jokes, have less interesting pursuits, or be a less entertaining hostess.

"She has greater things with which to concern herself than the possibility of catching a cold," Caroline scoffed.

Bingley turned to face her. "Such as?"

"Such as her respectability. I have said before that her behaviour shows a shocking indifference to decorum."

"And I have said before that it shows a level of affection for others that is very pleasing."

"You have?" Jane enquired, but she was ignored.

"Charles, you astound me," Caroline said. "Surely, even you can comprehend the injury such wilful gaucherie will do to her reputation?"

"Oh, for God's sake, Caroline, she went for a walk. Sometimes, I declare you are more fastidious than Darcy."

"Am I? I thought he would spit when he heard she had brought the girl into the house."

Bingley flinched. Jane was sure of it.

"Nonsense. Darcy was only concerned that Elizabeth might be caught in the rain." He must not have convinced himself, for soon after, he added, "Think you it was her other activities that displeased him?"

At last, a chink had appeared in Elizabeth's armour where Bingley might actually see it. "It certainly seemed so," Jane said quietly, which only increased Bingley's disquiet, thereby exacerbating her own umbrage and provoking her to say more. "We must not blame him. Mr. Darcy has been very kind to indulge Lizzy's disregard for propriety this long, but he has a right to expect his wife to comport herself properly—as *other* wives take the trouble to do for *their* husbands."

"Well said, my dear," Caroline interjected. She turned to her brother. "But I hardly think it would be well-advised for us to dwell on the Darcys' marriage."

A look passed between them that Jane could not interpret. Moments later, Bingley backed into the nearest chair and crossed his arms. "What would you have us discuss, Caroline?"

"You had best keep to the weather, Charles. It is safest."

Fortunately for all, the weather seemed intent on providing them with as much to talk about as it could with its blustering winds and sporadic thunder and lightning—even, when the conversation looked to be flagging, throwing in a brief bout of hail for extra measure. No further mention of Elizabeth's impropriety, or anyone's opinion of it, was made as they waited with various degrees of anxiety for their hosts' return.

Bullscroft farm was a little over two miles from Pemberley. Alone and in good weather, Elizabeth might ordinarily have walked there and back within an hour. With Powell's daughter in tow, who was but five or six years old if Darcy's memory served him correctly, he supposed he could add half an hour to that. Even so, she ought to have returned by now, but she had not. The danger of a fever to her and the baby terrified him, but the farther he went without finding her, the more concerned he became that something even more serious had befallen her, for she was nowhere to be seen.

His alarm reached new heights when he came to the Rush, a ford so named for the sudden violent currents that arose there after heavy rain, rendering the otherwise easy crossing treacherous. As he feared, the water gushed ferociously, shin-high over the stone crossing. He could see no sign she had come to harm there, but it gave him no relief, for it then became just another place that Elizabeth was not. "Curse it, woman. Do not do this to me!"

When he came within view of the farmstead with still no sign of her, he gave in to a moment's panic. Acknowledging that a greater search effort was required, he urged his horse on faster to the house, where he might summon assistance. A child within yelped when he hammered on the door, but there was no room in his thundering heart for contrition. He had not a moment to lose. Too slowly, his knock was answered, and Mrs. Powell opened the door.

"Good 'eavens, Mr. Darcy! Come in out the rain!"

She dipped a hurried curtsey and stepped aside. Darcy removed his hat and ducked beneath the lintel. Inside, he straightened and froze. There, before a fireplace, with not a hint of dampness about her and a look of astonishment upon her face, sat Elizabeth. Only ingrained propriety prevented him lunging forward to drag her into his arms, though restraint rendered his first words exceedingly brusque. "Mrs. Darcy. You are here."

"I am," she replied, gently manoeuvring a small child aside and rising to stand before him. "As are you, for which I cannot account. Has something happened at the house?"

He knew not whether he wished most to rail at her or to kiss her. "Nothing other than its mistress is feared lost in a storm."

Her eyes widened. "You thought me out walking in this? How you must have worried! I would have sent word, only"—she lowered her voice to barely a whisper—"I thought you would know I should never be so foolish."

"I assumed it began after you set out. You left Pemberley some hours ago, and neither of the ladies thought you meant to tarry here long."

She gave a small, sardonic huff of laughter. "I do not doubt it! But no, that was not my intention. Only, Bess and I had such adventures on our walk, it took us twice as long as it should have to get here, and by then, the rain had begun, so I stayed. The children have kept me well entertained though. Master Timothy has sung to me, and Master John allowed me to hold his pet frog."

Tearing his eyes from her for the first time since entering the house, Darcy became aware that two young boys were in attendance also. He bowed formally and thanked them for keeping Elizabeth safe.

"I kept 'er entertaineded too!" the child by the fire squeaked.

"Indeed you did!" Elizabeth said happily. "And would you like to show Mr. Darcy the sketch you made?"

The girl nodded and came forward, timidly bearing a slate on which was chalked some manner of beast with stick limbs, large teeth and flaming eyes.

"Very impressive!" Darcy told her. "What is it?"

She drew herself up proudly. "Miss Bingley."

Elizabeth's shaky outpouring of breath ill-concealed her laughter and in no way assisted Darcy's attempt to contain his own. He bit the insides of his cheeks and sucked in a sharp breath through his nose, though it was Mrs. Powell's stammered apologies that truly saved him.

"Do not distress yourself, madam. I am sure your daughter intended no impertinence." To the child, he whispered that it was a remarkable likeness and promised to send over some paper and crayons that she might practice her skill at drawing. Her eyes widened in wonder, and she spun away to regale her mother with news of her good fortune.

Darcy declined Mrs. Powell's subsequent offer of refreshments upon discovering that the storm had exhausted itself. Leaving his regards for her husband, he bade them farewell, and within a few minutes, he and Elizabeth were headed for home, his horse following behind them. He walked rapidly, wildly impatient to reach the bend in the lane that would take them out of sight of the little girl yet waving from the farmhouse door, but Elizabeth forestalled him.

"You are angry with me," she said, as soon as they rounded the corner.

"No, I am not angry."

"But you were when you arrived."

Her disquiet puzzled him, for she was not usually much cowed by his temper, even when he was genuinely vexed. "You must understand: I had been searching for you in vain for half an hour in that storm, Elizabeth. You were not dressed to be out in the rain, you were alone, and you are with child."

She looked down. "Forgive me, Fitzwilliam. I forget on occasion that I am no longer Elizabeth Bennet of Longbourn."

More mystified than before, Darcy stopped walking and tugged her gently to face him. "I happen to be very in love with Elizabeth Bennet of Longbourn."

Her mouth lifted into a small, rueful smile. "Yet, we both know Mrs. Darcy of Pemberley ought not to disappear about the country unaccompanied, endangering the master's heir. I do not blame you for being angry."

Darcy let go his horse's reins and took hold of her face with both hands. "I was not angry, Elizabeth. I was terrified. Do you still not comprehend what it would do to me were you to come to harm?"

A delectable little frown pulled at her brow. "Then, you are not displeased with me for walking so far?" He shook his head. "Or that I went with little Bess?" He shook his head. She bit her lip guiltily, a spark of mischief lighting up her eyes, rendering her absolutely lovely. "Know you that I served her chocolate in the Spanish Saloon?" He nodded. "You are not angry about that, either?"

"Are you planning on making a habit of it?"

"No."

He stroked her cheek with his thumb. "Then no."

She gave a little huff. "Well something vexed you, for it seemed as though you could not decamp from Mrs. Powell's parlour soon enough."

He held her gaze and lowered his face close to hers. "There you go again, woman, wilfully misunderstanding me."

There was time enough only for her eyes to widen slightly with comprehension before he kissed her. Fanning his fingers out over her cheeks, he pulled her closer, pressing his mouth hard against hers in a bid to dispel all trace of his earlier panic. Her arms wound about him, her weight fell against him, and it was several magnificent minutes before he recalled there were but twenty yards and a hedgerow shielding them from prying eyes. He allowed himself one last lingering caress, and then, though her kisses were ambrosia to his fear-ravaged heart, he drew back.

She smiled up at him archly. "I stand corrected. But if you will insist on always looking so grave when you are thinking of seducing me…"

"It is a very serious matter and one that occupies my thoughts a good deal of the time. I cannot always be smiling when I am so constantly beset."

"You poor thing!"

Offering his arm, he set them off along the path again. "It is some months since you mistook any look of mine, love. Might I enquire why you were so convinced this day that I should be displeased with you?"

She gave him a pained look. "Pardon me if I have offended you, Fitzwilliam. Actually, it never occurred to me that you would object until you arrived so fierce and severe. Then, I own, I did begin to worry Miss Bingley and Jane might be right."

"They told you I would be displeased?"

She grimaced and nodded. He felt his lip curl into a snarl at the unpardonable audacity of both Bingley women.

"I would not usually have paid the slightest bit of notice to Miss Bingley's disapproval," Elizabeth spoke on. "But Jane's was harder to overlook."

Darcy chose his words carefully, for his opinion of Jane Bingley had never tallied well with Elizabeth's. "Much though I respect her, your sister is in no position to judge what will please me. And if she believes that showing compassion to my tenants will not, then she has greatly underestimated the value I place in you."

"Perhaps she is an imposter, and my Jane is still at Longbourn. Either way, I do not think I shall be sharing any confidences with her on this—my goodness, look at the river!"

They had reached the Rush. Darcy did not look but instead lifted her onto his horse, swung up behind her and nudged the animal forward.

"It is grown so fierce!" she exclaimed, leaning forward in the saddle and peering over the horse's withers into the water. "It was not like this when I crossed with Bess. Look!"

"I have seen it," Darcy replied, pulling her back and pinning her firmly against his chest. "I spent a good while looking in it for you on my last crossing."

For several heartbeats, she made no reply and sat very still and very quiet in his arms. Too still and too quiet by far, in fact. He was unsurprised that, when she spoke, it was to tease him.

"You truly do have a penchant for the dramatic, do you not? You are determined to always think me injured—or dead!"

He held his tongue, glad she could not see his chagrined expression. She was perfectly right, of course, but the woman already knew she divested him of all reason and was heartless to cavil so. She said nothing more, though the look she gave him as he reached to lift her down on the opposite bank left him in no doubt of her vast amusement.

"Besides," she said as he set her on her feet, "if you recall, you did not give me leave to die again." Her grin promptly disappeared, and she proceeded to fulfil all his fears by taking one step and slipping on the muddy ground, stumbling directly towards the river. He tugged her sharply back towards him, but doing so lost him his own footing, and he skidded into his horse, off whose meaty shoulder he rebounded, colliding forcefully with Elizabeth before sailing past her to land unceremoniously on his seat in the mud.

If her hilarity was aught to go by, this was possibly the most diverting thing Elizabeth had ever witnessed. She laughed the sort of laugh that made no sound for want of air in the lungs, and tears streamed down her face. There was nothing to be done but fold his arms resignedly over his knees and watch his beautiful, vivacious wife slip and skate about on the muddy riverbank until she exhausted her mirth. When, after several moments, she did not look as though she would, he grabbed her hand and pulled her down into his lap, putting an end to her laughter by commandeering her mouth for his own purpose.

They walked home hand in hand with the sun hot on their backs once more, delivering his horse to the stables and stealing into the house through a side door. Not ready for their adventure to end, Darcy pulled her into an alcove and indulged in another leisurely kiss. It rapidly grew less leisurely, and he transferred his attentions along her jaw and down her neck. She made a little noise of pleasure in her throat that he felt on his lips and that was that. How the woman did what she did to him he would never know, but he was instantly aching for her.

"Think you we could sneak upstairs unnoticed?"

"You certainly ought to try before Miss Bingley sees the state of you," she whispered. "She would not approve of all that mud."

"When did you begin to care for Miss Bingley's opinion?"

"She has so many. They are difficult to avoid."

He would have laughed were he not so aroused. Instead, her wit made him want her more, which meant his thoughts had taken on a decidedly lascivious hue by the time she added, "Just this morning I heard her say that I am beneath you."

His nostrils flared. "That is where I prefer to have you." He savoured the look that earned him, but their interlude was not to last. A door banged open a short distance away, and a footman hurried out of the passage from the kitchen. After him wafted the distinct aroma of cooking, and that was enough to turn Elizabeth's fragile stomach. She groaned and clasped a hand over her mouth, mumbling an apology through her fingers.

"Go! Get thee upstairs," he whispered, nudging her in that direction. "I shall see to our guests."

She nodded and disappeared around the corner at a pace. A heartbeat later, Bingley came around the same corner, his face overspread with concern.

"Darcy, you are returned."

"We are."

"Good. And, is everything—is Lizzy well?"

"She is, thank you."

"You are certain? For I just saw her, and I must say she seemed rather distressed."

Conscious of Elizabeth's wish for discretion, Darcy dissembled with a vague reference to her being tired after such a long walk.

"She is not ill after being out in the rain, I hope," Bingley persisted, frowning. "She looked uncommonly pale."

"She was not caught in the rain." *She is with child—my child!* he wished to say, and though he did not, he found himself hard pressed to keep the exultant grin from his face. "Mayhap, the Derbyshire air does not agree with her. No doubt, she will become accustomed to it in time or learn not to walk so far in it. Stop fussing," he added when Bingley looked as though he would object. "Elizabeth is perfectly well. She has only gone upstairs to change. As must I, now I have informed you of our return. Pray excuse me."

"Good God, what happened to you?" Bingley exclaimed as Darcy passed him by, apparently noticing his muddied apparel for the first time.

"*Elizabeth* happened!" he replied over his shoulder. "I tell you, Bingley, no one else's wife seems to give them this much bother!"

Sunday, 6 September 1812: Derbyshire

Bingley rose with the rest of the congregation, grateful for the return of blood flowing to his legs, and since Darcy and Elizabeth had moved forward to speak to the rector, he offered Miss Darcy his arm and walked with her out of the church.

Their party numbered only four. Mrs. Annesley, he was told, had gone to Kympton with a friend. Jane and Caroline had both cried off altogether, the former claiming to be indisposed and the latter making no claims at all, only failing to appear downstairs in time to join them. Darcy had been in no humour to wait, and Bingley strongly suspected both his friend and his sister were still brooding over their exchange at dinner the previous evening.

He had little sympathy for Caroline. She really ought to have known better than to gainsay the Titan at his own table, but she would persist with her remarks on outmoded country town practices long after he decreed the matter of Elizabeth's escapades closed to further discussion. Darcy's rejoinder that Caroline would be well placed to learn some country town humility whilst staying at Netherfield had silenced the table completely until Elizabeth expressed an interest in his own venture in Nova Scotia, and the conversation had thankfully picked up once more.

Darcy's disinclination to discuss Elizabeth's kindness towards the little tenant girl troubled Bingley greatly. It seemed Jane and Caroline had been correct. He disapproved of her conduct. In an attempt to allay his concerns, Bingley had ventured to make some discreet enquiries. They had brought him little in the way of encouragement. Caroline had vigorously averred that Darcy's dissembling was due to shame.

"For what gentleman wishes to admit that his upstart wife has made an exhibition of herself and his marriage is a catastrophe?"

He had erred in broaching the matter with Jane. She had disliked his interest as much as he had disliked her answer.

"If Lizzy cared half so much about her husband's happiness as you do about hers, she might give him less about which to be displeased!"

Least reassuring of all had been Elizabeth's typically arch remark.

"Pray, take pity on him and allow him to forget the incident as soon as may be! He has suffered quite enough distress for one day as a consequence of my actions, and I daresay tomorrow will only bring more."

"Mr. Bingley?"

Miss Darcy was regarding him expectantly.

"I do beg your pardon. My thoughts were elsewhere."

"Not at all," she assured him, too polite to enquire further.

"I say," he said, "do you suppose your brother was angry with Lizzy at dinner last night?"

She coloured deeply. "Oh! Well, I…goodness! I do not believe so but mayhap. It is difficult to tell sometimes because of their manner of talking to each other. Lizzy is excessively sportive with him."

"And this he does not like?"

"He said he ought to have invited Mrs. Gardiner to stay since she had more respect for him than Lizzy does."

That Darcy required his wife's respect, Bingley was well aware.

"Just this morning I heard her say that I am beneath you."

"That is where I prefer to have you."

He had not been meant to hear that, of course, and a true gentleman would have forgotten it instantly. Yet, he could not forget how Elizabeth had dashed away with her hands covering her ashen face. What had his friend done? Married a woman whom he considered beneath him and doomed her to a life of disrespect and misery? Bingley's anguish was too great for him to say more, and he walked on in silence. Would that he had offered for Elizabeth when he had the chance…

"ACHOOOOO!"

The unheralded and almighty sneeze made Miss Darcy shriek and Bingley near jump from his skin. They both whirled around.

"Upon my life, Darcy! Were you worried we would not notice you were there?"

"Oh my, I hope you have not taken a chill from riding out in the rain!" Miss Darcy fretted. "Would that you had stayed in the dry as Lizzy did!"

Darcy deigned to answer neither of them. Bingley stared in dismay as, instead, he turned to Elizabeth, who had been grinning broadly up until that point, and said gravely, "Not a word from you, madam. Not one word."

"I should not dare!" she replied, her beautiful eyes brimming with challenge.

Bingley turned away and climbed into the carriage, unable to watch. How long could Elizabeth's wonderful, inimitable liveliness endure in the face of Darcy's constant disapprobation? He could not reconcile the man whom he had, for many years, held in the highest regard with this one, who seemed content to forever look down upon his supposedly beloved wife. It was an unbearable situation—the worst of it being, there was absolutely nothing he could do about it.

Netherfield, Hertfordshire
September 11

Dearest Lady Ashby,

We are back at Netherfield at last! I cannot thank you enough for the solicitous concern expressed in your last letter, which made what was indeed a difficult visit bearable.

Having admitted to her own selfishness when last I saw her, I had expected E might endeavour to make some improvement. Alas, she has improved in neither thoughtfulness nor manners. She made private jokes with the gentlemen, dominated every conversation, spoke impertinently to and of her husband with little mind to her audience, made no effort to behave as a woman in her position ought, and incorrectly assumed she would be universally admired for her independence.

You will know how deeply this behaviour distressed me, given my fear that her careless charms might once again draw B in. Yet, though at first he seemed excessively attentive to her, by the end, I was far less anxious. What you predicted, you see, is coming to bear. Her allure is fading. Your cousin reveals little of his feelings, but even he failed on a few occasions to conceal his displeasure, and if his favour is so rapidly diminishing, it cannot be long before B's dwindles entirely.

Forgive me if it pains you to discover this. I know you were hoping for better news, but such assurances I cannot provide. On the contrary, D is regularly embarrassed as a result of E's wilful disregard for propriety. If I tell you that, amongst her other transgressions during the course of our visit, she served refreshments to one of his tenants' children in the same room as her houseguests, then traipsed halfway across the estate, alone and in the rain, to escort the child home, necessitating that D ride out in the storm to search for her, you will have some idea of the indignities he faces.

Even B expressed concern for his friend's displeasure with E and the frequency and bitterness of their disputes. He has invited them to stay with us on their way to your cousin's wedding in Kent, which I sincerely hope is attributable to his sympathy for his friend and nothing more. I do not relish another visit with all its attendant obligations of civility, yet I recall your counsel to avoid a rift with the Ds and recognise the prudence of ensuring it goes well. Indeed, it was precisely that advice that prompted me to demonstrate a measure of affection for E I did not feel on our final evening at P to compensate for the few instances of contention during my stay. Whether or not my efforts were successful I could not say. I wonder whether she even noticed.

All that remains to be said is what consolation your friendship has been and continues to be during these trying times, for which I thank you most sincerely.

Affectionately yours,
Jane Bingley

Monday, 28 September 1812: Hertfordshire

Autumn had well and truly settled in Hertfordshire by the time the Bingleys returned from their travels. The trees were every shade of orange, brown, and red, dusty paths had turned to mud, and the air grew chillier by the day. For Jane's youngest sister, there was but one consequence of changing seasons worth considering: changing gowns. Thus, presently, Jane was ensconced in her bedchamber while Lydia rummaged through her closet for a different, mayhap warmer, definitely finer gown than any of her own to wear to the next assembly in Meryton. With Mrs. Bennet closely supervising the search, there was little for Jane to do but sit on her chaise longue and watch.

"La, what is this old thing doing in here?" Lydia exclaimed, backing out of the closet and sneering at the gown she held up before her. "'Tis two years old at least! Look at the sleeves!"

"There is nothing wrong with the sleeves. They are very charming," Jane demurred.

"I do not care how charming they are," said Mrs. Bennet angrily. "Mrs. Bingley of Netherfield cannot wear gowns from one season past, let alone two! Lay it on the bed, Lydia. That one can go to the maid."

Lydia did as she was bid then returned to foraging. Jane sighed. Her mother had not the head for money matters. Her enduring love affair with French lace was proof of that.

"Mama, it is a perfectly serviceable gown. With very few adjustments, it could be worn for half dress."

"Half dress? You could not wear that to bed, never mind to dinner! You would not be fit to be seen! Really, Jane, you must better attend to these matters. It is no wonder you are not yet with child if that is the sort of thing you are wearing!"

Jane had no response to such a shocking and offensive tangent and sat speechless and indignant. Mrs. Bennet glanced conspiratorially over her shoulder to where Lydia was yet buried in the closet and then shuffled closer to Jane. When she spoke again, it was in a low voice and with such vastly exaggerated enunciation as made her harder, not easier, to understand.

"We have spoken before of men's desires and how to entice them. The same is just as true after you wed. Bingley will not come to you if you do not make yourself alluring. And you need him to come to you, Jane, for unless he is prodigiously blessed, he will not get you with child from the next room."

"He does come to me," Jane whispered, mortified.

"Evidently not often enough or you would be increasing by now."

"Mama, we have not yet been married three months!"

"And you must not go any longer. You must dress to better tempt him." A shrewd smile overtook her countenance. "In fact, when Lizzy arrives on Friday, ask to borrow some of her gowns. He will like that."

Jane's blood ran cold. "I have no wish to dress like Lizzy."

"I know, dear, but it might not be such a poor scheme."

She inhaled deeply, attempting not to sound too breathless when she enquired whether her mother believed Bingley favoured Elizabeth.

"It hardly matters which of you he prefers," she replied. "He married you; thus, it is you who must provide him with an heir!"

Jane came to her feet with a wordless cry, appalled beyond measure. Her dismay, and perhaps the sudden movement, made her light-headed. Close to swooning, she fumbled for the arm of the chaise longue and dropped back into her seat, sick to her stomach and with tears stinging her eyes. Her anguish was rudely interrupted when her mother shoved a bottle of smelling salts under her nose, bringing her lurching forward, retching, and the awaiting tears cascading down her cheeks.

"What is the matter with Jane?" Lydia enquired.

"Hush, child!" Mrs. Bennet admonished. She bent over Jane, peering at her suspiciously. "Are you sure you are not already with child? Now that I notice it, you do seem very pale and mayhap a little thickened about the waist."

Jane closed her eyes. "It is possible," she mumbled, supposing it was—hypothetically—and hoping it might satisfy her mother enough to make her go away. It did not.

"Oh, *Jane*! I knew it! You clever, clever girl! Lydia! Lydia, did you hear?

Jane is with child! Oh, heavens above, what happy news!"

"Kitty and I wondered who would be first," Lydia replied. "She thought Lizzy, but I thought you, Jane. And I was right! You have beaten Lizzy to it!"

A heartening prospect indeed! "Well, it would be agreeable to have done *something* better than the flawless Mrs. Darcy. Let her take a turn at being shone down." Jane regretted her petty outburst when Lydia gasped, looking thoroughly taken aback, but her mother only smiled and leant to pat her hand.

"It is very common to feel a little waspish at the beginning, dear, very common indeed. Ooh, wait until your father hears this news!"

"Pray, do not tell Papa!" Jane cried urgently, recognising she must end the charade before her mother falsely raised half the town's expectations. "Indeed, do not tell anyone, for it is not true!"

Her mother looked hurt, as though Jane had done her an injustice by depriving her of such momentous intelligence, but her expression soon softened. "I understand. It is too early to be certain. Let me assure you, though, you are showing all the signs." She cut off Jane's attempt to object again with a sharp shake of her head. "I shall not mention it to a soul." Lydia scoffed loudly. "And neither will you, Miss Lydia, or you will not be going to the assembly at all!" She stood abruptly. "Come, come, let us leave your sister to rest."

"But I have not chosen a gown!"

"Oh, hang your gown, girl! Your sister is with child! What do I care for your gowns?"

"Ugh! I shall ask to borrow one of Lizzy's then," she retorted. "Hers are bound to be finer than Jane's anyway."

Mrs. Bennet forcibly hustled her from the room. Jane stared after them. Her mother's misapprehension would resolve itself soon enough when she did not begin to increase. The matter of Bingley's itinerant affections seemed destined never to resolve itself, recurring with nightmarish persistence to torment her. Feeling her heart harden a little further, she stood and rang the bell for her maid—to whom she gave the gown that supposedly made her so vastly unappealing, along with every other dress in her possession with similarly outmoded sleeves.

Friday, 2 October 1812: Hertfordshire

Darcy regarded the bustling streets philosophically as the carriage trundled through Meryton. His memories of Hertfordshire were many and varied, but he was able to reflect on even the unpleasant ones with a certain amount of complacency, for Elizabeth nestled sleepily in his arms with his child nestled safely in her belly and his happiness was complete.

He had grown exceedingly fond of her habit of sleeping curled up against him on long journeys. He was thankful his sister had elected to visit the Castletons rather than accompany them to Kent, leaving them free to enjoy such intimacy. As the carriage turned away from the town towards Netherfield, he began to gently rouse her, diverted by her drowsy reluctance. "Truly, I cannot comprehend how you sleep so soundly in a moving carriage."

"I never used to be able to or even wish to." She yawned, sitting upright and stretching. "I believe I have your child to thank."

He smiled to hear her speak so assuredly of it, for despite all indications to the fact, she had yet to feel the quickening and was adamant they ought not to celebrate until she did.

"Am I presentable?" she enquired, beginning to fuss with her hair and clothes.

"You look divine." She truly did.

She reached for her bonnet. "I hope Georgiana has settled well at Hornscroft."

"I am sure she has," he replied, frowning at her non sequitur.

"Ought we to have insisted upon Mrs. Annesley going with her?"

"Now you profess reservations on that score? After the energy with which you defended her wish to go alone?"

"Well, no—only, I do so wish her to have an agreeable visit."

He watched her fingers fumbling with the ribbons under her chin. After a moment, he gently nudged her hands aside and tied the bow for her. "She will enjoy it more than she would have enjoyed Rosings. But, I do not believe it is her visit that troubles you."

Elizabeth frowned and opened her mouth as though to object, but the carriage's lurching halt distracted her enough that when she spoke again, it was with a rueful grin. "For a man who once readily mistook antipathy for love, you have become vexingly perceptive. Shall I ever be able to hide anything from you again?"

"I hope not."

The door was opened and a servant appeared in the aperture, bending to unfold the steps.

"What strange creatures we are, traipsing about the country, chasing dissension and hostility, when we could so easily have remained at home and avoided all of it," Elizabeth whispered.

"Another of my suggestions you opposed, I believe," Darcy teased as he climbed down from the carriage.

"Righteousness is of no value in retrospect, you know," she replied as he handed her down.

"Obstinacy in the moment is preferable then, is it?"

"Pray tell me you have not argued the entire way from Pemberley!"

They both turned at the sound of Bingley's voice.

"Not the entire way, no," Elizabeth replied archly. "I slept for some of the time."

Half an hour later, Darcy sat in Bingley's study, grimacing at the contents of his glass. "What in God's name is this?"

"Cognac."

Darcy raised one sceptical eyebrow. "*This* is from France?"

"No, it is from Sir William."

He set his glass aside. "It is good of you to put us up so soon after your own travels."

"Not at all. I know Lizzy must be eager to see her family again."

Darcy regarded his friend with a carefully neutral expression. He questioned whether Bingley was even aware his wife was not presently on good terms with her sister. Did they not talk to one another of such matters? "Speaking of family, I had expected the Hursts to be here."

"Hurst has taken Louisa back to London. He did not trust the midwives hereabouts to be of use when she enters her confinement."

"That bodes ill for you, then. I hope you have better luck finding a decent one locally."

"What? Why would I…what do you…what?"

"It is probable you will have need of one for Jane at some point."

"Oh! Yes, of course!" He gulped down the remainder of his drink and twisted around to dispense with his empty glass on the desk behind him. He placed it atop a pile of papers whose ink instantly began to run where drips of the unspecified liquor had pooled around the bottom.

"Bingley, your correspondence!"

"Oh, blast!" Bingley sprang to his feet and snatched up the glass, but—too late. The top three or four sheets of paper beneath it were now attached to its base, and when he hefted it clear of the desk, a whole sheaf of documents was dragged up into the air with it, all of which promptly cascaded to the floor.

Darcy shook his head, chuckling quietly, if incredulously, at his maladroit friend. He abstained from teasing and crouched to help gather up the scattered paperwork, though when he came upon a sheet bearing naught but an exceedingly ill-drawn blue and orange face, he could not refrain from comment. Snatching up one or two last papers, he pushed himself to his feet. "Were you half cut when you created this masterpiece, Bingley?"

"What is that?" his friend replied from the floor.

Darcy showed him; Bingley's face flushed beetroot red.

"Dare we enquire what is going on here?"

Elizabeth's interruption came from the doorway, where she stood with her sister, her arms folded and one exquisite eyebrow arched high in amusement. Darcy bowed a formal greeting. At his side, Bingley scrambled to his feet and gave some kind of absurd wave.

"Bingley is…" He glanced at the disordered bundle of papers his friend clutched to his chest, one of which, most divertingly, chose that moment to escape from his grasp and flutter conspicuously back to the floor. "Filing."

"Thank heavens. I thought for a moment he was asking for your hand."

"I should have said no if he had. I could never marry a person who draws even more poorly than I do." Ignoring Bingley's embarrassed groan, he held up the pitiable scribble for the ladies to see.

"Oh! That is Anna's sketch of me!" Elizabeth exclaimed.

"Yes," Bingley said. "You dropped it here at my picnic in the summer. I meant to return it to you. But forgot. Obviously."

"You are very good, sir, but I have a hundred others just like it. You need not have troubled yourself."

She then informed them—because Jane did not—that tea was to be served in the morning room and suggested, if the gentlemen had completed their business, they all remove there. Before anyone could agree or disagree, Bingley proceeded to drop most of the papers in his arms *again* whilst attempting to shuffle them into a neat pile. Darcy watched Elizabeth press her lips together. Her eyes, when they met his, shone with laughter.

"Blast!" Bingley grumbled again. "Go ahead. I shall join you all directly."

Darcy crossed the room and gave Elizabeth his arm. It was only as he held out the other for Jane that he spared any thought for the fact she had not spoken a word since coming into the study. She observed Bingley in silence with an inscrutable expression, though the spots of colour pinking her cheeks might be indicative of some pique. It was a few heartbeats before Jane removed her gaze from her husband and, without a word, accepted Darcy's arm. It was not his business. On that point, he was painfully clear. With a determined effort to draw no conclusion whatsoever about Jane's demeanour towards Bingley, Darcy led the two women from the room.

Saturday, 3 October 1812: Hertfordshire

The gentlemen went for an early ride the next morning with the agreement that they would all convene in the dining room to breakfast together at ten. Thus, Elizabeth descended the stairs alone. Her feelings were so different from the last time she trod the same path that she could not help but smile. It had been the last morning of her stay to nurse Jane to health, almost a year ago, and she had never been so eager to leave behind a place or a certain person. Presently, she begrudged every moment apart from him.

That her relationship with Jane had soured to a similar state of acrimony as hers and Darcy's at its worst pained her deeply. They had not explicitly argued at Pemberley, but neither had they properly recovered from their quarrel in London, and the new coldness in Jane's manner continued to dissuade Elizabeth from sharing her happy news. She had come here without expectation of a revival of intimacy, only the desire for matters to deteriorate no further, which was the sum of what she had thus far achieved.

A footman opened the door as she approached the breakfast room, revealing her husband already seated at the table. He stood immediately upon seeing her, giving an almost imperceptible shake of his head. She slowed to a halt and waited while he disappeared from view around the table, then appeared again in the door, striding towards her.

"Whatever is the matter?"

"Eggs," he replied in a low voice.

"Oh! Yes, that might have proved embarrassing. Though everybody will just as soon think you are unwell now. What reason did you give for leaving so abruptly?"

Much to her amusement, he looked somewhat confused by her enquiry. "I am not in the habit of explaining myself to people."

She bit back a smile. That was precisely the sort of behaviour she had previously considered proud and uncivil, but in light of his generous motivations, she had not the heart to point it out to him. "Well, I am very grateful to you, Fitzwilliam, but your forethought does not solve the problem of my still being hungry."

"Which is why I brought you these." He presented her with a napkin that contained two buttered muffins. "Would you care for an impromptu picnic?"

She nodded eagerly, and they continued on arm in arm towards the front of the house but got no farther than the study before their progress was interrupted. The door was torn open and through it swept Jane in a terrible agitation of spirits. She almost ran directly into them, let out an enfeebled cry, and staggered backwards. She likely would have fallen had Darcy not caught her and helped her into a nearby chair.

"Jane!" Elizabeth cried, kneeling before her.

"Shall I fetch Bingley?" Darcy enquired.

"Yes, quickly!"

"No!" Jane's protest was firmer than Elizabeth's plea. Darcy hesitated.

Elizabeth tried again. "Jane, you are ill. Pray let us summon him."

"No! There is nothing the matter with me, Lizzy." Her assertion was greatly discredited by her pallid complexion and trembling hands. Elizabeth reached for one, only for Jane to snatch it away, insisting, "You surprised me, nothing more."

Elizabeth acquiesced with a sigh and stood up. Jane did likewise, brushing non-existent creases from her skirts before excusing herself and disappearing up the stairs.

"What in heaven's name was that about?" Elizabeth whispered.

"I am the last person likely to know." Darcy turned back to the front door, placing his hand upon her back and gently directing her there. "Mayhap, she is also with child."

Elizabeth whipped her gaze to his. "That might be it! She was very pale. And faint." For a moment, she was wounded that Jane would not confide such a thing to her, but feeling the hypocrisy of her grievance, she soon set it aside. "I should like it to be true," she said once they were in the garden. "It might bring us closer again to have children so near in age."

Darcy said nothing but gave her a sympathetic look and squeezed her arm. Nothing more was said until they came upon the avenue dissecting Netherfield's gardens, and Elizabeth's spirits rose once more. "We walked here last autumn. Do you recall?"

"Vividly," he replied. "You ran away."

"Such appalling manners."

"Better you than either of Bingley's sisters." She looked askance at him, and he added, "Neither of them is half so pleasing from behind."

Thus, they found themselves turned to matters more agreeable to both, Jane's queer turn put from their minds. Nourished by naught but the stoutest love and two buttered muffins, they passed an hour wandering the gardens until time would dawdle for them no longer and they were forced to return to the house and attend to their respective pursuits.

THE LADIES HAD WITHDRAWN AFTER DINNER, LEAVING MR. BENNET, HIS two sons, and a quantity of liquor of dubious origin to commune in masculine seclusion. The occasion had proved to be one of negligible delight. He took a swig of the pungent concoction in his glass and made a final attempt to goad his young companions into conversation, enquiring how many birds each had brought down that afternoon.

"Two–and-twenty," Darcy said at the same time as Bingley mumbled, "Six or seven."

"Ha! True to form, gentlemen! One has his bird in the bag afore the other has decided which to aim for." Neither rose to the bait, which drained all Mr. Bennet's remaining hope of finding sport in their company. His suggestion that they join the ladies was met with universal assent.

All seemed as one might expect when they entered the drawing room. Elizabeth and Mary were deep in conversation on one sofa. Kitty and Lydia were draped over opposing arms of another. Jane and Mrs. Bennet were huddled together in a pair of chairs before the window, whispering about something that was having a very different effect on each of their countenances. Miss Bingley stalked the edge of the room, thus far unsuccessful in what appeared to be a search for another way out.

The gentlemen had not taken more than a few steps into the room when this scene of humdrum domesticity was shattered by Mrs. Bennet's voice.

"I knew it! You *are* with child!"

Judging by the looks on the faces of the two people best placed to know about such a development, Mr. Bennet thought it very unlikely, but since his opinion rarely had any influence on what his wife wished to believe, he saved his breath to cool his porridge. Instead, he sauntered over to claim a seat with the most advantageous view of every countenance in the room, spoilt for choice between the varying expressions of horror, vexation, surprise, and smugness.

"Mama, please!" cried Jane, possessor of the horrified countenance.

"Oh, there is no need to be coy about it, Jane! We are all family here. You may as well tell everybody while we are together."

"Mama!" Elizabeth exclaimed, her tone echoing her vexed expression. "How could you? 'Tis not your place to announce such a thing!"

"Oh, fie, Lizzy. Nobody else was going to!"

"Exactly!"

"Jane?" This rather feeble plea was from Bingley, presently boasting the exceedingly surprised countenance.

Before Jane could respond, Lydia of the smug countenance interrupted. "I know not why you are pretending to be upset, Jane. You said yourself how pleased you were to have outdone Lizzy."

At this, Darcy's countenance, which had heretofore displayed only vague distaste, darkened into an ominous glower. He moved farther into the room, which, rather disconcertingly, seemed to shrink as he did so. Mr. Bennet lifted up the glass he had carried in with him from the dining room and squinted suspiciously at the sallow beverage therein.

"*Lydia!*" Jane exclaimed. "I said no such thing!"

"Yes, you did. You said you were glad to have done something better than 'the flawless Mrs. Darcy.'"

"Oh, Jane!" said Mary, radiating ecclesiastical reproach.

"Ignore her, Jane," Kitty advised. "She is only saying it because, if you are not with child, she will have to give me back my bonnet."

"I am not lying!" Lydia complained, twisting around to snarl at her eldest sister over the back of the sofa. "I know what I heard! You were talking about shining Lizzy down!"

"Turn around and be quiet, girl!" Mrs. Bennet screeched. "Jane is not to be distressed."

"Mother!"

"Charles, for heaven's sake, do something!" Miss Bingley hissed, probably wishing her search for egress had been more fruitful.

Mr. Bennet fancied she would have more luck requesting assistance from the potted plant next to which her brother was standing, provided he did not swoon into it first, which at present appeared to be a distinct possibility. He turned to share the observation with his second eldest child, and it was then he truly appreciated that he had lost his Lizzy to her successor, Mrs. Darcy. She neither laughed at nor joined in nor censured her sisters' squabbling. Instead, she rose to her feet, accepted her husband's arm, and without another word, walked calmly from the room—showing Miss Bingley how simple a thing it could be.

Sunday, 4 October 1812: Hertfordshire

"Absolutely not."

Elizabeth suppressed a sigh. Though her own anger had abated somewhat overnight, Darcy was every bit as furious as he had been the previous evening and adamant that her family be given no further opportunity to distress her. She rose onto one elbow and waited for him to take his eyes off the ceiling and look at her.

"I cannot leave matters as they are. My feelings notwithstanding, I grow more convinced by the moment that something must be very wrong to make Jane behave in such a way. I must at least attempt to speak to her."

"How many attempts must you make before you will concede the futility of it?"

She gave a small unhappy shrug.

He brushed the curls from her cheek. "I shall not spend another evening watching you pace the floor in agitation because your sister cannot keep a civil tongue."

"Think you I do not share the same concerns about your returning to Rosings?" she said, keeping her tone gentle.

"I am not in a delicate condition. You must consider the child."

She almost laughed. Of late, she had thought of little else, grown impatient for the quickening that it seemed would never happen. She had spent a good ten minutes peering in the mirror yesterday, searching for signs of increase that were simply not there. "I assure you I do—very constantly. But it would distress me much more to leave without an explanation. Besides, Jane is in the same condition. We shall have to argue delicately."

Tenderly, he pulled her down onto his chest, wrapping his arms around her. She felt him sigh his resigned acquiescence into her hair.

"What will you say to Mr. Bingley?" she enquired after a moment.

"As little as possible."

"Fitzwilliam, none of this is his fault. He clearly did not know Jane is with child, and he cannot be held responsible for the things she says. It must be very awkward indeed for him to be in such a position. You might at least assure him we do not blame him."

"Your generosity of spirit is astonishing, Elizabeth." It sounded anything but a compliment.

She laughed, though it soon trailed off with her next thought. "It will have to be if I am to keep my temper when I speak to Jane."

He did not object again. He only held her tighter.

Speaking to Jane turned out to be rather more difficult than Elizabeth had envisaged. She did not attend church with them or come out of her room when they returned, and she sent her excuses at dinner. Afterwards, when Miss Bingley remarked that she hoped Jane soon recovered from her sudden illness, Elizabeth could no longer restrain her vexation.

"This is absurd!" she hissed under her breath to Darcy. "Jane is not unwell. She is sulking. She will be complaining of her nerves and calling for salts next!"

"Elizabeth—"

"No! I beg your pardon, but I can go no longer without hearing what she has to say for herself." She promptly made her apologies to Mr. and Miss Bingley and marched up the stairs to Jane's room.

There was a long pause after her knock, long enough to afford reason a little latitude over her pique. Had she not begun that very morning to suspect something dire must be troubling her sister? And saliently, had she not learnt by now the danger of hurling charges in anger before being in possession of all the particulars? By the time Jane reluctantly enquired who knocked, she had her temper under far better regulation.

"'Tis I, Jane." There was no reply. "May I come in?"

A flash of livery and the sound of whispering at the far end of the passageway decided her. She would not stand there begging for all the staff to see. She pushed open the door and entered. Her sister sat at her dressing table, unmoving. "Jane, please turn around."

"What do you want, Lizzy?" she said, her voice distant and severe.

"I would talk to you."

"I am not feeling well. Can it not wait?"

"It would have to wait a good while, for I am leaving tomorrow, and I shall not see you again for many months." Jane made no answer. "That is your wish, then?" Silence.

Elizabeth bit back an angry remark, determined to remain composed. "I do not wish it, Jane. I do not wish for you and I to continue thus. I miss you." Her entreaty was met with more silence, yet she saw in her sister's shifting carriage that she was not unaffected. She took a few steps nearer. "Will you not speak to me?" She would not, apparently.

"Very well, if you will not, then I shall. I do not wish to believe what Lydia claimed you said of me, but your behaviour of late makes it impossible to discredit." She did not deny it. "Will you not tell me why you are so angry with me and in such a rage to shine me down?" Naught but the sound of forced breathing. "Why, Jane? There was never any rivalry between us before. Why should it matter to you now? I assure you it does not matter to me which of us is liked best, if only we could like each other!"

Elizabeth had never known Jane to be so cold. Still, she did not speak or turn to face her. Ever more certain the struggle was lost, she made one last heartfelt attempt. "I would not be on bad terms with you, Jane, especially now. Pray, let us not be at odds at what will be such a special time for both of us."

Jane stiffened and turned her head very slightly as though to ensure she had heard properly. "Both?"

"Aye. For I am with child also."

There was the longest pause.

"Get out."

"Pardon?"

"Go. Leave me." Her tone was implacable. Still, she did not turn round.

Elizabeth felt as though she were in a dream. "Will you not at least—"

Jane stood abruptly and spun to face her. "I said get out! Get out!"

The vehemence of her outburst forced Elizabeth several steps in that direction, but she was too stunned to go any farther of her own volition. She stared aghast at her sister, whose fine features were contorted beyond recognition by frightful, ugly emotion.

"Why?" she enquired breathlessly.

"Because I cannot compete with you any longer! I have none of the allurements that, for some reason, make you so vastly appealing. I am not sarcastic or gauche or coquettish or artful."

Each charge hit Elizabeth harder than the last, harrowing up every shred of anger she had so valiantly attempted to keep at bay. She opened her mouth, a furious protest on her tongue, but Jane had not finished.

"And neither am I with child, you stupid, selfish girl!"

"What?"

"Had you not been so utterly self-absorbed, you might have grasped that Mama was mistaken and saved me your boasts! Instead, with your usual disregard for anybody's feelings but your own, you have forced your way in here and crowed of your latest triumph."

Elizabeth clenched her fists so tightly that her nails dug into her palms. "Believe me, I wish I had not, for you have not even mustered the good grace to congratulate me."

Jane laughed someone else's laugh, her smile twisted into a bitter sneer. "Congratulations then, Lizzy. You have now trounced me in every possible way."

"Trounced you? Think you I got with child to outdo you? Can you not conceive that Darcy and I might have had other inducements? The world does not revolve around you!"

"There is *nothing* of which I am more aware!" Jane all but screamed back. Tears had begun to roll freely down her face, though she did not sob. They seemed to fall quite independently of her ire. "It revolves solely around *you*—only you are too rapt with your own existence to see it!"

"Listen to yourself! You are all resentment and bitterness!"

"And you are all coquetry and satire!"

Elizabeth gaped in furious disbelief. "And you wonder why I am loved better than you?"

Before she had closed her lips on the last word, Jane's palm landed hard across her face. Searing pain bloomed over her cheek, and she staggered several steps backwards in surprise.

Either time slowed or her heart sped up alarmingly as Elizabeth met the gaze of the stranger who had struck her.

No apology was forthcoming. Instead, Jane said quietly, "I asked you to go."

Slowly, deliberately, ignoring her shaking hands, Elizabeth turned her back on Jane and left the room, closing the door firmly behind her.

When, after an hour, Elizabeth had not returned from her sister's room, Darcy sent her maid to fetch her. When the maid returned to say Elizabeth was no longer with her sister, Darcy swore and went in search of her himself. She was in the first place he looked, furiously pacing the only area of floor still lit by the library's dying fire. Unsure what manner of comfort she might require, he stood at the edge of the hearthrug, crossed his arms and waited.

She saw him on her next turn. "Do not dare tell me I ought to have listened to you and stayed away," she said, continuing to pace. "I am in no humour for sermons."

His eyebrows rose. "Nor I for preaching, I assure you."

"And do not scowl at me so! I shall not harm the babe by walking."

"No, but you might harm it if you do not calm yourself."

"Regrettably, Fitzwilliam, not all the world is as unexcitable as you. You may be able to sit calmly and write long letters when you have been insulted, but the rest of us like to fume and pace!"

Thus, it was confirmed that Jane Bingley had indeed insulted her yet again.

"I am as disposed to pace as to write letters," he replied evenly. "As well you know. You have teased me for both."

Elizabeth stopped abruptly, clenched both her fists, and huffed an exasperated growl at the ceiling. "And now I am reduced to insulting you because I am too vexed to think sensibly!" She rubbed her temple with the heel of her palm and added in a subdued voice, "Forgive me."

Darcy unfolded his arms and stepped forward to wrap them around her. "I have told you before, I am not afraid of you."

Her frame was taut with anger, and it was some moments before she relaxed into his embrace. "Dearest Fitzwilliam, your arms could cure a thousand ills. What would I do without you?"

"Go for long solitary walks and hum to your heart's content, I should imagine."

She gave a small breathy exclamation and clung to him more fiercely, whispering of her love. He tightened his embrace but said no more.

"I ought to have listened to you and stayed away," she whispered at length.

"You ought to have returned to me instead of coming here alone."

"I did not wish for you to see me pacing. I promised you I would remain calm."

"You did. You are well though, I trust?" He dipped his head as he enquired, attempting to catch her eye, but she would not meet his gaze.

"In the way you mean, yes," she replied.

A less reassuring answer he could not imagine. He lifted a hand to her chin and tenderly but firmly tilted her face up. She resisted at first but then yielded with a sigh and allowed him to see her countenance. When he did, cold fury flooded his gut.

"She *struck* you?"

"Aye." Her flat tone spoke volumes as to her bitter disillusionment.

"What the devil possessed her?"

"I told her I am with child. And she is not, and she despises me for it."

Darcy felt a vein in his neck throb. "She did this *knowing* you are with child?"

Elizabeth nodded.

He could not immediately respond, so livid was his rage. When he felt able to speak without cursing, he unclenched his teeth. "We will be leaving at first light, we will not be returning, and you will not be seeing your sister again before we depart."

Elizabeth wrapped her arms about herself and turned to the dying fire, its dwindling light just enough to set aflame the tear that ran down her cheek. "You will hear no argument from me."

10

Prejudice, Thy Power Is Sinking

Monday, 5 October 1812: Kent

Colonel Fitzwilliam watched his cousin step down from the carriage and look up at the house with unconcealed contempt. He did not blame Darcy for his rancour and admired his decision to come at all, though it did not surprise him, familiar as he was with his fierce loyalty. He was also familiar with his disinclination for forgiveness; thus, he was not at all sure what to expect from the visit. He set his drink down and made his way to the entrance hall.

"Fitzwilliam!" Darcy exclaimed, shaking his hand. "We did not expect to see you here."

"It was a recent decision. Grandmother was determined to attend, but I had the devil of a time wriggling out of my engagements."

"Your grandmother is here?"

He grinned. "Ineludibly so."

"And Lady Catherine consented to this?"

"In no way, shape, or form! But she has used all her energy complaining and has none left with which to drive her out."

"Is she very ill then?" Darcy enquired gravely.

"Montgomery informs me she has good days and bad."

"And where is Montgomery?"

"He has taken Anne and my grandmother to Hunsford village. You may as well take the opportunity to settle into your room and change before dinner." The housekeeper had engaged Elizabeth by then in a discussion about lady's maids or some other such trifles, and Fitzwilliam took the opportunity to discreetly enquire how well Darcy had weathered his stay in Hertfordshire.

"Another time," he replied darkly.

Never had there lived such a proficient at conveying abject loathing in the mere curl of a lip; Darcy's scowl told a thousand words, and it did not take a genius to deduce something dire had occurred. And now he must suffer Lady Catherine's censure also!

"*De Charybde en Scylla*, eh?"

"*Précisément,*" Darcy replied flatly and turned away to escort his wife upstairs.

Since their falling out in the summer, Darcy and Lady Catherine had been in company but once, at Ashby's ball, and Fitzwilliam did not believe they had exchanged more than a few venomous glares on that occasion. With Lady Catherine's continued campaign of calumny and decidedly underhanded tactic of being incurably ill, he knew not whether this encounter would go much better. Watching them reunite that evening, therefore, made for an anxious few moments.

Darcy stood guard over Elizabeth with a storm seething in his eyes and a snarl prowling about his lips. Lady Catherine came in on Montgomery's arm, her new infirmity almost the first thing one noticed about her after the raging umbrage emanating from her in waves. As heavily as she dropped into her chair did her gaze fall disdainfully upon Elizabeth, on whose shoulder Darcy immediately placed his hand, as though to prevent her from even contemplating rising.

"You came then?" Lady Catherine said curtly.

Darcy had affected the ominous stillness that marked him as one of the few people of Fitzwilliam's acquaintance capable of unnerving him.

"Lady Catherine, you will greet my wife and me properly, or we shall leave."

Her countenance coloured crimson. "I hardly know how," she croaked.

"Your *wife* is my incumbent's cousin, a tradesman's niece! What am I to call her?"

"Mrs. Darcy," he replied in an eerily low voice. Fitzwilliam was rather surprised he had stayed to answer at all.

"I certainly shall not! My daughter was to be Mrs. Darcy. My sister was Lady Anne Darcy. This…*girl* from nowhere at all is not worthy of the name!"

"You shall not be the judge of who deserves my name, madam."

"I ought to have been, given how ill you have chosen!"

In a move that clearly demonstrated she was not afraid to defend herself, her husband, or their marriage, Elizabeth raised a hand to cover Darcy's where it gripped her shoulder and interrupted them both. "Lady Catherine, whether you like it or not, I am now your niece. I should be very happy if you were to call me Lizzy as Mrs. Sinclair does and pray we might waste no more time discussing it."

Her ladyship looked as though she had been asked to dance the waltz—with Lord Byron, in a whorehouse, naked. She turned to regard Mrs. Sinclair with disgust. "You call her Lizzy?"

"Do not be jealous, your ladyship. I have several nicknames for you also," the older lady replied.

"To shorten one's Christian name shows a vulgar coarseness of manners." Lady Catherine narrowed her eyes at Elizabeth. "It is precisely this sort of disdain for decorum with which you disgrace my nephew."

Privately, Fitzwilliam laughed at how well Elizabeth knew her husband, for she observably tightened her grip on his hand, tethering him in place. "Come now, madam," he said. "What is to be gained by continuing to make such charges? There is no foundation for them."

"No foundation?" Lady Catherine cried with a scornful laugh that devolved into a noisy and unpleasant clearing of her throat. "How is it, then, that I hear naught but tales of her shameful disregard for propriety, her constant arguing with Darcy, her struggles to perform the simplest of duties as mistress?"

A brief glance at Darcy prompted Fitzwilliam to hastily inspect the wider vicinity to ensure no firearms lay within his reach. "That is absurd," he said to his aunt. "Where have you heard such nonsense?"

"All of London has heard it!"

"Your ladyship," Mrs. Sinclair interjected, "I really must disabuse you of the notion that your circle of three acquaintances constitutes *the whole of London*."

Montgomery, also glancing anxiously at Darcy, added his quiet yet stern voice to proceedings. "And may I remind you of my hopes for reconciliation, madam? I beg you would accept Darcy's consent to make peace before he rescinds it, and for all our sakes allow these vile rumours to be forgotten."

"Would that these were rumours, sir!" Lady Catherine croaked, pulling a handkerchief from her sleeve and holding it near her mouth. "But I saw for myself evidence of one of her violent altercations, the tale of which I have since heard repeated abroad. And let us ask Darcy to deny it was necessary for him to drag her from the arms of another man mere days before his wedding."

Elizabeth's eyes opened wide, and Darcy's fury took on a wild edge of incredulity.

To Elizabeth, Lady Catherine continued. "I am no stranger to the particulars of that infamous affair, young lady. I know it all. How you willingly received that man's addresses, the patched-up arrangements made to keep you away from each other afterwards—"

"That is enough!" This Darcy actually shouted. He broke free of Elizabeth's hold—or she released him, Fitzwilliam was not sure which—and stepped towards Lady Catherine. On either side of him, all other occupants of the room sank away from him into their chairs like the Red Sea parting.

"Unless you wish me to leave this place forever, to refuse Montgomery and Anne the assistance they desire, for our families to be publicly and permanently divided, you will apologise to Elizabeth. You will welcome her with all due respect as my wife, and you will desist your reprehensible incivility this instant!"

But for Lady Catherine's rasping breath, there was silence as she and Darcy glared at each other in a monumental test of wills. It was Anne who broke the stalemate. "Please, Mother. I am grieved enough at the prospect of losing you. I would not wish to lose my cousin also."

It was a painful and courageously honest observation—and most effective. Lady Catherine sagged in her seat, and though her expression was cold and her words clipped, she nonetheless ceded her enmity.

"I apologise, Mrs. Darcy." She moved her eyes to her nephew before adding, "I am glad you are come," whereupon she fell victim to a virulent spell of coughing, which Fitzwilliam would have attributed to the avoidance of further capitulation had he not espied the spots of red on her handkerchief. "I have exceeded myself," she sputtered. "Excuse me."

Anne and Montgomery led her from the room with the promise of re-joining everyone for dinner once they had her settled. The door closed. Fitzwilliam let out a slow breath. Lady Catherine had apologised. Darcy had not renounced the de Bourghs for all eternity. The only bloodshed had been on Lady Catherine's handkerchief. All in all, the encounter could have gone significantly worse. With a relieved shrug, he moved to join Darcy and Elizabeth.

"I am well, truly," she was saying. "Only a little tired."

"Then you must rest," Darcy asserted, looking far more concerned than a simple claim to fatigue justified.

"You cannot think I mean to desert you after that?" she objected.

"You must rest," Darcy repeated, rather severely. "I shall have a tray sent up for you."

"Fear not," Fitzwilliam assured her. "I believe between me, the dinner table, and Lady Catherine's cognac, he will be adequately consoled."

Elizabeth smiled gratefully but did not seem ready to acquiesce.

"I should leave them to it, my dear," advised Mrs. Sinclair, pushing herself to her feet with her cane. "Men are never satisfied with things until they have ranted about them in their cups. I shall dine with you upstairs if you have no objection to it. All the promise has gone out of the evening anyway now that her ladyship has shuffled off to bed. With any luck, she might shuffle a bit too far and topple right off the end of her mortal coil."

"Bloody Hell! I ought never to have brought her here!" Darcy exclaimed as soon as the door shut behind the two ladies.

Fitzwilliam went directly to the sideboard, of the opinion that getting foxed and grumbling about the whole sorry mess was a fine idea. "She seemed to hold her own."

"It should not be necessary for her to *hold her own,*" Darcy shot back, accepting the drink Fitzwilliam handed him and taking a substantial swig. "This hostility is not good for the…it is not good for her health."

"I must say, I have never considered Elizabeth to be a fragile sort of woman. Why the sudden excessive concern?"

His cousin stared into his glass for a moment or two, his expression softening into a small but exultant smile. "She is with child."

"Bugger me, already?"

Darcy's slight shrug seemed to ask what else he had expected. Fitzwilliam shook his head at yet another example of the man's nauseating proficiency in all things and offered his hearty congratulations. "Do not blame yourself for having brought her here. I daresay, now the worst is over, Lady Catherine will calm down."

"That had better be the worst of it. Another word of her vile philippic and we shall leave directly."

"Oh, I rather think she will back down," he said lightly, wandering over to seat himself at the pianoforte. He poked at a few of the keys. "You certainly made your point, old boy."

Darcy's brow contracted. He took an angry gulp of his drink and stalked to scowl out of the window into the night. "It is unfortunate that we came here directly from Hertfordshire. Events there left me in no humour to hear another word spoken against Elizabeth."

Fitzwilliam closed the instrument and leant on the lid. "I think it high time you told me what the devil happened at Netherfield."

Darcy's frown deepened, accurately presaging the grim account he proceeded to give. When he was done, Fitzwilliam stared at him, appalled. "And this was her elder sister, you say? Not any of the ghastly younger ones?"

"It was Jane. Bingley's angel."

"Good God! How did you act?"

"I informed Bingley that I would no longer recognise his wife or receive her into any of my houses."

Fitzwilliam raised his eyebrows and blew out his cheeks. "How did he like that?"

"Very ill, though he did not cavil."

Snatching up his glass, Fitzwilliam left the pianoforte and joined Darcy in staring out onto the moonlit lawn. "That must have been very difficult. You have been friends a long time."

Darcy breathed in deeply through his nose and nodded. "We have. But Elizabeth is my priority now. I shall tolerate no further injury to her honour or her person." He quaffed the rest of his drink and snarled. "Neither shall I tolerate Greyson's loose tongue."

"I very much doubt Greyson has said a word after the little chat we had with him. Lady Catherine much more likely had that tale from Collins."

"What about the rest of the claptrap she claims is circulating about London?"

"I daresay that is all invention—borne of jealousy, most likely. You broke a lot of hearts about Town when you married Elizabeth, you know." Darcy levelled a stare at him. "'Tis true! There was universal despair amongst the ladies of the ton the day your announcement was printed in the *Times*. Miss Periwinkle attempted to take her own life by pricking her finger with her embroidery needle. Miss Wilson declared she had nothing left for which to live and threw herself off a pavement into a puddle. Lady Frances cried herself to death." That earned him an eye roll. "Lord Tewkesbury's heart just about stopped altogether. He had five hundred pounds on your marrying Miss Bingley."

"Stop."

"That one is not even a joke."

It turned out his grandmother was correct. A stiff drink, a spot of discourse, and Darcy was almost smiling again.

Tuesday, 6 October 1812: Kent

The sun shone bright and warm the next morning, oblivious to the pall of gloom enshrouding everyone at Rosings. Eager to escape the house, Elizabeth left early to call upon her friend Charlotte Collins but found her not at home. On learning from the servant that she had gone into Hunsford village, Elizabeth walked there in the hope of seeing her but to no avail. Eventually, exercised but divested of none of the confidences she had hoped to divulge to her friend, she walked back in the direction of the house.

There, leaning against the stile separating the parsonage from Rosings Park, she found her husband awaiting her. He cut a dashing figure in his snugly fitted trousers, precisely placed hat, impeccably defined side-whiskers, and knee-buckling little smile.

"I was considering sending out a search party."

She refrained from suggesting he ought to consider employing a permanent staff for the purpose. "My apologies. I thought you were busy with Mr. Montgomery."

"We are done." He pushed away from the stile and came towards her. "Are you too tired to walk a little farther?"

"No, I should like that very much." Indeed, she was happy to stay out of

Lady Catherine's way for as long as possible. "Where shall we walk?"

"Any path you choose but that one," he replied, nodding at the one leading to Rosings. She grinned at their like minds and then, curious to discover what changes the different season had wrought on one of her favourite haunts, set out in the direction of the grove that lined the park.

IN TRUTH, DARCY WAS NOT IN A HUMOUR FOR WALKING, TALKING, OR indeed anything but ordering his trunks packed and departing forthwith. It seemed every time he came to this cursed place, he must wrestle with violently conflicting notions of affection and duty and without much history of success. He had hoped some time alone with Elizabeth would improve his humour, and indeed, it did until he recognised her chosen destination. Then, with the remembrance of her unbearable rejection growing more vivid with every step, his spirits grew gloomier than ever.

"How went your discussions with Mr. Montgomery?" Elizabeth enquired.

"Well enough. He has the capital to save Rosings, provided it is managed carefully."

"Hence his desire for your assistance?"

Darcy inclined his head but said nothing more. His attention had come to be fixed upon the gate at which he had handed Elizabeth his letter.

"Will you help him, despite your aunt's behaviour?"

"I shall." This pleased her, he could tell. What he would not have given *then* to show her he was not devoid of all proper feeling!

"You are not happy," she said gently, startling him from his reverie. "I am sorry the visit has not started well."

"It is not that which troubles me presently," he admitted, smiling ruefully at his own foolishness.

She stopped walking and turned to him, all anxiety. "Then what does?"

"It is this place. My memories of it are inexpressibly painful to me."

She lifted a hand to his cheek, and though her next words were teasing, her voice was as soft as her touch. "Oh, Fitzwilliam, you dear, silly man! I thought all that was forgotten?"

"Forgetting is not my forte, as well you know. I left this place believing I had lost you forever."

"Yes, you do have a penchant for losing me, I have noticed."

He choked out a surprised burst of laughter. "Would that I had known then how I should come to be the constant object of your wit, teasing devil of a woman!" He pulled her closer, then one arm at a time, took hold of the front edges of his greatcoat and wrapped them around her, cocooning her against his chest. "What would you have said had someone told you after that night you would be back here half a year on, wife to me, and increasing with my child?"

She looked up at him dubiously. "If that is *all* I had been told, I think I would have been justified in being excessively alarmed."

His smile faltered. She was perfectly right, of course, yet it made hearing it no less painful, for it served as further proof of how she had despised him at the time. She saw it, God love her. She saw it and immediately redressed the injury.

"Though, had I been told how blissfully happy you would have made me in that half a year, how wonderful it would be to be held the way you hold me and kissed the way you kiss me, how honoured I should feel to be carrying the child of the best man I have ever known, had I been told how very dearly I should have come to love you, I believe I might have been more sanguine about it."

It frightened him how fiercely he loved her. It had then and it did still. He made no attempt to find the words to express it, however; he doubted any existed sufficiently profound. Instead, he took her by the hand and drew her to the nearest tree, from which he plucked one of the last remaining leaves. Silently, he pressed a tender kiss to her brow and the leaf into her hand, closing her fingers around it.

"Fitzwilliam?"

"Yes?"

"Kiss me. The way you do."

Darcy's spirits seemed to improve drastically thereafter, and Elizabeth's certainly did. They enjoyed a far pleasanter stroll through the grove than any they had shared the previous spring and returned to the house in excellent humour.

A happy sight greeted them upon reaching the lawn. Mr. Montgomery and a small boy, whom Elizabeth presumed must be his son, were playing a game of cat and mouse. Too busy watching his father over his shoulder to pay heed to where he ran, the boy promptly careened headlong into Darcy's legs, which had rather the same effect as a blancmange being hurled at a boulder—one moved not at all, and the other crumpled in a messy heap on the ground. Elizabeth crouched to help the boy to his feet, brushing his breeches clean.

"Jonathan, do be careful!" Mr. Montgomery called as he made his way towards them.

"It is very nice to meet you, Master Jonathan," Elizabeth said. "I am Mrs. Darcy. And this is my husband, Mr. Darcy."

"You have introduced yourselves, I see," Mr. Montgomery puffed, arriving at the scene rather short of breath. To his son he said, "Mr. Darcy is Miss de Bourgh's cousin."

Much to Elizabeth's delight, the boy gave them a dear little bow and then craned his neck to look up at Darcy.

"You are too big to be a mouse," he declared. "I shall be the mouse. You be the cat." Then he turned and toddled away across the lawn, leaving the three adults regarding each other—one apologetically, one sceptically, and the other vastly diverted.

Elizabeth raised an expectant eyebrow at her husband. With a sigh and a perfectly solemn countenance, he removed his hat and greatcoat and handed them to her, then exploded into a run across the lawn. Jonathan squealed and tripped over his own feet attempting to escape. Mr. Montgomery soon joined them, and Elizabeth watched with melting heart as two of the most serious and dignified men of her acquaintance darted about the lawn, drawing shrieks of happy laughter from the little boy. She could not help but suppose Darcy's anticipation of fatherhood contributed to his rare eschewal of decorum, and her stomach did another of its little pirouettes as she fell a little further in love with him.

Only as she looked about for a seat did she notice the solitary figure occupying a bench on the far side of the lawn. She presented a lonely picture, and Elizabeth set out at once to speak to her. "Good morning, Miss de Bourgh. May I join you?"

"Mrs. Darcy," she replied, nodding at the space next to her by way of permission but not moving to make it any larger.

Not overly surprised and certainly not deterred, Elizabeth lowered herself onto the bench, balancing Darcy's hat and coat on her lap. Having imposed this far, she felt obliged to begin the conversation, but not knowing the least bit about her, was unsure which subjects were safe. She settled on enquiring after her health.

"I am as well as I ever am. Which is not very," answered Miss de Bourgh.

"I beg your pardon, I was not aware you were unwell."

"I am not unwell. I am simply not well."

"I see." *Such a contrary creature!* "You must be greatly anticipating your wedding tomorrow."

"Must I?"

"I hope for your sake that you are. Mr. Montgomery is a very kind, unassuming gentleman. I hope you will be very happy together. From what I hear, it sounds as though he has grown very fond of you."

This remark brought Miss de Bourgh's head whipping around and the first splash of colour to her cheeks Elizabeth had ever observed. "He has?"

"Why, yes. Darcy tells me he speaks very highly of you indeed. I understand he values your calmness of temper in particular." This evidently flustered her, leading Elizabeth to wonder whether she had ever received a compliment on aught, other than the things her mother believed she might have accomplished had her health allowed it. "Master Jonathan seems a lovely, lively little boy."

"He is certainly the latter."

Elizabeth smiled. "Most three-year-olds are, I think."

"Are you much in the company of young children?"

"I have been, at various times. I have three younger sisters and four very young cousins."

Miss de Bourgh picked at a fleck of dust on her pelisse then looked into the distance with a sniff. "I never thought I would have children. I know not what one is expected to do with them."

A small laugh escaped Elizabeth's lips before she could prevent it. Such a curious mix of uncertainty and arrogance she had never seen. "Does Master Jonathan have a nanny or a governess?"

"Both."

"Then all there is for you to do is love him."

Her companion's only response was to look moderately terrified.

"Miss de Bourgh," Elizabeth said cautiously, "our husbands are good friends. It is probable you and I shall be thrown together quite often as a result. I cannot but think it would be tedious to be always in each other's company and never at liberty to enjoy it. Do you not agree?"

"Come to the point, Mrs. Darcy. I do not care for clever tongues."

There really was no further proof required that she would never have truly appreciated Darcy had she married him. "Very well. I should like it if you and I could be friends."

Elizabeth had rather expected her to be offended by this proposal, and she was surprised when spots of colour once more pinked her cheeks, for she looked more abashed. It occurred to her that perhaps Miss de Bourgh did not have many acquaintances she could call 'friend.' "Mayhap, in time," she pressed gently, "we might learn to be mothers together." She received no answer but counted it as a great victory that neither did she receive a rebuff. "Shall we begin now?" she enquired, gesturing with a nod towards Jonathan.

Miss de Bourgh gave the smallest of nods. As they walked onto the lawn, a slight movement behind her caught Elizabeth's eye. She looked up at the house and observed Lady Catherine peering from an upstairs window. She smiled up at her and inclined her head. Her ladyship's eyes narrowed furiously, the curtain dropped back down, and she disappeared from view. Elizabeth sighed, then just as quickly smiled and turned to forge ahead with Miss de Bourgh, counselling herself that the walls of Badajoz were not brought down in a day.

Tuesday, 6 October 1812: Hertfordshire

"Oh, Sister, I cannot recall ever seeing her so withdrawn, not even when Mr. Bingley went away last autumn."

"Is she very distressed? What did she say?"

"Very little—only that it is certain she is not with child. Her courses arrived on Sunday."

Mrs. Philips shook her head sadly. "Well, she is not the first woman to be mistaken about such a thing."

"It breaks my heart to think how her hopes have been dashed."

"And yours, my dear."

"Yes, mine too! For I was certain she must be increasing. She showed all the signs! She even asked me on Saturday last how long a woman must usually wait to feel the quickening."

"I see why you were so convinced. She obviously believed it to be true."

"And now all our hopes are dashed."

"Only temporarily, Sister. With any luck, you will not have to wait long for better news—from Lizzy if not Jane."

"What use is it to me if Lizzy has a child, for I shall scarcely ever see it! I am getting too old to be forever traipsing hither and thither about the country."

"I am sure her husband will be vastly pleased to hear that," said Mr. Bennet, walking into the room and taking up a position before the fire. "Perhaps that is why Mr. Bingley delays. He may wish to find a house farther away before he begets another excuse for you to visit him."

Nothing Mrs. Philips could do would settle Mrs. Bennet's nerves after that remark. There was nothing for it but to help her sister to bed and request a tonic from Hill that would allow her to sleep off her disappointment.

Thursday, 8 October 1812: Kent

Fitzwilliam stifled a yawn. He wished he had not fought so prodigiously hard to remain awake throughout the wedding ceremony, for a brief nap then might have afforded the stamina required to endure this—the dullest celebration in the history of matrimony.

Lady Catherine and all her cronies, whom she had been adamant must attend to sufficiently mark the vastly prestigious occasion, had collared him and Elizabeth on the sofas. Elizabeth, however, was too busy fluttering her eyelashes at Darcy across the room to pay any heed to the conversation, leaving him the sole casualty of the ladies' inane chatter, and he was rapidly losing the will to live.

"Of course," Lady Catherine croaked, "had Anne's health allowed her to be in London more, she would have attended the opera very frequently and enjoyed it better than most, for she has a discerning ear."

"That is not to be doubted," Lady Metcalfe replied. "And had I had a daughter, I am certain she would have been blessed with superior taste and enjoyed everything that is fine."

"Will you visit the opera while you are in London?" Fitzwilliam enquired of Elizabeth, attempting to regain her attention and not being wholly successful.

"I hope not," she replied absently. "I cannot abide the opera."

"Cannot abide it!" Lady Rutherford repeated, aghast.

"Everybody in our sphere enjoys the opera," Lady Hartham said. "No woman can consider herself accomplished who does not appreciate the finer arts."

Lady Catherine said nothing, but then her lips were so contorted with disdain, Fitzwilliam thought she probably was not able.

"What of your husband?" Lady Metcalfe pressed indignantly. "Would you deny him the pleasure of it?"

"By no means, ma'am. If he wishes to go, I am sure we shall."

"Well, I hope you do, for only by taking the trouble to attend will you begin to appreciate it as you ought."

Elizabeth inclined her head.

"You must see *Idomeneo*, in that case. It begins towards the end of the month and is certain to be superior to anything else being performed."

"I thank you for the recommendation, though my husband generally prefers Handel's operas."

"Miss Ben—Mrs. Darcy," Lady Catherine interjected. "It is vexing enough that you must give your *own* opinions so freely. Do not presume to begin giving my nephew's as well. He is perfectly capable of speaking for himself."

"Lady Hartham," Fitzwilliam said hastily, feeling guilty for having embroiled Elizabeth in the discussion, "have you heard from your son recently? How fares he in Lisbon?" As hoped, this set the ladies off on a different tangent. He turned slightly and whispered his apologies to Elizabeth. "I quite fed you to the wolves. You must allow me to make amends. Shall I cause a distraction that you might escape?"

"Too risky," she replied with a grin. "But if you feel you must atone, you may fetch me a drink."

"Certainly. Wine?"

"Do not trouble yourself, Fitzwilliam," Darcy said, arriving from nowhere to hand Elizabeth a glass.

"Oh, where is mine?"

"I was not aware you were thirsty."

Fitzwilliam looked between them, amused by a fleeting notion that they must communicate via blinks—one for "thirsty," two for "hungry," and three for "your aunt has slighted me again, immediate rescue required."

"There you are, Darcy," Lady Catherine said loudly. "What have you been discussing with Lord Rutherford all this time?"

"The new theatre on Drury Lane, madam."

"Oh, yes, my husband is an avid patron of the arts," Lady Rutherford said, adding with a sly glance at her friends, "and he especially enjoys the opera. Indeed, he considers it as one of the first refinements of polished societies. Would you not agree, Mr. Darcy?"

"Of course he would," Lady Catherine answered for him. "My nephew is a great lover of the opera and attends regularly."

Fitzwilliam caught Elizabeth's eye, rather enjoying the twinkle her amusement afforded them.

"I expect you will go to see *Idomeneo* when it begins," Lady Metcalfe said to Darcy.

"I have no plans to, madam."

"Oh, that is correct," she replied in a tone of condolence. "Your wife has just been telling us she does not much care for the opera. We must not blame her. People of certain spheres do not generally have the opportunity to attend. Though I must say it is very good of you not to complain about the deprivation. I am sure I should not be so gracious about it."

Fitzwilliam held his breath, awaiting the cataclysm Darcy's scowl portended, yet in the end, a steady glance from Elizabeth was all it took to stay his reprisal.

"I merely prefer Handel's operas," was his only reply.

Fitzwilliam was still smirking over that inadvertent victory for Elizabeth when Montgomery and Mrs. Sinclair hailed them from across the room, prevailing upon Elizabeth to play the pianoforte. Darcy wasted no time in leading his wife to the relative safety of the instrument. The other ladies fanned out to find seats from which to criticise her performance, leaving him alone with his aunt.

Her ladyship spent the next several minutes unable to speak as she succumbed to a fit of coughing that Fitzwilliam suspected she had been withholding for some time. He fetched her a drink and stayed with her until she recovered.

"Anne seems very content," he said when she was composed.

"No thanks to the contemptible strumpet at my pianoforte."

He breathed a silent sigh and persevered. "Content nonetheless."

Lady Catherine sniffed disdainfully. "Would that Darcy could be."

"He is, madam."

"Do not attempt to mollify me, Fitzwilliam. It is my lungs that fail me, not my eyes. A fool could see he is not happy."

"If you will pardon me for speaking frankly, your incivility towards his wife is hardly likely to cheer him. Nor your ill health."

The latter seemed to surprise her though she quickly covered it with affected hauteur. "I am glad to discover he is not lost to all proper feeling. He ought to be distressed that I am ill."

"We all are."

"She is not," she said, waving her hand towards the instrument. Fitzwilliam was unsure whether she was referring to Elizabeth or Mrs. Sinclair, and since at least one of them was not the slightest bit troubled, he opted not to answer at all.

He caught sight of Darcy watching his wife play. Contrary to Lady Catherine's claim, he looked positively serene, which diverted him, for Darcy was not a man naturally given to serenity. To his mind, Elizabeth's influence was there for all to see. Would that he could dispel some of his aunt's prepossession that she might observe it herself.

"You know, I was there when Greyson importuned Elizabeth," he said, surprising his aunt for a second time. "I rather think the incident has been elaborated by the fool who relayed it to you." Lady Catherine made no response, but her expression invited him to explain. "The man was in no way encouraged, and there was naught prurient about the incident on either side. He had the temerity to offer for Elizabeth under Darcy's nose, despite their already being engaged. She refused and walked away, Greyson took hold of her arm to prevent her from leaving, and Darcy intervened to demand that he go. That is all there was to it. "

She received this information in silence, her lips pinched and her brow creased. Fitzwilliam thought he might as well take advantage of her rare quiescence. "As to her being struck, the officer in question was violently drunk and attacked her in the street. She can scarcely be blamed."

"Of course she can! What was she doing anywhere near a drunkard in the first place?"

"Attempting to defend Darcy's good name, I understand." He rather liked being able to surprise his aunt this often. "She is not the coquette you believe her to be. Indeed, you do Darcy a grave injustice in continuing to think ill of her."

"Do I? Regardless of whether those reports are true, her descent, her connections, her vast unsuitability cannot be denied. It will not be long until it is widely known how poorly she has adapted to Pemberley. When he is ridiculed in every corner of the world by every person who knows him, Darcy will regret marrying her. It cannot go otherwise."

Fitzwilliam shook his head. "I know not what nonsense has been passed your way, but I assure you, Darcy has nothing but praise for Elizabeth's endeavours at Pemberley. Doubtless, she has lessons to learn, but she is a perfectly capable, clever woman. There is no reason to doubt she will learn all she needs to with time. And you cannot but think Darcy will be a positive influence on her."

Her ladyship faltered slightly but quickly arrived at another objection. "What of the visits of her uncle and aunt from the city?"

"I daresay the walls of Pemberley will not crumble," Mrs. Sinclair said, hobbling up to join them. "Unlike *your* walls, which seem to be crumbling of their own accord without any such provocation."

"Oh, take her away, Fitzwilliam!" Lady Catherine wheezed.

He thought that an excellent idea and duly did as he was bid. A backwards glance, indeed several more glances over the remainder of the day, revealed an uncommonly pensive Lady Catherine intently observing a certain gentleman and his new wife.

Friday, 9 October 1812: Hertfordshire

"It is absurd," Caroline said, following her brother into the room and closing the door behind her. "This is the sixth day in succession she has remained in her rooms."

"Yes, I am aware," he replied wearily, dropping into a chair.

She walked behind the opposing one and leant over it with both hands on the back, glaring at him. "You cannot allow it to continue. The servants are beginning to talk."

Charles's head fell back, and he stared at the ceiling. "Let Jane stay in her room for as long as she pleases. I have no wish to see her."

"What you wish is neither here nor there. You must put it right! Is it not enough that you married so far beneath you? Must you satisfy everybody's contempt by allowing it to be known the marriage is falling apart before the first twelvemonth is out?"

He only sighed.

"Charles!" She slapped the back of the chair. His head whipped upright. "What efforts have you made to persuade her to come down? Have you even spoken to her since she locked herself away?"

"No."

For a moment, Caroline squeezed her eyes shut in vexation, repressing the urge to hurl something at him. "Never did I think the day would come that I should be defending Jane's character to you, but for heaven's sake, she is not a monster! You cannot mean to ignore her indefinitely."

He sat up, all indignation. "She slapped her sister!"

"And? Never was there a woman more in need of a slap! I should rather give her a medal."

"Caroline!" Her brother launched himself to his feet, though he appeared unsure what to do next and merely stood frowning uselessly.

"Oh, Caroline *nothing*. When will you overcome this ridiculous fascination with Eliza Darcy?"

"I am not fascinated!" he cried with more than enough affront to convince her of quite the opposite. "I require no romantic inclinations to persuade me that slapping one's sister, a guest in one's house and the wife of one's husband's oldest friend, is a reprehensible thing to do!"

"It was an impolitic thing to do certainly, but she was distressed. Would you punish her forever and ruin all our reputations over one instance of passion? I should have thought you would be pleased to discover she had some!"

"What had she to be distressed about?"

Caroline regarded him incredulously. How he had reached three-and-twenty unscathed with such a gaping want of penetration, she would never know. "Well, let us consider. Could it be that her delightful mother announced to the entire family that she was with child when she was not? Or that her sister then tactfully informed her that she is? Or simply that, in general, she is cursed with the most lamentable relations in the kingdom?"

Her brother abruptly lost all colour from his countenance and slumped heavily back into his chair. "Lizzy is with child?"

She threw her hands in the air. "Lord save us! It ought to be nothing to you if she is!"

"It is nothing to me—except a surprise. Darcy did not mention it."

"For which we must all be thankful, for if you had swooned in this manner before him, he would certainly have wished to know why!"

"How do you know of this?" he enquired weakly.

"As I said, the servants are talking, and they will continue to do so for as long as you give them cause. Pray, end this stupid quarrel before it becomes a scandal."

"And how do you suggest I do that when she will not see me?"

"I thought you said you had not attempted to speak to her?"

"I went to her twice before she and Lizzy argued—on Saturday evening after her family left and again on Sunday morning. Both times, I was refused admittance. She will not see me."

Caroline peered at her brother very closely. "Why not? What have you done? I sincerely hope I shall not hear of any more maids being dismissed without reason."

He jumped slightly and looked at her wide-eyed, though whether in affront or alarm she could not be sure.

"I have not done anything!"

"Then why is she displeased with you?"

"Would that I knew! Perhaps if what you say is true, it is because she is not yet with child."

"Then for heaven's sake get one on her!"

He pouted. "It is not that simple."

She clenched her teeth. Throwing something at him was becoming more and more of a temptation. "I have heard it is."

"That was not my meaning!" he cried, colouring deeply. "I meant—blast it, Caroline, I do not know that I wish to…to—we are not even speaking!"

"I know! For six whole days, I have had to look out of the window to discover what the weather is doing."

"Pardon?"

"Oh, never mind it. Would that you only cease blaming her for one trifling little spat and make your peace before you become the laughing stock of the world."

"You are quite alone in thinking this a trifling concern, Caroline."

"In this house, I am generally alone in thinking, but do surprise me."

"Darcy has excluded Jane from all his houses."

Caroline's heart lurched into her mouth. "What? Why on earth would he do that? What is it to him if his wife has words with her sister? Imagine if Mr. Hurst banished me from Farley House every time I squabbled with Louisa!"

"Yes, well, as Darcy himself informed me, one does not slap the mistress of Pemberley and remain welcome there."

Caroline stared at him for a moment then threw her arms in the air. "Tremendous! I do not believe I could conceive of a better way to ensure we become social pariahs, except perhaps if we were to contract leprosy and begin moulting limbs on the dance floor at Almack's."

Her brother opened his mouth to speak, but since it was exceedingly unlikely he meant to say anything of value, she shouted over him. "Debarred from Pemberley! Have you any idea how low we shall sink in the eyes of the world if this is discovered? Remedy this! Before anybody learns of it!" She spun on her heel to leave but turned back when he called her name. "What is it?"

"Is the staff talking about anything else?" He looked excessively conscious.

"Why? Is there something else for them to talk about?"

"No, I was only—no, nothing. Would that I had listened to you and never come back to Hertfordshire!" He dropped his head into his hands—which was fortunate, for it meant it was marginally better guarded when, in the next moment, a pin cushion, replete with a full contingent of pins, was violently flung at it.

Sunday, 11 October 1812: Kent

Elizabeth's week at Rosings had never promised to—and had certainly not—delivered any significant improvement in relations, but neither had it been without its small advancements. With Mrs. Montgomery, she had formed the beginnings of a tentative understanding that, with a good deal of time and an even greater measure of patience, might eventually become something approaching a delicate sort of friendship. Darcy and Mr. Montgomery were steadily rekindling the familiarity they had enjoyed before one went abroad, and Elizabeth could not but be pleased to have gained such an amiable, steady gentleman for a cousin.

Lady Catherine still looked on her with the utmost disdain, but she had mostly given over casting aspersions about her abilities in favour of not speaking to her at all and observing her with disconcerting application. Darcy was convinced it was to find fault. Elizabeth was more hopeful, choosing to believe she was searching for something of which to approve, though if she had met with any success, she had not yet admitted it.

Elizabeth and Darcy's happiness only increased. Every day was punctuated with blissful private moments, shared jokes, and all manner of discussions from edifying to teasing. Of Master Jonathan they had both grown very fond, delighting in his sweet antics whenever he was brought down from the nursery and secretly anticipating the time when their child might play with his or her new cousin.

Thus, though Elizabeth was not sorry to be leaving on the morrow, neither was she sorry to have come, which was a better frame of mind than that with which she had departed Netherfield a week earlier.

"You are very quiet," Charlotte said as they emerged arm in arm from the church. "Nothing is amiss, I hope?"

"No, I was only thinking of everything that has happened this week—well, and since I was here in April, really. I have endured the worst and best moments of my life in these few short months. I never dreamt my life should end up so…altered. Oh, do not look so worried. I am the happiest creature alive, but I cannot deny it is overwhelming at times."

"I am not surprised you feel that way. Every woman experiences some change when she marries, but rarely so vast or challenging an adjustment as yours. You are bearing it with remarkable fortitude though." She patted Elizabeth's arm. "You endure his family's incivility with far more forbearance than they deserve. I should hate to see you lose heart now."

"No fear of that," Elizabeth replied with a grin. She lowered her voice as they joined the back of the crowd of people milling about in front of the lychgate. "My heart is well and truly bound to my husband's and in no danger of being lost."

Charlotte smirked. "Forever the romantic." Her teasing had not the chance to gain pace, for a young girl directly in front of them—about Lydia's age and with a similar grasp of propriety—drew their attention with a barely whispered exclamation.

"Did you see her? Even paler and more miserable than usual!"

"Aye, very ill indeed!" her equally indiscreet companion replied.

"Who was the gentleman with whom she was sitting?"

"Her husband, Mr. Montgomery."

"I thought she was supposed to marry Mr. Darcy?"

The second girl giggled. "Peter heard Mr. Darcy lost a wager to Mr. Montgomery and was obliged to give up his claim to Rosings Park to settle the debt."

"He cannot have been very distressed, for who would wish to marry that cross, sickly thing anyway? Perhaps it was Mr. Montgomery who lost the wager, and he was obliged to marry Miss de Bourgh in Mr. Darcy's stead!"

"It is unlikely," Elizabeth said, unable to hold her tongue any longer, "since neither the house nor the lady was theirs to wager. Mrs. Montgomery is a sensible woman from a distinguished family. She is quite at liberty to choose her own husband. She ought to be celebrated for having chosen to take on a little boy in need of a mother. I should wager he cares not one whit for the paleness of her countenance."

The two girls turned to face her and looked caught between astonishment, shame, and indignation. Just as Elizabeth thought the latter might triumph and cause a scene, Charlotte hastened to say, "Miss Webb, Miss Emily, allow me to introduce my very good friend, Mrs. Darcy."

Both girls abruptly took on a pallor not dissimilar to the object of their earlier ridicule, curtsied, giggled, and ran away. With a rueful smile at her friend, Elizabeth set off again through the throng of villagers to where her party's various equipages waited in the lane.

"You are not distressed by their idle talk, I hope," Charlotte said quietly.

"On the contrary, I am comforted to discover my sisters are not the only thoughtless girls in England."

The approach of the rest of the de Bourgh party prompted a hasty but heartfelt adieu between the ladies. They were both reunited with their husbands whilst Fitzwilliam and Mr. Montgomery gallantly handed the other ladies up into their respective carriages.

"Wait!" Lady Catherine demanded. Her ladyship fixed Elizabeth with a steely glare. "Mrs. Darcy will ride with me."

Thus, after a quick re-shuffling of passengers between carriages, Elizabeth found herself travelling the short distance back to Rosings alone with Lady Catherine, rather than enjoying a final stroll back through the park as she and Darcy had planned. Her ladyship said nothing for the first several minutes.

Elizabeth waited, wondering whether it was more likely that she meant to bestow a surprise blessing or take advantage of one last opportunity to abuse her. A hoarse intake of breath presaged what transpired to be the latter.

"Let me be very clear, Mrs. Darcy, I shall never approve of you. You are of absolutely no importance in the world. You are impertinent, you are appallingly liberal in your thinking, and you have, against every appeal to common decency and reason, put my nephew in an unpardonably tenuous position in society." She looked away for a moment, coughing slightly as she peered out of the window. Eventually she looked back. "I do concede, however, that I may have underestimated your character."

Had there been no sides to the carriage, Elizabeth might have fallen from her seat.

Lady Catherine nodded brusquely as though satisfied with her astonishment. "Were you aware I was behind you when you were speaking to Mrs. Collins just now?"

"Why, no, ma'am."

"I did not think so. You might still have spoken that frankly regardless, but she certainly would not have. You were discussing your situation."

"Aye, a little."

"You spoke with more modesty than I have heard you admit to before. I am relieved to have heard it. You ought to be overwhelmed."

Elizabeth frowned warily. "I am not sure I—"

"Because no matter how strenuously you deny it, you were not born to this sphere, and you cannot have been prepared for this degree of responsibility. Complacency would be disastrous."

"I assure you, I have never been complacent ab—"

"But you act as though you are! Your behaviour shows nothing but an unjust assuredness of your success and an equal indifference to your failures." She paused and took a deep, rattling breath, continuing in a far calmer tone. "I am relieved to discover you are without such conceit, after all. Modesty, where there is real inferiority of mind and situation, modesty will be always under good regulation."

Elizabeth stared at her. "That may be so, but I think you credit me with too much. When I said I was overwhelmed, I was referring to the rapidity and magnitude of changes to my situation. I did not mean to imply I was suffering from any peculiar feelings of trepidation or inadequacy."

Lady Catherine's eyebrows rose, and she gave a huff of displeasure that immediately dissolved into coughs. Elizabeth waited for her spasms to pass then calmly but firmly pressed her point. "I am far from complacent, but I am assured of my resolve to be the very best wife to my husband I can be, and as long as he is satisfied with my efforts, so shall I be."

"Mrs. Darcy, I invited you to ride with me with the particular purpose of acknowledging that I may have been ungenerous in my assessment of your character. Am I to be repaid for my condescension with ingratitude and defiance?"

"I am certainly not ungrateful, and I hope my endeavour to be honest will not be taken as defiance. But nothing would be gained by my accepting your approbation for modesty I do not possess. You would only be disappointed the first time I behaved otherwise, and that would pain Darcy all over again. Far better that you accept me as I am."

Lady Catherine narrowed her eyes at her and did not reply for an uncomfortably long time. "I am able to count on one hand the individuals who are unafraid to speak plainly to me. You are among them. I abhor impertinence, but honesty and fortitude are qualities of which I can approve. I expect that is why Darcy admires you. Growing up with me as almost his closest relative has taught him to esteem strong women. You, no doubt, remind him of me." There was no response to that, but as usual, her ladyship required none. "You also spoke in defence of my daughter."

Elizabeth had not been prepared for such an arsenal of topics and was relieved to espy the gatehouse from the window, for it signalled an imminent end to the startling interview. "I did."

Her ladyship grunted disdainfully. "I give you credit for that, though I cannot account for why you did it. You cannot have any regard for her, or you would not have poached her husband."

Elizabeth schooled herself to restraint. Truly, from Darcy's first proposal to this thorny olive branch, her new family had the most extraordinary gift for delivering insulting compliments. "Perhaps your daughter and I are not the best of friends, but I should not like it if rumours that sprung up as a result of our union were to injure anybody in this family and neither would Darcy. Besides, I happen to think it a very fine thing that Mrs. Montgomery will be mother to Master Jonathan."

Again Lady Catherine peered overlong at her before replying. At length she lifted her chin and sniffed. "You are correct. It is your fault such rumours exist. It is only fitting that you exert yourself to quash them."

That comment brought Elizabeth to the very brink of her forbearance. "And what of the many rumours about me? Will you exert yourself to quash those?"

"When I remarked upon your willingness to challenge me, I did not mean it to be taken as an invitation to do it more often! Do not imagine you can dress up your insolence as courage and expect me to tolerate it."

"It is neither courage nor insolence that motivates me to speak thus, but my affection for Darcy. Can you not see how your willingness to heed every rumour about me is wounding him? And to what end? Your fears that I might make him a poor wife are irrelevant now. We are already wed!"

"They are not irrelevant. Your marriage does not mean the rest of his family should give up caring about him!"

"That is not wha—"

"I promised my sister I would take care of her children. If Darcy had married Anne, they would both have been set up forever, as would Miss Darcy. But he would marry you. I have salvaged my daughter's future, but his and his sister's could not be more uncertain. It is unlikely I shall live out another year, and what guarantee have I that they will not end up ridiculed and despised the whole world over once I am gone? My fears could not be more relevant!"

Elizabeth rubbed her temple. "Madam, I comprehend your attachment to him—indeed, it is very touching—but I am his wife. I cannot see how turning the world against me will help him."

"Do not be absurd! I am not turning the world against you. I may hear things, but I do not repeat them."

"You repeat them to him, and that pains him more than you can know."

"He needs to hear them. He needs to know what people are saying."

"People might cease saying those things if somebody who knew better contradicted them!"

"This is not to be borne! I shall not be made to account for myself to you!" Her pique abruptly gave way to a convulsive, barking cough that still had not passed when the carriage stopped before the house. Elizabeth pressed her own, fresh handkerchief into Lady Catherine's hand, and when a footman opened the door, instructed him to close it again.

"Forgive me," she said softly once her ladyship had finally quieted. A burgeoning suspicion that she had ruined her only remaining chance to win her over had dispelled much of her anger. "I meant no disrespect. Only...Lady Catherine, you may very well never approve of me, but I beg you would accept that Darcy does and cease vilifying him for it. Trust him that the rumours about me are untrue. Visit us at Pemberley and see for yourself how well we do. Let us convince you we shall not give the world cause to despise us. His happiness would be complete if you would only allow this rift to be mended before it is too late."

Her ladyship took several shallow breaths and spoke slowly as though to prevent a relapse. "If nothing else, your tenacity has convinced me your regard for him is sincere. There can be no other possible advantage to opposing me on every subject."

"My regard for him is—" She broke off, unsure how to adequately express the depth of her feelings. "I believe you will tire of hearing me say how dearly I love him long before I tire of saying it."

Lady Catherine regarded her strangely. "I accept your invitation." She shuffled forward in her seat and rapped on the window. "I shall visit Pemberley at Christmas." The door was opened and she climbed out.

Elizabeth followed her with mixed feelings. She knew not which was worse: an unresolved schism between nephew and aunt or another prolonged stay under the same roof together.

"And in the meantime," Lady Catherine said as soon as Elizabeth's feet touched the ground, "try eating ginger."

"I beg your pardon?"

"It will aid with the biliousness."

Elizabeth's eyebrows shot up. "Oh! I—how did you know?"

Lady Catherine sighed impatiently. "I may have but one living daughter, but I have been with child more times than I care to recount. I am aware of the signs."

"I see. Thank you."

"You must take care, Mrs. Darcy. That is my great-niece or nephew. Your responsibilities to this family increase by the moment!" In accordance with Elizabeth's expectations, Lady Catherine's word was the last. She walked away into the house.

"Elizabeth, are you well?"

She spun around at Darcy's anxious voice in time to see him march onto the drive from the lane. "Oh, my word! Did you run the entire way?"

"It felt like it!" said Colonel Fitzwilliam, emerging from the same point a moment later.

"Are you well?" Darcy repeated. "She has not distressed you?"

"I am well. Somewhat surprised but perfectly well, I thank you."

This appeased him but little, and he continued to scrutinise her countenance with the utmost concern. "What was said?"

"Let us go inside, and I shall relay it all."

"That will not do," Fitzwilliam said, laughing. "He passed the walk dreaming up every rum motive conceivable for my aunt to wish to talk to you alone. You must put him out of his misery and assure him nothing dreadful occurred."

Elizabeth grimaced. "That is debatable."

"Why?" Darcy demanded. "What *has* occurred?"

She looked up at him with playful contrition. "I seem to have invited her to Pemberley for Christmas."

Rosings Park, Kent
October 12

To Lady Ashby

You have been industrious in your endeavours to unearth and report Mrs. Darcy's failings to me. A week in her company has disproved the vast majority of your information, calling into question your purpose, which, it can only be presumed, was to recommend yourself to me by undervaluing her. You are sorely mistaken if you believe such despicable schemes could ever win you my good opinion.

Your information, in substantiating my greatest fears, has afforded me three months of the most painful and, I now discover, wholly unwarranted anguish, which has unquestionably contributed to my decline in health. You have shown yourself to be petty and vindictive without any of the probity exhibited by she whom you have so assiduously maligned.

You have sunk beyond redemption in my estimation. Do not presume to write to me again. If I discover you have dared to engage in any further idle talk pertaining to any member of this family, I shall be extremely angry and shall act accordingly. When next our paths cross, I expect to discover your loyalty and discretion vastly improved. Should you require guidance in the endeavour, you may look to Mrs. Darcy for illustration.

Tell my nephew I am seriously displeased.

Lady C. de Bourgh

Tuesday, 13 October 1812: London

"There you are!" Elizabeth said when Darcy entered the parlour. She set her book aside and reached a hand towards him. "Where have you been?"

He bent to kiss her hand. She was curled up on the sofa, and he sat down next to her feet, placing his hand on her stockinged ankle. "I called on Bingley."

"Oh, he is in Town?"

He nodded, caressing her calf. Bingley's calling card had been awaiting him when they returned the previous day, but he had wished to discover the purpose of his friend's visit before troubling Elizabeth with it, lest it signified further antagonism from her sister.

"What brings him here?"

"He accompanied Miss Bingley to Farley House to attend her sister as she nears her confinement, though I suspect he simply does not wish to be at Netherfield. Relations are strained, I understand."

Elizabeth's brow contracted. "Because of my quarrel with Jane?"

He nodded again.

"I am sorry to hear that. Unpleasant though it was, it ought not to come between them."

"How could it not? Any man's esteem would be damaged by such a display of meanness."

Elizabeth puffed out her cheeks. "He will have to forgive her eventually. They cannot become estranged over an argument that is not even their own."

"You know how he dislikes disputes. I do not believe he knows how to resolve it—and before you enquire, no, I did not advise him on the matter."

She grinned at him. "In this instance, you might have been forgiven."

"Oh, no! It is for him to take his wife in hand, not me, and so I told him."

Some part of that amused her, for she raised a satirical eyebrow. "And what said he to that?"

"He got absurdly affronted and asked if that is how I treat you."

"And how did you answer?"

"I laughed. I could no more control you than I could control the weather."

She gasped in mock outrage and lunged forward to poke him in the ribs. He grabbed her wrist and tugged her with him to recline into the cushions at his end of the sofa. "I am sorry for Bingley," he continued as he laced his fingers with hers. "It is not in his nature to expostulate, yet he will have to address her conduct, for it will injure his respectability if she continues thus."

"And hers," Elizabeth replied quietly. "What a muddle." Her melancholy did not last, though, and with a deep breath, she pushed herself upright and twisted to look down at him. "I hope you invited Mr. Bingley to join us at the theatre tomorrow."

"I did not." He reached to toy with a few curls of her hair that had come loose. "I wished to have you to myself."

"Well, you cannot have me to yourself," she said, playfully knocking his hand out of the way and standing up. "I have asked my aunt and uncle to join us now, so you may as well invite him."

Darcy fixed her with a look, resisting the smile that tugged at the corners of his mouth, lest it stretch so wide it made him appear ridiculous. "You see? Utterly uncontrollable."

"Veritably wild," she replied, smiling wickedly over her shoulder as she left the room.

No more than two heartbeats passed before Darcy was out of the door after her.

Pevensey Hall, Ashby, Derbyshire
October 13

Jane

I am gravely vexed. Everything you have ever told me about your sister's arts has been proved true. She has somehow managed to inveigle her way into the affections of my husband's aunt and poison her against me! A believes D has likely done everything in his power to keep E's failures concealed from his aunt. That must be so, for how else could she, of whom that lady never approved, have achieved such an improbable coup?

I am threatened with action if I speak out. So be it! Let them all suffer in ignorance and be disgraced in the end. You and I shall know better! I never wondered at your disliking her. Now I applaud you for it.

In respect to the other matter of which you wrote in your last letter, my counsel is to spare it not another moment's thought. You are far from alone in suffering such a—let me call it a disappointment. It is a universally accepted fact of married life. But attend, Jane! It is also a universally guarded fact, never spoken about in polite circles. Keep your counsel in this matter, allow B to do likewise, and in the fullness of time, when your house is filled with your children (an eventuality I personally would advise delaying as long as possible), such disappointments will no longer be of any significance to anybody.

Be sure to write again with news of your sister's next calamity that we may laugh together at our being entirely removed from her ruin and disgrace.

Yours etc.
Lady Ashby

Wednesday, 14 October 1812: London

ELIZABETH HAD NOT COMPREHENDED QUITE HOW TIRESOME HER TIME IN Kent had been until she left. Eight-and-forty hours later her spirits had risen to more than their usual liveliness, and she was vastly anticipating her evening at the theatre. Indeed, such was her good will towards Darcy that she rather rued overruling his wish to come alone, but on that she thought it better to remain silent.

There was a small stir as their party entered the theatre lobby—Darcy's prominence and her novelty still sufficient to generate some attention—but she paid it little mind. It was uncommonly busy for the time of year, and she was assured something or someone more interesting would soon steal everyone's attention.

They made their way in the direction of the stairs, but before they reached them, someone quite literally threw themselves into their path, tripping over an unknown obstacle and almost barrelling directly into Elizabeth. Darcy pulled her to one side, though the fellow still caught her arm with his shoulder, spinning her backwards slightly. After several more tottering steps, he rediscovered his footing and turned with an apology on his lips, whereupon all three froze and a painfully awkward moment ensued.

"Elizabeth!"

She closed her eyes. Of all the ways in which he might have withdrawn from the unfortunate encounter without exciting Darcy's ire, addressing her so familiarly was by far the least likely to succeed.

"Mr. Greyson." She inclined her head very slightly.

"Greyson," Darcy all but growled.

"My apologies, Mr. Darcy," he sputtered. "Had I known you were here, I should never have attempted to speak to Eliz…to your…to her. That is, it was not my intention to speak to her at all—and certainly not to impose myself upon—"

"It is well, sir," Elizabeth interrupted to save him from his own runaway tongue. "There is no harm done. Pray, do not let us detain you from your own party."

He clamped his mouth shut, nodded, bowed, and backed away into the crowds.

"Are you hurt?" Darcy enquired, turning to her all apprehension, his eyes darting pointedly to her stomach.

"Not at all."

"Was that Greyson?" Bingley enquired, appearing next to them to puff up Darcy's affront with his own. "The deuced cheek of the man!"

"Where have my aunt and uncle got to?" Elizabeth said hastily, peering about in search of her relatives, in no humour to permit either gentleman's indignation any latitude.

Mr. Gardiner obligingly appeared, apologised for having been waylaid by a friend, and without delay, they all joined the hordes going up the stairs. About mid-way up, a whisper—half overheard, half inferred from the accompanying look of contempt—alerted Elizabeth to the possibility that her encounter with Mr. Greyson would not escape elaboration by society's rabid imagination. A second remark soon sprang up from somewhere closer, this time with unmistakable references to the mistress of Pemberley and some manner of illicit affair. She could just imagine her father's delight were he here to witness such a plethora of folly.

"Miss Bennet!" somebody called in a vaguely familiar voice.

She looked about.

"Miss Bennet!" the gentleman called again, coming down the stairs towards her.

"Mr. Craythorne!" She felt herself blush fiercely, for all she could think of in that instant was the last time she had seen him and his *very evident* admiration for her on that occasion. Being now a married woman, her understanding completed the explanation her aunt had given at the time of what his breeches had ill-concealed, and she could scarcely bring herself to meet his eye for embarrassment.

"What a delightful surprise!" he said, resisting being shoved forwards by the people behind him. "You look exceedingly well. Pray, what brings you to London?"

"I live here. I am married now. May I introduce you to my husband, Mr. Darcy?"

Mr. Craythorne's face fell upon hearing her news, fell farther still when he heard the name Darcy, and almost dropped off his chin when he looked up—and up—to meet her husband's piercing stare.

To Darcy, Elizabeth said, "This is Mr. Craythorne. He used to lease Purvis Lodge near Meryton."

Both men bowed, if perfunctorily, for they had gone past each other by then and Mr. Craythorne was soon engaged in greeting Mrs. Gardiner on the steps below, though he did throw a forlorn farewell over his shoulder as he eventually relented to the momentum of the crowd and disappeared down the stairs.

"He seemed excessively pleased to see you," Darcy remarked as they reached the top.

Elizabeth shrugged, not wishing to expound upon the gentleman's particular interest in her.

Presently, her aunt, uncle, and Mr. Bingley arrived on the landing, and they all moved to the saloon serving their box. It was not as crowded as downstairs, nor as noisy; thus, she clearly heard the remark that Mr. Greyson's bumping into her had been contrived to facilitate a daring exchange of letters beneath her husband's nose. She pressed her lips together in amusement. *My, bad news travels quickly!*

"Darcy! It is you!" boomed a large gentleman coming towards them using his glass of wine like a scythe to clear a path through the crowd. "I thought it was. What brings you to London at this time of year?"

Relieved that not every person was foolish enough to concern themselves with idle gossip, Elizabeth gladly consented to being introduced to Mr. Thatcher and eagerly joined his discussion with Darcy of the Montgomerys' wedding. Thereafter, the conversation moved on to matters interesting only to landowners, and the party naturally divided. Mr. and Mrs. Gardiner struck up their own exchange, and Mr. Bingley turned to Elizabeth to do the same.

"This is precisely why I prefer balls—less talking and more dancing."

"And precisely why Darcy dislikes them," she replied, turning to him with a grin. "However did the pair of you end up friends?"

"I sincerely hope Darcy has not deprived you of too many dances because he does not enjoy it himself."

"We are going to a ball in a few days, as it happens. If I am very lucky, I might persuade him to one dance." She resisted the urge to turn and stare incredulously at whoever it was behind her muttering about her carrying on with Mr. Craythorne *and* Mr. Greyson. "And what are your plans in Town?" she enquired, ignoring it. "Do you intend to stay long?"

"Regrettably no, I must return tomorrow."

"I am sorry 'tis with regret that you must return to Jane. Pray, do not allow our quarrel to come between you."

He grew excessively awkward and stepped closer, speaking in a hushed voice. "Lizzy, I am appalled by what she did to you. You are…and she…" His eyes flicked first to her stomach and then to the place Jane had slapped her. "I do not know that I can forgive her."

"I beg you would. I have just endured an exceedingly trying visit with Darcy's family, attempting to resolve the schism I caused there. Pray do not require me to undergo the same unpleasantness with my own family."

"Darcy said nothing of any difficulties at Rosings. What happened to you there?"

Saving her the bother of answering, two absurdly plumed ladies walked past arm in arm, brazenly discussing Lady Catherine's displeasure at the new mistress of Pemberley's reputed ineptitude. Mr. Bingley frowned after them and, shortly afterwards, at a young man dressed in regimentals, who could be heard telling his companions about a Lieutenant Wickham, who had attempted to murder Mrs. Darcy upon discovering she had forsaken him for her new lover, Mr. Greyson.

"You must admire their inventiveness," she said, raising an eyebrow.

"Hardly. I know not how you bear it."

"I pay it no mind, and I hope you will not either. Now, will you promise me you will forgive Jane? I should be far happier if I knew you were not at variance because of me."

He smiled sadly. "For you, anything."

Perceiving she had made him uneasy, Elizabeth thanked him and reinserted them both into conversation with the rest of their party.

Having concluded his brief aside to his wife and hearing Darcy's acquaintance mention railways, a burgeoning interest of his own, Mr. Gardiner eagerly engaged him on the subject. Their exchange was not energetic enough that he did not hear somewhere off to his right, Elizabeth's name mentioned, followed in rapid succession by Mr. Wickham's, Mr. Greyson's, Mr. Craythorne's and the tell-tale rumble of collective derision.

Mr. Thatcher seemed not to have noticed, but Darcy bore it less well, withdrawing completely from the conversation and frowning furiously at the crowds. Mr. Gardiner was vastly relieved when Elizabeth ceased running on at Mr. Bingley and turned her attention to placating her husband. Just as she attached herself to his arm, however, a pompous wigged gentleman sauntered past, blathering some nonsense about Darcy of Pemberley being duped into marrying into trade, somewhat thwarting her efforts. Darcy abruptly bowed to his friend, obliging Elizabeth to relinquish his arm and, to all appearances, any imminent hope of appeasing him.

"It was a pleasure to see you, Thatcher," he said with stiff formality, "but it is high time we all took our seats. I must bid you good evening."

"Delighted to have run into you again, Darcy." Mr. Thatcher bowed to everyone and departed, revealing the woman standing directly behind him to be pointing at their group, her sneering lips curling disdainfully around the word *trade*.

"Shall we?" Darcy barely waited for Elizabeth before stalking off.

Considering the vast condescension the man had showed in hosting them in his box, Mr. Gardiner was not about to take umbrage if he found that the ensuing attention chafed somewhat. Elizabeth, he perceived, was not nearly so ready to excuse her husband. Her expression as she marched after him was indignant.

"I believe that is our cue to go in," he said to his remaining companions.

He began edging his way through the crowd, envying Darcy his height, or perhaps his pique—whichever had enabled him to cut through at such a pace.

"The gossips are out in force this evening," his wife observed.

"The place is crawling with them!" Bingley agreed. "I pity Lizzy having to tolerate it."

"Do not distress yourself on her behalf," Mrs. Gardiner replied. "She is a sensible girl. She can tolerate a few silly rumours very well. I am more inclined to worry for Mr. Darcy."

"Darcy? Why?"

Mr. Gardiner chuckled and answered for his wife. "Because little though he likes all this tittle-tattle, unless he learns to better direct his affront, he will find himself with a very unhappy wife on his hands." He left unsaid the glaringly obvious explanation that the only thing ever to come of an unhappy wife was an even unhappier husband, assured from what Mrs. Gardiner told him that Bingley was already well aware of the fact. Sharing a knowing smile with his wife at the prospect of their vastly spirited niece giving her illustrious husband a dressing down for his ill temper, they nipped into the box ahead of Bingley and took their seats.

Bingley's trips to any theatre were sparingly few, and this one was doing naught to convince him he ought to change his habits. Whilst it was true that people gossiped with equal zeal at balls, at least there, one was never trapped in a blasted box, lit up by several thousand candles for every person present to scrutinise.

Elizabeth and her relatives were doing their best to ignore the whispers. Darcy sat in icy silence with his arms crossed, glaring fixedly at the stage and giving monosyllabic responses to every attempt at conversation, the lack of which exposed them all to the whispers rippling through the surrounding boxes.

By the end of the third act, Bingley had heard charges ranging from Elizabeth's total want of education and accomplishments, to her scheme to turn Pemberley into a poor house. One report even had it that Darcy had killed Wickham, the only one of Elizabeth's lovers not present, in a duel. Most painful of all were the recurrent murmurs of the Darcys' discontent, something with which no one watching them this evening could argue.

"It is quite different to the adaptation we saw in Cheltenham, is it not,

Lizzy?" Mrs. Gardiner said overly loudly, failing to completely muffle the strident remark from a gentleman in a box overhead that if his wife were such an incorrigible flirt, he would hand her over to her lover and wish him good luck.

"Aye, very different," Elizabeth replied with laudable composure.

"I hear they played it as Mrs. Siddons' farewell performance earlier this year." Mr. Gardiner chimed in as cheerfully as if somebody had not just replied to the other gentleman that if Mr. Darcy were handing his wife over to lovers he should very much like to know where he might join the queue. "I am surprised they reprised it so quickly, though it seems not to have done them any harm."

"Aye," Bingley said, adding as ebullient a voice as he could muster to their charade of equanimity. "It has drawn quite a crowd."

Their endeavours to appear unaffected left Darcy unmoved. He continued to glare petulantly at the empty stage as though incensed that Act Four had the audacity not to have yet begun. Bingley shuffled to the edge of his seat and leant to speak quietly in his ear. "Darcy, this is absurd. If you are intent on being in such high dudgeon, you may as well admit defeat and go home."

"I should like nothing more," he muttered back, "but, though it may have escaped your notice, not even the first performance has yet ended."

They had been speaking extremely quietly, but Elizabeth must have heard nonetheless. She leant close to Darcy. "If you wish to go, let us go. I have a headache anyway." She twisted round to address Bingley. "Would you be so kind as to take my aunt and uncle home?"

Bingley assured her he would, and after the arrangements were agreed with the Gardiners, Darcy stood up, sullenly tugging his lapels straight. Elizabeth made to stand also, but he prevented her with a gruff instruction to remain seated. "I shall arrange for the carriage and come back for you. I would not have you standing about if you have a headache."

A nice enough sentiment to be sure, though Bingley thought his surly tone rather belied his solicitude.

The curtain went up on stage just as the door to the corridor closed behind Darcy, preventing ordinary conversation. Nevertheless, Elizabeth and her aunt immediately struck up a fervid whispered exchange that Bingley strained to hear despite himself. He could not make out Elizabeth's opening remark, what with her back to him, only Mrs. Gardiner's response.

"I am sure it is not intentional. He must be excessively uneasy."

Though he still could not hear her words, the agitation in Elizabeth's voice as she whispered back was unmistakable.

"You forget what deference he is used to," her aunt replied. "You may be able to shrug it off without another thought, but you are being unfair to expect a man of his consequence to do the same. Rest assured, your uncle and I are not offended."

Frustrated at not being able to hear Elizabeth's responses, Bingley resorted to pretending to refasten his shoe, bringing him within earshot in time hear her reply emphatically that *she* was.

He sat up again, heart hammering with dismay. Elizabeth and her aunt looked around, and for a moment, he thought his eavesdropping had been discovered until he heard Darcy say behind him that the carriage had been summoned and realised it was at him the ladies were looking. He let out his breath and eased back into his chair, regarding the Titan sidelong while Elizabeth bade her relations good evening. There he stood, caught up in the injury to his consequence, impervious to the fact that Elizabeth suffered not only the scorn of the entire theatre, but that of her husband as well, and with a damned sight more forbearance than he!

Bingley scarcely wondered at Elizabeth's resolute composure. No doubt, were she to reveal aught of her own misery, Darcy would "take her in hand" as he had, only yesterday, suggested he do with Jane. He launched himself to his feet to speak, but it achieved him naught. Elizabeth was done bidding her relatives goodbye, and after a cursory farewell to him, she and Darcy were gone.

It was accurate to say Elizabeth did not leave the theatre quite as happy as when she arrived. She held Darcy's arm for the sake of appearances only, beyond caring for the tension in it that evinced his displeasure. Barring a curt instruction to his coachmen, he maintained an obstinate silence from the moment they left the box to the moment he stiffly handed her up into the carriage. She afforded him the same courtesy for the remainder of the journey home.

The consequence of her silence was the escalation of her indignation, as her mind substituted conversation with seething. She cared not what the rest of the world wished to say about her. She had told Darcy over and again she would be unmoved by any such disapprobation. But his petulant and public brooding over it, his unpardonable incivility to her relations, and her suspicion of Lady Catherine's influence in all of it had reduced her patience for his present ill-humour to a resounding nil.

Godfrey met them at the front door, enquiring with a well-trained blind eye to their early return whether they should like supper to be served directly.

"I have no appetite," Elizabeth said. Leaving Darcy to answer for himself, she took her leave and stormed upstairs to her bedchamber. She was unsurprised when her door clicked open again moments after she slammed it closed. She finished peeling off her gloves, dropped them onto her dressing table, and turned to face her husband, all defiance.

"Elizabeth, are you unwell?"

It was not how she expected him to begin. "Unwell?"

"Yes, unwell," he snapped. "You have claimed a headache and no appetite. These are common symptoms of illness, are they not?"

"I daresay. They are also common symptoms of serious vexation." His evident surprise exasperated her no end, provoking her to give poor Baker short shrift when she arrived, expecting to help her mistress undress. "How could it possibly come as a surprise that I am vexed?" she demanded of him once the maid had been unceremoniously dismissed. "Did you expect me to enjoy your incivility this evening?"

He frowned and looked aside, his jaw clenched. Elizabeth crossed her arms and awaited his answer, declaring with her silence that she required one.

"I was not aware my distraction was obvious," he said at length.

"It is not as though you made any endeavour to conceal it! You have sulked the entire evening!"

"I have not sulked."

"Call it what you will," she replied, beginning to tug pins from her hair and toss them forcibly onto her dressing table, "but you barely spoke two words together the whole night, you ignored my aunt and uncle, and you flinched every time I so much as touched you! I call that sulking."

"I apologise if I was not as attentive as you would have liked, madam, but my mind has been less agreeably engaged."

"You have suffered no more than I—less, I should say! Most of the rumours were about me, after all, and I have not hurled my rattle from the crib for the whole of London to see!"

"What rumours?"

No two words could have more effectively doused her anger. She lowered her hands and stared at him. "What do you mean *what rumours*?"

"I mean precisely what I said! I have no idea to what you are referring."

"I am referring to all the hostile attention we received this evening." He only stared at her, nonplussed, prompting her to press, "Are you telling me you were not aware of any of it?"

"I am sorry to say it escaped my notice," he replied, frowning. "What was said?"

"Nothing of substance—but much of it."

His countenance darkened. "It grieves me to here this."

"Oh, for heaven's sake, do not become vexed about it *now*," Elizabeth cried, returning to taking down her hair with still greater impatience than before. "There is even less advantage in allowing it to distress you *after* the fact!"

He looked affronted. "Let us both hope I am improved enough in character that the whisperings of a few imbeciles with pretensions to consequence can no longer distress me. I am grieved that you were distressed by it and that I was too distracted to act as I ought to have done."

"I was not distressed by it! I have told you many times I care nothing for the world's scorn."

"Then might I enquire why the devil you are upbraiding me, woman?"

"Because I thought you were distressed by it—unreasonably so. You certainly made it seem that way with your insufferable brooding. You ignored us all—all evening!"

He stepped towards her abruptly. "Is not discovering my wife has been intimate with another before me enough to consume my thoughts to the exclusion of all else?"

Elizabeth recoiled, unable to do aught but stare at him, no less bemused than incredulous. Her astonishment kept her silent too long.

"You do not deny it?" His anger did not quite mask the note of panic in his voice.

"I am unsure of what precisely you are accusing me, sir. With whom am I supposed to have been intimate?"

Her words, or tone, or perhaps both gave him pause. Doubt flickered across his features, and he did not sound at all sure of himself as he answered. "Mr. Craythorne."

Her mouth fell open. Yet, even as her affront rallied itself to be unleashed in its fullest force, she recalled his strained observation that Mr. Craythorne had seemed excessively pleased to see her. The insult of his absurd assumption notwithstanding, the burgeoning suspicion that her dear, sensible husband, paradigm of reason and man full grown, was suffering a jealous pique worthy of a stripling boy tempered her indignation with more than a pinch of amusement.

"I understood you did not care for rumours?"

"Would that it were rumour and not your own aunt's testimony."

"My aunt? What had she to say on the matter?"

"That it was thanks to Mr. Craythorne you knew far more about the marriage bed than a maiden ought to before she found herself in one!"

Elizabeth bit her lips together. In his defence, that did sound hideously damning. "Why on earth did she say that to you?"

"She said it to your uncle," he mumbled, "while I was speaking to Mr. Thatcher."

She raised an eyebrow.

"It is not my habit to eavesdrop," he said angrily, "but I heard Gardiner enquire of your aunt why you blushed so violently upon seeing Mr. Craythorne, and since I wondered the same, I made a point of listening to her answer!"

Oh, dear Lord, how she loved him—her dear, foolish, jealous husband, so wild with envy that reason had quite deserted him. Nevertheless, in a long line of strong contenders, this was possibly the most offensive of all the charges he had ever laid at her door, and she would have him admit the injustice of it before absolving him.

"And from that answer you took it that I had…what? Lain with another man out of wedlock? And this you thought me capable of concealing from you?"

After a moment's silence, he let out a harsh breath and lowered his head to pinch the bridge of his nose. "Had I felt less, I might have given it more thought, Elizabeth."

"Or indeed any."

He looked up at her then frowned, possibly at the grin she could no longer conceal, and stiffened indignantly. "I beg you would trifle with me no longer. Tell me Mrs. Gardiner's meaning!"

With a quiet sigh, Elizabeth raised her hands to feel for the few remaining pins in her hair—as much to shield herself from her imminent mortification as to finish the much-interrupted task. "Mr. Craythorne took a fancy to me some time ago when he lived near Meryton. He approached me in the garden one day and attempted to charm me with some pretty words—at least, I presume they were pretty. I have never been able to recall them, for it was not his speech that formed the memorable part of his address. His prevailing claim to affection was more inelegantly displayed in the distension of his breeches."

Darcy's appalled expression made her laugh a little. She set the last pin down and turned to face him fully. "I cannot say what his intentions were, for my aunt intervened almost immediately. But I later insisted she explain what I had seen. And after some persistence on my part, she consented to tell me *far more about the marriage bed than a maiden ought to know.*"

Darcy stared at her for a moment then closed his eyes and shook his head. "My God, forgive me. I am a damned fool."

Elizabeth well knew how he would now berate himself for accusing her thus, yet she could not be overly angry. In addition to the compliment of his possessiveness, reason had by then arrived to remind her of all the ways in which he had cared for her this evening that anger had prevented her admitting at the time—his concern for her fictitious headache, his having arranged for a hot brick to be placed in the footwell of the carriage home, his care for her well-being when she refused supper, his regret for not comforting her in the face of society's derision—all of it done whilst struggling under a most heinous misapprehension.

"Yes, you are. But you know how I love to laugh at folly." Unfastening her necklace, she turned to lay it carefully on her dressing table. "How fortunate for you that I am not so unreasonable about *your* previous lovers."

It was a passing remark, ingenuously made, and she did not comprehend its impact until she turned back and observed his horrified countenance.

"How did you—" He clamped his lips closed and ran a hand over his face.

She pulled a wry face and set about removing a stocking. "I may have come to your bed a maiden, but I did not come to it a simpleton."

"Elizabeth, I…it is not—"

"Fitzwilliam," she interrupted, holding a hand up to stay a conversation neither of them wished to have. "I harbour no resentment for the life you lived before you met me, but I have absolutely no wish to dwell on it. I ought not to have teased you." She bent to remove her other stocking. By the time she was done, Darcy was by her side, tenderly turning her towards him.

"You are the most remarkable woman I have ever known. I do not deserve your clemency after my behaviour this evening."

"It has not been your finest few hours as a husband, but there were a few redeeming performances. You have not done as badly as you think."

He was so very serious, his eyes black in the candlelight. "I love you."

She slid her arms about his neck and pulled herself up to lightly kiss the scar on his cheek. "I know. That is why you are forgiven."

He rested his forehead against hers and wrapped his arms around her, whispering his heartfelt thanks. "Though I would have you cease walking alone in gardens," he added. "You are entirely too prone to being propositioned in them."

"Fear not. I only accept propositions in churchyards."

He smiled the understated smile she loved so well.

"And bedrooms."

He stopped smiling and upon having his propositions agreed to, bestowed upon her such attentions as went a considerable way to earning him the clemency he claimed not to deserve.

11

Distinctions in Connubial Felicity

Friday, 23 October 1812: Derbyshire

The weather took a decidedly wintry turn towards the end of the month, hindering the Darcys' journey home with persistent rain and icy winds. They endured two days of uneven, occasionally jarring passage over deeply rutted roads and by the third day, to Darcy's dismay, it had begun to take a toll on Elizabeth. Sickened by the motion of the carriage, she had not once slept as she had become accustomed to doing on long journeys. Fatigue and nausea had rendered her pale of countenance and dull of spirits. When they stopped at noon to change horses, he insisted she order something substantial to eat but watched her poke it ineffectually around her plate.

"Did I tell you I had to prevent my aunt from writing to Jane?" she enquired quietly, breaking a piece of bread into two pieces and putting neither in her mouth.

"You did not."

"She mentioned it after dinner on Monday. She meant well, yet I cannot see that a reprimand could possibly improve Jane's opinion of me."

"Your sister ought to be concerned with improving your opinion of her, not the reverse." Elizabeth's miserable expression bade him regret speaking so severely, and he hastened to redirect the conversation. "At least the Gardiners' opinion of me is salvaged. They seemed to have forgiven my incivility at the theatre."

"They were not angry with you to begin with, least of all my aunt."

He chuckled quietly. "I confess I was relieved by our reception at Donaldson's ball on Friday, also. My behaviour seems to have done us no lasting damage."

"I was never concerned that it would. Your reputation has survived this long, and I speak with authority when I say that was not the first time you have been seen brooding in public." She smiled at her joke but weakly, then put her bread down and pushed her plate away with a sigh.

"Elizabeth, you need to rest. I shall take a room for the evening."

She snapped her head up. "Do not dare! We are almost home!"

"We are five-and-twenty miles from home."

"That is half what you call an easy distance."

"On good roads, of which we do not presently have the luxury."

"And if it rains again, which is very likely, the roads will only worsen."

He gritted his teeth. "You are unwell."

"I am not unwell. I am with child, and unless you intend for me to remain here until my confinement, I shall simply have to endure the journey. You worry unnecessarily. I am only tired. 'Tis nothing more serious."

"Excuse me, Mr. Darcy," interrupted a servant, "your coachman asked me to inform you your carriage is ready."

"Thank you," Elizabeth answered for him. "Tell him we shall be there directly."

Darcy shook his head resignedly and stood to offer her his arm. "Nothing more than tiredness, my eye. You suffer from terminal obstinacy, woman."

She grinned at him and whispered her thanks. Yet for all her bold assurances, the jouncing of the carriage continued to make her ill. By the time they reached the final coaching inn, her countenance had lost what little colour she had regained at the previous one. She even refused the opportunity of a walk, preferring to wait in the carriage while the horses were changed one last time. The properly kept roads surrounding Pemberley were rather too little antidote too late, he feared, for her pallor was not noticeably improved by the time they arrived at the house. Her spirits, however, were vastly buoyed.

"I have never been so happy to be home in my life!" she exclaimed.

He smiled, never tiring of hearing her speak of his home as hers. "I am sorry it was such a difficult journey, love."

"Even you cannot assume the blame for the weather. Besides, I believe it was I who refused to stagger the journey."

"True," he said, climbing from the carriage and turning to help her down.

She took his outstretched hand and leant forward to duck through the door. "But promise me we shall not go anywhere again in a—oh!" She cried out and sat back down heavily on the seat.

"What is the matter?" he cried, leaping back into the carriage. "Are you in pain?" His heart leapt into his mouth upon noticing her hand on her stomach. "Dear God, is it the child?"

"Yes, I—oh!" she gasped again. Far from looking distressed, however, her countenance was a picture of wonderment. She raised her eyes to his. "I felt it!"

There truly was no end to this woman's assault on his sensibilities. His heart returned to its rightful place with a thud and promptly swelled to overfill the cavity with elation.

"Oh my," she said softly. "It—oh, Fitzwilliam! I have been so anxious something must be wrong, today more than ever, but 'tis really true!" She reached for his hands. "I am so happy!"

Magnificent though her jubilant relief was, the intensity of his own feelings rendered Darcy silent and serious. All doubt was removed, all anxiety for the most uncertain stage allayed; his beloved Elizabeth would be mother to his child. Nothing and no one had ever been so precious to him. He lifted both her hands to his lips and kissed them with wordless reverence.

Twice more over the course of the evening did Elizabeth feel the fluttering of their child. Each time she gasped, not yet accustomed to what she described as a most uncommon sensation. Each time he reeled, likely never to grow accustomed to how profoundly he loved her. She fell asleep early. He stayed awake watching her until the very last candle guttered out, unwilling to miss a single moment of her existence, now so irrevocably and blissfully entwined with his own.

Longbourn, Hertfordshire
October 29

Dearest Lizzy,

Our happiest congratulations! You cannot know with what joy you have filled your parents' hearts. I am glad to hear Mr. Darcy is looking after you properly. Your task is to do everything in your power to ensure you provide him with a son. With that in mind, I have enclosed a list of every method I ever employed to beget a boy, which you must read in detail and avoid at all costs, for none of them work.

You will very soon find that all those fine gowns Mr. Darcy has bought you will no longer fit, likely never to again. Some might lend themselves to adjustment, but those that do not, I ask that you send to Jane, for she has not yet managed what you have achieved and could do with a little assistance.

She is exceedingly dull of late, Lizzy. Miss Bingley is gone off to Town to stay with her sister, who was delivered of a daughter this week, and Mr. Bingley manages to keep himself excessively busy for a gentleman without an occupation; therefore, Jane is often alone at Netherfield. Your sisters and I visit as often as may be, but all our best efforts have not succeeded in making her any livelier. A child would occupy her creditably. I cannot comprehend why she delays.

My head is aching today, and I can write no more. Pray do not resist your Mr. Darcy's attempts to take care of you, for I know you will not do it properly yourself, and I shall have no rest unless I know you are well.

Love,
Mama

Pemberley, Derbyshire
November 8

To Jane,

Be not alarmed that this letter contain any mention of those events which transpired at Netherfield. I have no wish to dwell upon them, and since you have offered neither explanation nor apology, I must assume neither do you. Nevertheless, we cannot continue to ignore one another, else family occasions will become impossible and our husbands' friendship will suffer. Moreover, I miss you, Jane, and I worry for you. If we can exchange letters without animosity, perhaps in time we shall be able to meet again as friends and forget these few difficult months. With the sincerest hope of achieving such an end, here is my beginning.

Darcy and I have been back at Pemberley for three weeks now. He indulges me almost every morning by walking out with me, and the countryside hereabouts is growing dearer to me by the day. The view from the rise behind the house has become my favourite in all the world, though the one from Oakham Mount will forever retain a special place in my heart.

We are to dine tomorrow evening with our neighbour, Mr. Peterson. He is shortly to be married to Miss Hawes, whom I have met twice now and like very well. I hope we shall see much of them and believe they will make charming neighbours.

I imagine it is much the same for you as it is for me, being thrown into new circles. Quite apart from becoming acquainted with all of Mr. Bingley's friends, with Charlotte and me gone, your own circle is depleted to fewer people your own age. I heard from Kitty, though, that Marianne Etheridge has returned from her uncle's establishment. Have you had opportunity to see much of her?

November 15

Mrs. Ferguson, whom I met in London but whose husband's estate is in Dumfriesshire, has written to invite us to their Twelfth Night Ball. I should have loved to go, but apart from being quite unequal to the journey, we shall have a houseful of guests of our own to entertain. There will be Aunt and Uncle Gardiner and the children, of course, then Lord Matlock, Colonel Fitzwilliam, Mrs. Sinclair and, I have recently been informed, Lord and Lady Ashby. Lastly, Lady Catherine, Mr. and Mrs. Montgomery, and their son, Master Jonathan, will join us from Kent. I hope especially, despite all our differences, to make their Christmas enjoyable since it is likely to be Lady Catherine's last. Indeed, I believe that is why Lord Matlock insisted that Lord and Lady Ashby join the party.

I own I am a little daunted by the prospect of being hostess to so many but anticipate it nonetheless. To have such a gathering, such a mix of characters, it ought to be entertaining at the very least!

November 18

Jane, the tone of Mary's most recent letter to me was rather downhearted. I believe she is missing our presence at Longbourn. I shall invite her here as soon as may be, but in the meantime, I believe she would be pleased to spend more time with you at Netherfield. Might you perhaps invite her to practice on the pianoforte there? Then you could sing with her, as you used to do with me.

November 20

I am a little forlorn today. Mrs. Annesley, Georgiana's companion of above a year, has given us notice. I shall be sorry to see her go, but we shall not replace her for, barring the weeks of my confinement, I ought to be able to act as companion whenever Georgiana requires it.

Just as she is leaving us, we must begin the search for a monthly nurse and nursery maid. I should be happy to employ one person to fill both positions, but though it seems a sensible economy to me, it has been impossible to achieve. Lady Catherine has provided a list of names as long as my arm, all of whom Darcy has dismissed out of hand based on the ill-fated experience with another of her recommendations, Mrs. Younge, if you recall. Have you been required to appoint any new servants as yet? I should be grateful to hear how you went about it.

November 21

I have given much more time to practicing the pianoforte since I arrived, and my playing is at last beginning to reflect my efforts. Even better, when Georgiana and I play together, we have perfected the art of arranging the pieces so that her proficiency disguises my weaker talent. We played a duet for Darcy after dinner yesterday and he seemed genuinely delighted with our performance. Whether we receive such generous praise from a less partial audience remains to be seen. I do not doubt that some of my imminent guests will prove suitably severe critics.

November 23

Much though I have taken pleasure in writing this letter as though it were for the Jane I knew before all our recent difficulties, sending it to the Jane I left behind at Netherfield two months ago is a truly daunting prospect. I dread that you will receive my news unwillingly and reply in bitterness. I dread more that you will not reply at all. Regardless, you can hardly respond to a letter that has not been sent, thus I have at long last summoned the courage to post it.

I hope you and Bingley are both in excellent health and wish you both a very merry first Christmas together.

Yours in love and hope,

Lizzy

Monday, 7 December 1812: Hertfordshire

It was several years since Jane had been in company with Marianne Etheridge, and she was surprised by how little the woman had altered. She had gained none of society's graces, despite her time in Town, and had returned home after two Seasons still plump, awkward, and single. It was polite of her to call, however, and were it not for Elizabeth's unsolicited and presumptuous counsel on how she might broaden her circle of acquaintance by seeking just such an audience, Jane might have been better pleased that she had.

"How are you finding it here at Netherfield?" Marianne enquired. "Is it strange to be away from Longbourn?"

"On the contrary, it is delightful to be mistress of my own house."

"I imagine it must be very agreeable," Marianne replied, though her tone gave the impression she was wholly indifferent to Jane's domestic felicity.

"And you?" Jane said. "Do you find Meryton much changed since you went away?"

"Very little, for which I am excessively grateful. I have never been suited to London society. I am only sorry it took me so long to convince the rest of the world of that fact."

Jane smiled. "As my very good friend Lady Ashby says, a woman ought to be sensible of her station."

"Indeed." Marianne looked at the clock. "Pray tell me, how does Lizzy? Her marriage is quite the talk of the town."

"Curious, then, that you feel the need to ask me about it," Jane replied before thinking, pained by the very mention of Elizabeth's popularity. She hastily affected a laugh to disguise her bitterness and added, "But she is at Pemberley and means to stay there for Christmas, I understand."

"One does not wonder why. I am sure that will be delightful."

Jane knew of at least one person who would not agree. In her most recent letter, Lady Ashby had expressed her dismay at having been summoned to Pemberley and joked of being made to sit down with the tenants for a "Christmas meal served with a garnish of gaucherie and a second course of impudence." Jane felt the vast compliment of her ladyship's admission of envy for her own, humbler arrangements.

Rather than speak any more of Elizabeth, she enquired as to the Etheridge's plans for Christmas, which they discussed until the clock struck the hour, and Marianne all but leapt from her chair, insisting she would not outstay her welcome, and left.

Jane would not have objected if the visit had lasted longer, for she was expecting no other callers that day and was rather offended by Marianne's resolve to go. She consoled herself with Lady Ashby's assurances that, contrary to what Elizabeth might think, it was not for her to associate with a woman who had been slighted by the rest of society.

Pemberley, Derbyshire
December 18

To Miss Mary Bennet

I thank you most sincerely for your last letter. Life at Longbourn sounds very lively. Until recently, I should have said Pemberley was quite different, but that has not been the case these past four-and-twenty hours. All but two of our guests have now arrived for Christmas, and yesterday there was such a commotion! I have not seen my brother so cross ~~since~~ for quite some time, but I am ahead of myself. Allow me to explain.

My aunt, Lady Catherine, arrived yesterday. I was shocked to see how frail she has grown. She was scarcely able to walk into the house, even with assistance. Whilst everybody was fussing over her, attempting to get her indoors and make her comfortable, your cousin Anna ran into the hall without looking and knocked her ladyship's cane from her grip. I was very sorry for her, for she had been an angel until then and chose such an unfortunate moment for a spell of mischief. The cane fell across her ear and made her scream until she was snatched up by her father and carried off to the nursery.

It was then that Lady Catherine discovered the Gardiners were staying at Pemberley for Christmas. Oh, Mary, she was so angry! I should never have thought, from that first sight of her, that she would have the energy for such a tirade as she then gave! I am ashamed to say she was very unkind to your aunt and uncle and demanded they leave. When my brother told her none of his guests would be leaving, she turned her anger upon him and Lizzy. Lizzy bore it with impossible civility, but Brother was not nearly so forbearing, and there was a terrible scene.

In the end, when nobody would yield to her demands, my aunt attempted to leave instead but was too weak to walk back to the door and almost fell. Mr. Montgomery and my cousin Fitzwilliam were obliged to escort her against her will to her room, where Lord Matlock (her brother) instructed her to remain until she could "recall in which trunk she had packed away all her dignity!"

Be assured, I have spent some time with Anna since, and she is quite recovered from her fright and the trifling injury to her ear. Lady Catherine will not so rapidly overcome her wounded pride, I fear. Lizzy, however, spent an hour with her last night—truly, Mary, your sister is fearless—and whatever she said seems to have persuaded her ladyship against leaving.

Your aunt and uncle have been astoundingly gracious throughout. You must be proud to be able to claim such relations. Excepting Lizzy and the children, they are the only two people here of whom I am not at least a little bit afraid. Even my brother—nay, I daresay especially my brother when he is as angry as he was yesterday—can be a fearsome creature. My cousin Fitzwilliam assures me matters will settle down in a few days, but his grandmother thinks otherwise and insists that, when my other cousin Lord Ashby and his wife arrive, the fireworks will begin in earnest.

I am not afraid, though. Not with Lizzy here. She has such a way of manoeuvring people out of ill-humours and encouraging them to good cheer. Already, she has persuaded my brother to overlook Lady Catherine's incivility and have her seated next to him at dinner this evening. All apprehension aside, I believe this year will be the liveliest and, I hope, the merriest Christmas Pemberley has seen in many years.

To answer your query: yes, Lizzy does very well. Very occasionally she tarries abed of a morning, but she assures me a little fatigue is quite common, and thus, you must be similarly assured that she is in perfect health. I share your anticipation for the arrival of a niece or nephew. Lizzy teasingly suggested that I watch Lady Catherine closely during her stay for ideas on how best to go about the business of being an aunt—at least, I hope she was teasing, but I would prefer to be more like Mrs. Gardiner.

Enclosed is the music for two cradle songs I thought we might learn and play for the baby when he or she arrives. Mention it not to Lizzy in your letters. Let it be our surprise when next you visit, which I hope will be very soon.

Wishing you a very happy Christmas,

Yours sincerely,
Miss Georgiana Darcy

Thursday, 24 December 1812: Derbyshire

"'Tis a play!" Fitzwilliam shouted. At Mrs. Gardiner's nod he gave a bark of triumph—it being his only correct guess of the entire game. It was a game to which everyone's (mostly) willing participation he could only attribute to the vast quantity of mulled wine and punch collectively consumed over the course of the evening. Whatever had brought on the singularly peaceable interlude, he approved of it, for against all odds, everyone seemed to be having uncommonly good fun.

"'Tis but one word," Elizabeth surmised from her aunt's raised index finger—and then, "One syllable."

"You might actually guess this one then, Dickie," mumbled Ashby from the chair next to Fitzwilliam.

"Fie, you have not guessed one correctly yet, either."

A host of calls loosely apropos of horses erupted around them as Mrs. Gardiner began enacting her clue.

"Mayhap my understanding does not run to a mercantile bent," Ashby said under his breath.

"Oh, untwist your ballocks, man. The Gardiners are very good people." Indeed, Mrs. Gardiner was presently proving what a very good sport she was, galloping back and forth before the fire, to everyone's delight. "Stallion?" Fitzwilliam guessed.

"One ruddy syllable, you ninny," Ashby grumbled. "And my manservant is a very good person. It does not mean I wish him to cease pressing my shirts and begin playing parlour games with me after dinner."

"Mare?" called Mrs. Sinclair.

"Upon my word, you are a fastidious arse," Fitzwilliam hissed, "Even Lady Catherine has condescended to converse with them. She and Mrs. Gardiner exchanged ten words *at least* over dinner."

Ashby snorted. "Lady Catherine only approves of the woman because she believes it is deference that makes her blush and mumble whenever Darcy addresses her."

Fitzwilliam had to smirk. He, too, had noticed Mrs. Gardiner's appreciation for his fair-favoured cousin. "Let her think it is deference if it makes the situation more palatable to her."

"Trot?" Mr. Gardiner tried.

"It makes it no more palatable for me," Ashby replied.

Fitzwilliam gave up attempting to placate him with reason and handed him his hip flask instead. "Here. Have something spiritual to cleanse the injury to your pride."

Ashby accepted the flask with a broad grin then shouted, "Charge?"

Mrs. Gardiner shook her head. *Still* she galloped about on the rug, now looking exceedingly vexed.

"Horse!" Lady Ashby said for possibly the third time, seeming bemused it was still not correct.

"Steed?" Montgomery guessed.

Again, Mrs. Gardiner shook her head and galloped furiously back the other way. Fitzwilliam heard Elizabeth hoot with laughter.

"Reins?" Mr. Gardiner attempted again. "Horse?"

"That has already been said!"

"Nag, then? Pony? Mule? *Goat?* I do not know! Do something else, for heaven's sake!"

Mrs. Gardiner ceased galloping and stood on the rug with her hands on her hips, glaring at her husband.

"'*The Provoked Wife,*'" Matlock called.

The room erupted into laughter, though a feeble exclamation, barely audible above the merriment, caught Fitzwilliam's notice. He turned to his aunt, sitting on his left, and enquired whether anything was the matter.

Lady Catherine withdrew an emaciated hand from her blankets and pointed at Darcy. "You are correct. He is happy. He looks the picture of my sister when he laughs."

The observation was as unexpected as it was moving, and Fitzwilliam knew not what to say.

His aunt, never plagued by such difficulties, spoke on. "And she is *jousting*."

"Pardon?"

"Mrs. Gardiner is jousting."

"Inspired, madam!" Fitzwilliam swivelled back to the room and called, "Joust" over the hubbub.

Mrs. Gardiner pounced upon it, waggling her ear forcibly.

"Sounds like joust?"

"Faust!" Mr. Gardiner roared, coming to his feet exultantly.

"About time, sir!" his wife replied, to the delight of the entire room.

Mr. Gardiner doffed an imaginary cap and scuttled past her in deep obeisance, apologising facetiously. He then began his turn by re-enacting the exact same gallop across the room as she had. A chorus of groans went up from everyone else, but Mrs. Gardiner instantly and correctly guessed *canter,* showing her husband how easy a thing it could be to make a sensible suggestion.

"The Canterbury Tales!" Fitzwilliam exclaimed, to an uproarious round of applause. "How can you find these two aught but agreeable?" he whispered to his brother before standing to take his turn. "I think they may be the most diverting couple of my acquaintance."

Ashby only grunted but notably refrained from demurring. Fitzwilliam left him to brood upon his prejudice, full in the belief that it was as much at risk as every other prepossession in the room of being overturned.

ALL THE HILARITY SANK IN DARCY'S AWARENESS NEXT TO THE SOUND OF Elizabeth's laughter. Her countenance glowed, and her eyes sparkled in the candlelight. Her merriment was wholly unaffected, demure—yet altogether without ceremony. He marvelled at it, for despite all their prior hostility, she was genuinely enjoying his family's society. Moreover, his family appeared, quite against their will in some cases, to be genuinely enjoying hers. It was all her doing. This was Pemberley as it was intended to be: a true family seat. And this was his family, with Elizabeth at its heart.

Because he was watching her, Darcy noticed her laughter ebb. She shifted in her chair and rubbed the swell of her stomach. He reached to lay his hand over hers and whispered a query as to her well-being. She bit her lip and slid her hand from beneath his to press his palm to her belly, whereupon he felt a small but unmistakable nudge. His heart thudded in his chest, and he waited, staring at his own hand, and was rewarded with another palpable shove. Overcome with wonder and delight, he raised his eyes to Elizabeth's. She was beaming, her countenance suffused with joy.

"Happy Christmas," she whispered.

It was a moment before he composed himself enough to whisper back how very dearly he loved her.

Absorbed in their own private rejoicing, they missed the end of the game, alerted to it only when Anne guessed Fitzwilliam's charade, and he roared an exasperated "Hallelujah!" After that, the festivities drew to a natural conclusion. The elders took themselves off to bed, and everyone else adjourned into the great hall to check that the Yule log was still burning and to enjoy a last glass off mulled wine before bed.

Fitzwilliam came to stand next to Darcy, giving him a firm slap on the shoulder. "I own I was not convinced even you could accomplish it, old boy, but a pleasanter Christmas I cannot recall."

"Do not believe me ignorant of the fact that is because you won your wager with Ashby."

"You wound me, Darcy! What wager?"

"Whether or not I would exclude at least one relative from the house before Christmas Day."

Fitzwilliam grimaced. "I am discovered, though still ten pounds richer than my brother."

"Not so, regrettably, for I wagered him fifteen pounds he could not make you give up your hip flask. By my reckoning that makes him five pounds richer and significantly drunker than you."

Fitzwilliam muttered an unseasonable imprecation.

Darcy returned the slap on the back. "I am delighted you are here, Fitzwilliam. It has been the happiest Christmas in my memory also."

Pemberley, Derbyshire
January 11

Jane,

I shall not pretend I am not deeply grieved by your silence, yet because I love you and because I cannot dispel my concern for your happiness, I am making another attempt.

I have weathered my first Christmas at Pemberley! We made merry on Christmas Eve, attended church on Christmas Day (and danced that evening, after all those who would despise us for it had retired), toasted the servants and tenants on St Stephen's Day, and feasted with our neighbours on Twelfth Night. On the whole, it was merrier than we could have hoped, though not without incident. I like to think, however, that Lady Catherine felt better for being able to inform me of at least three ways a day in which I erred.

I jest, but I found I did not mind her imperiousness half so much as I thought I would. She and I have had an exceedingly tumultuous acquaintance, but she is esteemed by so many of the people I have come to love, I cannot but be moved by her plight. Darcy and I sat with her in the gallery one morning, listening to her tales of all the people in the pictures there, including a few about Darcy's mother he had not heard before. Notwithstanding all her antipathy, I will ever remember those few hours with great fondness.

Now the decorations have been taken down, all my guests are gone, and Pemberley is quiet once more. Is it the same at Netherfield? We heard from Mary that Miss Bingley and Mrs. Hurst did not join you. I hope that did not make your celebrations any less agreeable. I wish you would write and tell me about it, though it seems probable you will not. I am not entirely without hope, though, for if I can make peace with a woman so wholly prejudiced against me as Lady Catherine, surely I can reconcile with my own sister?

Wishing you a happy New Year,
Elizabeth

Saturday, 23 January 1813: Hertfordshire

Pevensey Hall, Ashby, Derbyshire
January 21

Jane

I must say I was rather alarmed by the tone of your last letter. You sounded rather hysterical. Yes, I received your previous note but had not yet found the time to reply—nor, indeed, realised there was any urgent need to do so. Certainly, none of your news was remarkable enough to warrant any haste on my part. Neither was your eagerness to hear how dreadful my Christmas was likely to induce me to be prompt.

I do congratulate you, of course, on being satisfied with your first Christmas as mistress of your own house, though I do hope you will not make a habit of petitioning me for compliments. As your friend and better, you must allow me to tell you it is excessively coarse. Objectionable though your sister's self-sufficiency may be, it does at least make her easier to please.

I hope you are not too disappointed to learn that in truth I had a very agreeable Christmas. My stay at Pemberley was tolerable, but then the splendour of the place is such that even your relations being there could not lessen the elegance of our party. Your sister continues to be Lady C's favourite, but that also turned out to my advantage, for it saved me the inconvenience of her notice.

E yet boasts the same graceless independence and brazen coquetry of which you have ever accused her, but her novelty, and thus her potency, is diminishing. She is becoming less interesting by the moment, so let us speak of her no longer. Of much more interest was my attendance at Lady O's Twelfth Night Ball. I know you will congratulate me when I tell you of the favourable reception I enjoyed there.

"Mrs. Bennet is here to see you, ma'am."

Jane shoved her letter between the cushion and her leg, acting not a moment too soon. Seconds later, her mother burst into the room, coming to roost on the sofa next to her. "Good afternoon, Mama. Would you like some tea?"

"No, I am too vexed for tea. Your father has had a letter from Mr. Collins. That sly Charlotte Collins, whom we all treated as a friend for so many years, has begotten herself a boy child, and they have written to boast of it."

"I am sure they did not mean to boast."

"Oh yes, yes they did! We must already endure being turned out of our own home as soon as your father draws his last breath. There is no call for them to taunt us with heirs as well. And you can count on their knowing that you are not yet increasing. How cruel of them to gloat of their issue in the face of that failure!"

Tears sprang to Jane's eyes. "I would hardly call it a failure."

"Well, it scarcely qualifies as a success."

A tear dripped off her chin, followed by others she did not trouble herself to wipe away.

Her mother peered at her with some confusion. "Jane? Oh, Jane, Jane! Calm yourself! Let not those wretched Collinses' thoughtlessness distress you. You will be blessed eventually. If your sister has managed it, I daresay you will."

Jane let out an exasperated wail and shook her head. "No, I begin to think I shall never do as well as Lizzy. Even my Christmas celebrations were inferior to hers apparently."

"Never mind," Mrs. Bennet replied, patting her hand. "Perhaps you could go to Pemberley next year and spend Christmas with her?"

Jane barked a harsh laugh. "I am sure that would please my husband no end!"

She regretted her outburst immediately. To no one other than Lady Ashby had she admitted the truth of Bingley's inconstant affections, and her mother was the last person to whom she would have chosen to disclose it. Yet, Mrs. Bennet did not seem to be appalled by it, only mildly surprised.

"Oh dear. He still admires her, does he?"

"You knew he admired her?"

"I had an inkling, but I was sure it was a fleeting attachment. All men admire a comely figure, and goodness knows Lizzy has ever displayed hers better than you. But then, she had to learn, for she has not your looks."

"How could you allow me to marry a man you knew had feelings for another?"

Mrs. Bennet sat back, looking offended. "Because, had I not, you would very likely not have been married at all! Though you are making such a muddle of it, I am beginning to think that might have been for the best."

"Would that you had not imposed upon me to secure him with a well-aimed swoon then!"

Her mother looked genuinely bemused. "Is that how you ended in his arms on the sofa?"

"I should very much like to know that also."

Jane's heart pitched into her mouth, and her gaze snapped to the door, which had been closed moments before but was presently occupied by her observably appalled husband.

"You tell me *now* it was your design when you swooned that day to coerce me into marriage?"

"No, indeed!" Mrs. Bennet answered for her. "Only to *encourage* you."

"Mama!"

"You swooned deliberately?"

"Well, I…you see…"

"Your hedging is rather a confirmation of it."

"Perhaps I did, but only in panic, because you—"

"And you, madam?" Bingley exclaimed, turning to Mrs. Bennet. "Was it by design you brought Sir William into the room at that moment?"

"Indeed, it was not, sir!" she replied indignantly, and for a moment Jane thought she was vindicated. The moment quickly passed. "That was Mr. Bennet's doing. He forced his way past me, knowing full well what he was interrupting."

"*Mama!*"

"Pray leave us, Mrs, Bennet," Bingley said, his voice cracking on the last word.

Mrs. Bennet flapped and blustered and attempted to set all to rights, but in the face of both Jane and Bingley's resolute silence, she had no choice but to go.

"Charles?" Jane whispered into the supervening silence.

"What have you done?"

"It did not happen as my mother implied."

"All of this might have been avoided, had I but known."

She gasped. "Is that what you wish? That you could have avoided marrying me altogether? Is it that disagreeable to you?"

"Discovering I was duped into it has rather lessened my enjoyment of it, I must say."

"No, you are wrong! It was never my intention that we should be discovered, but I was expecting your addresses. Instead, you seemed about to change your mind and leave me again. I thought you must still not comprehend my feelings!"

"I did not! How could I when you were so cold and reserved all the time?"

"Could you expect me to behave differently after you abandoned me so cruelly?"

Bingley ran both hands through his hair, grasping two fistfuls and squeezing his eyes shut. Releasing them abruptly, along with a gruff sigh, he took two strides towards her. "Yes, I left. It was ill done, and I have never apologised properly for it. But I came back! I braved the reproach of your friends and family to return and court you in the best way I knew how. And you barely spoke to me! The only person who ever showed any pleasure in my return was Lizzy."

Jane lurched to her feet with a wordless cry. "Yes, Lizzy! Perfect, wonderful Lizzy! Why did you simply not marry her?"

"I would have, had you not come to the room where I awaited her and draped yourself all over me!"

It was not as shocking as it ought to be—only bitterly predictable. Had she not suspected all along he preferred Elizabeth? In retrospect, she supposed every other appalling consequence of his thwarted affections had been inevitable.

"Would that you had never come back," she whispered. "I could have lived far better with the memory of a man I believed loved me for a few short months than endure a lifetime with a man who does not love me at all." She dropped her face into her hands and burst into tears. For a while she could only sob, her distress heightened by Bingley's continued silence. After a few minutes, he did speak, but his words, far from comforting her, cast her into a tumult of confusion and alarm.

"The same graceless independence and brazen coquetry of which you have ever accused her?"

Jane gasped and looked up. He was reading from her letter!

"Are you in the habit of exchanging insults about your sister with Lady Ashby?"

His expression was furious, yet his defending Elizabeth vexed Jane as nothing else could, curdling her dismay into righteous anger. "Better to say I am in the habit of commiserating with her."

"Commiserating?"

"Yes!" she cried, wiping her tears away with the heel of her palm. "I know you will find this difficult to comprehend, but I am not alone in my aversion to her unending teasing and impertinence."

Bingley gaped at her. "Are you out of your mind, maligning Lizzy to this woman? She is Darcy's cousin!"

"Precisely!" She snatched the letter from him. "That is why she is as mortified by Lizzy's behaviour as I am!"

The more she said, the angrier Bingley's expression became. The angrier Bingley grew, the more indignant she became. "Think you any of Mr. Darcy's family approves of her determined coquetry? Imagine their horror when they learnt what trouble her flirting has already brought about from Mr. Wickham and Mr. Greyson! I assure you they are far less impressed than you were by her efforts at Pemberley and even more dismayed to hear how she argues constantly with her husband! So you see, she is not as—"

He thrust his face towards hers, his eyes huge and his complexion flooded crimson. "Good God, that all came from you?"

She recoiled and fell silent, stunned by his ferocity though too angry herself to regret any of what she had said.

"What possessed you to write such things of your own sister?"

"It is all true!"

"How can you be so obtuse? True or not, everything you have ever whispered in that woman's ear has now been spread over the whole of London! The Darcys are a laughing stock! I witnessed it myself when I was there in October—twisted versions of everything you just said, things only you could know—flung at Lizzy in contempt. I wondered then where it all began. Never could I have suspected it originated with my own wife!" He returned to clutching fistfuls of his hair. "They have been sunk into a scandal of your making, and Darcy is punishing Lizzy for it! You have made her the contempt of society and condemned her to her husband's resentment and disdain. Damn you, Jane, you have ruined your sister's marriage!"

"That seems just," Jane cried, "for she has ruined mine! She has condemned me to my husband's complete indifference! Why can you not care about my happiness half as much as you care about hers?"

"Still you accuse me thus?" he roared. "Upon my life, I forswore my own heart to preserve yours!"

Jane wilted in the face of his vehemence, dropping into the nearest seat and looking wordlessly upon his escalating fury.

"Ignorant as I was of your scheme to entrap me, I offered for you without excuse or objection and have endeavoured ever since to make the best of the situation—to love you, if I could!"

She shook her head helplessly as he wound himself into a greater and greater pique.

"I may not always have done it well, and God knows you have not made it easy, but nonetheless, I have tried! My sacrifice was evidently in vain if you are as miserable as you say. So be it! I see no benefit to prolonging our mutual agony. Allow me to relieve both our suffering and leave!"

His pronouncement was so unexpected that it rendered Jane speechless. She uttered not a sound from that instant to the moment the door closed behind him—not while he informed her he would remove to his London townhouse directly, not while he informed her he meant to remain there for the foreseeable future, not while he forbade her from obtruding upon his seclusion with either letters or visits, and not while he informed her she ought to go about the business of being Mrs. Bingley in the same way she ever had—as though his being her husband bore no relevance to the situation whatsoever. He was gone before dinner.

By breakfast the next day, Mrs. Bennet had learnt of his decampment, returned to Netherfield, and said enough words to compensate for Jane's want of them several times over. By the end of a week, Jane began to fear that, on this occasion, Bingley truly meant not to return.

Monday, 8 February 1813: Derbyshire

Elizabeth looked up from her breakfast as the door opened and tried not to appear impatient when her sister entered. She and Darcy both wished her good morning.

"Has Mr. Bingley been down yet?" Georgiana enquired as she seated herself at the table.

"Not yet," Darcy replied.

"I do hope he is not ill."

The door opened again, but it was only Maltravers with a letter just arrived for Elizabeth. She took it, feeling some apprehension upon perceiving her mother's hand, for the previous two from that quarter had borne little in the way of good tidings. According to Mrs. Bennet, Bingley had removed to Town after a disagreement with Jane and had sworn never to return, leading to all manner of unpleasant rumours circulating about Meryton. Having witnessed first-hand the ugliness of Jane's recent behaviour, Elizabeth and Darcy could not fault Bingley for wishing to escape it for a while, but they were nonetheless grieved by the apparent severity of their squabble.

Darcy had written to his friend, enquiring if there was aught they could do to assist. They had not heard a whisper in response until he appeared at their door the previous evening, unannounced and in a vast discomposure of spirits, begging that he be allowed to retire directly and promising to explain all in the morning. Thus, they were all on tenterhooks to hear what he had to say.

"He is not unwell. My man confirmed it with his this morning," Darcy informed them, replacing his cup in its saucer and enquiring with a raised eyebrow and a nod as to the provenance of Elizabeth's letter.

"Mama," she informed him, breaking the seal. She very soon after refolded it and set it aside in disgust.

"What news?" Darcy enquired gently.

"My Uncle Gardiner called on Mr. Bingley and was told he was travelling here. My mother has dedicated three whole sides to her displeasure."

"Nothing more about the nature of their disagreement?"

Elizabeth shook her head. "Only a demand that we send him back directly."

"Then we shall have to wait for Bingley to enlighten us. Regrettably, I can wait no longer. Peterson is expecting me at eleven."

A quarter of an hour after Darcy's departure when Bingley still had not appeared, Elizabeth encouraged her sister to attend to her pianoforte practice and went out for a walk—not five minutes into which, she came upon her errant houseguest. "Mr. Bingley! We thought you still abed."

"Er, no, I beg you would forgive me, I…"

"Do not make yourself uncomfortable, I meant not to upbraid you. We were only concerned."

He inclined his head but seemed no less ill at ease.

"I was about to walk around the lake. Will you join me?" He readily accepted, and as she hoped, the pursuit lost him a little of his awkwardness, though not enough to persuade him to speak. "You will have to satisfy my curiosity at some point, sir," she said at length. "Are we ever to know why you have come?"

"I came to see you," he said wretchedly. "I wished to see a friendly face."

"I can understand that. I am glad you know you will always receive a friendly welcome from us, though I am exceedingly sorry you do not feel there would be one at Netherfield." He looked glummer than ever. "Will you not tell me what it is that you and Jane have quarrelled about?"

He gave her a strange look, then sighed and frowned at the ground. "You."

Elizabeth's heart sank. No wonder Jane resented her still. "I thought you agreed to forgive her for what she did to me? She and I will never be able to forget it if you will not."

"I did. At least, I endeavoured to, but something else has since come to light that I cannot forgive." He looked at her, then away, several times. Then he removed his hat and ran a hand through his hair. "Would that I could avoid speaking of it, for I know it will give you pain."

"I am afraid you cannot escape speaking of it now."

He shoved his hat back on and sighed deeply. "It cannot be avoided anyway. You need to know. But is there somewhere we might sit?"

"If I am to be vexed, I should rather keep walking."

He looked uncertain, but since there were no seats in the vicinity, he had little choice but to acquiesce, and they walked on. She was glad of the activity when he eventually, and not very fluently, gave her to understand that Jane had been exposed as the source of every damning piece of gossip they had heard flying about London and regurgitated on Lady Catherine's lips.

"I had not thought Jane so bad as this!" she cried, pain and fury hastening her steps. "Though I had supposed her to be resentful of my station, I did not suspect her of descending to such malicious revenge!"

"Pray take care!" Bingley cried. "I would not have you trip."

She slowed a little, not for him, but because her baby had begun kicking as though in support of her indignation. She laid a hand on her stomach to soothe it.

"Are you well?" Bingley enquired in alarm.

"I am not *un*well, but I am scarcely happy!"

He directed a pained grimace heavenward. "Lord, I cannot forgive her for wounding you thus, first with violence, now with calumny, for which you have suffered doubly, what with society's disdain and Darcy's."

She frowned, bemused as to his meaning, until she recalled the last time they were in company. "If you are referring to our evening at the theatre, you must not concern yourself a moment longer. There was much talk, but Darcy's overhearings at least were easily gainsaid. The matter is quite settled between us."

"I am in awe of your forbearance, Lizzy."

Supposing him to be resigned against resolving his dispute so easily, she regretted boasting of her own marital harmony, and though the circumstances were hardly comparable, she found herself saying, "Do not suppose yourself incapable of the same. Grievous though Jane's indiscretions may be, they must not be allowed to come between you, not after all you endured to be together."

He made a derisive sound and looked away. "All I endured, indeed!"

"When you were persuaded she did not love you, I meant."

"I took your meaning, and had not your sister graciously informed me two weeks ago that she tricked me into marrying her, I might still have shared the opinion that such was the greatest injustice I have endured."

Elizabeth stopped walking. "Sir, notwithstanding my present feelings towards her, that is still impossible to credit."

He shook his head slowly. "You will recall the attitude in which she and

I were discovered the day we became engaged."

"I could scarcely forget it."

"It was not the happy celebration everybody took it to be." He blew out his breath and rubbed the back of his neck. "Moments before that, Jane swooned, or so I thought. She fell in such a way as toppled us both to the sofa."

Elizabeth made a noise of protest but he interrupted.

"She has admitted doing so by design. Then she…pardon me…then she kissed me."

"Why would she do such a thing? And, pardon *me*, but why would you object?"

He appeared confused by this and abruptly turned away. "I like your method of walking off vexation. Might we continue?"

She consented, and they walked for two hundred yards at least in silence before he ventured to speak again.

"Your sister's demeanour was altered when I returned to court her after Easter." He paused to heave a heavy sigh. "What with all the other unpleasantness and distractions that occurred during those weeks, I…well, suffice to say that by June, I had begun to question my wishes. It seems she perceived my indecision and conspired with her mother to act. Mrs. Bennet has freely acknowledged our being interrupted at that moment was deliberate."

"I do not recall that it happened in that way. My mother tried to prevent our going in."

He looked unsure for a moment but then dismissed it. "It scarcely matters. By then, Jane had thrown herself upon me, and it was assumed by everybody that we had reached an understanding."

"But why did you not explain the situation to my father? Or—very well, perhaps not him—but to Darcy."

"I could not tell Darcy!" He seemed to regret his tone and in a calmer voice added, "Not even he could have extricated me without severely injuring your sister's reputation. Or yours. Besides, I was not deficient in any feeling for your sister. I believed—I *hoped*—we might be content." In a pitiable voice he concluded, "I knew not then how embittered she would become."

If Jane had indeed condescended to despicable means to secure an offer, condemning herself to a marriage of vastly unequal affection, then Elizabeth hardly wondered that she should have grown jealous of her genuine happiness with Darcy. The injustice of punishing her for it with malice and disloyalty was insufferable. "I am very sorry for you," she told Bingley. "I understand now why you wished to leave."

"May I…do I ask too much to stay on a little longer?"

"You are more than welcome. You must return only when you are ready and not merely because I have forced you, no matter how my mother begs me to try." Thinking of her mother and father, she added, "There can be nothing more wretched than being unable to respect one's partner in life. I refuse to have any part in committing you to such a fate."

He did not reply for a time. When Elizabeth gave up glowering fiercely at the lake and looked at him, she was surprised to find him watching her with some concern.

"Would that I could offer you such words of comfort as you have given me, Lizzy."

How she pitied him then, for she had Darcy to ease the pain of Jane's betrayal. He had no one. "Perhaps we can be of comfort to each other," she offered and was pleased to see his expression lighten. Her anger was too great to accommodate much in the way of comfort at that moment, however, and she sought to end their tête-à-tête by suggesting they return to the house before breakfast was cleared away. The prospect of food persuaded him to abandon the subject, and they returned indoors without taxing themselves to discuss anything more significant than the whereabouts of the other members of the household.

"There, you see," Elizabeth said as they came through the front door. "I can hear Georgiana at her practice still."

"She is a good girl," Bingley remarked. "Vastly less trying than my own sisters were at her age."

He could not have known the very great anxiety this comment would cause her, and Elizabeth did her utmost to conceal any sign of it, but his reference to Georgiana's steadiness of character sent her mind racing down a most unwelcome path. She excused herself on the pretext of some menial task and went to her husband's study to fretfully await his return.

"And has he stopped her writing to anybody else?"

"He did not say, but that is not the worst of it."

"Pray cease pacing and come to it then."

Elizabeth obliged him insofar as she ceased pacing, yet she continued to prevaricate. "I am almost afraid to tell you, for I know how angry you will be."

Darcy was already a good way beyond angry—with Jane, with Bingley, with Mrs. Bennet, and with Ashby and his bloody wife. He watched Elizabeth bite her lip and rub her temples and grew angrier still at all those who continued to obtrude on her happiness. "Tell me."

"Jane knows about Georgiana's near elopement."

He closed his eyes and clenched his teeth.

"I am sorry, Fitzwilliam. I meant not to break your confidence, only on the very day I returned home from Hunsford, Jane and I met Mr. Wickham in the street. He was so vile, so charming, I could not bear to see Jane taken in; thus, I told her. But I trusted her then. I never dreamt she might—"

Darcy stepped forward and took her by the shoulders. "Calm yourself. I do not blame you for telling Jane. She is your sister. You could not have known how she would change."

She let out a shaky breath and gave a weak smile of thanks. "But think you she will tell Lady Ashby?"

"I know not."

"I should never forgive myself if Georgiana's reputation were tarnished because of me."

"It would not be any fault of yours if it were," he said firmly, pulling her into his embrace. "Leave it with me, love. I shall deal with it."

Knightsbridge, London
February 11

Ashby,

I am in no way surprised Darcy has written you such a letter if your wife has indeed been playing arson with his reputation, and neither ought you to be. I shall overlook the colourful rant you sent me on the assumption that you were not brave enough to direct it at him. Frankly, you ought to count yourself fortunate that his threats ended where they did and were not extended to include the removal of one or both of your ballocks.

May I presume, dear brother, that this is the reason for Lady Catherine's displeasure? Your wife is making friends hand-over-fist, is she not? I suggest you encourage her in future to better select her enemies. The wives of men such as Darcy are not generally prudent marks.

Do not trouble yourself writing to Father. He will not intervene and neither will I, for we both dislike your wife as much as you do. Knowing you prefer an uncomplicated existence, my advice is to shake off your indignation and concede to Darcy's embargoes. Opposing him will only cost you money and respect—and possibly a ballock.

Your younger and eminently wiser brother,
Fitzwilliam

Friday, 19 February 1813: Derbyshire

Darcy gritted his teeth. "Your turn, Bingley."

"Oh, I beg your pardon." Bingley ceased staring from the window and turned over a card.

Darcy played another of his and returned to waiting. After a minute, he cleared his throat.

Bingley turned over another card.

"For pity's sake, that was a king!" Darcy exclaimed, tossing his hand down in disgust. This was precisely the inattention that had forced a premature end to their game of Vingt-et-un and Piquet before that, reducing them in desperation to playing Beggar-My-Neighbour.

"It was? I thought I had missed my turn again."

"I comprehend now why you disdained the idea of foils. Woolgathering such as this would have seen you skewered within moments."

"'Twas you who turned your nose up at billiards."

"Thank God, else it might have been my cloth you skewered. Besides, I thought some air and exercise would do you good."

"It is February, Darcy. I have no wish to be outside—be it on a horse, on my feet, or on my arse by the lake catching frozen fish. I was quite content merely sitting here 'til you came along, resolved on entertaining me. I shall never comprehend your need to be constantly occupied."

Darcy maintained a blank expression, keeping his exasperation well hidden. He would have been equally content to leave Bingley to his musings, had not Elizabeth's vexation at her mother's latest letter persuaded him this discussion could be postponed no longer. Yet, having long ago lost all taste for interference, he was presently guilty of some vastly uncharacteristic procrastination whilst he summoned the will to delve into the quagmire of Bingley's *affaires du cœur.*

"Pray forgive my ill humour," Bingley said with a sigh. "You are very good to have me here. I would not be ungrateful, only I have much on my mind."

Darcy inclined his head.

"I have received a letter," Bingley sullenly informed him. "From Caroline."

"I see. She has discovered you are here then?"

"Aye, and she is displeased, to say the least. Jane is apparently gone to Farley House to escape the gossip in Meryton."

"Indeed? Elizabeth received word from her mother that Jane was gone to Town, but she made no mention of her staying with the Hursts." He could imagine with what delight they had received her and wondered whether Hurst might soon arrive at Pemberley seeking refuge as Bingley had done.

"Dare I enquire what else Mrs. Bennet wrote?" Bingley enquired.

Elizabeth had not shown Darcy the letter but had summarised her mother's position with telling consternation. Jane had gone to London, allegedly fanning speculation that Bingley meant to auction her off to the highest bidder, Mr. Bennet was imminently about to die of shame, thus the Collinses were banging down Longbourn's door, and Mrs. Bennet and her other three daughters were busy packing their worldly belongings in preparation for living out the remainder of their days at Pemberley. "Suffice to say she is eager to see you soon returned."

"Then, I am afraid she will be disappointed."

"You do not intend to return directly?"

"I do not intend to return at all."

Darcy tensed with the endeavour not to sit forward in his seat. "Ever?"

"Do not judge me, Darcy. It is no longer any secret that I did not wish to marry her in the first place."

Indeed. Darcy had been significantly less astonished by the revelation of Jane's scheming than Elizabeth. In his opinion, no despicable deed was beneath a woman content to strike her own sister, full in the knowledge she was with child. He only pitied Elizabeth her disappointment and Bingley his unenviable predicament.

Never mind that it was before noon, it was most definitely the hour for brandy. "Why did you not cease visiting Longbourn if you were decided against her?" he enquired as he poured them both a glass.

"Because of Lizzy."

He turned around. "Elizabeth?"

Bingley looked up sharply then launched himself from his chair and stalked to the window before Darcy could make out his expression. "Yes, well…while you were off being a lovelorn arse-about-town, I was supporting her family in the wake of your friend Wickham's attack, or had you forgotten?"

"I had not forgotten," Darcy replied, chastened though no less perturbed.

"I could not conscionably have abandoned Jane a second time whilst her sister lay insensible abed."

"Of course not." It was a reasonable explanation. Darcy fought prodigiously hard to ignore the unjust flicker of wariness occasioned by the recollection of Bingley pulling Elizabeth into his arms in the churchyard.

"I see now that my lingering must have prolonged her anticipation," Bingley mumbled. "I suppose it is what prompted Jane to act as she did."

"Impatience is no excuse for duplicity. She was very wrong to deceive you." Darcy handed him his drink and sat back at the card table. "But have you truly had no pleasure from the marriage? Is there no possibility that you might learn to esteem one another again? You did love her once, after all."

"Aye, but she is not the same person she was then."

"No, but there is every reason to hope she might improve. I did, once I was made aware of my faults."

"You mistake me, Darcy. I have no wish to redeem the situation. Even were she to revert to the sweet girl you thought smiled too much, she would not be the woman I want." He lifted his empty glass in query. "May I?" Darcy acceded with a nod. "Besides," Bingley added whilst he poured himself another drink, "people do not alter as much as all that. You are no less proud than you were. Lizzy has merely learnt to tolerate it better."

His conversational tone belied any hostility. Nevertheless, Darcy was wounded, appalled at the merest possibility of its being true. Such was his agitation that he missed what Bingley said next and was obliged to ask him to repeat himself.

"I said I plan to settle in Nova Scotia."

Darcy stared at him, endeavouring to judge whether he was in earnest.

"You will advise against it, I know," Bingley added, returning to the table. "But I have learnt the perils of yielding too easily to persuasion."

"I am glad to hear it. It is a shame you have not yet learnt to yield to good sense."

Bingley flinched. "You mean to lecture me on how the country is at war, I suppose?"

"No, I should think in that part of the country you would be as far from their army as we are from Napoleon's here. I meant only to express my sincerest doubt that going so far and giving up so much would ever improve your situation. It is a vast undertaking, not easily undone." When Bingley did not respond, he added more frankly, "This is not the same as hopping in your carriage and racing off to London on a whim."

Bingley pulled himself up indignantly in his seat. "I am aware of that!"

Darcy regarded him intently for a moment then leant forward and began gathering up the playing cards. "What will you do with Netherfield?"

"Let Jane keep it."

"You would purchase it for her or lease it indefinitely?"

"Er…yes."

"Where will you live when you arrive?"

"I mean to purchase an estate."

Darcy tapped the pack of cards into alignment on the table. "What will you do for companionship? You could not simply remarry."

Bingley reddened. "I do not recall expressing any wish to remarry."

He placed the cards in their box and returned the lid. "And what of Jane? Would you consign her to a life without a husband or children?"

"Let her tell everybody I have died and take another husband!"

"That would create far more problems than it would solve."

"Blast it, Darcy! After the way she has treated Lizzy, I know not how you can care!"

"Mayhap I have learnt some of Elizabeth's compassion." He leant forwards with his elbows on his knees and fixed his friend with a serious look. "The imprudence of my attempting to persuade you one way or the other speaks for itself, but I must say you do not appear to have given it much consideration. I beg you would not act with your usual precipitance here. Give the idea some more thought."

Bingley slammed his glass down on the table. "I have given it thought! I have done nothing but think on it these past two weeks whilst I have sat here watching you have everything I want and knowing I shall never have it!"

Darcy sat back, startled by his vehemence and heartily sorry for it. He was well aware of his own extraordinary good fortune and pitied his friend's plight, for it was probable Bingley would never know equal felicity with a woman such as Jane.

"I am sorry the succour you sought here has come at such a price. Yet, you must not permit my situation to influence yours. At the risk of sounding like persuasion, I will say this: you are a very good friend, and I should be excessively sorry to see you go."

Bingley stammered his thanks and promptly excused himself to seek out some of the air he had earlier disdained.

Darcy rubbed a hand over his face and stood up, pondering where he might find Elizabeth, that he could relay the whole of it to her—and rather uncharitably attempting to guess how much it would cost him to purchase Netherfield in the event that Bingley did not, that Mrs. Bennet's threat of coming to live at Pemberley need never come to fruition.

Saturday, 20 February 1813: Derbyshire

"YOU MUST GO. I ABSOLUTELY INSIST."

"I should feel as though I were deserting you." The look Elizabeth gave her made Georgiana feel silly. "That is, I know you do not need—"

"Dear Georgiana," Elizabeth interrupted, reaching to squeeze her hand, "I did not mean to imply that I would not miss you, only that you must not feel guilty for wishing to go. Miss Castleton is your friend, and her invitation is an excessively generous one."

"It is, is it not?" she replied, allowing herself to smile at the prospect of a week's dancing instruction from Mr. Thomas Wilson himself, alongside half a dozen of Henrietta's school friends.

"Indeed it is! I am quite jealous, which is why you must go. Then, you may relay to me in detail all that you learn." She fidgeted in her chair as she spoke, attempting to find a more comfortable attitude.

"Here, allow me," Georgiana offered, leaving her own seat to help better arrange her sister's cushions. "You poor thing! This is why I do not wish to leave you."

"When I am grown so fat I cannot even arrange my own cushions, I shall simply give up sitting in the orangery and take to my bed. It still would not be a reason for you not to go to Hornscroft."

For a fleeting moment, Georgiana felt chastened—until she caught herself and laughed instead, feeling rather pleased to have grown better used to Elizabeth's sportive manner.

"Besides," Elizabeth continued, "I shall not be without female company. Tabitha is coming to Pemberley."

A week at Hornscroft Hall abruptly quadrupled in appeal. "Mrs. Sinclair?"

Her dismay must have been obvious, for Elizabeth laughed outright. "She is not so very objectionable, you know."

"Mayhap not, but she is disposed to be quarrelsome. Ought you not to be avoiding such excitement?"

"On the contrary, I have great hopes the trouble she is bound to cause will provide a creditable distraction from any anxiety I might be feeling."

The remark took Georgiana aback, having never before seen or heard of Elizabeth suffering any uneasiness. "Are you very anxious?" she enquired softly.

Elizabeth wrinkled her nose. "Daunted, certainly, but I think there are few who would not be. I am endeavouring not to think about it overmuch."

"Will your mother come?"

"I am trying very hard to make sure she does not! I need my wits about me at the best of times when dealing with her, and I do not anticipate that being the case in the throes of my confinement. I shall not be alone, though, for my Aunt Gardiner has agreed to come at the end of March." After a pause, she quietly added, "I always thought I would have Jane with me."

Only since Mr. Bingley arrived at Pemberley had Elizabeth divulged what transpired between Jane and her at Netherfield. Georgiana could not have been more shocked or more indignant, though she had not expounded upon the latter sentiment to Elizabeth. "I am sorry for you, Lizzy. I know not what to say to ease your mind."

"It is the most painful thing in the world, but there is nothing to be said or done. But enough melancholy," she said, drawing herself up and leaning to pour them both more tea. "Are we agreed that you will visit Miss Castleton in two weeks?"

Georgiana grinned. "Aye, very well. Would that you could accompany me. You dance so beautifully."

"Not these days, I assure you. I am all clumsiness and inelegance."

"You judge yourself too severely. You are still remarkably graceful. If you will pardon my frankness, I have seen ladies far more unhappily altered by their increase than you. Your condition becomes you very well."

"She speaks true, Lizzy. It most certainly does."

Georgiana jumped. She had not heard Mr. Bingley come in.

"Our sanctuary is compromised, Georgiana!" Elizabeth cried, one hand held to her breast in feigned dismay. "The men have discovered us!"

"I come alone," Mr. Bingley protested, holding his hands up in surrender. "And I swear Darcy will not learn of your hiding place from me."

"Oh, my brother knows we are here. He had business in Kympton, or he would have joined us."

"Kympton this day, is it? I declare I have never known a man with more business than Darcy. He is scarcely ever at home."

Georgiana rather thought that, if Mr. Bingley troubled himself to rise earlier in the day, he would see more of his friend. Elizabeth was kinder in her response, gesturing for him to join them as she agreed that Darcy had many demands on his time.

"You are singularly forbearing not to demand more of it for yourself," he replied, choosing the chair nearest to Elizabeth.

"Come, you of all people know he would never neglect his responsibilities on my account."

"No, I do not suppose he would."

"Besides, he is not absent as often as that implies or so very far away. It is not as though he is gone off to another country, never to return."

Mr. Bingley paled. "Darcy told you?"

"He did," Elizabeth replied.

"Shall I call for another cup?" Georgiana said hastily, eager to remove herself from what suddenly promised to be a most awkward conversation. Her escape notwithstanding, the orangery was not so large that the distance to the door took her out of earshot.

"Are you angry?" she heard Mr. Bingley enquire.

"No, I am not angry," Elizabeth replied. "I am sad. I wish you did not feel you had to go."

"Forgive me. The last thing I would wish is that my leaving should cause you any distress, yet I know not how much longer I can live in this ghastly suspension."

"It distresses me to see you make a decision so evidently contrary to your happiness."

"It will be inconceivably hard to leave, I grant you."

"Then why do you not stay? At least until you are more certain of your feelings?" Elizabeth said gently.

Georgiana reached the door, but waited, curious what he would answer.

"I am in no doubt of my feelings, Lizzy, but I cannot countenance making you unhappy. I shall not go just yet. I shall tarry a little longer."

Satisfied, Georgiana opened the door and requested more provisions of the footman waiting without. She took her time walking back, vastly undesirous of obtruding onto aught delicate.

"I feel in part to blame," Elizabeth was saying. "Had I not argued with her—"

"We were discontented long before that."

"Aye, and had I not championed your suit with her so single-mindedly, regardless of the changes in her character or your regard, she might never have acted as she did, and you would never have suffered as you have."

Through the plants lining the path, Georgiana could see that Elizabeth was measuring out more tea from the caddy and seemed oblivious to Mr. Bingley's drawing closer to her, seemingly captivated by her every word.

"Had I not dithered in coming to know my own heart," he replied, "neither of us would have suffered as we have."

"Ah, good. You are still here."

Georgiana jumped for a second time. "Brother!" she exclaimed, turning to see Darcy come through the door.

"Forgive me, I meant not to startle you." He looked wholly unrepentant as he bowed to kiss Elizabeth's fingers. "How have you all been amusing yourselves?"

"Merely talking, Darcy," Mr. Bingley said. He had abandoned his chair and was examining whatever plant it was that clung to the back wall.

"Lizzy has been persuading me to accept Henrietta's invitation," Georgiana said. She chose to feign ignorance of Darcy's baffled glance at Elizabeth, as well as her mouthing *Miss Castleton* to him in return, thinking it a rather sweet exchange. "Her father has engaged a very fine dancing master in preparation for her coming out and allowed her to invite all her friends to partake in his instruction."

"That is exceedingly generous of him."

"It is a shame Lizzy will not be able to join me, though."

"I shall be sorry to miss it, Georgiana, but there is little hope of my dancing elegantly enough at present to do justice to such a master."

"What has your present inelegance to do with the matter?" Darcy enquired. "You were not heavy with child when you knocked Tobias onto the floor."

"He is right, Georgiana. Hornscroft Hall is too full of ornament and finery to be safe from me. It is for the best that I do not go."

Georgiana listened with but half an ear, her attention instead fixed upon Mr. Bingley, who observed this exchange with a rapidly deepening frown. She could not blame him for his disquiet; from his vantage, he could not have seen Elizabeth's broad grin, only Darcy's severe expression.

Such was always the way with her brother, she had learnt. Whatever joke he made was made with impenetrable solemnity, so that it was impossible to tell whether he spoke in jest unless one knew him to be stating an opinion not his own. It was an aspect of his character with which she had been wholly unfamiliar until Elizabeth came to Pemberley. Though her new sister certainly did not treat him disrespectfully, she yet wielded a mysterious and unashamed sort of power over him, daring to tease him, and in return, provoking him to some decidedly surreptitious teasing of his own.

When presently the footman arrived and they all convened at the table for refreshments, Mr. Bingley appeared to be struggling to conceal his confusion. Though it was a little ungenerous, Georgiana triumphed to see him suffering under the same misconceptions she once had, happy in the knowledge that she, at least, was no longer a bystander to her brother and sister's repartee.

Sunday, 21 February 1813: Derbyshire

Bingley threw aside his covers and scrabbled at the bed curtains in an attempt to find the join. They opened a yard to the left, courtesy of his man.

"Are you well, Mr. Bingley?"

"No! No, I am *not* well!"

Indeed, he was exhausted, having been unable to sleep a wink for recurrent nightmares of succumbing to the temptation to kiss Elizabeth—and then being murdered on the spot by Darcy. It was outside of enough! Could he expect his feelings to ever subside while he remained in such close proximity to her? Could he expect Darcy would not truly run him through if he ever came so close to exposing his desires as he had yesterday in the orangery? No, regardless of Elizabeth's plea, he must leave this place and soon! Snatching his dressing gown from Banbury's grasp, he seated himself at the desk in the corner of the room and pulled out a sheet of paper.

"Perhaps some breakfast would restore your humour, sir?"

Bingley answered distractedly that breakfast would be most welcome, and Banbury must have left to fetch it because, when he stopped to dip his pen, the man was no longer there. By the time he returned with a tray, Bingley was done. He handed him the three letters he had dashed off and sat down to eat.

"I cannot find my blasted address book anywhere, Banbury," he said, slicing into a hunk of gammon. "Be a good fellow and see to it they are addressed properly, would you?"

"Certainly, sir," Banbury answered. A moment later he added, "Mr. Forsyth, sir?"

Bingley looked up to discover him peering dubiously at the uppermost letter. "Netherfield's freeholder," he explained around his mouthful.

Banbury bowed slightly, and though he said no more, he did raise both eyebrows. It made Bingley nervous. The man knew far too much of his private affairs, which made him wonder what conclusions he was drawing. He forced his mouthful down before he had properly chewed it and choked out, "Why I write to him is no concern of yours."

"Indeed, I made no enquiry, sir."

"You did—of a fashion. You are doing it again now. Your eyebrows are all up in the air."

Banbury apologised and frowned.

"No, no, I do not require you to scowl. Leave your eyebrows where they were." He sliced some more meat and added sullenly, "I am enquiring about purchasing it if you must know."

"Indeed, there is no obligation for me to know, sir," Banbury replied coolly as he shuffled the letter to the back of the pile and regarded the next no less disdainfully than the last. "The harbour master, sir?"

"Yes, the harbour master!"

"Which harbour, might I enquire, sir?"

Bingley threw down his knife and fork. "Blast it, Banbury, that is not your business, either!"

"Undoubtedly not, sir. Though if you were to make it so, it would be much more likely that I should address it correctly."

Damnation! "Right." Breakfast had lost its appeal. He pushed the plate away. "Send it to Liverpool, if you would."

"Very good, sir."

Bingley watched closely as Banbury flicked to the last letter in the pile, anticipating a raised eyebrow, a frown, a sneer, a twitch, *some* indication of disapprobation, yet the man was taking his own good time peering at the addressee.

"My cousin, before you ask."

"I would never be so impertinent, sir." He pursed his lips and slipped the letters into his pocket.

"Dash it all, Banbury, I mean to settle in Nova Scotia, and that is all there is to it." In truth he had absolutely no desire to live out his days in a foreign country, yet trial and error had proved nowhere in England was far enough removed to keep him away from Elizabeth for long, thus abroad he must go.

Banbury inclined his head. "A shrewd decision, sir."

"Shrewd?"

"Certainly, sir. At such a great distance there is almost no possibility your troubles in Hertfordshire might follow you there."

Bingley felt himself colour. "Just dress me for services, would you?" he muttered, hauling himself to his feet.

"Services are over, sir."

"What?" Bingley whipped about to look at the clock. It was gone midday. "Upon my word, why did you not tell me the time when I sat down to write those letters?"

"I would never have presumed you could not tell it yourself, sir."

Bingley narrowed his eyes at him. He swore Darcy never had this much trouble with his staff. "Very well, dress me as you see fit. Only get to it, that I may be left in peace."

Banbury did as he was bid with mercifully little more impertinence and made to depart.

"Ah, Banbury, one other matter before you leave. I would have you take those letters to the receiving office in person. Entrust them to nobody else. Mrs. Darcy is not to get wind of my plans. I shall not have her distressed."

They parted ways after that, Banbury to wherever it was he went when he was not attending Bingley and Bingley to escape into the park to reflect, with no little alarm, upon the very great moment of the course upon which he had just resolved.

Wednesday, 24 February 1813: Derbyshire

"There you are. I thought you meant to join us in the library."

Darcy looked up from his letter. Whatever Elizabeth saw in his countenance turned hers from happy to alarmed in an instant, and before he had the chance to respond, she was hastening to his side.

"What is it?" she enquired, laying a comforting hand on his arm and peering at him with the utmost concern.

He raised a hand to cover hers. Then he changed his mind, tossed the letter onto his desk and used both hands to pull her gently onto his lap.

"I am summoned to Kent."

"So soon? Is she…?"

"Not yet, but the physicians do not believe it will be long, and Montgomery writes to beg my assistance in the preceding days." In answer to her puzzled look, he added, "He respectfully alludes to my experience in matters of probate."

"In other words, he does not know what he is doing and needs your help making all the arrangements."

Darcy smiled at her turn of phrase and inclined his head. "One wonders what his attorney is doing to earn his fee."

"Even the best attorney is no substitute for the counsel of a trusted and experienced friend."

"Then I am grateful he has so many others to call upon." She pulled an odd face, half frown half question. He could not fathom her confusion. "You cannot think I mean to go."

"I cannot imagine why you would not."

"Why do you suppose?" He spread a hand over her stomach. "I will not have you make the journey again after last time."

She smiled ruefully. "Much though I know you love my obstinacy, I am afraid I cannot argue with that. But that does not mean—"

"And I will not go without you. Thus, we shall both remain."

She gave him a pitying look. "I beg you would pardon me for putting this so bluntly, but it did not sound as though you would be gone more than a few weeks." She laid her hand atop his. "I believe this little one and I might look after ourselves for that long."

It was true; he did love her obstinacy, particularly when it was unconsciously done and she believed she was being complying. Still, he shook his head, unwilling to countenance any length of time apart while she was in so delicate a condition.

"Consider what you would be denying yourself, Fitzwilliam," she pressed softly. "One is not always blessed with the opportunity to pay one's final respects."

"I have made my peace with Lady Catherine. I will not go to Rosings without you." He did not like the way in which she regarded him and said peevishly, "Anybody would think you were attempting to get rid of me."

She smiled at him and kissed his cheek. "I know you will regret it if you do not go."

Of course she knew—she comprehended him perfectly—just as he knew she grew anxious despite her endeavours to conceal it. Yet, still she encouraged him to go. She was without doubt the most selfless person he had ever known. "Loveliest Elizabeth." He held her face and ran his thumb along her jaw. "I swore to myself I would never leave you again."

"I shall detest every moment you are gone, yet it is for but a few weeks, and it is not as though I shall be alone. Georgiana will be here for most of that time, Tabitha arrives on Saturday, and Mr. Bingley has promised not to rush off. I am sure, if you ask, he will agree to stay until you return."

The notion of Bingley being Elizabeth's protector in his absence sat exceedingly ill with Darcy, yet he could not deny the wisdom of it. Indeed, the enforced delay might give the man time to come to his senses and eschew his absurd plan to emigrate. He conceded with a sigh and a lingering kiss, after which she nestled against him with her head upon his shoulder.

"I shall be back in good time, whether or not she succumbs rapidly," he said. "If I miss the funeral, so be it. I refuse to be farther from you than this room whilst you are confined."

"I did not expect otherwise, but at least you will have said your goodbyes and helped Mr. Montgomery. Though, if you did happen to be there as long as three weeks, you could bring Mrs. Gardiner back with you. I am sure she would vastly enjoy three days in your sole company."

He shook his head, smiling at her teasing, and nudged her to stand up. "What have I been missing in the library?"

"Nothing of consequence. Georgiana has given up waiting for you and gone to practice the pianoforte. And when I left, Mr. Bingley was brooding, as he is disposed to do these days."

"Good," he replied, taking her by the hand and leading her from the study and directly past the library door to the stairs. "In that case, our absence will not be noted by either of them." There was much he would need to arrange if he were to travel to Kent, but if he must go, he meant for them to take full advantage of what time they had remaining before he departed.

Sunday, 28 February 1813: Derbyshire

The heavens were the purest indigo blue, bedizened with myriad stars and buttressed on all sides by the even darker silhouettes of the surrounding peaks. Moonlight bounced off the frozen lake, flooding the snow-frosted lawn with eerie blue light. There could not have been a more enchanting scene to behold or a more perfect vantage from which to view it.

Darcy's arms tightened about her. "Are you cold, love? You shivered."

Elizabeth shook her head. "How I shall miss you," she sighed, her breath frosting the window.

"You delight in torturing me, woman. It is objectionable enough that I must leave you tomorrow without pronouncements of that nature."

"I would not say I delight in it, though neither shall I say I am sorry. I shall miss you. Though, if you remind yourself often enough what a vexing creature I can be, you might not miss *me* at all. Then only one of us need be miserable."

"That will not work," he replied with a soft chuckle. "I decided almost from the first moment we met that you were the most maddening woman of my acquaintance. It did not prevent me from pining for you for the half a twelvemonth 'til we met again."

She twisted her head to kiss his cheek. "Then we must be thankful only *you* have improved in civility since. If you fell in love with me because you enjoyed being vexed, you might fall out again if I suddenly learnt to be agreeable."

His lips curled into a wonderful little smile, and he shook his head. "Maddening."

She turned back to the window and hugged his arms to her.

"Have I improved in other ways?" Darcy enquired after a moment. "That is, am I still proud?"

The question took her aback. "What makes you enquire?"

"A passing comment of Bingley's. But it has been troubling me, as you will comprehend." She tried to turn around, but he resisted it, his arms stiff. "I would have you answer frankly."

Her heart went out to him. He was ever as unforgiving of his own defects as he was of other people's. "A little, then," she said gently. "Very occasionally. But I do not blame you for it."

"So you have merely learnt to tolerate it?"

She did turn around then. "Yes, I daresay I have, but is that not what love is—tolerating, accepting, even holding dear one another's imperfections?" She placed her hands on his chest. "I would have you know your imperfections are better than most other people's finest merits, and I love them very much."

He cradled her face with both hands and fixed her with the full force of one of his inimitable gazes. "If my imperfections are tolerable, it is because you have made them so. I would be nothing without you."

"As would I be without you."

He shook his head. "You have no imperfections."

She slid her hands around his neck and pulled herself up until their lips were a hair's breadth apart. "I love you more dearly than I knew it was possible to love, Fitzwilliam."

After that, the view from the window was forgotten in favour of the unseen pleasures of the darkened bedchamber, and though Elizabeth could not see him, she felt his gaze as intimately as she felt him love her, and she knew he felt the same.

"God, I shall miss you," he breathed into her hair as they lay together in bed some time later.

"I am sorry I shall not be there to comfort you," she whispered.

"Knowing I have you to come home to will be comfort enough."

"I shall be here, growing fat and relying unreasonably on others to relieve the tedium of waiting."

"Voila," he murmured sleepily.

"What?"

"I forgot your impatience when I said you had no imperfections."

She smirked, and for his benefit, because he could not see her expression in the dark, poked him in the ribs.

He caught her hand and brought it to his lips. "I do not think you ought to rely much on Bingley for company. I am not sure asking him to remain was wise."

Elizabeth delighted in the turn of events that had Darcy bemoaning Bingley's solemnity. "He might be in a better humour when you are gone, for I begin to suspect our felicity is contributing to his wretchedness."

"Yes, he has said something of that sort to me," Darcy replied, yawning. "It has much to do with his reasoning for leaving, if one can call it reason."

Elizabeth had given considerable thought to Mr. Bingley's professed intention to leave the country. Though both Darcy and she were convinced it was a foolhardy scheme, neither of them wished to interfere so far as to tell him outright he ought not to go. In truth, there was only one person who could. "Fitzwilliam, if I write to Jane, will you deliver the letter to her while you are in London to make certain she reads it?"

She felt him adjust his head down to look at her, though he could not have seen much in the darkness.

"Have you not had your fill of being shunned by your sister?"

"More than enough. Yet, I cannot help but think she is the person best placed to convince Mr. Bingley to stay."

"You assume she wishes it. To the best of my knowledge, she has not written to him the entire time he has been with us."

"I know. But consider, she does not know of his plan to go abroad. I cannot allow him to leave without giving her the chance to try and stop him."

He rolled his head back to where it had been on the pillow, pulling her more snugly against him as he settled into his repose. "I should never refuse you anything, love. But I beg you, enough of the Bingleys now. I would not have them obtrude any longer on my time with you."

She stretched to kiss his cheek and whisper her thanks, then settled her head back onto his shoulder to listen to his breathing, already slowing as sleep overtook him. She would rise early to write to Jane. Until then, she meant to remain in Darcy's arms all the night long. Where she belonged.

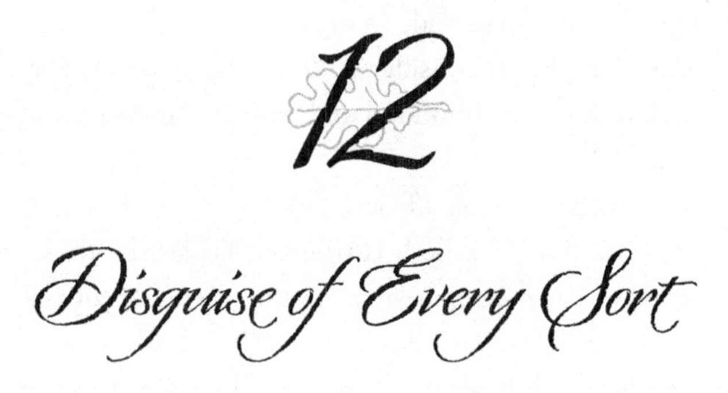

12

Disguise of Every Sort

Thursday, 4 March 1813: London

The nearer to Farley House the carriage took him, the hotter burned Darcy's resentment. He had not laid eyes on Jane Bingley since October when she slapped Elizabeth at Netherfield, and the intervening months had done naught to diminish his displeasure. Contrary to what Elizabeth believed, however, he was not averse to delivering her letter. Indeed, her request provided the perfect pretext to pay the visit he had been desirous of making for some weeks.

The carriage drew to a halt, and after presenting his card, Darcy was shown into a small room at the rear of Hurst's house where Jane Bingley sat at her needlework, for all the world as though her most pressing concern was where next to stick her needle.

Her serenity deserted her upon seeing him. "Mr. Darcy!" she cried, launching herself to her feet. "What are you doing here?"

Darcy waited for the servant to close the door, taking advantage of the brief time to bring his temper under regulation. Once the door had clicked shut, he turned his eyes upon her, feeling no contrition when she visibly quailed. He made no effort to moderate his tone, which even to his ear sounded exceptionally cold. "I would have your word that you will never cast aspersions about Elizabeth's good character again—by any means, to any person, or in any manner that might threaten her reputation or well-being."

"Oh! Pardon? I…I thought you must be come about Charles."

"I imagine you did. I have noticed your first thought always tends to your own interests. Your word, madam."

"I…I did not know any of what I said would be repeated! It was never my intention to gossip, only to confide in my friend."

"You are mistaken if you consider Lady Ashby a friend. She has been known to my family since childhood and long acknowledged by all of us as self-serving."

She had the temerity to look affronted.

"I might also add that Elizabeth is troubled far less by those to whom you whispered your vile misrepresentations than that you yourself believed any of it."

She frowned a little but seemed otherwise disinclined to remorse. He could not say he was surprised.

"I, on the other hand, take an excessively dim view of your propensity to gossip about my family *to anybody*. If it happens again, you will discover that being excluded from my homes is but the merest expression of my displeasure. Your word, madam."

She paled and gave it with a nod. He knew not why she should be alarmed. She could not have expected he would allow her to continue unchecked with behaviour so injurious to his family.

"And now, your word that you will not repeat what you know of my sister's dealings with Mr. Wickham to another living person." Her eyes widened, and she stared at him. "Do not pretend ignorance, madam. Elizabeth assures me you know."

"I do, but…you must think very ill of me indeed if you believe me capable of so cruelly exposing her. I assure you, I never would. I am not the sort of person who does such things to innocent young ladies."

"Evidently you are."

Her countenance contorted with emotion, and for one brief moment, he thought she might cry before indignation got the better of her and she began to bluster instead. "You do not know what I have suffered! It is scarcely my fault I have grown bitter."

"Do not dare suggest it is Elizabeth's! She has done *nothing* to deserve your contempt. You, whom she ever held in the highest possible regard and in whom, for some reason unfathomable to me, she *still* has not given up hope, have abused her in every imaginable method. You have disdained all the particulars of her new situation, from her home to her capacity to run it. You sabotaged her relationship with my family, you marred her entrance into society, and you have abandoned her when she most needs you." He lowered his voice. "You struck her, not only knowing that she is with child, but *because* of it."

She backed away, shaking her head. "You misunderstand! It is only that my husband has—"

"You would blame him also?" Darcy exclaimed, turning to walk with quick steps across the room to distance himself from her effrontery.

"As might you if you only knew what I have endured."

"What have you endured but Bingley's struggles to overlook the defects in your character and esteem you regardless?"

She laughed bitterly. "He does not esteem *me*!"

"That is hardly any great wonder. What, pray, have you ever done to earn his esteem?"

"I am his wife!" She appeared to think this would rouse him to compassion. Presumably, she did not suspect him of knowing how it came about.

"That alone does not entitle you to his unwavering affections. You cannot expect his good opinion to endure when you treat him and all those around you with such utter disdain."

"Sir, you are unjustly severe!" she cried, her eyes moist with unshed tears.

"In voicing such censure, perhaps, but not in thinking it. And since you have not scrupled in speaking ill of Elizabeth, I am not presently inclined to be overly sympathetic to your sensibilities."

"You do not understa—"

"No, I do not." Determined to hear no more of her self-pity, he reached into his pocket for Elizabeth's letter and held it out to her. "Neither does Elizabeth, yet such is her devotion to you that she has written again with news she considers imperative for you to hear."

Jane took the letter gingerly as though it might burn her.

"She wondered whether you had troubled yourself to read any of her others since you have never deigned to reply. I recommend that you read this one."

He turned on his heel and quitted the room without taking his leave. She deserved no such attention. He was unsurprised to discover Miss Bingley loitering outside the door and only wondered that her sister was not with her.

"I hope you are well, Mr. Darcy."

"I am, thank you. If you will excuse me, I must be on my way."

"Oh yes, of course. If I may, though…might I enquire as to my brother's whereabouts?"

"He is at Pemberley still, madam."

"With Mrs. Darcy?"

"Yes." She looked more concerned for her brother than he had ever seen her, prompting him to add, "He is in good health, despite his troubles. You need not worry for him."

She gave a poor approximation of a smile. "I do, though, Mr. Darcy. Pray, send him home as soon as may be. Pemberley is not the best place for him. He ought to be with Jane."

Darcy was no longer certain where the best place for Bingley was but gave Miss Bingley all the assurances she sought to avoid being further delayed. He later reflected, as his carriage sped across the Kentish countryside, that it was telling with what alacrity he hastened to his aunt's deathbed, infinitely preferring it to the scene of his objectionable audience with Jane Bingley.

Rosings Park, Kent
Saturday, March 6

Dearest Elizabeth,

Be not surprised if what I write is incomprehensible. It is late and I am weary, but I find I do not wish to end another day without speaking to you.

Lady Catherine is still with us, though barely. I am increasingly relieved that neither you nor Georgiana accompanied me. No quantity of pastille burners can mask the scent of illness in the house, and her appearance grows no less shocking upon subsequent visits to her bedside than when I first arrived. When my mother passed away, her mind wandered and her limbs trembled, but her person was otherwise unchanged. My father's death was so sudden I never saw him aught but hale. Lady Catherine is wasted away to almost nothing.

Nonetheless, you were correct. I am pleased to have come. She sleeps a good deal, but this evening she stirred sufficiently to acknowledge me for the first time. Our exchange was brief, for she can scarcely breathe enough to speak, but we were able to share a few thoughts. We touched on Rosings, Anne, Georgiana, our unborn child, and you. It does not surprise me in the least that what might be her last ever words to me were about you. "I am pleased you married Elizabeth. I always liked her."

I shall say no more on that. I trust we are of equal minds on the matter.

Montgomery and I spent two hours this morning with his steward and another three this afternoon with his attorney, all of which seemed painless in comparison to the ten minutes I spent with Mr. Collins afterwards. I am finding the role of adviser even more onerous than I had anticipated, not least for its tedium but also the unexpected remembrance of the days following my father's passing, which were dark indeed.

I have seen very little of Anne. It would seem her delicate health has not lent itself to the rigours of nursing a dying relative, and I understand she spends but little time with her mother. Your good friend Mrs. Collins, however, has been stalwart in attending her ladyship, despite not having been long out of her confinement and having a newborn infant in need of her attention. I mean to speak to her at church on the morrow to express my deepest thanks for her troubles. I have already given her your letter.

I have also given Master Jonathan the gift you sent for him, with which he was delighted, of course, though he was most disappointed not to have his Aunt Darcy in person. I am not sure how much of him you would have seen had you come, however, for he is largely being kept to the nursery, presumably to spare him from the general malaise in the house.

I should not object to such a reprieve myself. Much though I esteem my family here, the dismal circumstances have made poor companions of us all. Fitzwilliam has written to say he is delayed with imperative business at his barracks. Ashby will likely only come for the funeral, for he has never had much attachment to Rosings. My uncle has not made his plans known. This place has never seemed more remote.

I miss you more than words can express, Elizabeth. I have not heard from you—which you must not take as a complaint, for I know you prefer to add to your letters over a number of days—but I miss your voice. I miss your good sense and your teasing. Being here without you to talk to recalls me disagreeably to the time before you were mine. Thank God, that is in the past. I count the days until I am home with you and feel no compunction for desiring it, for it would be a mercy if Lady Catherine were released from her suffering sooner rather than later. From what I saw of her this evening, it cannot be much longer.

I trust you are receiving sufficient attention from our guests to allay your impatience and not overburdening yourself. I know you will laugh at me, but I cannot refrain from reminding you of your promise to send an express should any need occur.

Good night, dearest Elizabeth. I am away to my bed—with any luck, to dream you are there with me. Pray take every care of yourself and our beloved child.

As ever, I adore you.
Fitzwilliam

He tucked the leaf he had plucked from the vine in the conservatory into the folds of the letter and sealed it securely within. Then he climbed into bed and succumbed to the blissful oblivion of sleep.

Saturday, 13 March 1813: Kent

Four days had passed after Lady Catherine succumbed before Fitzwilliam was able to escape his duties and journey to Rosings Park. His father remained indisposed after a recent relapse, and Ashby had been indecently eager to claim Fitzwilliam's delay as his own, thus the two brothers had not arrived until the eve of her ladyship's interment.

The funeral had been what most funerals are: gloomy and tedious. On this occasion, thanks to Mr. Collins's interminable orations, it was also so protracted as to prevent half the mourners travelling home that day, forcing them instead to trespass overnight upon Rosings' empty rooms and Anne's less-than-enthusiastic hospitality.

Darcy, having been there the longest and being therefore the most desirous of leaving, was by far the least forbearing of the delay. Fitzwilliam was therefore surprised not to find him in better spirits as they readied to leave after breakfast the next day. His mind, however, seemed fixed on one thing and one thing only.

"I am certain all is well, Darcy," he said as he trotted down the stairs ahead of him. "Her letter has obviously been lost in the post."

"They cannot *all* have been lost in the post."

"Is she likely to have written more than one? You have not been gone a fortnight."

Darcy's voice, when he answered some five or six steps farther down, was divertingly peevish. "Yes, it is likely she wrote more than one."

Fitzwilliam inferred from this that Darcy had written several, and his concern was founded mostly on disgruntlement that his wife was not as mawkish as he.

He stopped at the foot of the stairs, a short distance from the gaggle of mourners milling about by the front door, donning their coats and hats and bidding their hosts farewell. "If aught were amiss you would have been informed. In cases such as these, no news is good news."

"No news is damned troubling, as well you know."

"She was in perfect health when you saw her twelve days ago. Men are sent to war on less reliable information than that." Darcy looked wholly unmoved; thus, he added, "Have you heard from nobody else at Pemberley?"

"No. I have written to them all, but too recently I fear, for I have yet to receive any replies. No post has arrived here today. I hope to find something awaiting me in Lon—" He ended abruptly. "Why are you grinning at me in that stupid manner?"

"Who do you mean by *all*?"

"The staff, your grandmother, Georgiana, Bingley."

Fitzwilliam could not constrain his laughter. The poor boy was a lovesick fool.

"What is this about Bingley?" Ashby enquired, peeling away from the crowd by the door and ambling over to join them. "What has the idiot done now?"

Darcy did not answer. Fitzwilliam glanced heavenward in exasperation. There had persisted an iciness between the pair of them these past two days of which he was grown excessively weary. "Darcy has written to him to enquire as to the state of play at Pemberley."

"Indeed!" Ashby snorted. "That man is more trouble than he is worth. Still, with any luck, he will be gone by the time you get back, Cousin."

"Darcy? A moment of your time before you go, if you would?" Anne called.

It was a fortuitous interruption, forestalling the angry retort heralded by Darcy's steely glare. Fitzwilliam wished Ashby would cease provoking him, but knowing his brother's petulance was directly proportional to the injury Darcy's recent letter had done to his pride, he thought it more probable that it would continue for some time to come.

"I doubt Bingley will be gone," he said quietly once Darcy had turned to speak to Anne. "Indeed, I think I have understood that he has not much idea of ever returning to Netherfield again."

"Yes, I know," Ashby replied, taking his proffered hat from a footman and lowering it precisely over his impeccably oiled hair. "He is taking the Hertfordshire chit and decamping to Nova Scotia." He tugged the brim to a suitably jaunty angle and turned his back on the servant to receive his greatcoat about his shoulders. "Bon voyage and good riddance, I say. Though why he would not simply wait and find himself one in a less interesting state when he arrives there is anybody's guess. The man is a fool."

Fitzwilliam raised an eyebrow. "You are singularly well informed, Brother. I believe you are mistaken, though. Darcy did not mention to me that Bingley was contemplating taking anybody with him."

"What does Darcy know?" Ashby muttered, tugging on his gloves. "I heard him say just now that he has not heard from his wife at Pemberley in two weeks. Mine had a letter from Bingley's but two days ago."

"They are not supposed to be writing to each other!"

"Sod Darcy and his bloody decrees," Ashby grumbled. "Am I to stop every man's wife putting pen to paper?" He resorted to pouting like a schoolboy thereafter, glaring sullenly at Darcy as he and Anne joined them.

"What have you there?" Fitzwilliam enquired, indicating the small velvet drawstring bag Darcy had evidently received from Anne.

"A brooch my mother gave to Lady Catherine when she married. She desired that it be given to Elizabeth."

"Why?" Ashby scoffed. "She did not even like her."

Fitzwilliam cringed, but he was surprised when Anne answered, not Darcy. "My mother had many objections to Mrs. Darcy, but disliking her character was never one of them. Indeed, by the end, she had formed a stout respect for her—a sentiment I suspect was as much attributable to Mrs. Darcy's consistently principled qualities as to the invaluable contrast to *your* wife's consistently vexatious ones."

Ashby coloured deeply, and his lips went from pouting to snarling, but he did at least refrain from voicing his umbrage to his newly grieved cousin, instead settling for glaring yet more viciously at Darcy. Darcy walked away, leaving Fitzwilliam to bear the brunt of his brother's prodigious indignation.

"Do shut up, man," he interrupted at length. "It does you no credit to carry on in this manner. I comprehend that you took objection to Darcy's letter, but it is not Elizabeth's fault that her own sister conspired with your wife to spread gossip all over Town."

"If Darcy does not like gossip, he ought not to have married so far beneath him."

"And if you do not like your wife being unfavourably compared to other women, you ought not to have married such an irksome termagant."

"Oh, go to the devil, Dickie. You really are an arse."

Thus, though he had travelled here in his brother's carriage, Fitzwilliam returned to London in Darcy's, whose humour thankfully improved every mile farther north they went. The spat with his brother did not trouble him a jot, for such was their customary mode of discourse. Ashby would likely have forgiven him by dinnertime. He would no doubt forgive Darcy also in due course, and unquestionably before Darcy forgave him.

That thought provided Fitzwilliam with the first true moment of wistfulness in the whole affair. For though they would resolve their differences eventually, Lady Catherine would have scolded them all back into harmony far sooner had she still been alive.

Saturday, 13 March 1813: London

"You know where it is," Darcy said, leaving Fitzwilliam to pour his own drink as he walked directly to his desk and the stack of letters there upon.

It had been a longer than usual journey home as a consequence of Rosings' stable master sending out every other carriage before his, meaning they arrived at every coaching inn last in the procession of all Lady Catherine's other London-bound mourners. Fitzwilliam had readily accepted his offer to dine at Darcy House before returning to Knightsbridge, though he declared his need for sustenance was not half as great as his need for alcohol since he had emptied his hip flask before they left Bromley.

"Anything?" his cousin enquired.

Darcy finished rifling through the letters and tossed the lot back onto the desk. "No." It was only the expectation of finding news awaiting him here that had allayed his alarm in Kent, but there was nothing from Pemberley.

He rubbed a hand over his face and attempted to reason away his disquiet.

"There you are then, you see? I was right."

"How so? I have no letter from Elizabeth."

"And neither do you have a letter from my grandmother or Bingley telling you some harm has befallen her. Cheer up, old boy," he added, proffering a drink. "There is nothing more troubling afoot than the discovery that your wife is a dreadful correspondent."

Though he disliked it intensely, Darcy would rather that explanation than have his misgivings substantiated. That she would have written was in no doubt, yet he supposed she might not have written often. Indeed, she could not have much news except in an emergency, and then she or someone else would have sent an express. And as Fitzwilliam had said, it was possible, even likely, that a letter had gone astray. Yet, one solitary note of commiseration seemed scant comfort from a woman more commonly overflowing with compassion. And two or more letters were unlikely to have been lost.

Comprehending that reason might not prove sturdy enough armour against his encroaching sense of foreboding, he reached for the drink his cousin held out and took a sizeable swig. "Come," he announced. "Let us eat."

"Give them a fair chance to get it on the platters, Darcy. We have only been here five minutes."

"Let us do something else then. I have no wish to sit about brooding."

Fitzwilliam grinned roguishly and pointed to Darcy's scar. "How about I give you a matching gash on the other cheek? That one gives you a shocking failure of perfect symmetry."

Darcy gave him an answering smile. "My imperfections have a new advocate, but by all means let us see if your countenance can be evened up a little."

A little under two hours saw both men back in Darcy's study, exercised, fed, and sufficiently distracted from their troubles to enjoy a last quiet drink together before the colonel returned to his barracks. "I may have had one too many glasses of wine with dinner," the latter said, "but I do believe I shall miss the old bat."

Darcy looked up from the letters he had retrieved from his desk and smiled ruefully. "She was too imposing a character not to leave a noticeable void in her absence."

"True, true. Visiting Rosings will not be half so much fun without having to run the gauntlet of her disapprobation."

Darcy did not reply, for he had come across a letter from an unexpected quarter.

"Bad news?" Fitzwilliam enquired.

"I cannot decide. It is from Colonel Forster. Wickham is being tried for attempted murder."

"Surely not! His punishment was meted out months ago, the matter was done and—"

"This has nothing to do with his attack on Elizabeth," Darcy interrupted. Holding up a hand to stay his cousin's questions, he read to the end before summarising. "He has seduced another young girl and been caught up in some violence with her brother."

"I see." Fitzwilliam sucked in his breath. "I hate to say it, Darcy, but he ever had a whiff of inevitability about him."

Darcy folded the letter closed. "He has asked that I meet his bail."

"He what? He ought to hang for insolence alone!"

Darcy pushed himself to his feet and crossed to one of the bookcases flanking the chimney to retrieve the stack of other correspondence from Forster that was filed there. He set the letters down on his desk and pulled at the ribbon tied about them, slowly unravelling the bow. "I shall not be paying his bail. The girl has died after a miscarriage."

"Good God!"

There was nothing more Darcy could add to that sentiment. He was done with Wickham and could only be thankful his father was not alive to see him sunk so low.

The pile of Forster's letters collapsed as the ribbon untied completely, spilling in all directions over his desk. His eye went immediately to one that was too crumpled to be folded neatly, knowing exactly which it was but not recalling how it had come to be filed with the others, for his recollections of the day he read it were hazy at best. He picked it up, unable to resist reading it. Even now, its contents left him cold. *She never awoke.*

He shook his head and refolded it, chastising himself for even looking. As he restacked the pile and added Forster's latest to it, another letter drew his notice whose seal had not been broken. He turned it over and was perplexed to discover it addressed in Bingley's distinctive hand, though even more untidily than usual. With the strongest curiosity, he opened the letter, smiling at first glance, for the spatters of ink, diligently noted time of writing, and general effusiveness of the first few lines told him Bingley was far into his cups when he wrote it. By the start of the second paragraph his amusement had well and truly died.

Netherfield
~~June 5~~ June 6, 3am

Darcy

You must congratulate me, for I am engaged! Or at least I shall be tomorrow, once I ask her, which I mean to do, for my mind is made up at last. Indeed, I cannot recall, as I write this, why it was not made up before. She is everything a woman ought to be—handsome, witty, comely, clever, handsome—and so wonderfully affectionate! I never see her that she is not pleased to see me also. I never knew a woman who enjoyed my company so well or made me feel so welcome.

It is unpardonable how long it has taken me to comprehend my feelings. I suppose my wish not to disappoint her sister a second time made me reluctant. Can you guess what has made me acknowledge them at last? A song! One I heard sung in the tavern this very evening. A coarse, bawdy song of which I ought not approve, yet I cannot condemn it, for it has taught me my heart at last. Henry Lucas calls it 'The Bennet Ballad.' ~~It has a verse for each of her sisters. Miss Lydia is said to.~~ I shall write it out as best as I can recall it.

~~Marry the fifth~~ Take the fifth for a wife only if you dare, For a man bound to her will needs must share, Wed the fourth if you value not common sense, For ~~silliness~~ (there is something about folly here) Take the third for a wife to atone for your sins, She'll preach you to death but yield not her quim, (ha!) Marry the first and be every man's envy, 'Til ennui strikes and witless rends ye, (this has been my struggle!) Hail the man that marries the second, She is the jewel, alluring and ~~feck~~ fecund, She'll fill your days with laughter and wit, And by night, beguile ye with that arse and those tits!

Is that not a fine verse? You will object to it, I know, but then you are not as drunk as I. And even you cannot deny it is witty. Inaccurate, though, for I am constantly beguiled by her figure, day and night. Not that I do not anticipate her night time charms being unparalleled! She is an angel, and I shall marry her and make her mine! The next time I write, it will be with the news that I am engaged to Miss Elizabeth Bennet!

Bingley

It was necessary to read it twice before he was able to grasp the full magnitude of the revelation. A thousand remembrances of past conversations, insinuations and looks swirled in his mind's eye, demanding that he reassess their import, but there were too many to make sense. Arrant fury overwhelmed him as every thought in his head coalesced into one, abhorrent memory: Elizabeth in Bingley's arms.

"Good God, Darcy, what in blazes does it say in that letter?"

He looked up to meet Fitzwilliam's troubled gaze. "I will kill him."

He thrust the letter at his cousin and turned in mute rage to slam both hands down on his desk. The nearest candlestick skittered sideways, its flame guttering. There he stayed, forcing air in and out of his nose. He could not speak. There were no words to express what he felt and no way of unpicking the knot of deception such a letter presented. The bastard was there now with Elizabeth!

He shoved himself away from the desk and stalked across the room. There was not enough space to contain his savage indignation. The sheer audacity of Bingley taking up in his house, dining at his table, conversing, joking, playing cards, *dancing* with Elizabeth—all the while wishing she were his! It was a worse betrayal than Wickham's, who at least had done him the courtesy of being furtive.

Behind him, Fitzwilliam let out a long, low whistle. Darcy whirled about, having almost forgotten he was there. "A whistle?" he challenged, barely able to contain his fury. "The discovery that my brother by law, who has been one of my closest friends for above ten years and who is presently at my house under orders to safeguard my wife from harm, has in truth coveted her since before we wed draws from you naught more than a puerile whistle?"

"Untwist your ballocks, Darcy. I do not make light of it. It is objectionable in every way. Yet, it is evidently drunken prattle written, if I am not mistaken, before he knew of your attachment to her."

"I care not when he wrote the damned thing. He is in love with my *wife!*"

Fitzwilliam flicked the letter straight and ran his eyes over it again, shaking his head. "Nay, it says nothing of love in here. 'Tis naught but sot's ardour. I daresay Bingley has lusted after most every woman of his acquaintance at some point or another in his cups. He no doubt forgot the sentiment as soon as his head cleared."

Darcy wished with all his being that were true, yet foreboding had pursued him all the way from Kent, and it would not be so easily satisfied.

"Indeed, he must have," Fitzwilliam insisted, "for it was her sister he married."

"He did not intend to." Icy tendrils of alarm knifed through Darcy's gut. "Jane threw herself at him and contrived to be discovered. He had no choice."

Fitzwilliam squeezed his eyes closed and pinched the bridge of his nose. "Are you certain? I cannot imagine why a woman such as Jane Bingley should need to entrap a husband."

Jane's pitiful objection last Wednesday rang in Darcy's mind: *He does not esteem me!* "She must have known he meant to offer for Elizabeth."

"There is no evidence of that beyond these few impolitic ramblings," Fitzwilliam said, gesturing at him with Bingley's letter, but Darcy's mind was already far beyond that point.

"He all but admitted it the night before the wedding," he muttered incredulously. "How could I have forgotten? He drank himself into oblivion and came to me complaining that he doubted his affection for Jane."

"Perhaps he was merely nervous of marriage."

"That is as I assumed at the time." He sneered bitterly. "No wonder he claimed he could not speak of it with me."

His cousin made a dismissive noise and stalked to the sideboard, slapping the letter into his chest as he passed him. "This is all too tenuous for my liking, Darcy. You are too apt to see the worst in every situation. Besides," he said as he refilled his glass, "Bingley is hardly the most discreet of men. If he was enamoured of Elizabeth, more people than Jane would have seen it."

Such a comment was guaranteed to send Darcy's mind whirling off into the annals of his memory, searching for evidence of just that. Regrettably, he found it.

"Mr. Bingley is at Longbourn, sir, mourning the loss of Miss Eliza."

Even the damned butler had known it!

"True to form, gentlemen! One has his bird in the bag afore the other has decided which to aim for."

Facetiousness had masked that speaker's better knowledge admirably, but retrospection stripped all such allusions bare. "Bennet knew," he said with utter, sickening conviction.

"And pray, what sudden penetration that was not previously in your power has led you to this unhappy conclusion?"

"Retrospect is a pitiless exponent, Fitzwilliam," he retorted, in no humour to be persistently gainsaid. "When I sought his permission for Elizabeth's hand, Bennet remarked that had I offered sooner, I might have saved Bingley weeks of indecision."

"So Bingley dithered about a bit? It is not unreasonable to think he was uncertain of his reception, having abandoned the lady once already."

Darcy clenched his teeth. Each of Fitzwilliam's objections was sound, yet he could not share his sanguinity. Too many unexplained anomalies were piecing together, though God knew he wished they would contrive to make a different picture. "I asked him recently why he continued visiting Longbourn after he had decided against Jane."

"And? What reason did he give?"

"Elizabeth."

"What, just that?"

Darcy nodded. He would much rather his cousin had continued adamant in the belief there was naught troubling afoot. As it was, the doubt flickering over his countenance tied his stomach in knots. "I must get to Pemberley," he announced, reaching for the bell pull.

"You cannot mean this instant?"

"I can and I do."

Fitzwilliam stepped in front of him, preventing him from summoning anyone. "Darcy, be reasonable. I grant you, this looks very ill, but all of it could be perceived in a different light. There is no need to do something as foolhardy as rushing off to Pemberley in the dark on the basis of one addled letter and a few spurious suspicions."

"Only they are not few, and they seem ever less spurious. I cannot think of one good reason for half the occasions Bingley has arrived at my door in the last year. He has followed Elizabeth halfway around the country and back, invariably appearing in places we have told him we will be, always contrary to the plans he has previously claimed and never with any real purpose."

"He could as easily have been following *you* about as Elizabeth. You have ever spent a good deal of time together."

"If that were the case, he would be here and not at Pemberley with her."

"No, I cannot believe it," Fitzwilliam said, shaking his head. "Not of Bingley. He would not be so devious as to impose upon your hospitality if it were the case. If, indeed, he was attracted to her at one time, we must assume he has overcome it."

A dreadful feeling of nausea accompanied Darcy's next remembrance. *"Even were she to revert to the sweet girl you thought smiled too much, she would not be the woman I want."*

He rubbed a hand over his face.

"You are inclined to think otherwise?" his cousin enquired.

He took a deep breath, for it was strangely difficult to speak. "When I urged him to give the idea of going to Nova Scotia more thought, he replied and I quote: 'I have done nothing but think on it whilst I have watched you have everything I want, knowing I cannot have it.' I assumed he referred to my general contentment."

Fitzwilliam's eyebrows rose. "I should like to say he might have been, but there is only so long I can continue to defend him without looking a churl," Fitzwilliam replied. "I suppose we might credit him with *some* morals for attempting to extricate himself from the wreckage and take himself off to another country."

Darcy gave a bitter laugh. "Oh, yes, he was all benevolence—until Elizabeth suggested he stay and he abandoned all his plans in an instant. At another word from her, he would probably stay forever."

"Yes, well, she would never ask it, and you would never allow it, so pray waste no time brooding on it. Besides, did Ashby not say something this morning about him being gone by the time you got back?"

"What does Ashby know?" Darcy strode across the room to snatch up the poker and unleash some of his anger upon the fire.

"That is precisely what he said of you," his cousin said behind him.

When he said nothing further, Darcy looked over his shoulder, and upon seeing Fitzwilliam's brow contracted into his deepest frown yet, turned fully to face him. "What is it?"

"Nothing dire—only, now that I recall what Ashby said, I think you have less reason to be concerned."

"And what did he say?"

"That Jane wrote to Philippa last week to inform her Bingley was taking her to—hold fire, is Jane with child?"

Every sinew in Darcy's body went taut. "Not to my knowledge. Why?"

Fitzwilliam said nothing, only paled and stared at him in alarm.

"What did Ashby say, Fitzwilliam? Verbatim, if you would."

"As best I recall he said, 'He is taking the Hertfordshire chit and decamping to Nova Scotia.'" He swallowed. Darcy waited. "Then he said something along the lines of it making more sense to find a girl who was not already with child when he got there."

All the air left Darcy's lungs in one violent exhalation, and a hideous pall fell over them both. Fitzwilliam looked at him with an expression of horror that presumably matched his own.

"Bloody hell, Darcy, I thought he was talking about Jane. He might have been. Are you absolutely certain she is not with child?"

It was possible, Darcy supposed. Yet, it was many weeks since she and Bingley were last in company, and he had not received the impression from him that they were often in the same *room* before that. Was it possible that since reading Elizabeth's letter they had reconciled and agreed to go away together? The alternative did not bear thinking about. He tossed the poker aside, sending plumes of ash into the air from where it landed in the grate. "I am for Farley House. I would speak with Jane. Will you accompany me?"

"Try and stop me."

This time Fitzwilliam rang the bell for Godfrey. While they waited, Darcy, as if to exasperate himself as much as possible against his erstwhile friend, chose for his employment the examination of all the letters Bingley had written to him since his return to Hertfordshire. It was fortunate their horses were saddled as expeditiously as they were, for the endeavour achieved naught but the unchecked escalation of his dread.

"But you would have heard, Darcy. I say again, no news is good news." Much though Fitzwilliam comprehended Darcy's concern, he remained unconvinced that there was sufficient foundation for any of his worse suspicions, and he was reasonably confident that, if Jane were unable to allay their fears, Ashby's reply to the express he had sent before they set out would clarify matters for them.

"*Still* you maintain that?" his cousin said darkly. "After all this, you are content to believe that a complete want of communication is not even a trifle concerning?"

"What do you propose? That Bingley has stolen every sheet of paper and pot of ink in the house that nobody could send for you? Has he also hobbled all the horses and bribed all the staff to prevent their going for help?"

"Bingley has the trust of my entire household. He could take Elizabeth away from Pemberley and tell everybody I had authorised it, and nobody would blink an eye."

"I think Elizabeth might have something to say about it." He thought he saw Darcy flinch.

"She also trusts him. They have found an affinity in both being betrayed by Jane."

"That does not mean she would agree to his bundling her onto a boat! Besides, he does not have my grandmother's trust. I assure you she would not sit by quietly and allow him to sail off into the sunset with your wife!"

"I do not know what has happened, Fitzwilliam! I do not know what he plans or what lies he has spun to achieve it. What I know is that I have received no letters from Elizabeth in two weeks, and that means something is wrong." He urged his horse to go faster, forcing an end to the conversation.

Fitzwilliam pushed his own mount to match his pace, not so easily deterred. "You are assuming that a want of correspondence necessarily means Bingley has acted against her in some way. The two matters may be wholly unconnected."

"Then I have two reasons to be concerned—what has prevented her from writing and what he may yet be planning."

"For God's sake, she is heavy with your child! Even Bingley could not turn a blind eye to that."

"He is impetuous enough to do anything once the thought to do it occurs to him. I will not allow it. The child is mine and so is Elizabeth."

It seemed perturbing memories were not solely Darcy's prerogative, for this remark recalled Fitzwilliam to an incident he had thought passing strange at the time and which in this new light appeared downright damning. Having followed his cousin to Hertfordshire the previous year and waited at Netherfield all afternoon for him to appear, Fitzwilliam's first question had been whether Elizabeth was truly dead. Darcy had responded that she was "very much alive and very much his," at which Bingley had inexplicably groaned and excused himself to bed, claiming a wish to be spared Darcy's raptures.

Was it possible Bingley truly held an enduring romantic attachment to Elizabeth? Lamenting Darcy's engagement to her whilst sober was a very different matter to scribbling a drunken ode to her tits. He was still frowning over it when Darcy directed them into a row of mews where they were divested of their mounts and escorted through a small passageway between the row of houses opposite and up the steps at the front to Hurst's door.

"Jane will not be pleased to see you," he muttered as they were ushered towards the drawing room. "Not if your account of your last meeting was accurate."

"That is not my concern," Darcy replied.

It turned out not to be hers, either, for the only two occupants of the room were Hurst and his wife. They both expressed their surprise at receiving such guests at such an hour, but nonetheless assured them they were welcome. Darcy refused their offers of refreshments, wasting no time in explaining his object of speaking with Jane.

"I am sorry to disappoint you, Darcy, but she is not here," Hurst replied.

"There you are. You see, Darcy," Fitzwilliam said, feeling inordinately relieved. "It is she who has gone off with Bingley after all."

"Ah, no…forgive me, sir, but Jane has not gone anywhere with my brother," Mrs. Hurst said, dashing his reprieve. "She has gone back to Netherfield. Might I enquire where it is my brother is supposed to have gone?"

"Aye," Hurst added. "We understood he was at Pemberley."

"Where is Miss Bingley?" Darcy enquired abruptly.

"Why, she escorted Jane to Hertfordshire," Mrs. Hurst replied warily.

"Is there nobody here who can tell me what is going on?" he growled. Fitzwilliam rather thought the Hursts must be thinking the same, but his cousin gave neither of them any time to enquire before fixing Mrs. Hurst with a steely glower and saying, "When I was here two weeks ago, your sister made a remark about Pemberley not being the best place for Bingley to be. I would know what she meant."

The lady's cheeks were instantly overspread with a most dreadful shade of guilt, and she looked to her husband in alarm.

"Best speak up, madam," he told her. "It seems serious. Tell them everything."

That did not bode well. Not well at all.

"Well, I…I do not…the fact of the matter is…" She wrung her hands. Darcy looked as though he wished to wring her neck.

"Hurst?" Fitzwilliam prompted.

He took the hint and lay all before them with laudable brevity. "Bingley is in love with Mrs. Darcy. Has been from the off."

Fitzwilliam shifted to the balls of his feet, taut and alert as he watched

Darcy close his eyes and become stock still but for the grinding muscle in his jaw.

"Has he done something stupid?" Hurst enquired.

"Is he *likely* to?" Darcy demanded, suddenly and fearsomely reanimated by the mere suggestion of it.

Hurst did not quail, though there did not look to be much blood left above his collar. "Caroline seems to think he might cause some trouble. She wrote to tell him to come home, but he never replied. I apologise," he added when Darcy bared his teeth. "Once Bingley got himself tangled up with Jane, there did not seem any way of mentioning it without causing more harm than good."

It was a blatant lie. An addle-pate could have guessed their true motivation for silence was the preservation of Darcy's favour.

"To whom?" Darcy roared, clearly of a mind.

"Darcy," Fitzwilliam said, gesturing at Mrs. Hurst who was visibly trembling. "There is nothing more to be done here. Let us go."

With naught more than a quick appraisal of each person in the room and a single nod of concurrence, Darcy turned and left.

"Bad form, Hurst. Bad form!" Fitzwilliam said before following his cousin from the house.

"This does not make it any more likely that he has absconded with her," he remarked to his mute and unmistakably seething cousin as they steered their horses back across Town. "It is an abhorrent abuse of trust, but he has not acted upon his feelings in a year. There is no reason to suspect he will do so now." Darcy did not respond. "I had not thought Hurst the sort for such deception," he continued. "It is reprehensible that he should have concealed this from you. That said, I cannot comprehend why Jane never said anything—to Elizabeth, if not to you."

"Never mind either of them. I would know what the hell Ashby is about, keeping this from me."

Fitzwilliam had been hoping he would not raise that issue. "It cannot have been his intention to keep it from you, or he would not have mentioned it to me."

"Intelligence such as this ought to have been brought to my attention as a matter of urgency, not tossed away in a careless aside half a week after the event."

"He, too, may have thought the letter referred to Jane. Do not rush to accuse him before we know the facts."

Darcy scoffed contemptuously. "The facts are that he begrudged my severe words against his wife and thought to punish mine in return. Do not attempt to convince me otherwise. We both know I am right. He must be lost to every feeling of decency and family honour to be so indifferent to Elizabeth's well-being."

With his brother's remark, "good riddance," and observation that Darcy ought never to have married Elizabeth fresh in his mind, Fitzwilliam was painfully aware of what little regard Ashby had for her. Nonetheless, he was deeply grieved by the possibility that he should prove capable of such casual betrayal. "Will you go to Netherfield to see Jane?" he enquired, changing tack.

"No, I shall go to Pemberley to see Elizabeth."

"I shall come with you if you will have me along. When do you leave?"

"Had we left when I wished, we might have been into Hertfordshire by now."

He sighed quietly. "I am sorry, Darcy, but Elizabeth would never forgive me if I allo—"

"First light. Do not be late. I shall not tarry."

Monday, 15 March 1813:
Somewhere between London and Derbyshire

Darcy awoke with a jolt, his heart thundering in his chest as he tried to dispel the memory of a nightmarish figure that was half Bingley-half Wickham, kissing Elizabeth against her will. All was black but for the feeble light of the torches at the front of the carriage bleeding through the edges of the blinds.

"What time is it?" Fitzwilliam enquired with a yawn.

Darcy took out his watch and peered at it, but it was too dark to make out. It had gone two in the morning when they left the last inn, but the brick in the foot well was still warm, and there was not a hint of dawn on the horizon. "Not past three, I think."

"Where are we?" Fitzwilliam said, hooking a finger behind a blind and peering out into the night.

"Not near enough."

Indeed, despite having set out at the break of dawn yesterday and spending the entire day and night on the road, it was not likely they would reach Pemberley until late that afternoon.

"All will be well, Darcy," his cousin said quietly.

"He tried to take her, Fitzwilliam. It is already long past *well*."

"Yes, he did but he failed."

"And who is to say he will fail next time?"

Everything had changed since leaving Farley House on Saturday evening. He had gone to bed that night plagued by fears that Bingley would attempt to steal Elizabeth away with him and awakened on Sunday morning to have all those fears transformed into fact when Fitzwilliam arrived, stony-faced and bearing a letter that had been awaiting him at his barracks.

March 11
Pemberley

Thirson,

Mrs. Darcy has just received a communication from her husband informing her that, despite his aunt being dead at last, he does not mean to arrive home until the middle of next week. I am at a loss as to why this should be. After his lunatic friend's escapades, he ought to be hastening home to ensure his wife's well-being, not dallying by her ladyship's graveside lamenting her long-overdue passing.

You will, of course, have heard from him what has happened, for I know Mrs. Darcy has written to inform him. You will agree this Bingley creature is unhinged. What madness convinced him to impose upon her, I know not—and in her present condition! Somebody ought to see to it that he is actually gone, lest he make another attempt to get her on board a boat. By which I mean I have seen men less set upon a purpose resort sooner to more forceful means to achieve it. One can expect nothing but trouble from a man capable of such preposterous aspirations.

Pray tell your cousin to leave off weeping over Lady Catherine's corpse and get himself back to Pemberley forthwith. I shall have someone write this out again and send a copy to Knightsbridge, lest this one arrives at Rosings after you have left.

Yours in perplexity,
Mrs. T. Sinclair

They had been in a headlong sprint to Pemberley ever since. He and Fitzwilliam were exhausted. His own horses had long been replaced with post, and his desperation to reach Elizabeth increased with every second that ticked by.

What manner of imposition she had suffered at Bingley's hands was not revealed in the letter, only that he had not succeeded, and Elizabeth was evidently well enough to be writing to him about it. There was small mercy in knowing she had indeed sent at least one letter, though the mystery of why he had not received it, or any subsequent ones, gave him an entirely new reason to be alarmed.

One-and-twenty hours' travel with nothing to do but agonise over things he did not know had left Darcy sick to his stomach with worry and angrier than it was sensible to be in such a confined space. Sleep brought him no relief. It only tortured him with the same picture of Elizabeth in Bingley's arms over and over again. He feared he would go out of his mind if they did not begin to make better time.

"He cannot succeed," Fitzwilliam said, "for they are forewarned this time. He will not be able to get within fifty miles of her. Besides, we cannot be sure he will make another attempt."

Darcy did not respond. This was a topic they had abandoned more than once, for it offered nothing in the way of hope. Mrs. Sinclair's letter was dated March 11. Having received no response from Ashby to the express sent on Saturday evening, they had no option but to treat his remarks in Kent as fact—and he, based on information received well after the first attempt to abduct Elizabeth, had averred in the future tense that Bingley meant to take her to Nova Scotia. No matter which way they looked at it, this only seemed to confirm Mrs. Sinclair's concerns that he meant to attempt it again.

Darcy let his head drop back onto the cushions. He stared into the pitch-black interior of the carriage, wishing for the thousandth time that he had never sent Bingley back to Hertfordshire. Brooding over how soon the cur's feelings must have changed after he got there proved an endeavour of pure torment.

"Hurst is right. He has always admired her," he said into the darkness. Fitzwilliam did not reply. Darcy was not entirely sure he was still awake, but he did not wish to sleep or dream himself, thus he continued. "I reread all the letters he sent me from Hertfordshire. They were all about Elizabeth.

They hardly mentioned Jane at all but to say she was reserved."

The carriage rolled on. "It was his suggestion that we all marry on the same day. I never did get a straight answer from him as to why he wished it." He clenched his fists. "And I knew he thought her handsome. I have often heard him compliment her. It was he who first recommended her to me."

The horses clattered through the lightless countryside, but he saw nothing of their inexorable progress. He knew only smouldering resentment. "He even kept a crayon sketch of her on his desk that one of the Gardiners' children drew. I can still remember Jane's expression when I discovered it. I could not understand why it vexed her so." He closed his eyes. He thought he might as well, for the image of Elizabeth in Bingley's arms now haunted him whether or not they were open. "How could I have been so blind?"

"We all were."

Not asleep then.

"If he hurts her—"

"Stop torturing yourself, Darcy. All will be well."

He pressed a fist to his mouth lest the dread constricting his throat escape. He knew not what he would do if it were not.

Pemberley's driveway had never seemed so tortuous. They wove in and out of woods, around crags, over streams, and for the first time in his life, Darcy found himself envying Rosings' contrived and formal avenue.

He could feel Fitzwilliam's eyes on him. He let him watch and continued staring from the window. They crested a rise and the roof reared into sight. Pemberley still stood at least. He pulled the window down and leant out to call to the driver. "Not the stables! Go directly to the front!"

He returned to his seat but kept his hand on the edge of the lowered window, drumming his fingers on the frame. As though in a dream, they scarcely seemed to advance despite the cracking of the whip and thundering of hooves. Trepidation filled his heart and crowded his mind, every hope of seeing Elizabeth instantly superseded with the sickening thought of finding her in Bingley's arms.

There was no one to be seen. The windows were empty and dark. The gardens were devoid of workers, the lawn devoid of visitors. There were not even any cursed ducks on the lake. No one opened the front door as they rolled through the gates and began to slow. That was as much as Darcy could bear. He stood, thrusting his hand out of the window to reach for the handle. The door flew open and he leapt out, hitting the ground at a run, taking the steps two at a time.

As he neared the top, the front door finally opened, and he almost stumbled, for through it walked the last person in the world he expected to see. Cold fury flooded his veins. With a roar, he leapt the remaining steps and charged at Bingley, slamming him into the wall and pinning him there with a forearm to his throat.

"Where is my WIFE? I know you mean to take her! Tell me where she is!"

Bingley did not fight him or look afraid or even ashamed. With a stirring of horror, Darcy realised he was crying.

"You are mistaken," he croaked past Darcy's stronghold. "She is not with me. She is dead."

13 Mistaken

Wednesday, 3 March 1813: Pemberley

His fifth tour of the lake brought no more relief than the previous four. Bingley remained wretched, still utterly befogged as to how he found himself in such a hellish bind. No man intends that his every choice should lead to calamity, yet it seemed that, at every juncture where he might have acted prudently, external influences had steered him into misadventure.

Had his sisters not been so adamant Jane neither loved him nor was worthy of his love, his heart might never have been laid open to the charms of another. Had Darcy not encouraged him to return to Hertfordshire, assuring him of a warm welcome and successful suit, or had Wickham not assaulted her, putting her in need of his rescue and protection, it might never have been Elizabeth to whose charms he succumbed. Had Jane not forced his hand, had Darcy not claimed Elizabeth for himself, had Jane not grown bitter and cold…the list of obstacles to his felicity were endless.

He cuffed a low branch from his path. It rebounded to slap him on the back of the neck as he stomped past, sending him tripping forwards and doing naught to improve his humour.

Even his decision to leave had been thwarted. No sooner had he booked passage on the next ship from Liverpool than he had been prevailed upon to stay. Though he risked forfeiting the vast sum laid out for a first class berth if Darcy did not return within a fortnight, he had agreed to the delay, for he was not prepared to abandon Elizabeth in such a delicate state, even if Darcy was.

He required no instruction to look to her well-being. His first thought upon waking each day was to attend to her happiness and to provide the appreciation and companionship she did not receive from her husband. With that in mind, he undertook to spend every available moment in her company. And how well they did together! Always, they found something about which to converse. Always, she was interested in what he said, never with any of the ridicule he had come to expect from his sisters or the indifference he so often perceived in Jane.

It was the cruellest form of torture being trapped here, admiring her in such close neighbourhood yet forbidden from expressing or, God forbid, acting upon his feelings. Likewise, it would be torture to leave, knowing he would never see her again. That might be less painful if only he could be sure of her happiness. Yet, he would leave full in the knowledge that her husband did not respect her, and she was as miserably allied as he.

The deplorable affair marked the death of his good opinion of Darcy. For above a year, he had struggled with conflicting notions of respect and disappointment, but the latter had finally triumphed. Deep as their connection ran, Bingley could no longer excuse the pride that overshadowed any concern his erstwhile friend ought to have felt for his wife's happiness. Over and again, he had watched Darcy put duty before any thought to her. Familial obligations, estate business, spurious social commitments—anything with half a chance of gratifying his need to be indispensable—seemed sufficient grounds for neglect. Presently, it was the draw of a reviled and dying relative justifying his absence.

Resentment gave haste to his ramblings. Bingley gave up the narrow path and stormed onto the lawn, railing at how the rest of the world rode roughshod over his life. But for Darcy and his blasted jaunt to Kent, he might have been in Liverpool by now. Damn him and his self-serving conceit, ever directing people hither and thither to suit himself. Where was it written that all lesser mortals must dance to the tune of the Titan's whims?

What right had he to look to his own pleasure when all around him were so damned miserable?

He had not the time to draw any conclusions. As he walked towards the house, the mistress of it herself suddenly came forward from the path that led behind it to the orangery. So abrupt was her appearance that it was impossible to avoid her sight. "Lizzy! I did not expect to see you."

"I live here now, you know," she replied, amusement dancing in her eyes—eyes that, despite how distractingly beautiful her teasing rendered them, Bingley could not but notice were tinged with red.

"Have you been crying?"

Her amusement ebbed. "Oh, pay me no mind. I am being silly." As she said it, she folded a piece of paper he had not noticed was in her hand and slipped it into her pocket.

"Upon my word, I am sorry if I embarrassed you, but I shall not ignore it if something has upset you. Come now, what are you crying over?"

She smiled sadly and whispered her admission to the ground. "Darcy."

It was but one word, yet it was enough to stir his indignation into a furnace of resentment. What the devil had the man done now—written to her with his disapprobation lest she become complacent in his absence?

"It is too much!" he cried. "I cannot bear to see you—*you,* loveliest, fairest Lizzy, condemned to this misery and disregard! It is the hardest thing in the world to watch you suffer so!" She stared at him and said nothing, which left his mind unfettered to make its next improbable leap of reasoning. "Come with me! By God, why did I not conceive of it before? You can escape this insufferable oppression if you come with me to Nova Scotia!"

Her countenance was the dearest picture of confusion—part frown, part smile. "This is a strange sort of joke, sir."

"Indeed it is not a joke!" He stepped forwards and reached for her hands. "Come with me, Lizzy. *Be* with me!"

She snatched her hands from his and stepped backwards. "Why would you ask such a thing of me?"

It seemed the whole world ceased what it was doing to watch. Never had Bingley thought this moment would come. Yet, here she was, lovelier than ever, anxiously awaiting his assurances. He regarded her earnestly, willing her to comprehend his sincerity. "Because I love you."

She made a little noise but after that seemed unable to catch her breath.

She looked somewhat horrified, though he supposed that was to be expected, for what he proposed was seriously audacious. He was somewhat horrified by it himself, yet he could not find it in himself to retract it. "I love you!" he said again, giddy with exhilaration for being finally at liberty to declare it.

"Did you fall and hit your head while you were on your walk?"

"No!" he cried, almost laughing at her sweet disbelief. "I am in complete earnest! Indeed, it cannot be wholly surprising. You must have suspected, for I know I have made a poor job of concealing my feelings."

Her expression was now all frown and no smile.

"Pray, be not angry with me for not declaring myself sooner. I know it would have brought you comfort had you known you were loved properly by *somebody* all this time, but I could never perceive any advantage in it. I never thought we would have such an opportunity as this to act." He stepped towards her, closing the space she had put between them. "But that does not mean I did not feel it. Every moment of every day, almost since the beginning of our acquain—"

"Stop!" She threw her arms in the air and turned to stride away from him towards the house. "I cannot listen to any more of this!"

He hastened after her. "I have shocked you. Forgive me! Only I have so long despaired of ever being happy that, now I see there is hope for us, I cannot but rejoice."

She neither slowed nor looked at him. "You have lost your mind, sir. I beg you would stay away from me."

"Nay, Lizzy, I am of sound mind! I comprehend what I suggest is scandalous, but we need not care for that! We would be gone to where nobody would know what we had left behind. We might even be able to marry!"

She stopped abruptly and turned to him, agape. "Are you *proposing* to me?"

He gulped. "Well…yes. Yes, I suppose I am."

"He was right!" she cried. "I shall never walk alone in a garden again!"

Elizabeth stormed through the house, growing angrier with every door through which Bingley pursued her.

"Wait, I beg you," he pleaded.

"I insist you cease this madness this instant!" She slammed another door closed between them and stood still, breathing hard. Her furious march had brought her all the way to Darcy's study. Though not consciously done, she was relieved to be able to put his vast desk between herself and Bingley when he ignored her plea and followed her into the room. "Come no nearer or I shall scream."

"Lizzy, I—"

"Do not call me that. I am Mrs. Darcy to you and shall never be *anything* else!"

He had the nerve to look unhappy about that. "I comprehend that you are apprehensive of what Darcy will do, but—"

"I know precisely what my husband will do, and believe me it is *you* who ought to be apprehensive. I am more concerned with what you intend to do." She stepped towards the bookcase to pull the bell for someone—*anyone*.

He held up his hands. "Pray do not summon anybody! I have gone about this very ill, I know, but I beg you to consider! This may be our only chance to be together."

The bell was forgotten. Elizabeth came out from behind the desk that she might direct her fury without impediment. "You are gravely mistaken if you suppose the mode of your declaration is all that prevents me from consenting to *be together* with you, here or anywhere."

"I agree there is a great deal at stake, but the reward would be worth the sacrifice."

"I see no reward in it, sir!"

"Because you will not believe that I love you."

"No, I will not, for it opposes every feeling of decency I possess."

"To blazes with decency! I love you!"

"Cease saying that! You cannot justly claim any regard for me and, in the same breath, prevail upon me to betray my husband! And while I carry his child!"

"I would love the child as my own. You must not concern yourself in that regard."

"Upon my word, you are speaking of incest and child abduction! I think my concerns perfectly justified!"

"When you put it like that, I grant you it is not an ideal situation, but it is the only chance we are ever likely to have."

"What is?" This most welcome interruption came from Mrs. Sinclair. She bustled into the room and perched with decided purpose on a sofa.

"He says he loves me!" Elizabeth cried.

"Indeed," Mrs. Sinclair replied, fixing Bingley with a dubious look. "Although I cannot presently think of any *good* way of declaring such a thing, I am quite convinced that chasing Mrs. Darcy through the house, bellowing at her for the whole world to hear, was a dreadful one."

"I know!" he said, running his hands through his hair. He turned to Elizabeth. "Forgive me! I have no excuse but that I love you."

"But I do not love *you*!" Bingley stared at her, evidently astonished, and she growled with vexation. "I shall not pretend to be surprised that the possibility of my indifference never occurred to you. I have come to expect that men will presume they can command a woman's affections at will."

"But everything in your manner has—"

"Nay, do not blame my manner, sir! I shall not have the blame for this!"

"But you are always pleased with my company!"

"I am pleased with many people's company. It does not mean I am in love with them."

"But have we not shown these past few days how well we do together?"

Elizabeth felt nauseous. "Yes, I have ever thought of us as dear friends. But if you have been imagining yourself my lover every time I so much as laughed at one of your jokes, then I can no longer think of our acquaintance with anything but abhorrence."

"But you asked that I stay."

"And you imagined I did so because I desired that we have a criminal conversation?"

He had the wherewithal to look abashed, but he did not deny it.

"I *suggested* you stay because you seemed hesitant about leaving."

He stepped towards her, a disconcertingly intense look on his face. "I did not wish to leave you."

"Your obduracy in this matter is most alarming, Mr. Bingley," said Mrs. Sinclair. "Might I suggest a return to the caprice for which you are renowned and allow Lizzy to disabuse you of your fascination before any further damage is done?"

"If I have misunderstood your feelings, I am sorrier than I can express," Bingley continued, heedless of her warning. "Yet, I beg you would not squander this opportunity for a want of the deepest love. We have been friends, I am certain of it, and I would be willing to live as such. Surely, you could tolerate the arrangement if it meant escaping Darcy's disesteem?"

Elizabeth could not immediately think how to respond, for so much in what he said offended her. "You will have to explain your meaning, sir," she said at length.

"I have seen how he treats you. You need not protect him on my account."

She gaped at him, her cheeks burning hot and her indignation hotter. "I have no need to protect him on anybody's account. He is the best man I have ever known."

That appeared to confuse him greatly. "But he abandoned you to go to Kent!"

"His aunt is *dying!*"

"I would not have gone."

"I can well believe that! It would require too much in the way of consideration for other people!"

"Oh yes, Darcy is all consideration. He considers every duty under the sun more important than you."

"I have the deepest respect for his sense of duty."

"Even though he spends more time jaunting about the country fulfilling it than paying any attention to you? Why do you continue to defend him? I know you have been made miserable. I have seen it."

"When?"

"Not ten minutes ago, for a start, when you admitted to weeping over whatever he wrote, or did not write, in that letter," he said, pointing to her pocket.

Incredulous, Elizabeth withdrew the darling sketch Beth Powell had given her that morning and unfolded it for him to see. "This? A picture of Darcy holding my hand, drawn in the crayons he gave one of his tenant's children out of the goodness of his own heart? Aye, it made me cry—because I miss him!"

It observably gave Bingley pause but regrettably did not deter him completely. "No. I *know* you have been distressed by his aloofness. I have seen him brush off the touch of your hand. I have heard him forbid you from speaking. I have seen you feign a headache to escape his company."

She shook her head, which only encouraged him to oppose her more vehemently.

"What then of his pride, of his regret for marrying outside his precious sphere? Though you claim to have resolved the matter, I have not forgotten how he blamed you for all the rumours we heard at the theatre last year. Would that were the only occasion I had seen him punish you for your lesser consequence, but I have heard him lament it too many times."

Elizabeth could offer no better response than incredulous silence.

"Truly, Mr. Bingley, your persistence is verging on the deranged," Mrs. Sinclair voiced for her.

"Very well," he said to Elizabeth, "I shall not go on listing all the ways in which he disesteems you, for you know better than I how little he respects you. You, who said to me that there is nothing more wretched than being unable to respect one's partner in life!"

Disbelief and affront drew a wordless cry from her lips. He seemed in absolute earnest yet spoke of his oldest friend as though he were a stranger. "I was referring to my mother and father when I said that, not myself!"

"Need I remind you," said Mrs. Sinclair, "that Mrs. Darcy is with child? I must insist you stop this before she becomes any more distressed."

"Her condition has not prevented Darcy from quarrelling with her nigh on constantly! I have never heard you object to his conduct!"

"I am old, not senile. What is your excuse?"

"Tabitha has no need to object to Darcy's conduct, for there is naught objectionable in it!" Elizabeth cried. "I shall not pretend we never disagree, but it is seldom and never without swift resolution. You have mistaken teasing and debate for discord. You have wilfully misunderstood everything you have seen to justify your treacherous feelings."

"But it was you who said when I arrived at Pemberley that we could comfort each other now that I was come."

"I meant we might comfort each other for having been ill used by Jane, not Darcy! I love my husband in a way you are unlikely ever to comprehend. But I am under no obligation to justify my happiness to you. Rather, it is you who must justify your betrayal. How could you? He has been the very best of friends to you. He has lent you his counsel, his time, his companionship, his houses, even his reputation, from which you and your sisters have squeezed all conceivable profit. He trusted you. How could you contemplate stealing his wife and child?"

A flush of something that ought to have been shame, but which she thought was more likely petulance, reddened his countenance. "I did not plot and scheme to steal his wife and child. The notion was but an impulse of the moment. Indeed, my design was to leave! I have passage booked on a ship sailing on the fifteenth of this month."

Despite her experience of having her impressions of people completely overturned in the course of one conversation, this volte-face was proving particularly difficult to countenance. She had always considered Bingley such a kind and amiable man. The discovery of such a profound selfishness was excessively painful.

"You were simply going to leave without telling anybody? What about Jane? Have you no scruple in abandoning her?"

"She will not care! She has loathed every moment of being married to me. I wonder that she went to so much trouble to bring it about." He shook his head and almost sneered. "How she will repent if ever she discovers you would not have had me anyway."

"What is your meaning?"

"She only threw herself at me to prevent me from offering for *you*."

Elizabeth's babe kicked and writhed, mayhap stirred by the rushing of blood in her veins, loud to her own ears and doubtless thunderous to his. "You did not mention that when you arrived here, spinning us your tales of woe," she said coldly.

He paled but said nothing, though Elizabeth supposed there was little he could say in defence of such duplicity.

"She has known *all* this time that you loved me?"

"Er...well...it would seem so, yes."

"Oh, Jane!" she whispered, sick to her heart.

Bingley squirmed and looked miserable and offered no excuse.

"You have stolen my sister from me! You, who knew how heartbroken I was at our estrangement, have stood by and pretended to be puzzled by her bitterness and jealousy, all the while knowing the cause!"

"That is not true! I was not aware she knew of my feelings until we argued just before I left Netherfield. How would I have suspected? What woman in her right mind would trick a man she knows does not love her into marriage?"

His obstinate ignorance brought tears to Elizabeth's eyes. "One who loves him very, very much."

"She did?"

"I daresay she still does. Else she would not care that you do not." She took a deep breath and swiped away a tear, determined not to weep on his account. "How could you? You have betrayed us all." He could not have looked more wretched, but she could summon no pity for him. "Get out of my sight, Mr. Bingley. Better yet, get out of my house."

She really thought he might begin to weep when he mumbled a pitiful query as to where he ought to go.

"I have long been an advocate of your leaving the country," Mrs. Sinclair opined. "The idea has had few supporters as I understand it, but I suspect exile is presently the safest option available to you."

Bingley nodded glumly. "I shall leave England as planned in two weeks."

"I think not, sir," Elizabeth objected. "You must see it is your duty to return to Netherfield and be a proper husband to my sister."

"I should let him go, Lizzy," Mrs. Sinclair demurred. "He is of no use to anybody this side of the Atlantic."

"He is of use to Jane."

"A ringing endorsement, by all accounts!" She levered herself to her feet with her cane. "Mr. Bingley, you have the privilege of being the most unparalleled idiot I have ever known. And since I have been alive for the best part of a century, I urge you not to underestimate the scope of such a commendation."

Bingley sent Elizabeth a plaintive look. "For what it is worth, I truly love you."

"It is worth nothing, Mr. Bingley. Nothing at all."

She took the arm Mrs. Sinclair held out for her and left, resolutely refusing to shed a tear until later when she was securely closeted beneath the covers of Darcy's bed.

Friday, 5 March 1813: London

Caroline Bingley arrived home in a foul humour, having passed the previous two hours being out-ranked, out-shopped, and out-flirted by her friends. "Where is everybody?" she enquired, flicking her things at the butler.

"Mr. Hurst is at his club, ma'am. Mrs. Hurst is taking the air with her daughter, and I believe you will find Mrs. Bingley in the parlour."

She inclined her head and walked with little anticipation of pleasure to the parlour. Her expectations were not disappointed. She found Jane hunched over a letter, sobbing uncontrollably into a handkerchief from which a needle still dangled on a thread from a corner. With a resigned sigh, Caroline sat next to her, patted her knee with the furthest ends of her fingertips and enquired what was the matter.

After one or two false beginnings, Jane managed to communicate that the letter was from her sister. "Mr. Darcy gave it to me yesterday, but I have only now had the courage to read it."

"I take it whatever made you delay opening it has come to bear?"

She shook her head. "I knew not what to expect, but this is worse. She writes that Charles is seriously contemplating going to live in Nova Scotia!"

"I see. You may cease your fretting this instant if that is all that has distressed you. Charles has never seriously considered anything in his life. Even if the thought has occurred to him, he will get no further than choosing which of his neck cloths to pack. He will come home; you may rely upon it."

"In that case, what comfort will it be to know it was only irresolution that made him stay?"

Caroline weighed her low opinion of Jane's fortitude with the need for frankness and decided the latter was more pressing in the present circumstances. "Pardon my saying so, but if you do not begin to give him a little encouragement, irresolution may well be the best for which you can hope. My brother has a great natural modesty of which Louisa and I have ever despaired. He is the sort of man who requires considerable urging to resolve on anything." In response to Jane's look of bewilderment, she added, "Your determination to be as cold and indifferent a wife as ever lived is not likely to convince him to love you."

Perhaps she might have worded it better. The tears returned.

"Cold and indifferent?"

"My dear, you are hardly what one would call a demonstrative wife."

"But you impressed upon me the importance of not being one! You disdained my meekness! You instructed me in my tone of voice, my address and expressions—in all the things that would make me more acceptable to your sphere. Indeed, Lady Ashby was adamant that becoming more fashionable would earn me his esteem!"

"With all due respect, Lady Ashby does not know my brother. He evidently liked you better when you did nothing but smile at him incessantly. By all means, continue as you have been in public, but if your wish is to make Charles love you, I am afraid you will have to indulge him occasionally."

Histrionics rendered her next speech all but incoherent, though Caroline gleaned the gist: Jane's efforts to be a good wife had only pushed him into her arms.

"Whose arms?" she enquired, certain she already knew the answer.

"Lizzy's!" Jane cried, collapsing face first into the handkerchief. Caroline pried it from her grip lest she poke herself in the eye with the needle.

"I had hoped he would overcome that little fascination before you discovered it."

"You knew about it too?"

"Regrettably." She wondered who else did.

"For how long have you known?"

"Since he decided to offer for her and somehow got himself engaged to you instead." Colour flooded Jane's countenance, and Caroline wondered belatedly whether she had only worsened matters. "Forgive me; I assumed you knew about that."

"I did," Jane whispered. "It is what we argued about at Netherfield, though I suspected long before then that he had feelings for her. I have been so anxious to make him admire me more than he does her. How insufficient have been all my pretensions to becoming a woman worthy of being loved! Had I only shown him more affection than I felt instead of less, he might never have done what he did!"

"What he did? What do you mean?"

"He got a child on her!" she howled.

"What? Mrs. Darcy's child is my *brother's*?" They were all doomed.

"No. He got a child on the next best thing—Miss Greening."

Caroline stared, nonplussed.

"Amelia. The maid at Netherfield. The one who looked like my sister."

Well, how completely, absolutely, utterly splendid. The buffoon had truly outdone himself on this occasion. "Is that why you dismissed her?"

"No. I dismissed her because she looked too much like Lizzy, and I did not want Charles to have any reason to be reminded of her. But either I acted too late or he sought her out afterwards, for she is with child."

"This is disgraceful. How—when did you discover it?"

"In September when Lizzy was at Netherfield. Mr. Darcy found a stupid little picture of her on Charles's desk that my cousin had drawn, and I knew instantly why he had kept it."

She sniffed grotesquely. Caroline gave her back the handkerchief, needle and all.

"I went to his study to find it—well, to burn it, in truth, I was so cross. But instead, I found a letter from a Mrs. Pence, who wrote that Miss Greening had felt the quickening and asked that the agreed funds be forwarded."

Caroline grew angrier by the moment. She wished her brother had shown half as much flair for cunning before entangling himself with the Bennets. "But you do not know when it happened?" Nor if it had continued, she dared not add.

"No. I have tried to guess. I asked my mother how long one usually waits to feel the quickening, but she misunderstood why I was asking and announced to everybody that I was with child."

Caroline recalled that evening all too well. This new information only made her loathe Mrs. Bennet more. "Is Charles aware that you know?"

Jane shook her head. "I could not bear to hear him admit it."

Caroline peered at her dubiously. "I confess I am struggling to account for your having been so concerned with earning his esteem, given all this."

"As have I on occasion, but I—well, I suppose it is simple, really. I love him. I do not believe I know how not to. I have loved him from the very first moment I met him."

Caroline's every moral fibre protested as the words, "He does not deserve you," reluctantly crawled off her tongue. "Why on earth did you not mention it to anybody else?"

"I told Lady Ashby. She said it was a part of married life and advised me never to speak of it."

"Well, she would! On dit, her husband has half a dozen children from the other side of the sheets. I doubt his taking lovers troubles her in any other way than whether her pin money is diminished."

"You used to speak more highly of her."

"She is a viscountess. I speak highly of her rank and influence. As a person, she is more comparable to a lemon. She adds flavour to other things but is sour and horrid on her own."

That this should surprise Jane was exasperating. It seemed, despite her low expectations, that Caroline had still managed to underestimate her new sister's naivety. She wished she had not, for much of this misfortune might have been averted had she more firmly pointed Jane in the direction of the real world from the start. "I am surprised you did not tell your sister."

"I might have, had she not come to my room that evening, after my mother made the announcement, to tell me she was also with child. It was too much. In one day, I had learnt that Charles still admired her and had got a child on her facsimile. She might as well have told me they had lain together." She let out a little whimper and added, "It was childish and unjust of me to blame her. Yet I *slapped* her for it."

"I daresay it did not do too much harm."

"But it has!" She lifted her crumpled letter and read from it. "*I shall never have the words to explain how deeply your jealousy and mistrust have wounded me. You are no longer the sister I once knew. You have lost all your goodness, and I have lost my Jane.*" She burst into tears again and dropped her hands and the letter back to her lap. "I have blamed her for everything, but Mr. Darcy is right. This is more my fault than I ever comprehended."

"An observation worthy of a good deal of solitary reflection, I am certain," Caroline replied, her limited supply of compassion abruptly exhausted at the thought of expending an ounce of it in defence of Elizabeth Darcy.

"You are right," Jane gasped between sobs. "I hardly know myself anymore."

"I am for Bath tomorrow," Caroline grudgingly admitted. "Allow me to take you as far as Netherfield. Indulge your reflections in the peace and quiet of the country while you prepare yourself for Charles's return."

"You are convinced he will?"

"I am. And if you are determined to make him love you, you had better work out how to return yourself to the artless country moppet you used to be before he does."

Wednesday, 10 March 1813: Hertfordshire

"This is it, ma'am," the footman said, opening the carriage door and indicating one of several buildings flanking a dingy-looking inn.

Jane looked up at the grimy windows set in rotten frames then down to the letter retrieved from her husband's desk. It was a poor quarter of Hatfield indeed, yet there was no doubting this was the place. If anything, that only strengthened her resolve. Gathering her cloak about her, she stepped down over the stinking runnel of slop separating the houses from the street and knocked on the door. A stout, officious-looking lady in a pinafore and mop cap opened it.

"Mrs. Pence?"

"Aye. Can I help you?"

"Is Miss Greening at home?"

"Who might be asking?"

"Mrs. Bingley."

There came two gasps—one from Mrs. Pence and the other from beyond the door.

"I am afraid she is—"

"Oh, let her in, Sally," the person inside said. "I can see Mrs. Fordwich salivating at her curtains across the way."

Jane was promptly ushered into a small, ill-lit room, and the door was closed behind her. The gloom inside was slow to lift its veil but eventually revealed a woman heavy with child, who looked far less like her sister than she recalled. Her chin was too pointy, her nose too large, and her eyes, unlike Elizabeth's, had nothing extraordinary in them. The sight affected her nonetheless, though not with jealousy as she had expected, only with crushing remorse for never having seen her sister similarly in bloom.

"You can't stop me from goin'!" Amelia declared, all defiance.

"Going? Nay, you misunderstand the purpose of my visit."

"Do I? Why else would you 'ave come?"

"I am come to see that you are being properly provided for."

This was the culmination of a week's heart-breaking reflection. Her days of railing against the injustices of the world were done. The candid censure of her nearest and dearest had shown her that. It shamed her, but she had come to comprehend that her transgressions, though of a different nature, were every bit as egregious as Bingley's. She was resolved to put matters right. It was her dearest hope that, if she could prove she had accepted and forgiven his mistakes, he might be persuaded she was still, at heart, the woman Caroline claimed he once loved.

"Why?" Amelia demanded suspiciously.

"Because my husband took advantage of you, and neither you nor your child deserves to suffer for that."

Of all the responses she had anticipated, contempt had not been one.

"You really are a gem, ain't you?" Amelia scoffed. "I s'pose you would think that, sittin' up in your big 'ouse with your pretty jewels and expensive gowns, waitin' for life to be 'anded to you on a platter. Well, the rest of us live in the real world, Mrs. Bingley. Life don't just fall in the laps o' girls like me. Those of us as live 'and to mouth needs take every chance we's given. And in case your mother never learnt you in these things, men such as your 'usband are goldmines o' chance."

Mortifying though this speech was, Jane did not miss the significance of the revelation. "He did not seduce you then?"

"I don't know 'bout that. 'Tis devilish tricky to end up like this 'less the man's inclined to tumble." She placed a hand upon her swollen stomach. "You could just as easy take the blame, mind, if you'd rather the fault not lie with 'im. It was you what left 'im wanting."

"Me?"

"No advantage to actin' surprised. 'Twas me you sent to give 'im the note you wrote excusing yourself from your duty. Truly, what was you thinkin', expectin' 'im to go without on 'is wedding day? There are other things you can do, y' know."

Jane closed her eyes. Her wedding day!

"Deprive a man of what 'e wants," Amelia continued, "and you can bet your last penny 'e'll look for it elsewhere."

And she *had* deprived him of what he wanted that day, had she not? Elizabeth! What a different light this shed on the regret expressed in his answering note!

"I s'pose you think you got your revenge when you 'ad me dismissed? But see who's laughin' now!"

"I do not take your meaning."

"Seems you've been deprivin' 'im too long. 'Your 'usband's decided 'e prefers me, after all, an' 'e's taking me to live with 'im in Nova Scotia. An' there's nothin' you can do about it."

Her instinct was to disbelieve it, yet she could not account for Amelia knowing of those plans she had only recently discovered herself, and her hands began to shake. "No, you are lying. It cannot be true."

"No? Look at this if you don't believe me."

Jane accepted the letter Amelia withdrew from the top of her corset and read it twice from beginning to end, making certain she had not missed nor misunderstood any part of it.

"So you see, Mrs. Bingley," Amelia said, snatching it back and secreting it once more next to her bosom, "I've no need of your pity. I'm being very well provided for, thank you."

Jane refused to cry. Instead, she turned and left before her heart broke to pieces all over the parlour floor of her husband's lover.

Netherfield, Hertfordshire
March 10

To Lady Ashby,

Pray forgive my impertinence in writing. I know in your last letter you said you no longer had the time to correspond, but I beg you would indulge me this once, for I have nobody else to whom I might turn.

I have discovered B means to leave the country and take the woman you know as 'A' with him. I have seen his letter to her with my own eyes. He wrote that if she agreed, it would be in his power to restore her reputation and raise her condition in life, that they could invent a story to explain her situation that nobody would question and that he dearly hoped she would agree to go with him to Nova Scotia, where the child might be raised without prejudice. I would not have believed it, but I recognised his hand, and E has written separately to warn me of his plans to leave.

I know not what to do! Quite apart from the ruination of my reputation should he leave, I do not wish him to go! Though my head rages against it, my heart will not have any other way than that I love him still! I long for another chance to convince him that my affections are genuine.

He is at Pemberley, or at least his letter to A was sent from there, but I know not for how long he will remain there. According to that letter, he sets sail later this month. I beg you would advise me as to how I ought to proceed, for the prospect of losing him forever is too painful to comprehend. Pray, what ought I to do?

Yours sincerely,
J

Friday, 12 March 1813: Hertfordshire

IT WAS A BRIGHT, CRISP MORNING, NOT QUITE SPRING BUT NOT WINTER, either—just cold enough that their conversation billowed white on the air between them.

"Oh, Mary," Jane said. "Can you forgive me for treating Lizzy so ill?"

The kindly Mrs. Annesley had once counselled Mary that not everybody took solace in moralizing at moments of high emotion, thus she refrained from voicing her thoughts on the evils of jealousy and resentment and instead did what she thought Elizabeth would have done. She hooked her arm around Jane's and gave her a smile of the warmest sisterly consolation. "Yes, and so will she when you explain it as you have done to me."

"Would that were so, but I have been so awful, I do not see how she ever could."

"Then you are underestimating her still. She will be as sorry as I am that you have been this ill-used." Jane winced, and Mary pressed gently for her to explain why.

"I do not want you to hate Charles," she whispered. "I may be the biggest fool there ever was, but I believe what he said to me before he went away—that he has tried to love me. And I wish to believe—I *do* believe—he is only going because I have made him feel there is nothing for him here."

"If that is your wish, then as long as you love him, I shall love him also."

"Thank you," she replied, yet in the next moment, let out a soft but unmistakable sob. "It will not make any difference *who* loves him if he is not here!"

Mary had no comfort to offer that was not pure conjecture. "What did Lady Ashby say?" she enquired instead.

"That she would write to Lizzy and ask her to prevent Bingley from leaving."

"Well, that is something, is it not?"

Jane shook her head morosely. "I do not wish him to stay because Lizzy asked it of him. I wish him to stay because *I* did."

"Well then," Mary said, giving her arm a little squeeze. "You had better ask it of him."

"YOU AIN'T SERIOUS?"

"I was instructed to arrange transportation," Peabody said flatly, being careful to reveal no hint of amusement as Amelia flapped about protesting her outrage. "In the absence of further details, I took the liberty of procuring the most expedient means."

"But I can't travel on the *mail coach* in my condition! I ain't baggage!"

He raised an eyebrow. "That is moot."

"Why can't I travel in one of Mr. Bingley's carriages?"

He did then allow himself a small chuckle. That a catchpenny housemaid should think getting poisoned by the master of the house entitled her to ride in his carriage was absurd. "Neither was available," he said. "He has one with him, and the other, by this time tomorrow, will be transporting the mistress to Pemberley."

Amelia whirled to face him. "Why's she goin' there?"

"Oddly enough, she did not see fit to confide the particulars."

"Don't play the fool, Mr. Peabody; it don't suit you. I swear, if she's goin' there to try an' stop me—"

"Then she will be disappointed. Mr. Bingley already awaits you in Liverpool."

"Oh, well and good, then." Frowning, she added, "You didn't tell 'er 'e weren't there, did you?"

"She expressed a purpose of travelling to Pemberley. I am not in the habit of second guessing my employer's wishes."

"Careful, Mr. Peabody," she said, eyeing him slyly. "You're in danger of makin' me think you care for me, after all."

"Heaven forefend, Miss Greening. I do, however, care for my position, and the master was most particular that nothing should prevent you from boarding that boat."

This ought to have been ample warning, yet she still seemed surprised when he took her by the elbow and directed her firmly towards the coach, propelled her up the steps, and shut the door after her. "Do have a pleasant trip, madam."

Sunday, 14 March 1813: Lancashire

Darkness descended over the city in the hours Bingley sat waiting. His view of the street was gradually usurped by the candle-lit reflection of the inn's parlour. What had been an empty room when he came down from his rented rooms above stairs was now teeming with the worldly mix of people common only to port towns.

The door opened, and his stomach dropped when a man and a woman walked in, but he was not Banbury, and she was not Amelia. He slumped back into his seat, wondering what the deuce was taking them so long.

Someone put a tankard of ale down in front of him. "On the house, sir. You look as though you need it."

He looked up into the now-familiar countenance of the innkeeper whose establishment had been his home since he left Pemberley and whose ale had nursed him through some excessively painful meditations over those ten days. "Much obliged," he said, raising the drink in salute.

For a good many of those days, self-pity had consumed him, his heart heavy with the knowledge that Elizabeth did not love him. It had taken him longer than it ought to fathom why that hurt less than he thought it should. It was because he had never once considered whether or not she might.

He was sure he could not be wrong about Darcy. The Titan's cold, unabashed disdain towards his wife could not be otherwise explained or excused, but if Elizabeth did not object, who was he to assume she might love him any better? Having accused Darcy of undervaluing her, he was ashamed to acknowledge that he was equally guilty of wilfully misunderstanding Elizabeth's feelings.

Yet, if he had misunderstood Elizabeth's, he had completely disregarded Jane's. Quite when it had happened he knew not, but he seemed to have detached himself completely from her as though she were someone else's wife and her happiness were not his to ensure, her pain were not his to soothe, and her heart were not his to protect.

Lord knew how prodigiously he had attempted to lay the blame at her door. It had not been his fault, after all, that she had condemned them both to such a miserable union, but reason simply would not allow it. Over and again, she had insisted it had not been her design to entrap him, only to convince him of her feelings. And wherefore had it been necessary for her to do that? Because consciously or otherwise he had transferred his attentions to Elizabeth.

Not content with abandoning her the first time, he had come back, raised her hopes a second time, and then flagrantly mooned after her sister in full view of all her neighbours. She would have been exposed to their utter derision had he succeeded in winning Elizabeth's hand. And yet, it appeared that was not why she acted as she had. If Elizabeth was to be believed, it was not the world's disdain Jane feared but his. She had wanted nothing more than for him to love her. Instead, he had married her without the proper affection and, within hours, violated his wedding vows.

All endeavours to convince himself that his fleeting infidelity was of no significance to anyone were come to naught. He could no longer hide from the egregiousness of his transgression. Amelia had come to his study, fluttering Elizabeth's eyelashes at him and all but begging to compensate for Jane's indisposition. In succumbing, he had condemned himself to a union of dissatisfaction and misery.

His shame could only have been greater if Jane were to actually discover his indiscretion. This woman—who, when he first met her, had been the epitome of gentle goodness—had lived for a year suspecting she was neither loved nor respected by her husband. She had become an embittered shadow of her former self, and it was all his doing. She and Elizabeth had become estranged by jealousy and mistrust, and it was all his doing. Elizabeth despised him, and it was all his doing.

Now Darcy was going to kill him, and if *he* did not, Caroline would. There was no denying he would be safer in Nova Scotia. He lifted his tankard to sup his ale, and when he put it back down again, Banbury was there, wittering something about the mail coach being delayed.

"Mr. Bingley, if you ain't goin' to stand for me, you'll 'ave to pardon my sittin' down," a woman behind Banbury said. She sidled awkwardly onto the opposite bench, untied her bonnet and slung it on the table.

"Lord, I beg your pardon. I did not recognise you!" Bingley exclaimed, and truly, he had not, for Amelia was not carrying off her increase nearly as well as Elizabeth.

A hot meal and cup of mead seemed to assuage her affront. Once she was suitably revived and Banbury dismissed, their more serious business could no longer be delayed.

"I am pleased you have accepted my offer," he began. "It is a vast undertaking, but I believe it will be for the best."

"It were a fine offer, sir."

Bingley removed from his pocket the papers he had had drawn up and spread them on the table. "Your ticket is paid for, and I have hired you a companion and a man to chaperone you on the voyage. My cousin will meet you there. You are to give him this letter. It asks him to arrange your money and see to your housing. He will also—"

"I don't understand. Ain't you comin' with me?"

He looked up. Amelia had gone very red. "Well, er…no. You must see that would be impossible."

"I don't see nothin' o' the sort. You said you wanted me to start a new life with you in Nova Scotia!"

"I am afraid you are mistaken, madam."

"I ain't mistaken! Mrs. Pence read it for me, and she said that's what you wrote! Look here!" She scrabbled in her reticule and withdrew his letter, which she unfolded onto the table and jabbed repeatedly with her finger.

Bingley duly read what he had written, and indeed it said, "*I have booked passage for later this month and dearly hope you will agree to go with me to Nova Scotia, board the boat, and allow me to provide you a new life.*"

"Oh. Right. Ah, well this is dashed awkward. Forgive me, Miss Greening. That was meant to say Liverpool."

"But it *says* Nova Scotia!"

"Yes, I can see that. What can I say? I write in the most careless way imaginable. I am awfully sorry." She looked awfully angry. "But consider all I *am* offering you—the promise of a better life, an income, a home of your own, schooling for your child. And your reputation! Here, you will never be more than a fallen housemaid. There, you could begin again and be a respectable woman with whatever history you choose."

She stared at him sullenly. "You're quite one for forsakin' people, ain't you?"

He chafed at that. "With all due respect, madam, you cannot claim any peculiar attachment to me. We are hardly good friends."

Without dropping his gaze, she parted her travelling cloak, revealing far more clearly her distended stomach, over which she rubbed a hand. "I weren't talkin' about me."

He looked back at her, wondering what more she wanted from him. "Have I not said I shall fully support the child?"

Her mouth set in a hard line, and she wrapped her cloak back around herself, crossing her arms over the join. When she had remained silent for above two minutes, he enquired whether she would still agree to go, not quite managing to keep the impatience from his voice.

"Will you still pay me?" she shot back.

"Of course. All the arrangements still stand, only I shall not be part of them."

She turned aside and shrugged, which with her arms crossed over her stomach as they were, made her shoulders almost touch her ears. "S'pose so."

"Thank you."

"What will you do?" she enquired sullenly.

"Go home to my wife." Though he could not imagine, after all the ways in which he had abused her, that Jane could possibly still love him, it was, as Elizabeth had said, time for him to be a proper husband. What Darcy had said at Pemberley was true also. He had loved Jane once. Perhaps, in time, he might earn back her esteem. He meant to try for her sake and Elizabeth's.

"Shame she won't be there," Amelia scoffed, ruining all his gallant schemes in one breath. "She's on 'er way to Pemberley."

"Good God, why?"

She shrugged again. "To stop you going to Nova Scotia, probably."

"What the deuce made her think I am going to Nova Scotia?"

"That letter," she replied, nodding at the offending article.

He did his utmost to speak calmly, though he felt anything but calm. "How did she come to see that letter?"

"I showed it to 'er when she called on me. Came to see I was being provided for. Least that's what she said."

He pressed a fist to his mouth and swore against it. *Jane knows!* His shame was now complete. All this time he had justified his behaviour towards Jane by telling himself she had grown into a woman he could not love, but she was not changed at all! What other person alive would discover her husband's infidelity and think only to the well-being of those involved? She remained as good-hearted as she had ever been! And mayhap, he dared allow himself to hope, not beyond forgiving his mistakes.

The remainder of his discussions with Amelia were conducted with no less awkwardness than was to be expected in the circumstances, yet all in all, matters were concluded with infelicitous haste. In less time than they had taken embroiling themselves in the situation to begin with, they had agreed to terms and parted ways.

"Make arrangements to travel at first light," Bingley informed his man upon reaching his rooms. "I must return to Pemberley."

"Is there something there you have forgotten, sir?"

Yes, he thought. *The only person left in the world who might yet love me.*

Monday, 15 March 1813: Derbyshire

Impatience had become less of an imperfection and more of an affliction for Elizabeth. Husbands, babies, news—all were presently exhibiting a most vexing disdain for celerity. Regardless of the grey clouds on the horizon, she was determined to walk out that morning before she went distracted from inaction.

"This letter has just arrived, Mrs. Darcy," said Maltravers as she came into the hall. The letter she took, but she waved away his offer of an extra shawl. "The master's instructions, ma'am," he said with some embarrassment. She smiled wryly and draped it over her arm.

"Might I enquire where you intend to walk, ma'am?" he said as he opened the front door for her.

She looked slyly at him. "Also the master's instructions?"

He inclined his head. Grinning at the very great pleasure of being cherished thus, even in Darcy's absence, she informed Maltravers of her destination and stepped out onto the front steps. Only then did she look at her letter. She was alarmed to see Lady Ashby's seal, for they had never corresponded. She tore it open, fearing instantly for Darcy's safety. Alarm turned to shock and shock to fury as she read of Bingley's intentions to leave the country after all and to take a mistress and natural child with him!

With an angry growl, she whirled about to go back into the house, but the shawl had tangled about her legs. The world tilted. She saw Maltravers' horrified expression, then the music room window, then the sky. She flung her arms wide, banging her wrist painfully on the balustrade. She grabbed it and cried out at the fire that burst through her shoulder as momentum wrenched her to face the other way. Her grip on the rail held, but her feet were gone from under her, and she slammed down heavily onto a step, knocking all the air from her lungs.

Maltravers appeared in front of her and soon after Mrs. Reynolds, both enquiring urgently whether she was hurt. She was not sure. Upon reflection, her wrist and shoulder both throbbed abominably, yet they were the least of her concerns. She waited, caught her breath and prayed until, with the most profound relief, she felt her baby wriggle its protest at being so violently flung about. What little air remained to her escaped in a shaky laugh. "I am well," she whispered.

She was led, gingerly, back inside to a chair where Mrs. Sinclair met them. "What is all the commotion? What has happened, Lizzy?"

Satisfied she had done herself no serious harm, Elizabeth's mind jumped directly beyond her fall to that which pained her most. "Mr. Bingley has been unfaithful to my sister!"

"We already knew that."

"No, he has a mistress! She is with child! He is taking her abroad. He lied! He was to go home to Jane, yet all the while, he was planning to go away with this…this *woman!*"

Mrs. Sinclair pulled an incredulous face. "The man is incapable of resolving on anything. Two weeks ago, it was you he wished to go away with. Before that, he planned to go alone. At some point, I suppose, he must have wanted your sister. I am beginning to feel quite put out that he has never wanted to go anywhere with me."

"Poor, poor Jane!"

Mrs. Sinclair looked distinctly sceptical but did not argue and instead enquired how Elizabeth had come to discover this news on the front steps of Pemberley.

"Lady Ashby has written, asking that I prevent him from leaving. They must all think he is still here. I must write to Jane." She shuffled to the edge of her seat. Mrs. Reynolds, hovering fretfully nearby, stepped forward to offer her assistance. Elizabeth was glad of it, for upon standing, she experienced a most shocking expulsion of fluids that rendered her faint with alarm. "Oh God, what is it?"

"'Tis the baby, ma'am," Mrs. Reynolds replied, looking disconcertingly troubled.

"Oh no! 'Tis too soon, is it not?"

"You tell us, my dear," Mrs. Sinclair said with a knowing look.

"Try not to worry, Mrs. Darcy," Mrs. Reynolds said more helpfully. "It is earlier than expected, but there is no sense in giving yourself any more to be anxious about than necessary."

Never had Elizabeth wanted Darcy more. The prospect of birthing a child was terrifying enough without fearing that it was not fit to be born. She sat down again. "I am not ready. It will have to wait." She ignored the look that passed between the two ladies. "My aunt is not yet here," she said, failing to keep her voice from trembling. "Who will attend me?"

"I shall, if you wish it," Mrs. Reynolds offered.

"I shall, even if you do not wish it," said Mrs. Sinclair.

Elizabeth would have continued to object had not a sharp pain frightened her into silence. "I think I would prefer to go back to waiting," she said quietly once it had passed.

"I fear young Master or Miss Darcy has other ideas, ma'am," Mrs. Reynolds replied.

Shaking with apprehension, Elizabeth allowed herself to be led upstairs to embark upon a wholly different exercise than she had thought to enjoy that day.

Even in the pallid light of late afternoon, Pemberley was magnificent. Jane regretted not having told Elizabeth how very well she liked it on her last visit. It was but one of innumerable things she regretted. She turned away from the window, her palm burning from the memory of striking Elizabeth's cheek. She had no notion of what she would say to her sister, or indeed if she would even be received given Mr. Darcy's unequivocal exclusion. Yet, there had been no alternative but to come. There was too much to be said between her and Bingley to stay away.

"Mr. Bingley left Pemberley a little less than two weeks ago, madam," she was informed upon reaching the house. She stared at the butler in mute dismay, all her carefully prepared words rendered useless. There was nothing more she could do. He was gone. What would become of her now?

Maltravers cleared his throat.

"Pardon me," she said quietly. "Would you be kind enough to inform my sister I am here?"

"I am afraid the family are not receiving visitors today, ma'am."

The sound of scraping furniture, incongruous against the stillness of the rest of the house, drew Jane's attention to a pair of footmen rolling the great hearthrug out from under the hall chairs. "Is there to be a ball?" she enquired foolishly. It mattered not what Elizabeth was doing. It did not involve her. Maltravers looked excessively conscious. "Ahem…no. There was an incident—that is, Mrs. Darcy was unexpectedly taken to childbed."

She looked back at him in surprise. "Presently? Why did you not say? Pray take me to her this instant." He hesitated, and she said, more urgently, "I am her sister; it is quite proper. Please, sir, I must insist!"

She grew steadily more anxious as she was led through the house, but all concerns that her presence might be unwelcome vanished when Elizabeth's cries first reached her ears. She hastened her steps. The footman paled upon reaching the door, evidently unsure what to do next. She dismissed him and, without a second thought, pushed the door open.

Her sister was propped on a bed of sorts, her hair drenched with perspiration and her countenance contorted in pain.

"Lizzy!"

Elizabeth's head whipped up, and their eyes met. For a heartbeat, Jane feared she might spurn her coming. Then she burst into tears and held out her hand. "Jane! You are here!"

Jane rushed to take it. "I am, and I shall stay if you will let me."

She nodded and gripped her hand tightly but seemed unable to speak further. Jane looked around. An older woman, Mrs. Sinclair, if she recalled correctly, glared at her reproachfully from the other side of the bed. The housekeeper was there, a maid—and no one else. "Where is the midwife?" she enquired in alarm.

"There is nobody available," Mrs. Reynolds said in a low voice. "They are all either engaged with other women or nowhere to be found."

"There must be somebody!"

"We are trying, Mrs. Bingley. Two weeks hence and the accoucheur and monthly nurse would have been in residence. We have sent a man to fetch one or both, but they are in Sheffield, and that is assuming they can be found and are available to come."

Elizabeth let out a held breath that stretched into a rasping groan. "It hurts!"

Jane looked in alarm at Mrs. Sinclair. "I do not know what to do."

"Nothing new there, then," the old lady mumbled.

"Talk to me!" Elizabeth cried. "Distract me, I beg you. What are you doing here?"

Jane winced in shame, for the answer ought to be that she had come for her. "I came to stop Charles leaving," she admitted. "But that matters not at the present moment. 'Tis you—"

"Of course it matters, Jane. I am so very sorry for you. You deserve a better man."

"I know that is not true. I have been awful."

Elizabeth did not argue. Instead, she squeezed her eyes shut and grimaced savagely. A long, tortured groan bubbled through her gritted teeth.

"Good girl," Mrs. Sinclair croaked, patting her other hand.

Elizabeth's groan escalated into a strangled scream that went right through Jane.

"Oh, Lizzy!" She leant over her, peering closely, looking for what she knew not. Mrs. Reynolds appeared by her side, proffering a damp cloth. She thanked her, deeply obliged for something to do, and put it to use cooling her sister's brow.

"Why did you not tell me?" Elizabeth enquired in a gasping, breathy voice.

"I confess I was ashamed my husband did not love me."

"Perhaps, then, you ought not to have tricked him into marrying you," Mrs. Sinclair said tartly.

"I did not trick him!" To her sister she said, "You must believe I had no idea we would be discovered. I was only trying to convince him of my esteem. I feared he would leave me again otherwise. Lizzy, I am so sorry. For everything. I have treated you abominably. Can you ever forgive me?"

Elizabeth squeezed her hand and nodded but was breathing too heavily to respond with words. Her countenance twisted into a rictus of agony, and Jane could only observe her in wretched suspense until the spasm passed.

"I forgave you as soon as I learnt his heart was untrue," Elizabeth gasped at length, collapsing back into her pillows.

"Thank you, dear Lizzy. I do not deserve you."

But she was already in pain again, her crying out now more of a growl. And though it was muttered through clenched teeth, Jane could hear her keening for her husband.

"Is it supposed to hurt this much?" she enquired, turning to Mrs. Reynolds in alarm.

"I have no children, ma'am. I would not know." She looked at Mrs. Sinclair.

"I birthed mine over half a century ago. You cannot possibly expect me to remember."

"Am I dying?" Elizabeth asked, her eyes wide with fear.

"We are all dying," Mrs. Sinclair replied. "Only some of us are doing it more quietly than others."

"Miss Baker, run and see if anybody has been found to attend Mrs. Darcy," Mrs. Reynolds shouted at the maid.

"Jane, I'm frightened!" Elizabeth cried.

As was Jane, more frightened than she had ever been, but it was long past time she acted like the sister Elizabeth deserved, and she was determined not to fail her. "Do not be. If Mama can do this *five times* then I am quite sure Mrs. Darcy of Pemberley can." She lifted a lock of drenched hair from Elizabeth's face and stroked her cheek. "And you are my brave Lizzy. You can do anything."

Elizabeth let out a sob. "*There* you are, Jane! How I have missed you!"

Georgiana was delighted to be returning to the serenity of Pemberley. Her stay at Hornscroft had been wonderful, but so many girls together in one place were exhausting. She knew not how Elizabeth had tolerated it, growing up at Longbourn.

Still, she had not expected the house to be quite as quiet as she found it. She had rather hoped Elizabeth would come to meet her, for there was a good view of the driveway from the saloon in which they usually sat. Perchance, she was in a different part of the house and had not seen her approach. That not even Maltravers was there to direct the unloading of luggage, however, was more than passing strange.

Hughes, her lady's maid and travelling companion, left to make enquiries below stairs. Of a mind to find her sister, Georgiana thought to look first in the orangery, but before she got farther than the foot of the grand staircase, Hughes came dashing back into the hall.

"Mrs. Darcy has been hurt, Miss Darcy!"

"What?"

"She fell down the front steps!"

"Oh my! Is she badly hurt? Where is she?"

The sound of someone coming down the stairs made them both look up. Elizabeth's maid Baker was galloping down at a pace. Hughes opened her mouth to speak, but Baker pre-empted her.

"Not now, Molly, I must see if they've found a physician yet. They need one for Mrs. Darcy *this instant.*"

"Is the mistress in a bad way, then?"

"I'll say! They all think she's dying!"

Georgiana gasped, her hands over her mouth in horror. Elizabeth could not die!

"An apothecary has been found," Hughes informed her. "Mr. Maltravers and Mr. Barnaby are interviewing him as we speak to make sure he knows his business. But let me fetch him. You had better go back up to Mrs. Darcy."

"Aye, very well, but hurry!" She disappeared back upstairs.

Hughes looked to Georgiana. "May I—"

"Yes, go, go! Make haste!" She herself set off after Baker, her mind blank but for the fear of anything happening to Elizabeth or her baby. Again, she was arrested, however, this time by the most unexpected arrival of Mr. Bingley.

"Miss Darcy! I hope y—"

"I beg your pardon," she interrupted, "but I must leave you. Lizzy has been injured. I must go to her."

"What has happened?" he cried, hastening across the hall towards her.

"She fell down the front steps."

"Good Lord! Is she badly hurt?"

Georgiana tried her utmost, but could not prevent herself from bursting into tears. "The maid said she is dying!"

Mr. Bingley's countenance drained of colour. "Dear God, I should never have left. Where is she?"

"I do not know, I am only just returned myself. I was on my way to find her."

"Miss Darcy! And…Mr. Bingley!"

Georgiana started and turned. Mrs. Reynolds was coming down the stairs.

"I did not know you had arrived, Miss Darcy."

"Only moments ago," Georgiana assured her. "I heard what happened. I was coming to find Liz—"

"No!" she exclaimed. "You cannot see her, Miss Darcy."

"But—"

"She is well attended, I assure you, but you are far too young to see such things."

"Upon my word," cried Mr. Bingley, "is it that serious?"

"She is near the end, sir," she replied, looking at him meaningfully. "As you might imagine, she is suffering a great deal."

"Dear God," he muttered. Georgiana did not know *what* to say.

"Pray excuse me," Mrs. Reynolds said. "I must fetch the apothecary myself. This delay will simply not do."

She had gone only one step before Baker reappeared at the top of the stairs. "'Tis too late for that, Mrs. Reynolds!"

Georgiana fumbled for a grip on the handrail, thinking she might fall.

Baker noticed her then and bent heads with Mrs. Reynolds to whisper the remainder of her dire message. Nonetheless, Georgiana still heard her say, "Not breathing." And there was no mistaking Mrs. Reynolds' cry of, "Oh dear Lord, the poor girl!" With a last instruction that Georgiana was not to follow her, the housekeeper disappeared up the stairs with the maid. Georgiana turned to Mr. Bingley, too horrified to speak.

He did not look to be faring any better. "Forgive me, Miss Darcy," he murmured, shaking his head, "I cannot—Oh God, I must get some air." With which he turned and stumbled towards the front door.

Less than a heartbeat later another door flew open, and Hughes rushed past her, followed closely by a man who must have been the apothecary.

Then the house was quiet once again. Georgiana remained where she was, halfway up the stairs, shaken, alone, and terrified.

"She is dead."

"No, she is bloody not!" Darcy snarled, ramming Bingley against the wall again. "I did not give her leave to die again!"

He was vaguely aware that Bingley dropped to the ground once he released him but spared it no further thought as he wrenched the front door open and stormed into the house, bellowing for Maltravers. He was not there, but Georgiana was, weeping hysterically on the stairs. He ran to her, resisting the pull of despair with all his strength. "Where is she?"

His sister only sobbed and shook her head.

"Mr. Darcy?"

He spun around. Barnaby and Maltravers had both materialised at the foot of the stairs.

"Mrs. Darcy is in the laying-in chamber, sir."

"The laying-in chamber? Is she—good God!" Bingley's words and Georgiana's tears rendered that news the most terrifying Darcy had ever received. He turned and ran. Yet, the nearer he got to the corner of the house where every mistress of Pemberley had birthed its heirs, the more fearful he became, for there was no crying out to be heard, either from Elizabeth or an infant. There was only silence.

He had not time to consider what he might find within the chamber. All he knew was his visceral need to be with Elizabeth, and no sooner had he reached the door than it was open and he was inside.

"Fitzwilliam!"

There she was—pale, evidently exhausted but, in stark contrast to all his deepest fears, alive and incandescent with joy, a child, *his* child, in her arms.

"Elizabeth! Thank God!" He was at her side before he knew how he got there, cradling her beautiful face and scrutinising every inch of it for blessed proof of life. "Are you well?"

"Aye, now that you are both here, I am." She smiled the most transcendent smile he had ever seen grace her countenance. "Meet your son, Fitzwilliam."

My son. He tore his eyes from her and looked down. It was apparent he had only just missed the birth, for what little could be seen of the child in the folds of bloodied linens was still covered with gore. But his eyes were open, and he was looking directly at him. He was the most wondrous sight Darcy had ever beheld.

"Perfect, is he not?" Elizabeth whispered.

Darcy looked up at her. Never in his life had he known a love such as he felt for Elizabeth and now their child. He nodded. "Without defect."

"He is a credit to you, Lizzy," someone else said.

Darcy looked up in surprise. He had not noticed Jane Bingley was there. Indeed, he had not noticed anyone was there—not Mrs. Sinclair, not Mrs. Reynolds, not the several maids—and certainly not the man, whom he seriously hoped was a physician of some sort, doing something alarming to his wife under a sheet at the foot of the bed.

"He is," Mrs. Sinclair agreed. "Promisingly troublesome from the off."

"Oh, tsk! We thought he was not breathing at first," Mrs. Reynolds hastily explained, "but it was only that he did not cry as most babies do."

Darcy turned back to look at the child in alarm. "Is he well?"

Elizabeth grinned and nodded. "He simply had nothing to say that would amaze the whole room."

Still, she had the ability to fell him with one utterance. He leant forward to rest his forehead reverently against hers. "God, I love you, woman."

She pressed a gentle kiss to his scar. "And I you."

Immeasurable though his relief and elation were, Darcy could not long overlook the events that brought him racing home nor the traitor awaiting him downstairs. He sobered as he considered the magnitude of what he had almost lost.

"Did Bingley hurt you, love?" He regretted that his question made her smile falter. He could not have cared less that it made Jane gasp. Elizabeth whispered that he had not. His relief was profound but short-lived, for in the next instant, she winced and gave a little gasp. "Are you in pain?"

The man cleared his throat. "Mr. Darcy, I presume? It is perfectly normal. Parturition is a many-staged process. You might prefer to step outside for a short time until Mrs. Darcy is ready."

"And who are you, sir?" he demanded, standing to his full height.

"He is the only available apothecary in all of Derbyshire," Mrs. Sinclair piped up. "And it took a good long while to find him. For heaven's sake, do not scare him off now."

Elizabeth huffed a tired little laugh and reached for Darcy's hand. "Do not go too far."

"No fear of that, woman. I shall never go far from you again. Every time I do, you die."

Bingley had never given much thought to how he would meet his maker. Now that the moment was upon him, the only uncertainty remaining was at whose hands it would be, for there presently seemed every chance Colonel Fitzwilliam might beat Darcy to it.

He sat as still as he could, mostly so as not to further aggravate his glowering sentry but also to minimise his discomfort. His throat and head were bruised from being flung against the wall, and he thought his arm might be broken from being hauled to his feet and manhandled into this antechamber. His ribs were almost definitely cracked from the blows Fitzwilliam had already dealt him, and his heart was broken for Elizabeth.

The door banged open. His innards liquefied. Darcy completely filled the aperture. The turn of his countenance was awful.

"Darcy," Fitzwilliam said, coming to his feet and putting a hand on his cousin's shoulder. "I am truly sorry—"

"No need," Darcy interrupted, never taking his eyes off Bingley. "Elizabeth is well. A little tired after delivering my son but in fine health."

Elizabeth was not dead! Bingley breathed a vast sigh of relief then wished profoundly he had not. Both men puffed up even further with affront and surged forward to loom over him.

"I am *this close* to running you through," Fitzwilliam growled, holding his finger and thumb half an inch apart to demonstrate Bingley's precarious mortality. "You have no right to be relieved. She is not yours!"

"I should be relieved under any circumstances at such happy news," Bingley mumbled.

Darcy's lip curled contemptuously. "Would you leave us, Fitzwilliam?"

It was decided then. The Titan would be his executioner. The door closed behind the colonel. Bingley flinched when Darcy moved, but he came no closer, only turned his back and stalked to the window. There he remained, ominously still.

Unsure of what exactly he was presumed guilty, Bingley thought it safest to say nothing at first. Yet, the longer Darcy remained silent, the more anxious he grew until he could stand it no more. "Darcy, I—"

"How long?"

"Pardon?"

"How long have you been planning to take her from me?"

"That is not how it was."

"No? Then pray explain this!" He whirled around and slammed his hand on a nearby table.

Bingley's ribs protested when he leant sideways to read the crumpled letter Darcy had slapped down, but that was nothing to the horror that settled in his stomach as it dawned on him what the letter contained. Imprecise memories floated back—of a bawdy tavern song, an argument with Louisa, and an instruction to Peabody to post the letter professing his love for Elizabeth to the man she would go on to wed.

"Do you still deny you have admired her since before I even returned to Hertfordshire?"

"Well, it—"

Darcy's hands landed on the arms of Bingley's chair, bringing their faces nose-to-nose. "I ask you again. How long have you been planning to take her from me?"

"No time at all, for I did not plan it!" he answered, scraping his chair backwards and scrambling out of it.

"Of all the depraved, incestuous schemes," Darcy snarled, circling on the spot to follow his progress. "To make off with your wife's expectant sister! How did you ever think such a plan would succeed?"

"I swear to you. I never planned it!" He edged away along the wall. "It was but a stupid suggestion made on the impulse of the moment!"

"Was it? Then how is it that my cousin's wife received a letter from Jane begging her to thwart your *plan* to take Elizabeth away?"

Bingley banged his head against a wall sconce. "Ow!" He ducked under it. "I have no idea!"

"Enough with your damned lies!" The manner in which Darcy clenched and unclenched his fists was frankly terrifying.

"I am not lying! I truly cannot explain it. No, wait—it is possible that Jane wrote to her about Amel—" He stopped but not soon enough.

"About what?" Darcy demanded in a tone that brooked no objection.

Bingley swallowed—or tried to. Curse his reckless tongue! "Amelia."

"Damn it, I am in no humour for equivocation, Bingley! Who the bloody hell is Amelia?"

"She was a maid at Netherfield." He prayed to God Darcy would not recall which maid. "I, er…we had a dalliance of sorts. It was reprehensible, I know. I would never usually…with the…only she was more than commonly willing—most determined, in fact."

"Jane's letter mentioned a woman with child."

"Er, yes. There was that small complication. I only found out about that after arriving home from my wedding tour. She came to the house while we were away. But I dealt with it! Well, I thought I had. I was not aware anybody else knew. Indeed, it might never have been discovered had I not decided to send her away, but Lizzy gave me hope that Jane might yet love me, and I thought, to stand a chance of keeping it that way, it would be best to ensure that she never found out. So I wrote to Amelia and…offered to send her…to…"

He ran out of words. He rather wished he had run out of them sooner. The force of Darcy's glare had begun to actually hurt. His tone, when he spoke, was glacial.

"You laid with the maid who looked like Elizabeth."

It was a statement, not a question. He remembered. *Oh, God!* A bead of sweat trickled between Bingley's shoulder blades. "It was not such a remarkable likeness—" He was sliding down the wall, blinking away a blinding flash of white light before he comprehended that Darcy had hit him. Then came the pain. Then, worse still, came the Titan's rage.

"Did you imagine it was Elizabeth?" he roared. "Is that what was in your head whenever you were in her company?

Bloody hell, his face hurt. He rolled onto his hands and knees. His head swam, and his ribs screamed. "No, I—"

"As you sat at my table and slept under my roof, whenever you danced a reel with her, were you pretending to yourself that you had laid with her?"

Darcy loomed over him, his raised voice fearsome, but nothing to the murderous look in his eye. Much like a cornered cat, Bingley struck out. "Yes, then! Is that what you wish to hear? There were times I imagined an intimacy that was not mine to envisage." And he instantly regretted it.

Darcy slammed his palm into the wall above his head. "She is *my wife*, for God's sake! Does that mean *nothing* to you?"

Flinching against a blow that did not come, Bingley got a foot underneath him and hauled himself to his feet with a grunt. "But I never acted on it!"

"You tried to abduct her, for Christ's sake!"

"Abduct her?" he cried, clutching at his ribs and sidling away. "Blast it, Darcy, what do you take me for?"

"I heard no word from Pemberley for *two weeks* before reports of your reprehensible actions reached me. If I discover that you hurt one hair on her head in that time, I swe—"

"Good God, I did not, and I would not!" He pushed away from the wall, taking a wide berth around and away from the Titan. "You received no word because I took her *letter*, not because I tried to take *her!*"

Had he a needle and thread to hand, he would gladly have sewn his own mouth shut, for nothing that came out of it did him any good, and Darcy looked about ready to tear him in two. "It was not my design to cause you any anxiety. I took it on a whim. It was left out for posting. I saw it as I left the house, and I knew Lizzy must have written of what I said to her, and then I—well, I thought that if you read it, you would kill me."

"I might."

That, at least, would stop his damned runaway tongue! "I am sorry, Darcy! I took the letter. It was wrong, and I should not have done it, but I did not attempt to abduct Lizzy! I thought she wanted to go!"

"You thought *what?*"

"I thought she was miserable!"

Darcy stared at him with much the same expression of incredulity as Elizabeth had when he suggested the same to her. "And you claim to love her? You do not even know her."

"I fully comprehend that now. She made it perfectly clear that I was mistaken. But it is not so very difficult for somebody to misjudge a woman's feelings, is it Darcy? Had you not done the same with Jane, none of this would have happened!"

He took several hasty steps backwards when Darcy lunged towards him, bellowing furiously. "Was this retribution enough for you? Taking my wife and child from me? I suppose, given the indifference with which you have just parcelled your unborn child off to another life, I ought not to be surprised that you did not blink an eye at the prospect of stealing mine."

The backs of Bingley's legs hit a chair; he could retreat no farther. Darcy stepped close, his eyes savage. "My *son*, Bingley, my *heir!*"

Bingley recoiled. 'Til that moment, there had seemed a world of difference between a swollen belly under a travelling cloak in a public house in Liverpool and a living, breathing child of such import as to make the Titan spit and rage. Amelia's remark about forsaking his child became suddenly the most heartrending thing in the world. With what callous disregard had he sent his own child away! With what unspeakable indifference had he almost taken Darcy's! He collapsed into the chair and looked up at his friend, who was all but panting with emotion. Yet to Bingley's dismay, it was no longer fury suffusing his countenance, but profound anguish.

"They are the two most precious things to me in all the world," Darcy said in a voice low and hard. "Have you any idea what it would do to me were I to lose either of them? I would rather see Pemberley razed to the ground."

Something turned over in Bingley's gut. Never before had he seen his friend thus, and therein lay the rub to all his senseless presumptions. In his very own words, *"If one were to dub inscrutability the harbinger of indifference, Darcy could be labelled the most unfeeling of all men."* He did not disdain Elizabeth. He loved her!

A nauseating torrent of remorse overtook him. How could he have thought so ill of this man, whose rectitude he had ever aspired to emulate—who had ever been the most stalwart of friends? How could he have been so wilfully blind to his own iniquity? "Forgive me, Darcy. I have been an absolute cur, but none of it has been consciously done. It is as you once said. I am impetuous. I do not think of consequences when I act."

"And now you have been careless with my family, and I will not tolerate it."

Bingley's heart reared up into his throat. He gulped it down and pressed himself back into his chair as far away from Darcy as possible. "Do you mean to call me out?"

"I suppose you would ask that," Darcy spat out. "I ought to, for you have used me in the most despicable way imaginable. But I do not share your recklessness. I shall not risk my family's interests to gratify my abhorrence of you."

Bingley could not recall a single time when Darcy had spoken severely of him. It wounded him grievously to hear it now—not because it was untrue but because Darcy was the very best of men, and in treating him thus, he had carelessly, foolishly, irrevocably squandered his friendship. "What would you have me do?"

Darcy sneered. "Still, you are asking me that?" He stalked to the door. "Leave. After that, I care not as long as I never see you again."

He left the room, and just as Bingley thought his day could get no worse, Jane appeared in the doorway.

FITZWILLIAM CEASED TALKING WHEN THE DOOR WAS PULLED VIOLENTLY open. Mrs. Sinclair, Jane, Georgiana, and he all looked at Darcy as he exited the antechamber.

Darcy looked at him. "Get him out."

He nodded, but it was his grandmother who spoke.

"Oh, you have not killed him then? How disappointing. Young men nowadays never seem to want to do anything properly."

"Have at him," Darcy replied. "I have better things to do." He turned, offering Georgiana his arm. "Come. There is somebody I should like you to meet." He left without a backward glance at either of the Bingleys.

Fitzwilliam turned to do Darcy's bidding, only to discover that Jane had anticipated him. He made to stop her, but Mrs. Sinclair laid a hand on his arm. "*This* I should like to see."

He grinned by way of assent and leant against the outside of the open door to observe how the encounter would go.

"Good day, Charles," Jane began.

"You are bleeding!" he replied.

Mrs. Sinclair shook her head and muttered that he was an imbecile.

"Oh no," Jane explained, "that is not mine. I helped Lizzy birth her baby... but *you* are hurt." She knelt before her husband and peered at his rapidly closing black eye.

"I cannot believe you care."

"I have never stopped caring."

"I am a fool for never seeing it."

"I am a fool for never showing it."

"They are both fools. Hallelujah!" Mrs. Sinclair huffed impatiently. "We could have told them that a year ago and saved ourselves all this bother."

"How better could you have shown it than by coming here?" Bingley said.

"I wished to stop you going away with…" Jane succumbed to a few sobs before choking out, "with Miss Greening."

"Who the devil is Miss Greening?" Fitzwilliam hissed to his grandmother.

"The maid from Netherfield with a likeness to Lizzy. The dolt got a child on her."

Fitzwilliam shook his head in disgust. There truly was no end to Bingley's blundering.

"I never planned to go anywhere with her," the idiot prattled on. "I meant to send her away to prevent her ever coming between us."

"Ah, now I see!" Noticing his grandmother's querying look, Fitzwilliam whispered, "Long story, but this means Darcy will no longer have to kill Ashby."

"I am quite sure your brother did nothing to deserve such a reprieve," she retorted and returned to watching the simpering ninnies beyond the door.

"I wrote to you in London to tell you I would be back this week," Bingley informed his wife.

"I was not in London. I was at Netherfield."

"Speaking of letters," Mrs. Sinclair said quietly, "did you ever get mine? All Lizzy's seemed to go astray."

"I did," Fitzwilliam answered. Then he grinned at a sudden thought. "Though not 'til after Darcy found a most enlightening one from Bingley." Leaning close to his grandmother, he whispered the "Bennet Ballad" into her vastly appreciative ear.

"Why did you come back here?" Jane enquired.

Fitzwilliam reached the line about Mary Bennet's chastity, and Mrs. Sinclair sniggered.

"For you. I heard you were coming here," Bingley replied, drawing a sob from his wife.

Fitzwilliam reached the line about Jane's vapidity, and Mrs. Sinclair snorted with mirth.

"Can you ever forgive me?" Bingley pleaded.

Fitzwilliam reached the line about Elizabeth's virtues, and Mrs. Sinclair burst into gleeful laughter. "Oh, that is superb!"

Both Bingleys looked at her with mixed consternation and mortification.

"Can you ever love me?" Jane said more quietly to her husband.

"How could I not love somebody who still loves me after what I have done? I know not why I ever *stopped* loving you."

"Because ennui struck and witless rent ye!" Mrs. Sinclair announced triumphantly.

Bingley instantly turned red. His wife looked confused to the point of wretchedness.

Shaking his head at his grandmother, Fitzwilliam put an end to the Bingleys' lamentations by instructing them it was time to leave. Jane's protests were unceremoniously deflected. If Elizabeth wished to see her, she would no doubt write. Until such time, her welcome was exhausted. Bingley had the sense not to object.

"I am truly sorry, Fitzwilliam," he mumbled as Jane climbed into their carriage. "I never meant to use Darcy so ill."

"You will be sorely disappointed if you hope for some great speech of exoneration from me, Bingley. This cannot be fixed with a trifling apology. Leave this place and my cousins be, or I shall finish the job for which Darcy had not the stomach."

Bingley paled, nodded, and climbed up after his wife. Fitzwilliam instructed the driver to ensure they left the park, then went back inside. He found his grandmother in the Spanish saloon, sipping a glass of gin and chuckling intermittently, much to the bewilderment of Georgiana, who had joined her there.

"Is Elizabeth well?" he enquired of the latter.

"Perfectly so," she replied.

"A toast then!" he declared. He poured two measures of sherry at the sideboard and handed one to Georgiana. "To Darcy!"

Mrs. Sinclair raised her glass. "Aye. Hail the man who wed the second!"

Georgiana frowned. Fitzwilliam began to regret arming his grandmother with the "Bennet Ballad." "And Elizabeth!" he said, raising his glass a second time.

Mrs. Sinclair raised hers also. "Aye, for she is the jewel, alluring and—"

He coughed loudly. She gave him a look of affected affront but capitulated nonetheless. "And their son," she said instead.

Fitzwilliam smiled broadly as he earnestly echoed her toast. "And their son."

Elizabeth lay at Darcy's side, her head on his chest and his arm firmly about her as they both gazed upon their son, nestled in the crook of his father's arm. Every feeling of joy and relief was hers to be united with the two people most precious to her in all the world. Darcy's stillness was expressive of his prodigious emotion. She almost did not wish to obtrude upon it but felt too much to remain silent.

"He looks so much like you. See how he is *almost* smiling. 'Tis you to a T." She felt Darcy's lips curl into a mirroring expression against her temple.

"What do you think pleases him?" he said quietly.

"I daresay he is laughing at his papa for always imagining such theatrical misadventures for his mama." Her head jumped slightly when Darcy gave a brusque little laugh.

"Tease if you will, woman. I am too happy to care."

She looked up at his dear face, suffused with delight but also tired. "You are happy now, but I shall not tease, for you must have been very worried."

He hushed her gently. "All that matters is that you are both well."

There came a sweet little gurgle from the bundle in his arms, distracting them both from weightier matters for a while. Elizabeth's heart felt fit to burst as she looked upon her darling child, blinking at the world as though surprised to see it there. Tiredness blurred her thoughts, and she drifted for a while in dreamless sleep, yet her head was too full of things she wished to say for it to last. "You know that I *did* write, though, do you not?" she whispered.

"I do. Now cease fretting."

"But it troubles me, Fitzwilliam. It was such an awful time for you. I cannot bear to think of your waiting for words of comfort that never came."

"I was more concerned for your safety than your condolences, but it is all explained in any case. Bingley stole your first letter, the second likely arrived at Rosings after I left Kent, and the third almost certainly arrived in London after I left there, for we departed at dawn on Sunday."

"He stole my first letter?" She sighed angrily. "His duplicity knows no bounds!"

"Think on him no more today, love. I mentioned it only to ease your mind, not to make you angry."

"Very well," she agreed, too fatigued and too happy to speak long of aught unpleasant. She placed her palm on her son's belly and spread her fingers, gently soothing him through the swaddling. He was so warm, so tiny, so perfect. "I promise to write more often next time, though."

"That will not be necessary. I was in earnest when I said I would never leave you again."

She smiled up at him, a tired but joyful smile.

He looked at her with the greatest tenderness and pulled her more tightly against him, rubbing his hand gently up and down her arm. "You are exhausted, love. What I endured is of no consequence in light of what you must have suffered."

"That matters not either, for look at my reward." She stroked her beloved son's tiny hand. He immediately clamped it around her finger, stirring a fierce swell of emotion that bade her exhale unevenly. "How I love you both!"

Darcy pressed a kiss to her temple and one to their child's forehead. "Dearest Elizabeth, you have given me everything. You *are* everything to me. I am so in love with you."

Satisfied that everything necessary had been said, Elizabeth surrendered to her fatigue and fell asleep to the blissful sounds of her son's sweet snuffling breaths and her husband's strong, steady heartbeat.

DARCY WATCHED WITH HEARTFELT DELIGHT AS HIS WIFE AND SON BOTH drifted to sleep in his arms. Nothing he had endured—not his aunt's passing or his fearful passage from London or Bingley's treachery—could detract from his elation.

His son was miraculous—hale despite his early arrival, perfect in form and gratifyingly like him in appearance. His feelings towards him were unlike any he had known before. Towards Elizabeth, his feelings were unchanged—immutable, immeasurable, profound. He loved her more than life itself.

Let the rest of the world go on with its deceits and misfortunes. He cared not for any of them. He and Elizabeth had their own family now, and they would continue as sublimely content as they were this day for all their days to come—in no way mistaken as to their happiness.

Acknowledgements

MISTAKEN MAY NEVER HAVE MADE IT OUT OF MY HEAD AND ONTO THESE pages without the help of some very special people. To everyone who helped me achieve it, I express my heartfelt thanks:

- Richard—for putting up with my silliness, for the sacrifices you've made so that writing can be my day job, and for your unwavering belief in me
- Kristi Rawley—for accompanying me steadfastly on this journey from inception to completion, for your capable and compassionate beta skills, and for loving *Mistaken's* Darcy and Elizabeth as much as I do
- Mum—for your honesty, for your constant and inexhaustible support, for the encouragement I needed to grow from the writer I thought I was into the author I am
- All my friends—for championing my dreams
- The members of A Happy Assembly—for your warm welcome, for the various contributions I received in the early stages of this journey, and for faithfully waiting for me to reach the end
- Michele Reed at Meryton Press—for seeing the potential in *Mistaken*
- My editor, Debbie Styne—for tolerating my obstinacy almost as well as Darcy tolerates Elizabeth's, for coaxing me down wiser paths, and for helping me polish Mistaken into a treasure of which I will forever be proud
- Ellen Pickels—for your eagle eyes and deft touch on the final edit
- Zorylee Diaz-Lupitou—for dressing up my story so beautifully with its wonderful cover

Perhaps most importantly of all, I thank Jane Austen. For your razor wit, stunning turns of phrase, and captivating characters, for the privilege of spending more time with your Darcy and Elizabeth, for the honour of incorporating some of your inimitable writing into this alternative journey for them, and for inspiring me to write, I thank you.